Cont;nue

Also published by Jeffrey Cummins
Leftwich Blues/Elfwitch Rules

EX-MAS SONG

by Jeffrey Cummins

ForgivenIAm Publishing House

This work is a product of its time and place and may include values, images, events, and language that are offensive to post-human sensibilities. Human reader metacognition is encouraged.

First E-Book edition: November 19, 2023
First Print edition: November 19,2023
First Hardback edition: November 19, 2023

Published by ForgivenIAm Publishing House, Salem

Copyright © 2023 by Jeffrey Cummins

All rights reserved. No part of this book may be reproduced or transmitted in any form or by any means, electronic or mechanical, including photocopying, recording, or by an information storage and retrieval system - except by a reviewer who may quote brief passages in a review to be printed in a magazine or newspaper - without permission in writing from the publisher.

This is a work of fiction. Unless otherwise indicated, all the names, characters, businesses, places, events and incidents in this book are either the product of the author's imagination or used in a fictitious manner. Any resemblance to actual persons, living or dead, or actual events is purely coincidental.

Scripture taken from the New King James Version®. Copyright © 1982 by Thomas Nelson. Used by permission. All rights reserved.

E-book ISBN 979-8-9853920-5-0
Print Edition ISBN 979-8-9853920-6-7
Hardback Edition ISBN 979-8-9853920-7-4

Printed in the United States of America

Dedication

"Glory to God in the highest,
And on earth peace, goodwill toward men!"
--Luke 2:14

To my wife, Tonya Cummins, and anyone who has suffered in fear in the twilight and the evening, in the black and dark night while waiting with hope against hope that the dawn cannot come quick enough: Yes, God can change a heart.

Cont;nue

Acknowledgements

Thank yous and shout outs go to Jan Brown for her excellent editing job and enthusiasm. Also, to advance readers Sharon Cummins, Callee Stephenson, and Emma Roberts for their feedback and encouragement. Special thanks to advance reviewer Gary Krupa. I am grateful for all the help I have received.

EX-MAS SONG

Table of Contents

FOREWORD

Dear Reader,

The original Christmas story begins with a gift.

A baby. A new life. With a fleshy heart as angels proclaimed,

 "Great tidings of joy."

Jesus was the first Christmas gift. God's gift to all people. A gift

of love. Because God gave himself.

And a chance for "Peace on earth, goodwill toward men."

If there was one Christmas gift that God wanted above all others

- - then it was love. So God decided to give away his best gift. Because

it is better to give than receive.

Remember, you can't out-love or out-give God. Does that mean

that God's love has been re-gifted all these years? Then, that's some

kind of love.

Worth more than all the diamond fields and the gold standard

and all the money the Federal Reserve could ever print. Because those things are the stuff of a stony heart, Dear Readers.

The Bible doesn't command us to celebrate Christmas. But it does instruct us to love God first and then to love others. Somewhere down the line, we chose to celebrate Christmas with gifts to one another.

It's just one day out of the year that we focus on having a fleshy heart. Can't we remember to love God and one another all the other three hundred and sixty four and a quarter days, too? Instead of living with a stony heart most of the year.

No one wants to be forgotten.

No one wants to get a lump of coal in their Christmas stocking.

No one wants to think they're not good enough to get a gift.

Everyone wants at least one gift.

One special gift. One thing over anything else that willmake them truly happy.

If Jesus was God's Christmas gift to the world, what would Jesus want for a birthday wish? "I give you a new commandment—love one another."

It was something he thought worth dying for: to give us new life and a fleshy heart.

Here's hoping that every day is Christmas for you. And that each and every Christmas, each of you Dear Readers gets that one special gift your heart desires.

"God bless us, Every one!"

Your Faithful Servant,
JC
03/30/11

FIRST VERSE—Giving Up the Ghost

1—The Way Of Lights

Well, to start with, I was dead.

Had been for about five minutes.

Blair, my ex #2, found me sprawled out on the couch. A butcher knife on the floor. Weeping cuts on my wrists. One of her strongest meds, Darvacet, spilled over the couch.

It wasn't very dignified.

But dignity had been the farthest thing from my mind at the time.

She went into true shock. Not her usual pantomimed routine.

I hadn't counted on a reaction like that and I hadn't counted on still being aware of what was going on around me.

After her initial shock, Blair got angry and that made her focus. She called for an ambulance and kept haranguing the dispatcher up to the moment it arrived.

She threw the door open and stood at the threshold with a plug of snow piled up inside the door frame and began to chastise the EMTs inside the ambulance.

She told them what to do and how to do it and that they'd better do it soon or they might was as well bring a body bag instead of a gurney.

And that was even before any of them had gotten out of the ambulance.

It had backed into the driveway. Crunching through snow that stacked up to the tire wheel wells. The taillights turning it a cherry red.

Then the back doors opened and two EMTS climbed down with a gurney.

The first EMT, a blonde headed man younger than myself, came all the way into the back of the house where I was and confirmed everything that Blair had been trying to tell them.

I had no pulse.

And I wasn't breathing.

So the general consensus was: I was very much in need of resuscitation.

Otherwise, I would stay dead.

The second EMT came in with the gurney. His face was grizzled and his white hair buzzed so short that it stood straight up.

Don't ask me how I could be aware of all this. It wasn't a dream. It was really happening. It was no different than watching some reality tv show or some documentary safe in a recliner with the remote in hand. Except Blair's vulgar adjectives weren't being bleeped out.

"No vitals, Bart," said the first EMT as he quickly bound my wrists.

"Time to juice up the paddles," Bart said as he brought the gurney alongside the couch.

I was in their hands now. Or more specifically, my stopped heart and my empty lungs were. Stony heart or fleshy heart, my heart was stilled.

They picked me up and put me onto the gurney. Then Bart ratcheted it up to chest height as they backed the gurney through the family room and then the kitchen and then the living room and then out the front door.

I was dead to the world.

And soon I would be room temperature.

Which would be still warmer than outside.

I had picked the night of a major snowstorm that was busy burying the entire St. Louis Metropolitan area under a foot and a half of snow to try and commit suicide.

It was falling from buckets. Choking the air. Coating everything on the horizontal.

Twelve inches had already fallen.

All was quiet. There wasn't a sound except for snowflakes falling atop one another.

The driveway was completely covered. The entire street was being buried while it slept. And when it woke, it would find itself under a thick silver blanket.

Bart pulled as the blonde haired EMT pushed the gurney through the snow to the back of the ambulance, idling its diesel. Because diesel drives the world.

Blair tried to follow out through their tracks. But she had no slippers on and only a flimsy old granny nightdress. The snow caked against her hem and swallowed up her bare feet.

That was enough for her. The cold bit through her panic and concern. She retreated back to the threshold, the furthermost edge of electric hearth and cubic warmth.

Blair demanded that she be allowed to ride along with the EMTs. But they told her no.

"Leave him to us," Bart said.

"But I can't drive in this. It's a freaking blizzard!" Blair complained. She always tried to haggle to get her way.

"Why don't you call for a friend or family to take you," the blonde EMT told her.

"Where are you taking my husband?" she wanted to know.

I was her ex-husband. But it wasn't like I could sit up and correct her at the moment.

"Our Lady's," Bart answered. "It's the closest place."

"You'll never get him there in time without a sleigh," Blair sneered and slammed the front door.

An overhang of snow fell off the roof and piled up against the front door.

The younger EMT looked at his older mentor.

But Bart knew better than to comment on such things. People didn't always mean what they said. If they did, hell would have frozen over long ago.

"Grab the other end here, Mel," said the older EMT.

The two lifted up me into the back of the ambulance. They shut the back doors and I saw the old emblem on the panel window. Hermes'caduceus: a rod with two wings at the top with a snake entwined around the pole. Hermes was the keeper of secret knowledge. And hidden treasure. And locked doors.

Although, before it had become a caduceus, it had been a snake on a pole that had been lifted up in a wilderness long ago so people might be healed. "Pharma" had meant healing and from there it had become pharmakon which meant "preparing drugs: remedy or poison." Then, afterwards, it became "pharmekia" with additional meanings of sorcery and a metaphor for the seductions and deceptions of idolatry.

This was the insignia that the medical profession had adopted for their own use long ago.

Mel locked down the gurney safe and snug and Bart closed the doors to keep in the roasty toasty air.

A middle aged African-American male sat in the driver's seat. He had on the same navy EMT jacket as the other two but a Santa hat sat perched at the tiptop of his bald head. "We ready?" he asked. "Fifteen miles to Our Lady's. But in this snow it's gonna seem like an hour."

"Ready to roll, Jasper," Bart said.

I was going for a ride.

Over the hills and through the snow.

Off to the hospital we go!

Sleigh ride, sleigh ride. Just hear them sirens a whistlin'.

Mel cut through my pullover and attached some sensors to me while Bart turned on a huge battery and picked up two paddles that were attached to it by cables.

As the machine registered a charge, Mel looked at the EKG.

It sang out in a high continuous tone.

That meant that I had flatlined.

I was clinically dead.

The machine registered a full charge and Bart laid the paddles on my bare chest. "Charge!"

Mel reached over and flipped a switch.

My Frankenstein's creature convulsed. Then it collapsed back down onto the gurney.

Suddenly, I was fifteen years old and sitting on a couch in my grandparents' house on Christmas Eve. We were passing out gifts and just beginning to open them. But not my Grandpa.

He had been in bed all day and had just gotten himself up to sit in his recliner in his blue terry-cloth robe and deer foam slippers. He was pale, his cheeks drawn tight, his lips pursed with every breath.

For him there was no joy tonight. No peace on earth. His fleshy heart growing weak and weary.

My parents were in the kitchen with my grandmother calling him an ambulance. Something sang out on the stove. A whistling tea kettle.

Then I was again laying on the gurney in the back of the ambulance while the EKG sang out again in monotone.

This was it.

I was really dead.

Kicked the bucket.

Bought the farm.

Croaked.

Checked out.

Chips cashed in.

They were gonna put me in a pine box for a dirt nap.

Getting ready to go into the fertilizer business.

Bart recharged his paddles watching the needle climb back up. "Juice him."

Mel flipped the switch.

And I was not in the ambulance. I was in the old family church, once warm and peaceful. But it wasn't now.

It was cold and grey. Built of gothic stone. The hard and straight pews were full of family and friends. While I waited at the foot of a dias.

There wasn't a pulpit or an altar. Only a baptismal. A circle of stones around a dark hole. Water dripped down to the bottom.

A melancholic march began. Everyone stood up. I was getting married for the first time. Again.

The bride came down the aisle. It was a dark robed anamorph, slender and lean. A webbed cowl hid the face. And long sleeves hide tapered fingers that did not bear a ring.

When the robed bride came to my side, the cowl came down. The cheeks held no warmth. The lips black from frostbite. The eyes blue and snowblind.

She was stone cold beautiful. More cold stone than beautiful. With a stony heart.

She was someone who would never speak to me in this world again. The only sound now was water dripping down into the well.

The candles inside the church flickered.

"No change," Bart hissed.

I was in the ambulance flat on my back.

Still flatlining.

Giving up the ghost.

Getting ready to ride off into the sunset.

Meet my maker.

Crossing the river Jordan.

Answer the roll up yonder.

Sprouting wings.

Ready to pull back the veil and join the choir invisible.

I was floating a few inches up above my body. I watched Mel do CPR. Saw the hairs on the back of his hands as he pressed down. Saw the flush in his cheeks from taking deep breaths.

I watched Bart recharged his paddles. Saw every line and crag in his weathered face.

Behind them, Jasper drove with sureness through the mounting snow.

The strobe lights blinked on and off across the white road. Over covered lumps that were buried cars. And over snow slopes that covered front doors and touched the roof corners.

It was a silent night. It was a holy night.

It was a wonderland.

And at every intersection, the ambulance's red and blue and white strobes were joined by the solid green of the traffic trees.

Bart laid the paddles on me again and juiced me a third time.

I walked down a narrow lane of some cheery old town lined brick masonry and thick glass shop fronts. It was late afternoon and the sky was a light grey.

I had on knit trousers and a pea coat. A top hat and a long scarf that hung to my knees. I followed a couple into a public house that had an old wooden sign above the oaken door.

The place was called Gingerbread's. It was warm inside and full of people. Some of the crowd toasted each other's good health with egg nog. While others shouted "Cheers" and knocked back shots of burning whiskey.

I stood at the back along with the other late arrivals. Everyone faced a low stage that bore five people.

One was a man sitting in an overstuffed chair next to a placard. It read: A CHRISTMAS TALE READ BY BOZ. The man sitting down in the rich velvet chair to read had chestnut brown hair that bobbed past his brow and ears. He was tucked inside a blue waist coat and striped vest. His cheeks ruddy and his smile impish. His fingers poked out of woven mitts and in his hand was a tiny tome.

"Faithful friends," Boz announced, "I will now endeavor to haunt you pleasantly with the spirit of this little book."

Next to him stood a red haired man who hid his balding head under an old mac dressed in a black turtle neck and dirty leathers. Behind him vamped a jazz trio. A drummer brushed his skins. A saxophonist breathed into his reed. And a double bass bowed with no fingers.

"Three wise men walk into a manger," the man rapped. "One has gold. One has myrrh. And one has frankincense. 'A merry prank,' said the virgin mother. 'You feel it along your spine,' said the espoused husband who had a mind to put her away privately."

Third time was a charm.

The EKG began to read a blip. Then began to track a signal up and down in a slow rhythm.

I no longer felt lighter than air. I felt a tug inside my gut. Something pulling me back to bone and muscle.

I could feel Mel's palms pressing on me. I could feel him grip my nose and breathe hot CO_2 down my air passages.

Something kicked started my heart. And I drew a deep breath of fresh air into my lungs.

Then I felt pain.

Mel steadied himself against the gurney to catch his breath.

"Welcome back, Mr. R.," Bart said and grabbed a radio. He began to call in my stats.

Jasper had just pulled onto Highway 15. We were on the outskirts of Belle-Valley now. Headed for Our Lady's Hospital. Which was next to the Shrine.

His visibility was no more than a few feet ahead and a few feet above the windshield.

The entire horizontal had been leveled out and raised by half a foot of white sticking snow.

His headlights were weak pinpoints against the spiraling mass and the wipers could barely keep the flakes from accumulating on the windshield.

Moving vehicles carried lumps of snow on their hoods and trunks. Snow filled tracks led off to ditches where cars had spun out and been abandoned. Road signs had been wiped by white frosty hands.

Drivers had no room to move over as their rearview mirrors were filled with strobe lights and AMBULANCE spelled frontwards. They dared not go into the drifting snow banks that disguised the road shoulder. All they could do was slow down and give Jasper enough room to drive down the middle of the road.

Only a fool would be out on a night like this if they didn't have to be.

For Jasper, Bart, and Mel, it was their job.

"Life's a gift," Mel said. "Why would anyone want to waste it?"

"Some people just ain't happy," Jaspar said. "Cuz they don't get what they really want."

"We're the richest country in the history of the world and you're telling me that people can't get what they really want?" Bart asked rhetorically.

"Maybe they ain't gettin' the right thing," Jasper said.

"Every Chrismtas everyone gets a ton of gifts. And the next day they can't wait to return them. It's never enough," Bart said.

"What if everyone just got one gift for Christmas?" Jasper asked.

"Could we settle for just one gift?" Bart asked.

"If it was the right gift. What we truly wanted way down deep in our heart," Jasper said never taking his eyes from the road.

"If you could just get one gift for Christmas, what would it be?" asked Mel.

"I'd trade this ambulance for a helicopter," Jasper said. "I could go anywhere with a 'copter. That'd be the living end."

Then Mel looked at Bart. The older EMT just shrugged, "Peace on earth. Just like it says in the Bible. Just for one night. How about you, kid?"

Mel smiled. "I want to sing 'How Deep is Your Love' by the BeeGees with you guys in a karaoke bar while drinking some eggnog."

Jaspar let laughter ring from the bell of his gut. "You alright, kid. You know that?"

Bart just smiled.

I suddenly felt very tired.

And very washed out.

After that everything went black.

2—The In-Take

I cracked my eyes open and found a plascinated head grinning at me.

It had no lips. Only muscles and teeth. So it had no choice but to smile.

It was the bust of a plastic head for medical demonstrations perched on a metal cabinet.

Backed up against a wall painted white with no windows.

I was in a different place now.

Far from my overstuffed couch back at home.

There had been that strange sensation of seeing everything around me.

And more than a few instances of flashbacks, or what I took to be flashbacks.

Since some of the things I'd seen hadn't actually ever happened to me.

I wasn't so sure if I was awake or still passed out at this moment.

My arms and legs were stretched out. My bare chest had goose bumps. My throat was dry. My wrists throbbed and had been bandaged.

But my soul was numb.

I was more alive than dead.

My pullover was gone and my shoes were off but I was not at home.

I was stretched out on an examining table inside a very small room with no door, with only a white modesty curtain.

At a hospital then.

Beyond the curtain I could hear drama and action. People living and dying, calling out for absent family members, and begging God to show Himself once and for all. Nurses and doctors running from table to table, calling for charts, calling for medicines, and calling insurance carriers.

EKGs blipped. Electronic bellows gulped and sighed air. Intercoms paged specialists.

I was in an ER. Just another patient on the night shift.

Rubber soled comfort shoes treaded their way to me.

"Never fails. The bigger the snow storm, the more suicides there are," complained a middle aged woman, presumably an ER nurse.

"It's because they're indoors too much and don't get enough sunlight," a lighter female voice explained. "The sunlight has lithium and keeps them calm."

"We'll just see if the patient has recovered. Then you can admit him," the first woman said.

She pulled back the curtain and I turned my head over to look. The first nurse was dressed in floral top scrubs and aqua pants that were stained with various bodily liquids. She was slightly overweight and had a sagging face. The circles under her eyes were caked with makeup. She had worked so many shifts back to back that she couldn't sleep when she tried to lay down because it was too quiet at home.

I could smell the perfume of the second woman. She was soaked in flowers and worekhakisand a long sleeve button shirt. She had a clipboard which meant she was administration.

Her auburn hair brushed her shoulders. Her pert chin and upturned lips sat above it. Her cheeks were pink and her eyes were a deep blue.

Alive or dead. Awake or asleep. I was being visited by an angel.

And I was not afraid.

The nurse had a large blue lanyard with OUR LADY and below that her name and a string of abbreviations.

The second woman with the clipboard had a different lanyard.   It was white with burgundy lettering.

HOPE COUNSELORS, INC. And below that was her name: JAYNE V. LCSW MSCW.

The first thing she did was smile.

And I felt a little better because of it.

The next thing she did was take a pen from her breast pocket and click it.

"Hello, Mr...," she began and looked down at her clipboard. "Mr. R.? Mr. Justin R.?"

I nodded. That hurt. My neck and chest were sore.

"I'm Jayne V. and I'm a therapist with Hope Counselors, Inc. We are contracted through Our Lady to do mental health care," she announced.

Mental health. So, I was really nuts. "Are you some kind of Catholic charity?"

My voice was full of sand.

Jayne V. shook her head. "No. We're a private mental health service. I'm here to do an in-take—just a quick interview before we can admit you." She released the ER nurse with a nod.

The ER nurse walked off to the next examining room to see who could be saved.

My lips were dry and it hurt to talk. "Is it still snowing outside?"

"Yes, it is," Jayne V. admitted. "It's a good thing I'm stuck here for the next 10 hours or else I wouldn't be able to get home."

"How much snow has fallen?" I asked next.

"You know, I don't really know. All I know that it's covering everything," she said. Then Jayne V. pulled up a chair next to the examining table. I didn't mind her getting close. Her perfume washed over me. "Do you think you're up to answering some questions now?"

There wasn't much else to do. I wasn't going anywhere. "Sure."

We began a round of question and answers for information. Then she would write it down.

"What is your full name?" she asked.

"Justin Earl R.," I said.

"Where were you born?" she asked.

"In a hospital," I said.

Jayne V. tried not to laugh. And waited for the right answer.

I had caught her off guard. "Here in Belle-Valley."

"What date?" she asked.

I gave her the date. It was getting farther and farther away from me each year.

Jayne V. asked me the necessary and obvious demographic information and then she asked me where I worked.

"America's Bank," I said. She seemed to hang on that fact for a while.

"What is your title?" she asked.

"Credit analyst," I said. It was a job boring enough to push anyone to the edge. And I danced there everyday of the work week.

"Do you have your insurance card?" she asked.

I felt for my wallet. It was still in my back pocket. Before I had tried to commit suicide I had kicked off my shoes but had kept my wallet on me.

I pulled it out and gave her my Blue Cross card. She took it and copied down the policy numbers. Everything in life was an alpha-numeric code. Worse, soon all would be an algorithm. *The algorithm of life.*

"Are you married, divorced, or single?" she asked.

"Divorced," I said. Married and divorced twice. But I would have been embarrassed to have to tell her that.

"Do you smoke?" she asked.

"Only when I'm on fire," I said.

"Do you drink alcohol more than twice a week?" she asked.

"Not since before Thanksgiving," I said.

"Before that?" she asked.

"Off and on. A lot when I do, though. To make up for the dry season," I said.

"Do you have a history of alcoholism in your family?" she asked.

"Yes," I said.

"Are you taking any illegal drugs now and if so which ones?" she asked.

"No," I said.

"Have you in the past and if so which ones?" she asked.

"Yes. Marijuana. Cocaine," I said. The usual stuff. It was easy to get. Hard to quit.

"Are you on any psychotropic medications and if so which ones?" she asked.

"None," I said.

"Does your family have a history of mental illness?" she asked.

"No," I said.

"Have you ever tried to commit suicide before?" she asked.

"No," I said.

"Have you ever thought about committing suicide before?" she asked.

"Yes," I said.

"How often?" she asked.

"Hourly, daily," I said.

"For more than a week?" she asked.

"Yes," I said.

"More than two weeks?" she asked.

"Yes," I said.

"Have you ever cut on yourself before?" she asked.

"Yes," I said.

"Often?" she asked.

"No. Just once before," I said. "About twelve years ago."

"Do you have problems sleeping?" she asked.

"Yes," I said.

"Do you feel anxious about things?" she asked.

"Yes," I said.

"Do you know what happened tonight? Do you remember the events?" she asked.

I shrugged.

I remembered.

I had tried to kill myself.

And I had failed.

"Would you like to tell me what happened?" she asked.

"I took a handful of darvacet and started cutting on my wrists with a kitchen knife. Then I was going to dip my fingers in my blood and write 'GUILTY' on the wall," I said.

"Where did you get the darvacet?" she asked.

"From Blair," I said.

"Who's Blair?" she asked.

The curtain was pulled back with a flush and there stood apple shaped Blair. She had showered and dressed. There was blush to her cheeks and snow in her wavy brown hair.

"I'm Blair," she declared. "Blair R." She still had my last name. The one I had been born with. It had been her fourth last name.

"And how are you related to Justin?" Jayne V. asked.

"I'm his wife," she said declared.

Jayne V. narrowed her gaze and looked down at her clipboard. "Justin says he's divorced."

Without a beat, without a blush, Blair stated, "We were married and recently divorced. But now we're together again."

Jayne V. did her best to keep a poker game face.

Without a further invitation, Blair took the floor. "I was the one who found him." A change came over her face. Her mouth puckered, her brows knitted, and her eyes watered. "I thought he was dead. He wasn't breathing. So I called the ambulance."

"You did the right thing," Jayne V. said.

"The ER nurse told me they had to shock him a couple of times," Blair reported. "He was probably dead for a couple of minutes."

Jayne V. maintained her stone face and wrote down the information. "Do you take darvarcet?"

Blair's eyes went big. "Why do you ask?"

"Justin admitted to getting in your darvacet and taking some before he tried to kill himself," Jayne V. said.

Blair flinched and turned sour. "I know. I didn't think he would. I've never had to lock up my meds before. But I will now."

Jayne V. worded her next question carefully. "What other meds do you keep in the house?"

"Seroquel. Zoloft. Lunestra," Blair said. One was a psychotropic. One an anti-depressant. The other a depressant to sleep. You could play Med-Scrabble with all the pills she had to take daily.

Jayne V. wrote it all down and asked, "Are you under the care of a physician or psychiatrist?"

"A psychiatrist," Blair said. "Dr. Frost. He sees patients here. Do you know him?"

Jayne V. ignored her. "Did he give you the prescription for Darvacet?"

"No," Blair said. "It was an old prescription I had from before."

"Have you seen any signs or indications that your ex-husband is a threat to himself or others?" Jayne V. asked.

"No, not to others," Blair said.

"Has he any shown violence to you? Or have you had to file a police report?" Jayne V. asked.

"No. We didn't begin to fight until we separated," Blair said. If she were a puppet without strings, her nose would have started to grow each time she opened her mouth at this point. Why was I letting her talk for me and say untrue things?

Jayne V. wrote down every word and asked, "How long were you married?"

"A little over a year. We were married last year in August. But then he left me this past June. And served me with divorce papers on our anniversary," Blair said in a hurt tone.

In fact, she had gotten the divorce papers just before our anniversary. By happenstance, not by plan. The only plan had been to get a painless divorce from her and get it done quick.

Things were quick in Blair's world. But they weren't painless.

She was a hurricane that had blown into my life. The divorce had been the eye of the storm. Now I was in the back half of the storm front.

"But now we're getting back together. Who knows? Maybe I'll get a wedding ring for Christmas," Blair said.

I almost choked on that. My stocking was going to be full of late notices if anything.

Jayne V. didn't bother to write that down. She turned her attention back to me. "I have your information, Justin. I am going to call Blue Cross and see what it will cover for mental health."

She left the small room and drew back the curtain.

And I was alone with Blair.

At least she had showered. She hadn't in the past two days. And had bothered to change out of her granny nightie into loose jeans and an Old Navy pullover.

"You had me so scared," Blair said.

"How did they let you in?" I asked.

"Silly," she said. "I told them that I was your wife."

If anything Blair was persistent in getting her way. Or just knew how to bluff well. I used to admire that until I realize she persisted in bluffing with lies.

I was surprised that the hospital hadn't called my parents. But the last time I'd been in the hospital I'd been a minor. Fifteen with a broken pelvis, so, yeah, call the parents or guardians because I was just learning how to make wise decisions.

Now I was adult.

Supposed to be making wise decisions.

Like getting back together with my second ex.

Well, if wisdom derived from experience and experience was begotten of failure, I should prove to be very wise indeed. If I lived through all of this.

"You'll need to call your parents and tell them we're back together," Blair said.

I was about to ruin their Christmas.

3—"No shoes. No shirt. No insurance. No service."

"When are you going to tell your parents?" Blair asked. Again with her persistence.

"I'm not telling them anything right now," I said. The less they knew the better off they were. I still wasn't sure about me. Maybe I could go crazy and they'd never have to know. Well, wouldn't they had found out if I had succeeded in killing myself? And who would have broken the news to them? Blair.

"Maybe I should call and tell them," Blair said.

I had no shirt on. My chest and back were freezing, though I did not seem to care. It was cold in the ER. I wondered how close the morgue was from here.

My bandaged wrists ached now, but would pulse with pain later and would never trust me around knives again. The rest of my body worked away on its own while my brain stuttered. It was hard keeping my eyelids off my cheeks.

The darvacet was working well. It gave me pharmaceutical peace on earth and goodwill to all laboratories.

But even in my haze and glow, I knew what she was up to. Now was not the time to give her power of attorney. Or any kind of permission whatsoever.

"Nuh, uh," I hummed. My throat was too dry to talk. And I couldn't even make a fist.

"They still hate me?" Blair mused. "They'll just have to get over it and accept that we're together."

The first statement was a rhetorical question.

The second was a claim and was more like wishful thinking.

I doubt my parents would answer a call from her or fall for a bluff.

"Why did you have to do this?" Blair moaned.

Did she think I was doing it to punish her? That I was following some grand master plan? That this was the best that I could do with the choices at hand?

"You wanna see?" I asked through numb lips and held up my bandaged wrists.

My wounds had been cleaned, stitched, and bandaged. But the ugly of it was plain to see.

Blair gagged and put her hand over her mouth. "Don't make me look at it!"

"Then don't call my parents," I said.

What Blair truly wanted was to get a reaction out of them when she told them we were back together. For Blair, life was a shot of happy, two shots of sad. Followed by a very bitter chaser. And she always made sure someone else picked up the tab.

She thrived on chaos.

Her life was a playground where the roundabout didn't spend the day her way.

Where the merry-go-round was broken down.

And the helter-skelter had put blisters on her fingers.

"Your insurance will get you admitted here," Blair said with confidence. She seemed to know the drill, was she speaking from experience? "Then you'll have to see a psychiatrist. And go to therapy."

That would be a new experience for me: letting a shrink walk around in my head. Blair would have to make room for him. "I don't know any psychiatrists."

"Tell them you want to see Dr. Frost," Blair said. Then she reminded me, "He sees patients here."

She was a wealth of information. A fountain of knowledge. But was the apple she offered tainted?

"Have you ever been here?" I asked.

As a rule, Blair avoided any and all direct questions. She'd been around enough lawyers and won enough settlements to not 'fess up to anything. Her credit report was in the tank because of public derogatories with liens from both public companies and private individuals. I only knew that from pulling her credit report at her behest after we'd first met. When I'd shown it to my supervisor at America's Bank, he said that it could be fixed. But what I should have done was run.

So, I asked her another question from a different angle. "Why do you want me to see your doctor?"

"He's a good doctor," Blair said.

This is how much good Dr. Frost had been for Blair. After we had married, and she had lost her second jobs in two months, I used my insurance coverage to pay for her to see a psychiatrist. She had been recommended to Dr. Frost by God knows who. And ever since she had started seeing the good doctor, he had tinkered with her medications and dosage level. Trying to find just the right combination by a method of adjustment (trial or error?) and substitution (error or trial?). What that meant was when I would get home from work, either the house was dark and Blair was comatose, or every light in the house was on and she was pulling everything out of the kitchen cabinets looking for signs of cockroaches. As of now, Dr. Frost had Blair taking a total of nineteen pills a day—just to function.

Good old Doctor Frost.

"Wouldn't there be a conflict of interest?" I asked.

After all, I would be airing my dirty laundry, some of which would naturally be about Blair, to the man who would be hearing all her dirty little secrets, some of which would naturally be about me. Dr. Frost would be getting it in both ears from both sides.

Blair just shrugged. "More money for him. Where's the conflict in that?"

The curtain was pulled back and Jayne V. returned. She did her best to smile at me and ignore Blair. She had a batch of new forms on her clipboard. "Good news. Your work insurance will cover you for a stay of up to five consecutive days for mental health. If you choose a psychiatrist in their approved network, the first three visits are free. After that, there is a co-pay. And if you enter our rehab and counseling inpatient program here, your first thirty-six hours of counseling are free. Once we are convinced that you are not a threat to yourself or others, you will have to return here for our intensive outpatient therapy one hour a night for the next three weeks. And you will be required to attend a local drug abuse support group. If you are willing, you need to sign here."

She handed over a form which had covenants of policy and snippets of law pursuant to disclosure and transparency.

Health care and counseling and insurance meant just one thing: Bureaucracy and endless forms that were in the process of being digitized to save trees and presented on i-tablets instead of clipboards.

The legal rights and responsibilities for each individual residing in the United State of America created a paper trail that could reach to the moon.

The moon might be full of cheese.

But the paper work was full of something else.

When all the paper work on all the earth was digitized, it would become a digital rabbit-black hole that would suck everything in.

"Do you know of a psychiatrist? You have to see one to get released from here," Jayne V. said.

"Yes. I want Dr. Frost," I said. *I won't go until I see him. I won't go until I see him. I won't go until I see him. So bring him right here.*

"Will my husband be admitted to the psych ward here?" Blair asked.

Ex-husband.

Psych ward? I hadn't counted on that. Of course, I hadn't counted on much beyond my suicide attempt. Maybe saying hello to God and Grandpa.

I did not relish the thought of spending the night in the psych ward. Of being put into a large room to join in the aimless shuffling of the living dead.

"Yes," Jayne V. said.

"Which part?" Blair said.

"Ward C," Jayne V said. "It has the lowest security threat."

"Not Kelter Ward C?" Blair asked.

Jayne V. looked at her. "Yes. You know it?"

"Yes!" Blair blurted. "I can't believe it's still here."

I looked at her then.

She had just given up a ghost of her own. It had slipped right on out. A crumb of naked truth.

And I stuck that crumb away intending to tack it somewhere onto the condensed life history that Blair had given me.

"Mr. R., are you feeling well enough to walk or should I get a wheel chair?" Jayne V. asked.

I tested my arms and legs. They still worked. But I wasn't about to go walking around without a shirt. No shoes. No shirt. No insurance. No service. "I'll walk. But I'll need my shirt. Or something."

I was quite the hairy fellow.

Jayne V. poked her head out of the privacy curtain and called for the closest attending nurse to grab a gown for me. The nurse came back jack-be-quick and handed me a white and turquoise gown with a design of squiggly lines. Meant to grab my racing thoughts and clear them out into a comfortable placid pattern.

I put my arms into the gown and Blair played mother and tied me up in the back. The material was coarse. And smelled of non scented laundry detergent.

I slid off the table and was back upon my feet, for whatever that was worth. The room swam around me. I took a step forward and my legs felt too wide apart. They were unsure of this new undiscovered land.

Blair took me by the upper arm, knowing better not to grab my wrist or forearm. "Careful, honey."

She was playing up the part of the dutiful ex-wife in front of the hospital staff. There was about five minutes of niceness in her before it would shut off. Servitude was fine as long it as somehow served her.

Jayne V. pulled the curtain back and I wobbled out of the examining room and into the heart of the Emergency Room.

The ER was set up as a hub and spoke. The center of the wheel held low desks and computers and filing cabinets as well as portable utility cabinets full of surgical tools and machines with laser precision cutters and portable lamps and magnifying lenses all just waiting to be carted into the half dozen examining rooms arrayed in spokes and be let loose.

Technology to the rescue.

The ER was quiet now. It was downtime. Between emergencies.

The staff was seated. Endorphins dropping. Yawns stifled.

With no one to save, there was nothing to do but boring, unrelenting digital compliance. Click. Check. Enter. Save. Open the next form.

Four of the examining rooms had curtains drawn. From behind the cloth, I heard one patient cough, another moan, and two were silent as the grave.

Two for two.

Tie game.

One might argue that you were either alive or dead in a place like this. But I had been somewhere in between. Of that, I was certain. And, of course, the argument was there was no in between.

If you could be resuscitated, then you were alive and if you couldn't, then you're very dead.

That argument made life cut and dry. Nice and simple. Only life wasn't always that way.

Jayne V. led us to the entrance of the ER. Beyond which was the waiting lounge. It was swamped with people who did not have the capacity or graciousness to wait without sighing, crying, complaining, or cursing. There were one parent families with children who were sick or bleeding or had broken bones to attend to while trying to fill out compliance on i-tablet or clipboard. There were pre-teens trying to convince their guardians that their symptoms had subsided so why couldn't they go home? There were elderly spouses encouraging their partner to tough out their painful conditions just a little longer. Some complained that since the refill had run out on their MK Ultra drugs, they had come to the ER to get free samples.

And what everyone had in common was that they had to wait for their names to be called.

To be validated.

To be recognized.

To be helped.

This was the real in between place. Waiting to be seen and until that happened, you did not exist.

Because of my condition and because of what I had chosen to do to myself, I had been able to skip ahead to the front of the line.

Shouldn't I have felt selfish?

I didn't feel much of anything.

Hadn't that been the plan?

Not to have to deal with anything anymore?

The disappointments.

The failures.

The hurts.

Give up on it all.

And just blank out.

Let go.

Sink down into oblivion.

But that wasn't what had happened.

I still had seen things.
Heard things.
And felt things.
What had that been about?
An out of body experience?
More like a near death experience.

I had been dead with no heartbeat. But I had been clinically dead? Had there still been brain wave patterns?

Maybe the stress of being shocked with the paddles had triggered a hallucination. Three, to be exact.

I had seen my past; I had seen my regrets; and I had seen places I had never been to in my life.

Right up to the time I'd awoken in the ER.

I hadn't wanted to wake up.

Not here anyway.

4—"From a Waiting Lounge to a Locked Door"

Yet here I was.

Walking down a hall with Jayne V. and her combed auburn hair and professional slacks and Blair, my ex #2, with her uncombed hair and dirty blue jeans and an Old Navy pull over hoodie. We followed the counselor down the white hallway into another officious atrium.

Ahead was a wide security door. Above it a tiny security cam perched in the eaves. To the right was an admitting window covered with shut beveled glass. To the left was a small suite of offices and conference rooms.

A small sign designated to whom the tiny lair belonged.
HOPE COUNSELORS, INC.

We had gone from a waiting lounge to a locked door.

Jayne V. walked us up to the sliding glass window. The beveled glass gave a hint of anamorphic silhouettes moving and living behind it. A long shadow slid the glass back and a middle aged woman with twenty extra pounds in the gut smiled at Jayne V. "Bringing in some new business?"

"Yes," she said. "He'll be staying a few days with us. His information should be in the system now."

"Always got room for one more," the worker said and checked her screen to confirm what Janet V. had promised. Then she handed Jayne V. another i-tablet. And slid the window shut.

Jayne V. gave it to me to sign electronically.

I looked it over while Blair read it over my shoulder.

Necessary compliance. A simple disclosure. And an agreement. That I was checking myself into the psychiatric ward of Our Lady's of my own free will. And that I promised to abide by the rules of the hospital. And I would not inflict harm upon myself. Or others. And I would not bring illegal substances into the ward or try to take them illegally out of the ward. And I would respect all the staff and all the other patients and regardless of race, color, or creed and not use hate speech.

Once I squiggled a digital date and signature with my forefinger—which may not what Michelangelo had intended--I handed the i-tablet back to Jayne V. who opened the beveled glass window with a knock so she could hand the i-tablet to the receptionist, who changed back to an anamorphic shape when she slid the glass shut again.

Jayne V. turned to face us again. This was where we were to part company. And where Blair could go no further. Unless she wanted to join me by admitting herself.

"They will send an orderly out in a minute to escort you in," Jayne V. said. "Kelter Ward C. is just through those doors."

"When can I come see him?" Blair asked.

"Visiting hours are twice a day. At 4:30 and 6:30," Jayne V. said.

It was almost eleven in the evening.

"I won't be able to see you until tomorrow honey," Blair said.

"I'll need some clothes," I said. "A couple changes at least. Can I bring my own pajamas?"

"Yes," Jayne V. said.

"And you'll need fresh underwear," Blair said.

Jayne V. suppressed a giggle.

"Don't forget those," I said. I couldn't stand the thought of having to wear dirty underdrawers.

"Can I come back tonight and give him some clothes?" Blair asked.

"Of course," Jayne V. said.

"Go on in, then, honey," Blair said. "And I'll be back in at least an hour. I'll have to get a four-wheel Uber drive. You don't want me driving in this."

First a *honey*. Then some sugar planted when she kissed me on the cheek as she walked down the atrium past the Hope Counseling, Inc. offices and out their appointed entrance door to the parking lot.

An Uber ride. More money down the drain. The stitches in my wrists pulled tighter and the pain burned a little deeper. The numbing blanket that the darvaceet had provided was beginning to withdraw.

"She seems very outgoing," Jayne V. said.

I nodded. "Right now, she's going out." And that was a good thing.

Jayne V. let a laugh escape. But just a little one.

The wide security door buzzed opened. From out behind it stepped a slim older African-American nurse and a middle aged male aide. She was smiling. He was not.

"Ready for the hand over?" Jayne V. asked.

"We'll take it from here," the coffee-creamed nurse said in a rich tone. Her lanyard read: ROCHELLE, RN, MENTAL HEALTH UNIT.

Jayne V. introduced us. "Nurse Rochelle, this is Justin R. Mr. R. this is Nurse Rochelle. She helps run the Kelter Unit. I'll be by tomorrow for ask some questions for Dr. Frost."

I stuck out my hand to Jayne V.. "Well, until the next session."

She shook it. "I truly hope the best for you."

"Come on in, Mr. R.," Rochelle invited. "And let us help you. You're in good hands now." She was past fifty. There were more than a few stray grays in hair. Her lean face was naked of makeup and jewelry or piercings and wore only a kind smile. I could tell she truly loved her job.

I felt envious. I hated my job at America's Bank.

And I felt small. There was nothing in my life that I loved enough to be dedicated to and excel in for its own sake. Nothing that I would be willing lay my life down for.

Maybe that was why I had been so tempted to just throw it away.

Rochelle walked ahead and I followed and the nameless pale-skinned aide brought up the rear.

We crossed the threshold and I was inside Kelter Ward C.

I expected to see the walking zombies. Soulless, will-less, burned out husks of human consciousnesses stumbling about in a psychotropic haze.

I saw none.

I expected to hear the howls and wails of the possessed huddled in their padded rooms with their arms locked across their bellies screaming out obscenities against their parents.

I heard none.

I half-expected Rochelle's goon/aide to grab me from behind in a half nelson and strong-arm me into a small room that had a table with leather straps for the feet, waist, wrists, and head. Next to that would be a huge oscillating generator with tubes and dials and a needle to read the charge to the poles. Coming out of the generator would be two cables, one red, one black, ending in clamps. That could be attached to my various extremities to give me a jolt of electrical shock treatment that would entreat me to ride the lightning. Pain travelling at the speed of plasma. Reaching down to the tip of my toes and bouncing back up to my brain and making my jaw clench and spasming every muscle. Not enough to burn out my eyes. But just enough to scramble my memories and leave blank spaces between the synapses.

I had come ten steps inside Kelter Ward C and that had not happened yet.

But I was still apprehensive.

Rochelle was at peace and the pale-skinned aide was ready, should I get even more apprehensive. After all, the hospital could not take it for granted that I was a threat to myself more than to anyone else.

If Kelter Ward C was supposed to be the lowest level of security in Our Lady's Mental Health Unit, did that mean there was a Ward B? And a Ward A?

Were they above us? What were they like? Was that were the hollowed out and hopeless did their endless shuffle? Was that were the violent and manic were constrained in dark padded rooms?

Did that mean that somewhere up in the attic behind maximum security doors that there was a secluded surgical room that held the generator and battery with clamps and a table with straps?

Kept in reserve. For when medicine might fail. Ready for use as an almighty mood reset.

Why not?

They had already shocked my still stony heart.

But neither Nurse Rochelle nor her aide familiar laid a finger on me.

Instead of slapping a straightjacket on me, they led me down a short hall to the day room. To the right was the nurses' station with walls of stat boards and notice boards, a tv monitor feed showing different camera angles of Ward C, chairs sitting behind a long counter protected with a thick glass window, and a steel door giving access to the station that could looked in case it needed to become an Alamo.

The patients' day room was small, almost like a bizarre boarding gate at an airport. The walls painted a bland beige and white without a single painting for a color splash, a dozen gouged and peeling lounge chairs, and two small tables facing an old 18 inch Sanyo on a rickety entertainment center.

Most of it was in deep slumberous shadows. A glare came through the big window of the nurses' station. Lit by a solitary lamp. The sign of a lonely night vigil. Rochelle's watch.

The entire ward was in sleep mode. Lights dimmed. Air whispering out its ducts.

All was still.

Tranquilized.

Sugar plumb fairies sedated.

Nutcrackers full of drowse.

Even the rats on the Ward were hunkered down for a long Christmas nap.

If I broke into an acapella rendition of "Jumpin' Jack Flash" now, it might get me bumped up a ward or two. Or a trip straight to the top. To the battery waiting in closet to touch and make converts.

The aide stood beside the open door to the nurses' station as Nurse Rochelle led me down a white antiseptic hall lit by a nightlight plugged into a socket. I counted eight rooms. Four to a side. With no doors.

She ushered me into the second threshold on the right. It was occupied by two empty single beds, two nightstands with two lamps and two dressers along the opposite wall. She went to the far nightstand and switched on the lamp.

"Lights out at 10 PM," Nurse Rochelle explained. "Now I understand you're waiting for your wife to bring you some clothes. We'll give her an hour. Then it will be lights out for you. We mustn't disturb the other patients."

"Thank you," I said and stood at the front of the bed furthest from the doorway.

"We can't feed you until morning. There is to be no food or drink in your dorm rooms. Is there anything else I can get you, Mr. R.?" she asked.

I looked at the bed. There was a thin blanket with a starched bed sheet. And one pillow.

"Do you think I could have an extra blanket?" I asked.

"Of course," Nurse Rochelle said.

"And an extra pillow?" I asked.

Nurse Rochelle calmly shook her head. "One pillow per bed. It cuts down on laundry costs. See that chord attached to the wall between the beds? That's the call button. Use it if you need me in a jiff."

Then she left me standing in the lamplight staring between a choice of two beds. My legs began to spasm. My wrists burned. The stitches pulled tighter. I was so tired. Years behind on sleep.

I looked at the other empty bed. Hopefully, I wouldn't get a roommate. I wanted to be alone as alone could be.

Between the two beds hung a beige cord with the call button that looked like a slender click-it marker. There was a small sign attached to the wall. *Emergency Use Only.* It had been tucked there for reassurance and hope in times of tight places or straits or trouble.

And above it was another object placed for reassurance and hope to be accessed only by faith. A holy icon. Of the Virgin Mary Holy Mother of Go. Wearing a white head shawl over a red tunic with a blue cloak slung over her shoulder. Her right hand tapped the center of her chest where flames licked a red heart and radiated out yellow light. Her left thumb and forefinger were erect. Her face was creamy white and serene. There was a slight blush on her cheeks, perhaps warmed from the flames within her heart. Her eyes soft and blue. Her chestnut hair pulled back. Her nose was long. Her lips ruby red and small. Her chin delicate. Behind her head was an occluded nimbus.

Mary of the Immaculate Heart. The namesake of the hospital and the adjoining shrine. She was beautiful.

Nothing like my ex #2.

Sometimes I couldn't remember what #1 even even looked like.

Then I felt the cool stillness of the ward. It was a restful slow rhythm. Somatic peace.

I wanted it to claim me. To lay me down and rock me. Tuck me in and sing me asleep.

I had lost track of how long I just stood there looking at the painting. Then came the soft tread of support shoes.

"You can lie down if you wish, Mr. R.," Nurse Rochelle said from the hallway. "I'll--" A soft ping like when an elevator door was about to open rang across the ward. "Excuse me. That's for me. I was just gonna say I'll wake you when your wife comes."

Then she was off to answer the call. Because she had made an oath to be a nurse.

I'd believe that when I saw it. Blair was probably at home updating her profile on CatchMe.com. Or pawning off the spare tv that my parents had given me when I'd moved back into my own home that I had left when we had separated and had to wait until the divorce legally gave me back my own house.

Twenty minutes later, I heard squishy soles of comfort shoes once again.

I was still standing in the same spot. Nurse Rochelle stopped briefly at the threshold and putting both her hands on it, ducked her head in and out to give the room a sweeping glance. I had already become a part of her routine.

This time, two pings from different rooms went off in successive beats. That would keep her busy. My arrival must have stirred up insecurities and questions and wants. But Nurse Rochelle could only deliver aspirin or Tylenol in place of warm milk and cookies.

Since it wasn't being used, I grabbed the pillow and pulled the blanket off the empty second bed. I pulled the covers back on my bed and fluffed pillows as much as the foam would allow. Then climbed in and pulled up the rationed blanket and sheet and pulled the extra blanket into place. It was stiff and coarse. Now I was ready for some rack time. Then I turned off the lamp.

I should have gone straight to sleep since it was so quiet on the ward.

But then, the silence was broken with another ping. And then another. And another. And one more for good measure. The pings did not stop. Someone, everyone, anyone, no one, was calling at the same time with incessant needs.

The pings continued until it became a chorus with no pause between the tones becoming all one long sustained note.

There couldn't have been that many people or that many call buttons on the ward.

Just an auditory hallucination? Stress triggering sleep paralysis? Why hadn't my subconscious decided to make me believe the wolf-man was underneath my bed waiting to snack on my hand if it fell out from under the blankets?

But I heard the sound of approaching steps once again.

The shoes squeaked under some weight as they came down the hall.

They stopped at my door again.

They should have continued on.

But they didn't.

Nurse Rochelle must have been standing at the door. Peeking in on me. Spying out my form in the darkness.

Maybe she could tell I had taken the pillow and cover from the other bed.

Maybe that constituted stealing according to the rules on the ward.

Maybe she meant to take the extra pillow and blanket away from me.

Or worse, she would send in her orderly familiar in to do her dirty work.

I turned over and switched on the lamp.

Someone stood in the doorway looking in on me. Only it wasn't Nurse Rochelle.

It was Grandpa.

Dead these nineteen years.

5—"It's the Little Things"

He didn't say hello.

He didn't run over to hug me.

He didn't tell a joke.

He didn't call me by name.

"You're worried she may not come back," was all he said.

At first, I thought he must have meant Nurse Rochelle.

"Maybe she's taking her lunch," I murmured. My mouth was lined with cotton and sleep.

"I've got just three words to say about her," he continued. "'No' and 'good.'"

Now I knew he wasn't talking about Nurse Rochelle. I knew who he meant.

"I love her," I said.

He raspberried the comment. "I love pizza. But it gives me gas. And it always had to be sausage pizza. Couldn't be anything but. First, it would bloat me. Then give me hellacious heart burn. Then'd come the gas. And your sweet grandmother would make me sleep out on the couch. That's where loving pizza got me. In the dog house."

"Grandma?" I asked incredulously. "No, she didn't."

"Yeah, she did," Grandpa said. "She was a no nonsense woman. Had to be to live with me. I can be tricky. But your grandmother had a heart of gold."

Or maybe a flaming heart.

Like the picture above my head.

Grandpa leaned against the doorframe. "So, Grandson, what you been up to?"

What a question.

"Not much," I said.

He tsked me and shook his head.

"Being stuck in a hospital stinks. And the food is the worst," he said. "And whenever you try to sleep, the nurses come round and poke you. Always taking your blood for tests. The last time I was in the hospital, a guy on the same floor as me woke up without a kidney. Somebody'd cut it out while he'd slept!"

He took a step into the room. A light blue terry cloth robe covered his pajamas and his feet were shod with Deerfoam slippers and there was an earbud in his right ear. Listening to a pocket radio stuffed into the pocket of his robe. Probably to a St. Louis Cardinals game. His beloved Cards.

"Grandpa," I began to ask. "Why are you here?"

"Because you're an idiot," he said. He wasn't one to mince words. They would either be something kind, funny, or pointed. "You're a grown man and you've totally given up."

"Maybe I've lost my faith or something," I said. When I was little, it was Grandpa to whom I gave all my questions. Was there a God? Why are girls different? What was it like fighting the Nat-zees in World War II? Why is there air?

And he would answer every single one of them. On the level. Without any bit of a fairy tale. I could always trust him.

"Lost your faith? Lost your mind is more like it. You let that woman take you for everything. Now she's come back for the crumbs."

"She's not like that all the time. When she gets upset she gets her back up. Like a cat," I said.

"A cat? More like a female dog. Biting the hand that feeds her and turning her nose up at whatever bones get throwed at her."

"You don't know her. You never met her. She just wants someone to love her," I told him. After all, he'd been dead when I'd gotten married. Both times.

He put a hand to his chin and laid a finger to his long wide nose. Grandpa had said that noses gave people's face character and that his had lots of it. He still had his whispy white hair swept back over his forehead. And he had never been tall. In fact, if I had gotten out of bed, I would be the same height. At thirteen I had his shoe size. Size seven and a half triple E. So, he gave me an old pair of Converse sneakers.

Grandpa had never met a stranger. He knew something about everyone and could always talk sports with anyone anywhere. He loved a fair-played competition.

His mind had been keen edged. And he'd kept his wits to his very last breath. During his last hospital stay when the doctor had asked how he felt, Grandpa had looked up from his crossword puzzle and said, "Copasetic." And then Grandpa had asked for sausage pizza for lunch.

"I don't have to meet her to know her, grandson," Grandpa said. Even dead, he knew a little about everything. And he was always right. "I hear your parents' crying. Hear them praying."

"The Bible says that when a man takes a woman as his wife they become one flesh, leave their mother and father, cleave to each other, and forsake all others," I reminded him. He knew the Bible backwards and forwards because he had taken me every to church every Sunday to hear it be read.

But just hearing it being read hadn't been enough. Maybe I should have lived it and put it in practice.

"Your parents would be so happy if that actually did happen. And it might have happened the first time if you'd given it a chance. Then you ran into this girl. And she was front page bad news.

"First you married her. Then you left her. Then you took her back. Now you're here. Because you're doing the same thing you did last time thinking you're gonna get a different result. That's the definition of insanity. No wonder your family thinks you're bonkers," Granddpa said.

"Speak some words of comfort to me, Grandpa. So I made a mistake. The same mistake. Twice. Can't they find it in their heart to forgive me?" I asked. The darvacet and whatever else they had slipped me in the ER was beginning to wear off. I could feel the fullness of my pain and hurt. My miserable thirty-three years of living weighted on my heart like a stone. Icy water rose up in the corner of my eyes. I guess my sorry choices had put myself in this mess.

"If you choose her over your family, they might forgive you. But they won't forgive her. And they won't forget it. You'll lose their respect forever. You really want that?" Grandpa asked.

That was Grandpa. Let 'er rip. Tellin' like it needs to be told.

I was mad. The tears squeezed out of my eyes all on their own. They were just the tip of the iceberg. There was a lot of hurt under the waterline. Deep and wide. Just waiting for the Titanic. "You weren't perfect either. We all know you were married before. After you died, Grandma sent Mom down to the safety box and she found your marriage license to your first wife in the safety box. You never told her or even your grandkids."

"Because it wasn't any of your mom's business. Or yours, or your brother's. It was in my past. The past is the past. My first wife had nothing to do with the life I got to make with your grandmother. God gave me a second chance and I made the most of it. Every day was a blessing for me. First, meeting your grandmother. Then having your mother after thinking we might not have be able to have any kids. And finally, through her, God gave me my two biggest blessings: my grandsons. And now you wanna try and throw this all back in my face?

"Yeah, I made a mistake. I was young. I loved sports. I wanted to be a professional athlete. Golf was my game. I was the club pro at Grand Marias on the East Side. Bet you didn't know that, did you? I could make some money at it. And I got some attention. Like Madge. Madge was beautiful. She knew how to turn heads and I liked that. She liked me because I was a winner and I looked good on her arm. When I won a regional tournament, we got married. Well, then I tried to qualify for a pro-golf tournament. Everyone I knew listened to the game on the radio. I got beat out in the first round. My friends and family forgave me. But Madge wouldn't. She wanted a winner. So, she hooked up with another player. I didn't find out about it till afterwards. We came home and her heart turned stone cold towards me. Then she started running with my friends. She had no respect for me at all. Or herself. One of them finally 'fessed up. Some friend. I was crushed. It was worse than everyone listening to me lose the state championship because everyone seemed to know about Madge but me. I was the last to know.

"I thought my life was over. Certainly, my golf career and marriage were over. My heart had gone to stone. I felt so guilty. It was like sets of chains around my heart. The last place I wanted to go was church, but that's where I ended up. I listened to the preacher talk about God's promise to give believers a heart of flesh to replace their heart of stone. I could have this if I got my mind right. So, I went forward to the altar and got down on my knees and asked God to forgive me and surrendered my life over to His Care. I made sure to let Him direct my every step every day for the rest of my life.

"So, I joined that church. In those days, people used to line up to meet new members. And that was when I met your Grandmother as she came through the line to greet me. She was so tiny, with hair so dark and her no nonsense eyes. But she was a true lady. A heart of gold. God had given her a fleshy heart.

"Then my cousin helped me get a job as a part time teller at Stockyards Bank. This was during the Depression when jobs were scarce. Even in the midst of all that doom and gloom, God blessed me.

"After that, I was able to get married to your grandmother. Everyday, I'd wake up, look in the bathroom mirror and tell myself, 'God has blessed you beyond measure. He is good all the time. All the time He is good. The best things come from Him. Like getting married to my little dark-haired lady and my job.' Then I'd go and fix her breakfast. Help her wash dishes every night after supper. She did right by me. And we never had even the tiniest spat. Remember, it's the little things that matter most," Grandpa said.

Then he said, "Like you not having pajamas. Or clothes for tomorrow. And just why is this?"

My tears had stopped flowing.

They had hardened in their tracks.

The well had been capped.

"Blair'll be back," I said.

"You sure about that?" Grandpa asked.

I didn't say a word.

"You're learning the hard that way that you can't make people do something they don't want to do. If you make them do it, they will resent you. See, most people don't wanna change. Not on their own. Only God can change a heart, and only if people will let Him. So, what you see is what you get. Do you really think Blair will change? She's a sow's ear," Grandpa said.

"I get it. You made a mistake. Got a second chance. And lived a great life," I said.

"Just like Job, I didn't ask for trouble, but it came anyway and turned my life upside down. And I was down for the count until I realized that God hadn't changed and I better get right with him. So, I let Him work on me until I had a fleshy heart.

"Let me tell it to you in baseball talk. Grandson, after striking out the first time, I made a grand slam homerun on my second at bat. With the bases loaded. Your mom was on third. Your brother on second. And you were on first. Madge was pitchin' against me. But your grandma was my battin' coach. So, it became a walk off grand slam. It won me the game. I am so blessed and thankful," Grandpa said. "Thank you, God. Forever and ever. Amen."

I realized that I had one more question for my Grandpa. A question that I had heard someone else ask earlier that night.

"Grandpa, what did you want most for Christams?" I asked.

Since he had been dead for nineteen years, surely he'd had time to think about it. Among other things. Like the history of the St. Louis Cardinals.

"I mean, if you could have just one Christmas gift right now then what would it be?" I asked my dead Grandpa.

He looked down his long nose. Rubbed the side of it with his forefinger. He was thinking very hard.

"Your grandmother's fudge," he finally said.

I nodded. "That sounds so good right about now."

"What about you, grandson?" he asked. "Do you even know what you want most?"

"Someone to love me for me," I blurted. It was honest and true. As are the first things we think of.

"Here, here. That's what families are for," Grandpa nodded.

Then I began to babble. "Blair is the only one who's ever understood me. We can make this work."

From out of the earbud in Grandpa's left ear came a crack of a bat and the roar of an opposing crowd sitting in the bleachers. It might have been the old colosseum-style Busch Stadium. Or it might have been the even older jewel box Sportman's Park. As Faulkner once said: *The past is never dead. It's not even past.*

Grandpa shook his head and wanted to spit. "What a crock! Cards just blew their lead. In the bottom of the eighth."

He turned the volume down. "I'm missing a good game by being here. So, you better listen up. Maybe you do belong here after all if you're willing to push over your own family for this crazy girl.

"What if she's home right now stealin' you blind? What if she left you here to rot?" Grandpa asked.

There wasn't much left for her to take after the divorce. I had managed to block her from all the accounts. And I wasn't about to put her back on them. Other than my pride or ego, it was slim pickings.

"You need to experience being bad off. You need to hit rock bottom. Get down so low that you can't tell the bottom from the top. Then maybe you'll open your eyes and see where you're headed. Cuz your future ain't lookin' so bright. Where you're goin', you won't be needin' no sunglasses.

"You remember Job? He went through all kinds of hell just to learn not to spit at the Voice in the Whirlwind. Job finally saw God for who He was and he learned his place: God the Almighty is way up there and we are just humans who are way down here. We don't have control over nothing except making a choice. You remember Jonah? He was in the belly of hell when he finally confessed that vanity had lied to him. Then he called out to God for salvation.

"Your heart is getting hard and calloused. More and more like a stone with every beat of the clock. What you need is a new heart. A fleshy heart. And only God can change a heart. And only if you let Him.

"You got just one more at bat. You know what that means?" He held up three fingers and kept waving them like an umpire giving a count. "Just three more strikes. You're gonna see three more spirits. You're gonna have three more visits, whether you want 'em or not. Just three more chances to make the right decision and turn your life around. So help me God, you better wait for a good pitch and swing away."

I heard soft squeaking of sneaker treads headed down the hall towards my doorless room. Grandpa ducked down the hallway and then someone else was at the doorframe.

It was Nurse Rochelle with an overnight bag. "Mr. R.? You awake? I hear you talkin' to yourself. Your wife dropped by. I got your change of clothes."

Grandpa was gone. Long gone. Dead and gone.

I put a cap on the well of my hurt and sucked up my tears and felt the stones in my heart.

But I couldn't hide my face.

<u>SECOND VERSE--The</u> <u>Ghost Of Christmas Fudge</u>

1-Shave and a Shower

It wasn't even my first full night in Kelter Ward C and already my room was a busy place. A stopover for spirits. Part of the nurse's night rounds. And a dumping place for my ex-wife.

I pulled back my covers and didn't realize that the circulation in my feet was so poor that I could barely feel them until I stepped down on the freezing linoleum. My feet were marble scraping against rock sheets. It was always the coldest just before dawn.

"No need to get up Mr. R.," Nurse Rochelle said. "She's not here."

"I thought you said she was," I said blurry with sleep.

"I said that she stopped by and brought you some clothes," she said. "She couldn't stay. It isn't visiting hours yet. So, I told her I'd take your clothes to you."

Grandpa's threat was still sounding in the well of my heart. Nineteen years dead and having never met Blair, he seemed to know her so well.

"We've got to scan the baggage anyway. Rules of the house," Nurse Rochelle added.

Some house, some rules. Locked down wards and rooms with no doors. And searching baggage for smuggled contraband. What was that old saying? *If you expect the worst, you'll never be disappointed.*

What could I do about it now? I had signed myself into this place, put myself under their care. And I wasn't getting out until I met with Dr. Frost and jumped through a flaming hoop for him.

My body was still drowsed. Every muscle tight and sore. The stitches pinching the wounds on my wrists.

"What time is it?" I asked.

"Six-thirty," Nurse Rochelle said. "Normally, we let patients sleep in till seven. But I wouldn't advise staying in bed any later than that."

"I'm an early riser anyway," I said. After years in rock and roll bands, I had come to the conclusion that I really wasn't that much of a night owl. Twelve midnight was my Cinderella hour. After that, I turned into a pumpkin. A brainless laughing fool living off the impulses from the lower cerebral cortex. I craved sunlight. Whenever the sun shone on my face, I couldn't sleep anymore. It made me wanna wake up and go forth and conquer. Or just get up and take a pee.

But there wasn't any sunlight in Kelter Ward C.

Every square inch of wall space had been painted light blue. Which was supposed to make me feel like it was a comfortable and cool and relaxing seventy-five degrees Fahrenheit. But the dim light of the dawn washed out the color and gave everything a grey tint.

Nurse Rochelle gestured back towards the hall and another orderly, this time a young African American male, hefted in my overnight bag and set it beside the dresser facing my bed.

"Thank you," I said wiping sleep from my eyes.

Nurse Rochelle answered for her orderly. "You're very much welcome."

Might as well get up and see Kelter Ward C in all its grey dimmed glory.

"Can I go ahead and take a shower?" I asked.

"Yes, you may. It's down at the end of the hall. Last room on the right. You'll have to wait to get buzzed in. You'll find towels and a robe in the anteroom. The water will only run for two minutes. And it will not be hot," she said as an African American orderly passed her as he headed back towards the nurse's station.

So much for taking a long hot shower.

They definitely didn't want anyone getting too comfortable.

A hot shower was a ritual I had created to cope with the stress and depression.

It helped me to breathe out and relax.

Make my muscles unknot.

Let my mind drift into a sweet oblivion.

It was about the only way I could get my body and mind to unwind.

Besides indulging in sex and drugs. Believe it or not, even indulging in sex and drugs gets old.

"Breakfast arrives at seven. We wake everyone up then. Give everyone a chance to eat. Breakfast gets taken away at eight thirty. First group meeting is at nine," Rochelle said.

"Group meeting?" I asked. My scalp was itchy. So I scratched it. My pillow sheet had been rough and my bed sheet had chafed at my cheek neck. "I thought I'd just take a nap until the good Dr. Frost gets here."

"Oh, no," Nurse Rochelle rebuked with a smile. "We want everyone to socialize. Best way to do that is to be out in the lounge as much as possible. It'll be good for you to be around people."

I didn't like that one bit. I didn't want to be around other broken people. Hear them babble and watch them drool. Comparing how much drugs they'd taken and how close they'd come to a successful suicide and how messy it'd been. Bragging rights. Stupid fights. Darkness over light. It was humiliating. Depressing.

Nurse Rochelle left me to my own devices. I put my overnight bag on the empty bed and unzipped it. I rifled through it quickly.

Blair might have packed some nacho cheese Combos but the staff had probably taken them. Bringing in food and open containers were expressly forbidden. On pain of death. *House Rules.*

She had packed my Addias runners, which was the only shoe wide enough to fit me true to size, so I wouldn't have to wear my thick soled Sketchers every day. There were two pairs of jeans. One pair of khaki Slackers. Three white t-shirts. One pullover. Three button down shirts. Four underwear--bless her—and four pairs of tube socks. Two pairs of pajamas: my navy Scooby Doo's and my black and grey Star Wars imprinted with the Death Star in all its imperial glory just before Luke Skywalker blew it up.

There wasn't a single book.

But there was a note:

My Dearest Justin,

Do not worry. The house will be safe with me. All because I love you. I am sorry for what happened. But I am committed to our being together. I hope you are, too! I know it's the right thing to do.

Love,

Blair

PS.

I would love to become Mrs. Justin R. again! Then your parents will have to accept us!

It was supposed to be a note of encouragement.

But it didn't give me a peaceful easy feeling.

Just the opposite. More like a pull in my stomach against falling gravity. Muscles knotting in the back of my neck.

Something made me wad up the paper. I looked around for a trashcan but there was not one in sight. But there was a nightstand with a pull-out drawer.

So, I pulled it out.

Someone had tucked a book inside it and then closed it again.

It was a Gideon's Bible.

It fell open towards the middle.

So, I picked it up and read.

Psalm 25

A Psalm of David

Unto thee, O Lord, do I lift up my soul.

O my God, I trust in thee: let me not be ashamed, let not mine enemies triumph over me.

Yea, let none that wait on thee be ashamed: let them be ashamed which transgress without paths.

Shew me thy ways, O Lord; teach me thy paths.

Lead me in thy truth, and teach me: for thou art the God of my salvation; on thee do I wait all day.

I'd grown up with stories of David in Sunday School. Shepherd boy to his father, minstrel and chief warrior to Saul, wise king to the nation of Israel, failed father to his family, murderer and adulterer to his army, a heart of worship for his God, and a sinner to boot. And through it all—the good, the bad, and the ugly--he wrote both psalms of beautiful praise and of heart breaking agony.

That the last I could understand.

That was the soul of a poet at work.

I wrote stories when I was happy and inspired.

And song lyrics when I mad or upset.

But I hadn't learned to give it all to God like David did.

When I was happy, I got drunk or high.

And when things were rotten I got drunk or high.

I conflated love with sex. And for someone to love me meant having sex with them. To say or hear, "I love you" during sex was the best it could get, I used to think. Which was a great high for my ego. Until either my partner or I would get mad and say, "I hate you."

And then I'd feel rotten…and get…well, you can guess the rest.

Drugs, of any kind, were like an elevator that took me straight up. But when I came down, the elevator would drop me straight down the shaft. I might laugh and be the life of the party while I was high but when I came down, I would cry and put a knife to my wrist.

So, sex and drugs and rock and roll…no matter which or what or how much I did, I'd end up feeling the same.

Cheated.

David had great faith. Both in God and in himself. Jesus said God loved David because he had a heart for God.

My faith in myself was small.

And my faith in God was even smaller.

God was no respecter of persons. He judged only what was in the heart. It wouldn't be hard to judge my heart—it was full of stones.

What I needed was a shower.

The stink of sleep and the grease of night were on my skin and in my hair.

I picked out a change of fresh clothes from my overnight bag and left my room with the door remaining open, as it had all night long, as all doors on the ward were, all but one. The only one that mattered.

The hall was grey, the linoleum cold. The iciness pricked the bottom of my bare feet. Blood was pumped harder from the tip of my toes until they hurt.

The entrance to the shower was the last down on the right. It was locked and I stood waiting before I began to wave at the security camera perched in the corner of the eaves. It buzzed and hermetically unsealed itself.

Inside was a dull antechamber with an open wardrobe full of folded towels and robes on peg hooks and clogs on the floor. Another security camera sat above the wardrobe. Below that were tubs full of bars of soap an inch long and travelling size bottles of shampoo.

I disrobed trying not to think of the security cam and who might be viewing it in the nurse's station at that very moment. Was it Nurse Rochelle or her pale-skinned counterpart? Then again, if the thought about God peering into my heart a hundred times a second never had stopped me from getting drunk or high, then the facility had a legal right to install a camera in the shower's antechamber.

I grabbed a bar of soap and a bottle of shampoo and opened the hard plastic shower door. It was more a plastic coated closet than a shower stall. Slippery and sleek.

I ripped the end off the soap package and slid the bar out. To turn on the water you had a turn huge dial. Which was set on a timer.

Two minutes only.

Nurse Rochelle hadn't been kidding around.

I soaped up dry and pushed the dial in.

The water was certainly not hot.

It bit into my aching muscles.

It reminded me that I was alive and what it was like to be one gigantic goosebump.

And that my powers of locomotion still worked and could work very fast when inspired.

I finished showering jack-be-quick and stepped out of the stall with the water still running. I grabbed a towel from the open wardrobe and was thankful for its pitiful warmth.

After I'd dressed, I balled up my clothes I had slept in and stepped back into the hall, the shower room hermetically locking behind him.

A grizzled orderly in snot green scrubs and plastic gloves pushed in a huge cart of trays. He bantered with Nurse Rochelle who came over to look at the catered food. Each tray bore a ticket with a patient's name and diet instruction and that meal's food order. She let the orderly know he had brought too many trays, that a few of the patients had been discharged yesterday. The orderly reminded her that the releases had to get down to admitting by eight PM the night before or a breakfast order would be put through. Anyway, he was just a humble food technician. Which meant he just schlepped the food.

Nurse Rochelle had not seen my approach from my room and down the hall to the day room but it was her duty to know where each patient was at all times, so she recognized my presence with, "Mr. R., we have a tray for you here. As of now, you have no dietary restrictions. But your doctor might place you on one later."

When I was stressed out and wasn't sleeping, my stomach would be in knots for days and I wouldn't eat. Couldn't eat. Worrying seemed to sped up my metabolism but shut down my thalamus, too.

I saw the trays. And the plates on the trays. And the covers on the plates.

I smelled hot food.

But it did not have an aroma.

I searched down one side of trays for my name. There were half a dozen names that had been designated certain diets: LOW SODIUM, LOW CARB, NO SUGAR.

I found mine in the middle of the other side.

Patient: JUSTIN R. Diet Restrictions: NONE. REGULAR MENU.

Apparently, God hadn't begun to punish me yet. I could have what passed as *regular* hospital food.

I looked over to Nurse Rochelle, "Can I eat it in my room?"

"You don't want to eat out in the lounge?" she asked.

There was just one person in the lounge. An older pale-skinned woman with withered skin and a birds' nest for hair. She might have been an unemployed Sybil newly kicked out of the Necromanteion.

Let's hope not.

I shook the thought and reference out of my head.

She gave me a disapproving look as I pulled off my tray and took it into my room.

There was no table or extra chair in my room. So I sat on the other bed that was still made and put the tray across my thighs.

I took the covers off the plates. And breakfast was revealed. A bowl of sloppy grits. Two rubbery pieces of bacon. A piece of dry toast cut in a triangle. A thumb sized tub of butter and strawberry jam. Two fingernail sized tubs of whipped butter. A small carton of regular milk. And an 6 ounce plastic cup of cold orange juice.

There were no illusions here.

This wasn't any attempts at award winning gourmet entries.

And neither was this fresh off the grill of some dirty spoon dinette.

It was what it was. And it was not what it was not, also. I'd make do with what I'd be given.

Then again, the grits could be seen as a definite sign. I loved grits. So, God had provided grits this morning. A small comfort. A small hope. A small sign that everything would be alright.

So, I remembered to give thanks. "God, thank you for the grits. I hope it stays down."

The butter went into the grits. Along with some of the milk. The jam went on the toast. The bacon was chewy and tough. It all went into my mouth and got washed down with a couple shots of orange juice.

Grandpa was right.

Hospital food was crap.

But it was bland enough to sit on my stomach and stay there.

Nurse Rochelle appeared at the door as I finished breaking my fast.

"Mr. R., I'm making my last rounds before I'm off for the day," she announced. "If you're finished, I'll take your tray. And I'll remind you that the first group session is at nine AM sharp."

She came in and I handed her the tray.

"Is there anything else I can do for you, Mr. R.?" she asked.

I rubbed my stubbly cheek. My facial hair was stiff and coarse. And I generally had five o clock shadow at five in the morning.

"My wife forgot to bring my shaving gear," I said. "Could I possibly ask to borrow a razor?"

"She didn't forget," Nurse Rochelle said giving me a look like I should know better. "We took the shaving tackle. It's not allowed on the ward. Nurse Michelle is just now coming on. I'll send her down with a razor."

Then she was gone with the empty tray.

In a few minutes down came a pale-skinned female nurse. She was as tall as me, which would be average height for a woman, a healthy build with no neck and no waist, and had frosted blonde hair with mangled bangs. Circles ran laps around her blue eyes. The price of the many changing shifts across shifting days.

Her lanyard read: MICHELLE, RN, MENTAL HEALTH UNIT.

"Hello, Mr. R.," Nurse Michelle said with the jolt of a strong cup coffee. "Rochelle said you needed something and I'm just the nurse to do it."

"I'd like to shave," I said.

She winked. "I'll be right back with a razor."

Other patients were stirring from their cocoons. Fighting the effects of pharmaceutical hibernation. A slow heartbeat, an ever slower metabolism, and a low blood pressure.

The call for breakfast had been passed door to door from sleepy bed to sleepy bed.

Anybody here yesterday already knew what to expect for breakfast.

They knew they wouldn't starve and a hunger strike would be countermanded. They also knew there was a chance there would be extra breakfast trays.

Nurse Michelle fetched two items. A disposable single blade razor and a travelling size can of shaving cream. I preferred a double razor or even a triple razor because my beard was so stiff and thick.

I took the items into the tiny bathroom. It had two sections. The first held an oval mirror and a plain counter with a small sink and basin. No cabinet underneath— hardly a vanity. The second was the size of a coat closet and held the toilet seat. Here one sacrifice to modesty and privacy had been made. There was a sliding door with a puny latch.

It was the only door in the ward that I could close and open myself. It promised to be a hiding place. A fortress of solitude.

I pushed the stopper in the sink and let the water run.

Nurse Michelle stood there and watched.

I sprayed some shaving cream in my left hand and applied it to my face, spreading the thick frosting with both hands. Then I washed my hands off in the water and swished the razor in it with my right.

Nurse Rachael watched my every movement.

My fingers were numb from gripping the razor. My wrists swollen and weak. And my hands shook.

I had to brace my right hand with my left. Handicapped, I continued on with my usual routine, shaving my left side first.

Nurse Michelle had not moved. I did not know why she hadn't left. Surely, she'd seen men shave before. Surely, I did no differently than any other man.

I tried to dismiss her. "You can go now. I can shave myself."

"Don't worry. I won't shave you. Unless I have to," Nurse Michelle said and folded her arms. "But I will watch you shave and I won't leave until you're done. Rules of the house."

She nodded at me the way Nurse Rochelle had when I had in innocence stepped over invisible boundaries forbidden by Kelter Mental Heatlh Unit law. I didn't remember seeing any of these "rules of the house" in the disclosure and agreement I had signed. But the floor nurse took a closed stance with her hands on her hips. The ball was in my court now. How far did I want to push it? She probably outweighed me by fifty pounds or more. But she had at least one watchdog orderly on stand-by. Ready to be unmuzzled.

Even with supporting my wrist, my hand shook. Causing me to knick myself more than I'd like. When I'd finished, I'd left half a dozen bloody spots under my chin and throat.

For me, shaving was a daily mutilation.

I swished the last of the cherry stained shaving cream off the razor blade in the murky water. Every bend of my wrist made them ache and my stitches pull on my wound. The fire of a rash from shaving burned my face as turned the faucet to cold to splash my face clean.

When I had finished washing and toweling off my face, Nurse Michelle held out her hand. I looked at her empty hand and she looked at the razor next to the sink.

"Mr. R., you need to give me the razor back," she announced.

"I can't keep it?" I asked. They had already taken my personal razor and shaving gear.

Nurse Michelle shook her head. "Rules of the house."

I looked into the mirror and saw that a couple of the knicks had stopped bleeding and had turned blacker than my mole.

Then I looked down at my bandaged wrists.

The staff of the Kelter Mental Health Unit wasn't about to trust me with anything sharp. They had sworn themselves to it. My life was their job.

My burning face. My cut-up neck. My shaking hands.

So, it was either my life or their job.

2-Lounge Games

***Having already showered and
shaved and eaten breakfast, I'd run
out of things to do.***

Normally, I'd be sitting at my desk at America's Bank. I doubt the bank would miss me. Now whoever got my workload might.

With nowhere else to go, I came out of my room and walked down to the patients' lounge.

The old withered woman lady was ensconced in a padded lounge chair watching "Good Morning, America" on the beat up 18 inch Sanyo. One of the hosts was doing a segment with a famous New York chef who was showcasing different recipes for French Toast on their mock kitchen set.

There was a small glass table with two chairs along the far wall. It was behind most of the other chairs which were placed to face either the tv set or the middle. It could be my small island of anonymity.

So I sat there and waited for the nine AM meeting.

The withered woman must have had great periperalvision or had sense a shadow falling on her or had felt a current of air because she said, "hi" to me from over her shoulder.

I said "hi" back to her shoulder.

Having never been in a psychiatric ward or a mental health unit or an insane asylum or whatever, I didn't quite know how to act.

One by one, the others on the ward filtered in.

The first to come in was a young boy with dark bed-head hair and thick block glasses. His left hand was tightly bandaged with all of his fingers sticking out. He kept his eyes from me.

The withered woman turned her head and showed a spark of maternal concern. "Hi, Timmy. How ya feelin'?"

Her voice was full of falling rocks, buzz saws, and scratchy records.

He shrugged. The eternal adolescent noncommittal gesture. "Okay, I guess."

"Ya 'posed to say 'With my hands,'" the withered woman said through what was left of her two front teeth.

Then she laughed at her own joke and a slapped her knee. It was more a hacking cough to shake some phlegm loose.

Timmy smirked, getting the joke and knowing it wasn't meant to insult him. He looked at me out of the corner of his eyes to see if he should be embarrassed or not.

I smiled and nodded, "Hi, Timmy. I'm Justin."

The kid was at least half my age.

"Hi Justin," the withered woman said at me. "I'm Lizzy B."

I had to look at her twice. Because the first time I didn't believe it.

She had been left out in the rain to rust.

She had been dug up by wild coyotes and drug in by alley cats.

She was the Wicked Witch of the North after the house had fallen on her.

She was dressed in dirty sweat pants and a blue tank top that exposed every wrinkle and scar and stretch mark over her leathery skin of her neck and shoulders.

Maybe once she had been young and fair skinned with long dark curly hair.

Or maybe she had always been this way since the day she was born.

Babies are born without teeth. Her entire bottom row was missing and whenever she smiled wide her tongue undulated with every cackle.

And many babies don't have much hair. Her curls were turning to grey steel wool and had thinned to the point where her forehead shone under the lights.

She caught me staring and didn't mind and turned back to the hosts on "Good Morning, America" who wouldn't be smiling into the camera if they had seen her sitting out in the studio audience.

A stout young woman walked in next. She had on a flannel shirt untucked over dark blue jeans. Her buzzed dark hair had a bent look from having been slept on. She had small eyes and mouth around a pug nose.

She smiled and said "hi" to both Timmy and Lizzy B.. Taking the lounge chair beside the empty chair at my table, she turned to me, "You must be the one they brought in during the middle of the night."

I nodded and stuck out my hand with a dovetailed wrist. "Justin R."

"Jacque A. B.," she nodded and took my hand in a sideways' grasp. "Sounds like 'Jackie'. Spelled like the French 'Jock'. JAY AY SEE CUE YOU EE."

She gestured with her eyes at my bandaged wrists. Then she pulled back her flannel shirt at the wrist to show me a puckering wound sewn shut. "I heard you died. They had to bring you back."

"Yeah, I guess so," I said with a little bit of that eternal adolescent understatement.

"Where'd ya go? Out?" cackled Lizzy B. Timmy T. tried to smile through the numbness of his medication. Jacque A. didn't smile.

"Turns out I didn't go anywhere but right here," I said.

""OD?" Jacque asked. Then she whispered, "You a suicide, too?"

"I've OD'd twice," boomed a male voice. "Last time, the doctors told me I damaged my heart and to cut out smokin'."

A tall young man strode into the lounge. He had on loose fitting jeans, dirty tennis shoes, and a raggedy shirt. He was nodding his head in time to the beat of his own drummer, holding a breakfast tray with one hand and stuffing bacon into his mouth with the other. "Like that's gonna happen."

"Bud C., you already ate!" Michelle warned as she came back up from the dorm rooms. "Put that back."

"Sedgewick got sent home. And they still sent him a tray," Bud C. grinned with a mouthful of bacon. "They'll just throw it away, won't they?"

He seemed the type who didn't ask for permission first. Or for forgiveness afterwards. He didn't care that he had gotten caught. Or he thrived on the extra attention. It was an ego-stroke until the next dare.

"Is there another tray left on there?" Nurse Michelle demanded.

Bud C. looked with eyes bigger than his stomach. "Yeah."

"Then that's the one for Cathy D.. So, don't touch that one," she warned.

Bud C. indicated the clockface on the wall. "She's got fifteen minutes. Then they'll take it away."

Nurse Michelle walked out of the Nurses' Station and pulled the tray from his hands. He played at resisting but let go after he snatched the last piece of bacon.

Bud C. kept eating as he moved around the lounge. Blonde curly hair dancing atop of his bopping head. He was head and shoulders above everyone else with an athletic build that was beginning to crumple.
His frame once beefy, now was jerky.

He came up to Timmy, who looked away from Bud C., and slapped him hard enough on the back to make the boy take a step back. "Top of the morning to you, Timmy!"

Then Bud C. pretended to sneak up behind old Lizzy B.

"Don't even try it, crackhead," she warned and cackled.

He ignored her warning and squeezed her around the shoulders. Lizzy T., like an old forgotten porch dog longing to prove her faithfulness once more, laid her head on his forearm.

"Good morning to you, you old tweaker," Bud C. said.

Working the room like a politician reaffirming alliances by promising favors, Bud C. ignored me and bent his head down by Jacque's ear and got in her personal bubble. "Why'd ya walk out on our card game?"

She didn't look at him. "Because it was time for bed, Hulk," she said.

"It's Bud C.," he said hurt. "You coulda stayed. Come by tonight and I'll straighten you out." He put a big hand on her inner thigh and squeezed. Jacque A. sat up and went wide eyed. "You won't be sorry."

I stood up and walked over to him with my hand out. "Pleased to meet you, I'm Justin R."

Bud C. looked me over, noting my black turtle neck, jeans, and Sketchers. "'All the kings' horses and the all kings' men.' I see they put humpty dumpty back together again. How long were you dead for anyway?"

I shrugged and then lied. "I couldn't even tell ya. I was out of it. Don't remember any of it."

Lizzy B. snorted at my answer. "Ha. They say you were non-responsive for five minutes."

Bud C. nodded. "Beats my old record. One day, I'm gonna do it right and not wake up." The he stuck out his hand. It was calloused and rough. "Pleased to meet ya, professor. I'm Bud C."

Taking my seat again I noticed the last of us had arrived. A young woman had slunk in wrapped in a blanket with her knees drawn up to her chin as she sat in a lounge chair with the folds of the blanket draped to the floor instead of her legs. Her face was washed out. Sleep filled her eyes. The mark of a pillow lined her face. Her hair all a tangle.

Bud C. turned around, saw her, and grinned. "Wakey, wakey, I took your eggs and bakey."

The young woman shaded her eyes with the back of her hand and squinted up at Big Bud C..

"Leave her alone, Big Bud," Lizzy B. growled.

"Not until she says hello," Bud C. said and stared her down. The young woman tried to shake Big Bud out of her gaze. But when he wouldn't take avert his eyes, she pulled the blanket over her head causing him to belly laugh.

"Cathy D.'s here. Good," said Nurse Michelle as she walked into the lounge. "Everyone needs to have a seat and then we can get started."

"Do we have to?" Timmy T. whined.

"You all had better pay attention," Nurse Michelle L. announced. She projected loud enough to keep sleepy Cathy D. from slipping back into a coma.

Everyone took a seat in a crude circle. Nurse Michelle walked around the inner part of the lounge shutting off the Sanyo and making Lizzy B. turn around. "First, you'll need to listen to me for a bit. Then I'll need your cooperation."

"How long is this goin' to take? I'd like to get a game of cards goin'," Bud C. said as he crossed and uncrossed his arms, his toe tapping out Morse code. He was restless beyond measure.

"However long it needs to," Nurse Michelle said. "If you're going to interrupt me and not pay attention, I'll keep you here to lunchtime."

That shut everyone up.

Big Bud C. even stopped fidgeting.

For a few seconds.

"I need you to all listen and to picture what I'm saying," Nurse Michelle L said in clear, slow speech. "Imagine you have a house. It's a nice home and you're happy there. Imagine someone you love. Friends and family. Your favorite pets. They live in the house with you. Now imagine all of the things that you love. Pictures, toys, chairs, tvs, baseball cards, dolls, anything you can think that gives you joy. It's all kept in that one house.

"Suddenly, a fire breaks out. You're able to get everyone out of the house. Every single person and pet who lives with you has gotten out safely. Now, the fire is ready to consume the whole house. Are you all with me? Do all of you have that image in your head?"

Everyone was quiet and was busy concentrating.

Imagining their perfect home.

Inside their head.

On fire.

Mine was my first childhood home. My parents were there. And my first dog, Charlie Brown. We were all standing outside watching smoke pour out of the windows. From under the front door and the closed garage.

Nurse Michelle had paused giving enough time for the dream homes to smolder and be consumed.

"The house is gutted. Going up in flames. If you had to go inside now for anything, you probably would get overcome with smoke and die. Now, what is important that's still inside?" she asked.

"My wedding pictures!" Lizzy B. said startled.

"My teddy bear!" gasped Jaque.

"My iphone!" snapped Timmy.

"My…children's…baby shoes," Cathy D. said as fast as she could.

Big Bud C. was weaving his head, probably gauging the heat and the intensity of the flames. Gauging how fast he had to run and how small he could make himself. Whatever was inside his burning house that he couldn't live without he wasn't saying.

Me, I wasn't about to say out loud either.

It was between me and God.

Only He knew my heart.

It hadn't taken me too long to realize what was my prize possession. My writings. The boxes of all the stories and novels I'd worked in vain over the last twenty years of my life.

All of my heart and soul were in those writings. And I was about to consign them to flames. In my mind, I was already running around the back to the sliding glass door that led to the living room. The handle would be burning hot. The glass blackening with smoke and soot.

But I had to risk it. If there was a chance to get inside and get to my writings, then I would take it.

Nurse Michelle listened to our responses and saw by our reactions that we were taking it very serious indeed.

"What is there that's so important to you that you have to risk your life to go back inside to get it?" she asked. "Books? Pictures? Furniture? Electronics? It can all be replaced. It's just stuff. The value is what you put into it.

"Remember, I said that everyone and your pets were able to get out. They should be more important than any stuff inside your house. And the most important thing you have is already safe outside. Can anyone tell me what it is?" Nurse Michelle asked.

Everyone went silent. Maybe they were thinking of an answer. Maybe they were too embarrassed to let her know they couldn't think of one.

"It's you," Nurse Michelle L. announced as she walked around the circle of lounge chairs, making sure to look everyone in the eye. "You're the most important thing that you have. You're the thing that can't be lost because you're irreplaceable."

I had totally missed where she had been taking it. I would have easily died to get my writings out of a burning house. They were a part of me that I didn't want destroyed.

"In a life or death situation, you're going to have to learn how to let go of things. And realize what truly matters. Nothing matters more than you or other people," Nurse Michelle said.

I felt ashamed. I was guilty of having emotional attachments to things. Of making things more important than people.

I had failed a simple mental exercise.

Everyone had it seems.

Inside the nurses' station, some RNs busied themselves with checking patient charts and getting out the pharmaceuticals out of a locked mesh wire cabinet and measuring them out into childsized disposable Dixie cups.

One of them nodded to Nurse Michelle. "Alrightie then, we're done for this morning. It's time for your meds and then your doctors will be along shortly to visit you."

Timmy T. raised his bandaged hand.

"Yes, Timmy," Nurse Michelle said. "You are still scheduled for surgery. The doctor has to try and repair that hand."

"Can I call my folks and have them come and visit me before the surgery?" he asked.

Nurse Michelle looked at the large LED readout above the nurse's station. It read nine forty-five. We'd just spent forty-five minutes in her visualization exercise.

"If you tell them to get here by eleven. Visiting hours are ten to twelve in the morning. And you're due in surgery by eleven thirty," Nurse Michelle said as she left the lounge to take her place in the nurses' station making sure to lock themselves in.

The other two RNs made room for her. Nurse Michelle slid the small window open at the bottom of the glass. Two nameless stoic orderlies positioned themselves on either side of the glass window.

The medicine shop was open for business.

Following the non-verbal cue, the patients lined up. With Bud C. first in line. Then Timmy. Then the girls. Even Cathy D. pulled herself out of the doldrums and onto her feet. She managed to shuffle over in fuzzy pink house slippers with the blanket wrapped around her and cut in line in front of Jacque A. who wasn't above stinking her tongue out at the back of the other's head.

I alone remained in the lounge. Uninvited to join the line and forgotten about. The life of my story.

One by one our meds were dispensed.

Given in little disposable cups.

Along with a disposable cup of water.

The sacrament ritual.

The holy and blessed pharmaceutical on the tongue placed.

Some knocked it back straight down the hatch with no chaser.

Some swished the water around in their mouth before swallowing.

Trying to sluice out the after taste.

But for most, their taste buds had been tainted. Changing from sweet and bitter to ash.

The aftertaste was their new taste.

"Did you take all yours, Buddy?" Nurse Michelle asked from behind the protective glass.

Bud C. opened his jaws and shoved his lips up and down with his thumb and forefinger as he stuck out his tongue and made it roll and flip to show a mouth empty of pills and full of bridgework.

Timmy try to shake his head clear of the taste. Lizzy B. smack her tooth-gaping gums. Jacque A. sneezed. And Kathy D. squinted her eyes and puckered her lips.

The straight line dissolved into a criss-crossing swirl of agents who quizzed each other on their prescriptions and shared the dosage amounts and bragged on the extreme out-liers of the side effects.

But not me.

I hadn't gone up to the window and I hadn't even been called.

I had not been fully initiated into the mystery of psychotropic therapy.

I had not yet participated in a pharmaceutical communion .

The ward door was unlocked and buzzed open.

And in walked Jayne V. with freshly combed auburn hair and fresh rouge and paint. She had on her business slacks and blouse and her tablet pouch slung against her left hip. She didn't miss a beat.

"Hello, Justin," she said spying me out from the others. "Are you busy? It's time for another follow up consultation."

"Nothing I couldn't move around, Jayne," I quipped.

And just like that we were on a first name basis.

3-Here Comes Doctor Frost

Jayne V. directed me to the top of the hallway between the Nurse's Station and the dorm rooms. She stood at the threshold of a small room with a small table and three small chairs and bid me enter. This room had a door because it was a consultation room. Protected by HIPPA. Patient confidentiality. Enforced by class action lawsuits.

In police stations they were called "interrogation rooms" for witnesses or suspects (everyone was a suspect) where the police sat behind a small desk in a tiny room and the suspect (everyone was a suspect) sat in a tiny uncomfortable chair. At least in the old Catholic church cathedrals, they had confessionals: a box separated in half by a screen for the priest to listen on one side as confessor and the one being shriven to sit in partial anonymity (with God, there is no respect of person and everyone is a sinner: neither person nor sin impresses Him).

Here the letters on the door read PATIENT INTERVIEW ROOM A.

In a police station everyone was a suspect.

In the old Catholic church everyone was a sinner.

In a hospital everyone was a patient.

In a mental health unit everyone was a mix of all the above.

She took the chair facing the door and kept her back to the wall.

I took a chair with my back to the door.

"Please close the door, Mr R.," Jayne V. said. Back to last names, again. Formality. Professionalism.

I closed it and turned to face her.

"This is a follow up consultation after our initial interview," she announced. "So, please don't get excited. You aren't excited are you?"

"No," I said. I was curious. Just a little.

"Describe how you are feeling," Jayne V. said.

"Tired. And sore," I said and pointed to both my wrists with the forefingers of each opposite hand.

She noted it all. Every word. Every movement and every look on my face.

"We could not give you anything for the pain or for anxiety since you had taken an overdose of darvacet earlier in the evening. A normal dose would be fifty or a hundred milligrams and the maximum prescription is one pill six times a day or three hundred milligrams. When they pumped your stomach and took your blood, they found enough darvacet for twenty-four pills which is four times the maximumdaily dose. You are lucky to be here talking with me right now."

"I don't know about that," I muttered.

"How did you sleep?" Jayne V. asked.

Her blue eyes searching out everything and seeking anything. My every word or every change of countenance. She typed it all onto her screen as a summary.

"Pretty crappy. I don't sleep well in new places. And the pillows weren't comfortable," I said.

"Anything else?" she probed.

I sighed. I had signed up myself for this, hadn't I? What had been the alternative? Keep trying to kill myself and remain a danger to myself if not others? Get a straight jacket slapped on me and thrown into a padded room upstairs in Kelter Ward A. Didn't I want help? So, I took a chance and made a trusting move forward. "I thought I saw my grandpa last night."

"I take it he's dead," Jayne V. said. Obviously, she didn't think I had tried to sneak him in as a visitor.

"Yes," I said.

"Has he appeared before this since he died?" Jayne V. asked.

I noticed her blouse was undone at the top buttons. And there nestled under her throat was a silver locket in the shape of a heart.

"Just in some dreams," I said.

"How about when you were awake?" she asked.

The heart caught the bright glare of the fluorescent ceiling light.

"Never," I said.

"Did he speak to you this time?" Jayne V. said.

The heart had a myriad of colors.

"Yes," I said.

"Is this first time you've had hallucinations?" she asked.

I knew she would think that Grandpa's coming to visit me had been a hallucination. And I knew what she thought it that meant for the state of mental health. But all I could think about was that Jayne V. was beautiful. That aside, if I was here to be helped and gain understanding that meant I had to tell the truth. And telling the truth meant being vulnerable. It meant having to trust others. Come what may.

"No," I said.

"When was the first time?" Jayne V. asked.

The exposed skin of her hands and wrists and neck was fair and white.

"Last night in the ambulance," I said.

"When you'd OD'd and they were trying to revive you?" she asked.

"When I was dead," I clarified.

"What did you see?"

"Everything. Blair going out of her mind. Again. The EMTs trying to save me and what they talked about. Then I saw my Grandpa. Except I was in the past. It was the last time I saw him alive. Then I was somewhere else I'd never been. I couldn't tell when or where it was supposed to be. Or even if I was myself. Last thing I saw was some kind of wedding. It was supposed to be me and my first ex getting married. But not like how it really happened. It was like some dark communion. My ex had some plans in store for me and I didn't want to be there," I said.

Jayne V. typed it all in hurry scurry. I could hear the click-clack of her well manicured nails against the screen. "You were married before?"

"Yes," I said.

"For how long?" Jayne V. asked.

"For about five years," I said.

Jayne V. changed tactics. "Is there any history of depression or insanity in your family?"

"Does senility count?" I asked.

Jayne V. smiled true and honest at that. "No."

"Then not that I'm aware of," I said.

She typed it all in. "I do not write prescriptions. That is Dr. Frost's job. But he may put on a serotonin inhibitor and some kind of tranquilizer to allow you to sleep through the night. Both will help with the anxiety and depression."

"What do I have then?" I asked.

"You're a clear candidate for clinical depression with periods of anxiety. Dr. Frost will have to examine you further along the lines of depression and suicide. But you've done the right thing by coming here. This is just the first step," Jayne V. said. Having finished, she flipped the cover back over her tablet. Then she flipped her wrist over to look at the LED display of her i-watch.

"Should I worry about the hallucinations?" I asked.

"Darvocet is an opioid," Jayne V. explained. "Weaker than oxycotin or morphine. But it does have hallucinogenic properties and considering how much ingested and the stress your body was under as it began to shut down, you probably had a NDE. Near Death Experiences are more common than what you'd think. It's much like sleep paralysis. Your brain doesn't know if it's awake or asleep. It's confused and trying to cope. Dr. Frost can explain it better than I can. He should be here shortly. You can wait here."

She stood up and moved to the door. "It was good to see you again, Justin."

"Will I see you again?" I asked.

"When Dr. Frost lets me know you are well enough to be released, I will set up your outpatient therapy," she said and left with a smile.

I decided right then and there I wanted out of here.

Today.

Tonight.

Any old time would do just fine.

That meant a lot of facing up.

To failure and bad choices.

Pain and guilt.

It meant coming clean, getting clean, and staying clean.

"Here comes Dr. Frost," I heard Lizzy B. T. crow. "You gonna release me soon, Doc?"

"I will see you later today," I heard a male say in a professional tone that settled the matter. "When it is your turn."

And in walked the good doctor. Long in the torso. Hands ending in stubby fingers bitten down to the quick and kept curled under. Pants not pressed. A white button shirt partially untucked in the back.

He might be a professional psychiatrist but he was a total slob.

The doctor blinked down at me through gold rimmed glasses and held out his hand.

"Mr. Justin R.," he began, "I am Doctor Henry William James Frost."

"You just said a mouthful," I said and took his hand.

He had the limpest handshake in the whole wide world.

His face was bland. Pock marked with scars. He kept his reddish brown hair clipped in no particular style other than short. The color was what the Brits would call "ginger."

Whereas I had been taken by auburn shade color of Jayne's hair and found myself taking in her appearance, I was being repulsed by the countenance of the good doctor. First impressions and all that.

It was time to stop daydreaming and start focusing on the here and now.

What did I most want for Christmas right now at this moment?

To get out of here.

If I wanted out, then I had to go through this man.

And Dr. Frost knew he was the man.

He took his sweet time about getting started. Sitting down in the chair and crossing his legs over his wrinkled pants, Dr. Frost took off his glasses and cleaned them on a wad of shirt hanging out over his belt.

He wasn't too concerned with his appearance.

Or the time.

His one accommodation to the luxury of rank and station was a golden stylus he used to tap on the digital keyboard upon his tablet. He was careful to pull back the flap and smooth it down as he cradled the tablet in his beefy hands.

"Just remember, I am here to listen. If you want help, you'll have to talk about your problems. If you don't talk about your problems, then I won't be able to help you," Dr. Frost said. With the ball in his court, Dr. Frost made the first move with a question. "Why do you think you're in here?"

"Don't you know why I'm here?" I asked.

He tsk-tsked at me without blinking an eye. Dr. Frost and Dr. Frost only got to ask the questions. His house, his rules. "I want you to tell me in your own words why you are here."

"Because I meant to kill myself," I said.

"Why did you mean to kill yourself?"the good doctor asked.

"Because I feel so guilty from all the bad choices. I'm a failure," I said.

"Why do you think you're a failure?" he asked.

"Because I've failed at everything I've ever tried to do," I said.

"When was the first time you think you failed at something?" Dr. Frost asked.

"Somehow, in third grade, I got fat. And so I became a target for everyone's jokes. My homeroom teacher even laughed at me one time so I stopped trying in her class. Meanwhile, my brother was the star athlete and got good grades. I got compared to him so much I wanted to be him. So, I tried to play basketball and one time I didn't want to go to practice because I had eaten too much spaghetti and I hated all that running. My dad got in my face calling me a quitter. So, I quit because that's what quitters do. I wasn't that good anyway," I said just babbling on and on.

"Why did they let you on the team if they didn't want you? Surely, you earned your place," the good doctor argued.

I shrugged off the achievement. "I was on the B-squad. And when you're on the B-squad your place is on the bench. So, B-squad means 'Bench Squad.' They put you in to let the starters catch their breath or when your team can't possibly loose, like in the last thirty seconds of the game. Being on the bench sucked."

"Why were sports so important to you then?" Dr. Frost asked.

"Most kids were all about sports. Everyone's parents came to their games. They were all ate up with cheering for their kids when they did good or yelling at the coach when they didn't like how something went. But there was no one cheering me on. Not when I failed all the time. My brother was good at basketball and golf because my grandpa would play ball with him and Dad would golf with him. But I just wasn't good at either. No matter how much I tried or practiced, I still sucked. I failed so much so often, it go to where I hated to even try," I said.

"So, you felt inferior and it made you insecure," Dr. Frost affirmed. That was some kind of affirmation, folks.

"I used to wake-up with headaches and I could drive up my temperature to ninety-nine degrees and convince my mom to let me stay home. I missed like forty-five days because I hated school. And my fifth grade teacher always compared me to my brother. She started off by saying, 'Oh, I just loved your brother! I hope you're just like him.' But when I struggled, she would yell at me in front of class—just like my dad would at home—'Why can't you get it! You're nothing like your brother!' So, I just shut down and wouldn't work for her. She was the worst teacher I ever had.

"I didn't have many friends. Even the younger kids in my neighborhood would tease me so I wouldn't even go out. So, when some neighborhood kids put together a summer soccer team, I convinced my dad to let me join. I wasn't tall enough for basketball but I was built better for soccer. I was on that team for four years," I rambled.

"So, you enjoyed soccer and built up some confidence," Dr. Frost summarized.

"I was decent at it. Even if I had to run more than in basketball. But my team sucked. We lost almost every game. We were the losers of the soccer league. Some teams would just laugh at us. That's what losers do, they lose," I corrected him.

"Did you ever want to be anything else than just good at sports?" Dr. Frost asked like it was his job.

"I wanted to tell stories after Grandpa took me and my brother to see the Star Wars movie when I was seven. I had never seen anything like that before. I was totally caught up by it until all I could do was live and breathe and eat Star Wars. So, I wanted to be a published writer.

"I could see the stories in my head but I couldn't get it down on paper too well. First, I tried to draw it out like the Star Wars comics I read. Only mine were stick figures and no one could understand what was going on. Then I tried to write it down and was brave enough to give it to my dad to read it. But he said I should tell what was going on not show it by writing 'BAM' and 'K-POW' like it was a comic. So, he gave me my first criticism.

"But then in junior high I discovered rock music and MTV played all these concerts of rock bands with huge crowds flicking their bics in the dark. So, now I wanted to be in a famous rock band right after I got out of high school. I'd do that until I was thirty and then write a best-selling and get rich and famous. Somehow I convinced my dad to let me take guitar lessons," I said.

"How did that pan out?" Dr. Frost asked as if he knew the outcome because after all, here we both were. All that was missing was a beer for me to cry into.

"The first time I played guitar in public I got booed of the stage. So, I switched to bass. And in high school, the first band I joined auditioned for the variety show. Then they kicked me out. So, I thought, maybe I better practice. In college, I got into bands that recorded their own songs. We made CDs of our own music. We'd get on the radio, we'd get interviewed in the newspaper. But my mom would only buy so many copies of our CDs. So, I always had to have a day job.

"My parents hated me being in bands. My dad and I would fight all the time about what I should do for a career. He wanted me to work at a bank and I kept thinking the next band I was in would get signed. Sex, drugs, and rock and roll. That became my to-do list," I said.

"Were you drinking a lot?" Dr. Frost asked.

"I had my first drink of alcohol at age thirteen. A neighborhood friend snuck out those party sized bottles of liquor from his Dad's liquor cabinet. And we got drunk. After that, he'd sneak some vodka into school and we'd get orange juice at breakfast in the cafeteria and we'd make screw drivers and pass it around. And I'd get drunk at school.

"But it was in college, that I really started to drink more often. When you're in bands, there's always a case of cheap beer at practice. And when you played in a bar, you'd either get half-price drinks or free beer tickets. And then someone always wanted to buy the band free drinks.

"It got to be where I'd drink at practice a couple of times a week. And I'd drink when I'd play out or go see bands on Friday night. Then, my brother would call me up on Saturday morning when I already had a hangover to meet him at a local bar and grill and we'd get there right when they open and drink all afternoon. My drinking was subsidized. I rarely had to buy my own drinks. Come to think of it, alcohol is probably the cheapest legal drug there is that's available everywhere.

"But just drinking booze gets old after awhile. So, other drugs came creeping in to call on me. Mostly, there was pot. But just smoking it to get a little buzz got boring. So, I started to eat the roach clips. Then, I'd just have pot brownies. And that always gave me a more intense high to the point that I'd hallucinate and have bad trips. In this last band, we'd do lines of coke now and then. Just a little bump to keep us going. And then about three in the morning, I'd drink some energy drinks mixed with alcohol to keep me going until it was time to go home," I said.

The good doctor had challenged to be honest about my problems. In order to do that, I had to talk about what I did. Now, why I did what I had done was another matter.

"What happened next? Did you finish college?" Dr. Frost asked.

"I went from having an A average and being on the Dean's List to getting scholastic probation because I was spinning my wheels and fighting with my dad. He didn't want me to be in bands and said I'd have no future in it. I wanted to at least teach English and be a writer. But my dad had been a teacher and had hated it, so he'd gotten into computers and worked for large banks. Naturally, he thought that's what I should do.

"It took me a long time to graduate. But I did. And got a job at America's Bank. Where I've worked for about the last ten years. And have hated every minute of it," I said.

"Why?" Dr. Frost asked.

"Because I have been living someone else's life. When I was ready to graduate, I quit the bands for a while. Quit drinking. And started dating a quiet church girl," I said.

"This was your first wife?" Dr. Frost asked.

"Yes, Lauren was her name. I dated her about three years while I finished school and then we were married for about five years after I started working at the bank," I said.

"And what happened to this first marriage?" Dr. Frost asked as was his wont.

"She wouldn't get done with school and get a proper job. So, I was the only one working. I found out that you can't make someone do what they don't want to. They get resentful. So, we lost respect for each other. I got back into bands and started drinking again. I wasn't happy at home, so bands gave me an instant gratification.

"We mutually decided to get divorced. Then I partied for the next year and a half. Started drinking and doing coke all night. I just got worse and unhappier. So, I quit the band and quit the drugs. Met Blair and got married about a month later. We were only married a year before I left her," I said.

"Why?" Dr. Frost asked.

"She's your patient, doc. You should know better than me how she is. Do you think she'll ever change or get better?" I asked.

"I am allowed to say this. Blair is very sick," Dr. Frost said.

"She can't keep a job. I saw her try to blackmail one of her bosses. I stupidly thought if I gave her a good environment, she'd be able to keep a job and we could build a life together. I stupidly thought, she has problems, I have problems. Maybe together, we can help each other. Stupid me, doc," I said.

"It will take a very special man to understand her and have the patience required to deal with her," Dr. Frost said.

"Doc, I can only tell you from experience. People do not change unless they want to change. And I guess it's scary to change. So, I gave her divorce papers on our one year anniversary. We got divorced. She gutted the house and I got an empty house. Then right before Thanksgiving, she knocks on my door. I move her in and here I am," I said and held up my bandaged right wrist.

"Do your parents know she's living with you again?" Dr. Frost.

"No," I said and held up my bandaged left wrist.

I don't know how long I had talked for. I don't know just how much good all this talking had done me. But I hadn't talked this much, hadn't thought this much, about things for quite some time.

There were wounds on my wrists because I had wounds on my heart. Some were very old wounds. And some were fresh ones. Some were scabbed over. And some of the scabs had turned to stone.

"Dr. Frost, do you ever see her holding down a job?" I asked. "Or will she always need a keeper?

"Right now, she can't deal with a lot of stress," he said.

So, there was the good, the bad, and the ugly. Blair was a passionate person. She laughed louder than the wind. But could turn angry on a dime.

When she was up, she was up and fantastic fun.

But when she was down, she wanted to bring the world down.

Straight to hell, the basket already in flames.

She understood me better than most people ever had.

But she could be tricky. I wouldn't trust her with my wallet again.

"I love her, doc," I said. "But will this be a conflict of interest for you to treat us both?"

"Are you still paying for her bills now that you're divorced?" Dr. Frost asked.

"Not anymore," I said.

"Then it shouldn't," he said. Then he added a caveat. "That is, unless you plan to remarry her."

I hadn't planned on taking it that far yet.

4-"You Don't Belong Here"

***After Dr. Frost cut me loose I
didn't know what to do with myself.***

Since time was on my side, I walked back into the Patients' Lounge and settled down in an empty chair against the wall. From here, I had a vantage of the hustle at the nurses' station and the bustle of everyone's coming and going from the dorm hall to the lounge. Piled up beside me was an oddball assortment of games, books, and old VHS tapes. On top was *Signs*, then *Mad Libs*, then *Catch-22*, and on the bottom was a children's book: *Stories from the Bible*.

My chair was the farthest away from the tv screen. Closer to it sat Jacque A., who said hello to me as she tried to settle into the groove of the hustle and bustle. Closest to the tv screen sat Lizzy B., who was absorbed in a news broadcast show where two paid experts argued away with pointless counter facts that proved only to whip both up into a frenzy. Maybe the newscasters were in need of prescribed meds and time inside Kelter Ward C themselves. Maybe the whole world.

"Doctor Frost gonna put you on some meds?" Lizzy B. asked me during a commercial break advertising Lunesta. The networks had the demographics of their viewing audience down cold. "Seen him come in."

"Yeah," I said. "I'm not looking forward to it."

My first ex had been outright scared of being put on meds. She had voiced that fear more than once after admitting that things weren't right in her head. The revelation of that moment lost upon me until right now. How long did my history of co-dependency stretch back?

"They got me on Prozac," Jacque A. offered. "No side effects yet."

Lizzy B. scoffed. "I been on Prozac, Xanex , Oxycotin, you name it. They won't put me on Oxycotin no more. Some things these labs make are just plain wicked."

"Bud C.! Leave that door closed!" called Nurse Michelle from the Nurses' Station probably watching a tv monitor feed of the hallway. "No one's going outside today!"

His voice grew stronger as he approached. "Wake up sleepyhead! Don't make me come in there!"

"Bud C.," Nurse Michelle warned. "Leave Cathy D. alone!"

"Just tryin' to help," Bud C. said. "We're not supposed to stay in our rooms."

He passed by the lounge smiling at us and kept right on walking towards the other end of the ward and tried the door there. It was locked.

"Place ain't even decorated for Christmas," Bud C. colored his complaint with an expletive. "And the shrine's right next door!"

"Both the Kelter Mental Health Unit and Hope, Inc. receive federal grant money," Nurse Michelle explained. "If you get government money then you play by their rules. Separation of church and state. We can't even say 'merry Christmas'."

"Well, merry flippin' Christmas," he growled and marched back down the dorm hall. Complaining with each step and his voice growing louder with each footfall, "So if we say 'merry Christmas', the government will stake us through the heart with some mistletoe. And if we dare wish someone a 'merry freakin' Christmas,' the government will boil us in our pudding. Season's greetings, you turkeys! Happy Holidays, you lunkheads! Merry Xmas and Happy Next Year!"

Their thumbs being pricked and sensing something wicked brewing, the two orderlies appeared from their hiding place to take their sentinel positions at the junction of the Nurse's Station and dorm hallway. They were only seen when they wanted to be seen. Otherwise, they remained invisible.

Lizzy B. shook her head at his wake. "Bud C.'s still tweakin'," she meant to tell Jacque A. but obviously didn't care who overheard. "Don't let him in your room. He'll steal your stuff. He only come to the ward so he wouldn't get sent off to jail again. Once he's out, he'll start usin' again and get back in jail."

"I'd like to be home for Christmas," Jacque A. C. said.

Before I knew it I said, "I don't even want to think about Christmas."

"Why? Aren't you married? Don't you have a family?" Jacque A. asked.

I shrugged. "We got divorced. Now we're back together. But my family doesn't like her one bit."

Jacque A. nodded. "It's the same way with me. My family found out I was a lesbian and freaked out. They said if I moved in with Nancy they would cut me off completely. Nancy said it didn't matter to her. But it matters to me."

"So you tried to kill yourself?" I asked. Just a generation ago, even a hint of someone being a homosexual was enough to ruin a person's life. They had been labeled deviants and placed in mental wards.

She nodded and sucked back a sob. "Nancy thought it was all her fault but it's mine."

I didn't know much about being a lesbian. But I knew a lot about being outcast and not fitting in. And how cruel people could be once they put a label on you and expected to you act out the role they had pegged you in.

I leaned over and put my hand on her shoulder. "I am sorry about your family."

Tired with the non-stop news shows where the newscasters vilified the free speech of people whose viewpoints they didn't agree with like gossipy know-betters, Lizzy B. turned the volume down and turned to both Jacque A. and me.

"Family'll turn on you like a dog. Mine don't want me no more. Can't find no good man to take care of me. And my son threw me out of his house on Thanksgiving day. Guess I'll be on the street come Christmas Day. Ain't got nowhere to stay, so, I'm stayin' right here, thank you. Three meals. Shower. And a bed," she said.

"Medicare. Government money says you can't be turned away."

"How long will you be in?" I asked.

"Medicare will let me stay up to ten days," Lizzy B. said. "How long will you be in for?"

"Jayne V. told me it will be up to my doctor," I said. I wasn't comfortable with saying "psychiatrist." None of the other patients had uttered the word: "psychiatrist."

Lizzy B. scoffed at that, too. "It's however long your insurance will cover you for."

"Three to five days I think it was," I said.

"Your doctor could let you out earlier than that," Lizzy B. said. "If you want out early then you gotta take your meds. And eat everything they give you. Don't sleep in. Get up in the morning. Take a shower. Get dressed. Go to all the meetings. And don't act up.

"Act up and they'll put you on Ward B. With the crazies. Up there they let everyone walk around in the dayroom and don't care if someone pisses on you or takes a bite out of you.

"Then there's Ward C. Isolation. Padded rooms. That's where they'll give ya shock treatment."

"They shock people here?" Jacque A. C. asked wide eyed.

"They don't do it for therapy. Just to keep ya in line," Lizzy B. said.

"As punishment?" I asked in disbelief. Was Abraham Stoker the director of the hospital?

The main door buzzed and clicked open. In walked Timmy T. accompanied by two adults. Smothering him was an older woman with uncombed hair and no makeup. Two steps behind was a balding and heavier set version of Timmy T., more grey and flab than the wiry cockiness of youth. I assumed the two adults were both husband and wife and mother and father, if it was legal to assume such things still existed.

Nurse Michelle met them just outside the Nurses' Station. "Timmy will do fine in the surgery. He can't have lunch. Or anything to drink. We'll prep him at noon and they'll come and get him for surgery at twelve-thirty."

"Will he back here afterwards?" the mother asked.

"We can transfer him to a regular room for recovery and observation. And if the operation goes well the doctor may release him tomorrow," Nurse Michelle told them. "You will have to leave the ward now. You could go to the cafeteria and get some lunch. Then you can wait outside of surgery once they start."

The mother hugged the nurse then touched Timmy's cheek with her hand. The father simply nodded to Timmy. The two orderlies warded the main door as Timmy's parents left. The orderlies kept their station until the door buzzed shut and hermetically sealed itself once more. I sensed the orderlies' job was the same as solider ants: to protect the entrances to the colony and repel foreign invaders and make sure the blind worker ants didn't slip out unless they had been dowsed with the right chemicals by the queen. Their function served, they melted back into the walls taking secret passages to other parts of the Ward ala Bronte sisters or Walpole.

Lizzy B. got up and hugged Timmy. "You'll be fine. Count yourself lucky your parents even came."

Jacque A. offered some encouragement and a hug. "Stay in touch," she offered.

Even Bud C. detoured from his stroll and slapped Timmy T. on the shoulder which must have smarted.

"They're gonna fix you up and you're gonna get out of here. So, don't go messin' up your hand."

"What did you do to your hand?" I asked.

Timmy T. had kept his head down the entire time he'd come back on the ward with his parents, now he looked me right in the eye. "My parents told me to stop seeing my girlfriend. I couldn't do it. I love her, man. They kept on pushing the issue. My girlfriend told me to show 'em I wasn't gonna back down. So, I took a Butcher knife and stabbed my hand." He held up his left hand and pulled back the wrapping with his right forefinger not unlike how Michealangelo would have envisioned it on a different Cistine Chapel ceiling panel. He pointed to the entry wound with his right forefinger. "Just missed the nerve. They will have to put some pins it."

"You did a lot of damage as it is," Nurse Michelle said.

"Is she worth it?" Bud C. asked and asked again, "Is she worth it?"

Timmy T.'s face screwed up bright red. "They won't keep us apart. I'd die for here, man!"

I thought, next time he just might.

"That'll show 'em!" Bud C. slapped him on the back. "Can't live without her, can't live at all."

"Bud C., don't get him upset. He's got surgery in two hours," Nurse Michelle said and led Timmy T. down the dorm hall. Then she walked back into the Nurses' Station and came out again with a small tray bearing two paper cups. "Justin, we get to start your medication. Dr. Frost prescribed them and your insurance approved it."

She picked up the paper cup with the pill and shook it so that the pills in it rattled. Then she handed it over. At the bottom were two white round film-coated tablets. I spilled them out into my palm. One side had two letters stamped into the tablet separated by a longitudinal fissure: **F|L**. The back side was stamped with the numeral **10**.

"This is Lexapro. You'll take one tablet three times a day. So we're doubling up on your first dose," Nurse Michelle said. "It's an anti-depressant. An SRI. Serontin Reuptake Inhibitor. And you've also been prescribed something to help you sleep at night."

I took the cup. Knocked the pills back and swallowed them dry before Nurse Michelle handed me the cup of water. Her duty done, she retreated back to her stronghold behind the glass.

Jacque A. asked me what I had just taken. I didn't want to say. But Lizzy B. had overheard and volunteered to say it wasn't a psychotropic and not habit forming but that it might give me constipation.

Lunch arrived.

Each tray was marked a different diet. Low fat. Low carb. Low salt. Sugar free.

Mine was still marked regular. Baked ham, mac and cheese, apple sauce, and a very large chocolate chip cookie.

There was a God!

Everyone had grabbed a tray except for Cathy D. who no doubt was still comatose in bed.

Bud C. had already crumbled up his cookie into his apple sauce and had slurped it up. He'd convinced Lizzy B. into surrendering hers. And now he was eying Cathy D.'s tray still on the portable carrier.

I occupied myself with *Catch-22*, leafing through it and wondering if it would be love at first sight.

Nurse Michelle kept trying to shoo him off the tray. Calling him a vulture. Finally, Bud C. raised siege and left but only after he'd already snagged the cookie and buried it in the crotch of his pants.

The orderlies wheeled Timmy T. out on a gurney toting an iv drip in his arm. He looked resigned to die for true love. Just to prove his parents wrong. His Dad didn't seem as if guilt could break him down.

The door buzzed and clicked open. Then they wheeled the gurney through it. The door shut again and I immersed myself back into the absurdity of American fliers trying to maintain their mental health without going insane.

"Justin R.," Nurse Michelle called from behind her glass window. "You have a visitor."

The door buzzed and clicked open.

For the life of me I did not know who on earth it could be. And for a moment I wondered if Blair had disobeyed me and gone ahead and called my parents and if it might be them who would be walking through the door now, in much the same manner as Timmy T.'s parents had done.

It was only Blair in a pullover hoodie and sweat pants with wet cuffs over her Nike shoes. Her blue eyes were red. The pupils dilated.

"Hi honey," she said. She hugged and kissed me. "So, this is the new Kelter Ward C. It's changed. Have you eaten?"

"Just got done with what they said was a ham and cheese," I said.

"Did it taste like a ham and cheese?" Blair asked.

"Not at all. Didn't even look like a ham and cheese to be honest. So, it may not have been a ham and cheese.

It might have just been something that the folks in the kitchen decided to call a ham and a cheese," I said.

"Have you seen Dr. Frost yet?" she asked.

I nodded. "Started meds right at lunch."

"What's he got you on?" she asked.

"Lexapro," I said.

"Never heard of it," Blair said. Which meant that Lizzy B. was correct in that it wasn't a tranquilizer or narcotic or psychotropic.

"Have you called your parents yet?"

I shook my head.

"Justin, babe, you've got to call them. And tell them we're back together. At least let them know where you are," she scolded.

I looked at her searching face, but all I could see was Timmy's bandaged hand.

She took a good look around the ward. "You don't belong here." A tear fell before she could wipe it away.

I was shocked. Was that some kind of admittance on her part about how bad things had gone last year, our first year of being married? Was she feeling a tinge of guilt? It made me want to be with her. I had to be with her. This had to work. This could work. If this was the price I had to pay then so be it. If Timmy T. could suffer through a damaged hand then maybe… "Think they'll let me call from here?"

"Of course," Blair said sniffling. "Babe, you've got to call them."

"I will," I promised.

"When?" she demanded.

"Supper's at five. They'll be home by then. I'll call after supper," I said.

"I'd better get back. I want to get back before dark," Blair said. "Still a lot of snow out there."

I walked her to the door

We hugged one last time. Then the door buzzed and opened with a click.

She left and the door clicked shut behind her. And I wanted to leave with her. Get out of here and go back to the home I had bought for her.

To the home I was barely keeping up mortgage payments on since I had racked up thousands in credit card debt after we'd gotten married while she'd been unable to hold down a job.

None of that was getting resolved while I was sitting in Kelter Ward C. I hadn't quite been thinking of resolving that when I'd slit my wrists. And all of that would be waiting for me like unopened junk mail and unwanted bills.

I walked back into the lounge and Bud C. was sitting upright with his hands folded in his lap next to Jacque A. C. They had been talking. And watching. "That your wife?"

"Sorta," I said. I didn't want to go into all the history. People only know as much as you tell them. They liked to make up the rest and fill in the blanks.

Jacque A. said it first. "She's pretty."

"Makes you wanna get out faster, don't it?" Bud C. said.

An old insecurity tugged at me. Just why did Blair have to turn around and rush home?

"Your parents don't like her?" Jacque A. asked. "She seems nice."

"My parents don't know we're back together. Or that I'm in here," I said.

"Dude, you need to live your own life," Bud C. said. "Do what makes you happy. Like me."

"Least you gotta life to go back to," Lizzy B. T. said during a commercial of *America's Funniest Home Videos.*

Bud C. leaned forward and brought up a horizontal palm to screen his mouth. "She's just an old tweaker. First husband got shot dead years ago in a crack house. Second one's in for a ten year stretch. Federal time. Her son just kicked her out. That's why she's here. If her Medicare gets turned off, they'll kick her out and she'll be back on the streets."

I was more engrossed in what was in his mouth rather than what was coming out of it.

His teeth were more stalagtytes than dental work. Crusted with film and discolored by tartar and speckled with black spots. His gums were brown. And several molars were missing.

The afternoon passed with Lizzy B. refusing to give up the remote to Bud C. by sticking it under her buttocks. Jacque A. tried to play cards with Bud C. who had to walk down the dorm hall between every hand. And Nurse Michelle succeeded in getting Cathy D. out of her catatonia long enough to shuffle down to the lounge where she curled up under a blanket.

I kept myself awake with kicking the anxiety of calling my parents.

The dinner cart arrived and Bud C. was first to get his tray. I saw him grab an extra roll and a handful of butter packets. Nurse Michelle called him out of line to give him dinner meds.

I got a tray with roast beef, mash potatoes, gravy, and peas. I double checked. The roll was still there.

The hospital food didn't have much flavor or color or taste. But it sat still on my stomach. After I'd finished, I set the tray back and went to the Nurses' Station.

"Can I make a call?" I asked.

"Local or long distance?" Nurse Michelle asked.

"Local," I said.

She handed me a clip board that read PHONE LOG. I signed it. "You can use the phone in the lounge."

I slipped back into the front of the lounge where an old corded phone was kept in a cradle on a small stand. Couldn't be a cordless phone or the patients could slip away unnoticed. And there had to be a log kept for legal purposes.

Picking it up, I punched in my parents' number and hope I wouldn't have to leave a message.

My mom picked up on the second ring.

"Hello, R. residence," she said.

"Hi, Mom, it's me," I said.

"Justin," she cooed, sounding as if I had just her made her day in calling her. "We were just getting ready to sit down to supper."

"Well, go ahead and sit down, I've got something unpleasant to tell you," I said.

"Maybe you should tell your father," Mom said. It wasn't that she didn't want to hear my news or not deal with it, it was just that she would have to explain it all over again to my dad. And she hated that.

It had been hard enough just to call and talk to her. I sure didn't want to have to talk to my dad.

"I've been very depressed. Really bad this time. And I did something stupid to myself and now I'm in the hospital," I began.

But she had already handed the phone over to my dad.

"Hello," he said. His voice was strong and officious. He was in managerial mode.

"Dad, I just told Mom so now I'm telling you: I've been depressed," I said.

"Everyone gets depressed," he said. Which meant: no excuse. There was no explaining it to my dad. You just had to tell him and flinch against the oncoming onslaught. It was like he was the big bad wolf and you were the little pig hiding inside a house made of straw.

"But does everyone try to kill themselves? It's so bad this time I tried to kill myself. I got taken to the hospital," I said.

"Where are you now?" he asked like I was late for curfew.

"I'm at Our Lady Hospital in the Kelter Mental Health Unit," I said.

"If you'd listened to me you wouldn't be there," he choked. In life, there was either His Way or No Way.

The connection ended and the dial tone filled my ears. Dad had hung up on me. My own dad. Like he'd washed his hands of me. Dad would have a short career as a therapist.

5-Bing and Bowie

Tidings of comfort and joy, indeed.

I had forgotten to tell my parents I was back with Blair.

Oh, joy.

There was no comfort in my heart. There was only a dark void.

"They'll be mad for awhile. Then they'll get over it," Bud C. said. "That's what families do."

"Don't count on it," Lizzy B. argued.

Bud C. waved her off. Then he was done offering advice, done sitting still, done with being in Kelter Ward C. He started up his rounds again. Looking for ways out and ways in and places to hide small things and which small things to hide.

Nurse Michelle stepped out from behind the glass window to call us altogether for an evening session.

We were shy one joker in the deck, Timmy T. having been transferred off the ward. Once Comatose Cathy D. showed signs of consciousness and joined us, Nurse Michelle got down to business.

"Since we can't decorate the ward for Christmas, let's talk about it. Please raise your hand one at a time and be respectful. What does Christmas mean to you guys?" she asked.

"Being with the ones you love," Jacque A. said.

"Lots of gifts under the tree for me," Bud C. said.

"Fightin' with my son," Lizzy B. growled.

"Cleaning and baking and standing in line to buy gifts and then having to wrap them," Cathy D. said.

We all looked at her. She'd said a mouthful.

Then they all looked at me. "Cookies and fudge."

Everyone seconded that with a grin.

"So, Christmas brings a lot of emotions and expectations. Maybe even some anxiety," Nurse Michelle said. "But what's it supposed to mean for the world?"

"Jesus' birthday," Lizzy B. T. said.

"It's better to give than receive," Jacque A. said.

"For unto us a Savior is born," I said. "Unto us a Son is given."

"Peace on earth and goodwill to me," Bud C. said.

"Having to put up tacky lights and play Christmas songs I'm sick of and pretending to like everyone," Cathy D. said. After not even two words in two days, she was probably through speaking for the week.

"Jesus wasn't a real person," Bud C. declared. "He wasn't even born on Christmas."

"Yes, He was. There's tons of evidence. He was the Son of God," Lizzy B. argued.

"Do you think Jesus really went around telling people to worship him and to remember his birthday?" Bud C. shot back. "Uh, no. Don't think so. He's about as real as the Easter Bunny."

"I believe Jesus really existed," Jacque A. said. "He was just a good man."

"Sure!" Bud C. nodded. "But he ain't God. And he ain't comin' back. Cuz he's tits up dead." Lizzy B. smoldered. "You hope He doesn't come back. Cuz He's gonna judge the living and the dead. Just what do you think He's gonna do with you, Bud C.?"

"God is love," I intoned like a protective blanket.

Bud C. repeated it. "That's right. God is love. He ain't gonna send anyone He loves to hell."

"Are you being respectful?" Nurse Michelle asked. "Take a deep breath. Hold it in. Now slowly let it as I count to ten."

Three of us took a deep breath and exhaled it over a ten count. Bud C. rolled his eyes. Cathy D. closed hers.

"We're moving on now," Nurse Michelle Laurenounced and held up a paper. "I have a Christmas quiz here. It's from Christmas movies and songs. Ready?

"One foggy Christmas Eve, who does Santa--" she began.

"Rudolph with his nose so bright," Bud C. answered.

Before she could finish with, "--- ask to help?" She paused and asked again. "The Grinch is as cuddly as-_"

"A cactus," Lizzy B. sang out.

"What is the most popular Christmas song of all time and who wrote it?" she asked and smiled that no one had been able to interrupt her.

"'White Christmas'," Lizzy B..

Bud C. made an ugly face. "I hate that song."

"It was recorded during World War II when all of the troops were overseas and it made everyone homesick," Lizzy B. T. said.

The last time I had been homesick was in first grade. And I couldn't wait for school to end early so we could go home for Christmas break. I thought I was going to miss it if school didn't let out.

"So?" Nurse Michelle asked. "Who wrote it?"

"Irving freakin' Berlin," Bud C. said. "It was my dad's favorite song. Which is why I hate it."

"What does Santa make and how many times does he check it?" Nurse Michelle asked.

Jacque A. burst out with, "A list. Twice."

"So he can find out who's naughty and nice," Bud C. said.

"Bud C., you're so naughty, you're gonna get a lump of coal in your stocking," Lizzy B. warned.

"On 'A Charlie Brown Christmas', how much did Lucy charge for a psychiatric session?'" Nurse Michelle asked.

"Five cents," Jacque A. said. "That's one of my favorite shows to watch every Christmas."

Lizzy B. snorted, "Doctor Frost would never charge no five cents."

"What was the name of the rabbit in the tv movie 'Frosty the Snowman?'" Nurse Michelle asked him.

Nurse Michelle waited. For anyone. All of us drew a blank.

"Pshaw," Cathy D. tried to give a raspberry but ended up slobbering on herself. "Can't believe none of you know it! Hocus Pocus!"

We all blinked. Of course, we'd known it all along. The answer had been hiding in plain sight.

"Well, I never liked 'Frosty' much. My favorite Christmas movie is 'It's a Wonderful Life,'" Bud C. said. "Use to sit up and watch it with my grandpa all the time. It was on every night before Christmas."

"Good, then tell me what was the name of the angel?" Nurse Michelle asked.

"Thomas," Bud C. said.

Nurse Michelle shook her head.

Everyone laughed. He was mad that he couldn't remember but neither could anyone else.

So I finally spoke up. "Clarence. Clarence Odbody."

Bud C. looked at me. "That can't be right. An angel named Clarence Odbody?"

"And when they were drying off their clothes, Clarence had a copy of 'Tom Sawyer' in his back pocket," I said.

"I don't want to play anymore," Bud C. sulked.

"I have a list of Christmas songs with the titles all re-arranged. You have to guess what they are," Nurse Michelle.

"I said I don't want to play," Bud C. said.

"Shut up and listen," Lizzy B. told him.

"Crystalized Vapor Homosapien with frozen precipitation," Nurse Michelle announced.

I waited while everyone looked at each other. Except for Cathy D.. She had already closed her eyes again.

"'Frosty the Snowman,'" I said.

"I hate that song!" Bud C. said. "Enough of this crap!"

He jumped up and walked from end one of the ward to the other.

Nurse Michelle kept an eye on him and dismissed the rest of us.

While Bud C. was coming down from whatever had wound him up for the past three days, Jacque A. suggested we all watch a movie. There weren't many choices. And not one we all could agree on. Lizzy B. hated *Mr. Deeds* (or anything with Adam Sandler), Jacque A. wanted to watch *Signs* (but Lizzy B. got it confused with *The Village* declaring it too stupid to watch a second time), and Bud C. was adamant that we all needed to watch *Saw III* (I hadn't even seen *Saw* or *Saw II* but predicted that *Saw III* couldn't be that different).

Signs won on the second round of voting after Jacque A. convinced Lizzy B. that it wasn't *The Village*, just the same director.

Bud C. turned on the DVD player and Jacque A. put the disc in. Lizzy B. tucked her feet under trying to make herself small on the recliner. I moved to a seat closer to the tv set. And Cathy D. continued to zone out

The movie had a quiet tension. What I got out of it was we should have faith in times of trouble or just going to pieces. And that we didn't always get the answer we wanted when we wanted it but when we needed it.

It wasn't a typical Hollywood movie. Hollywood movies operate on two principles: every movie must have a happy ending and every movie must have a sequel.

Generally, whenever Americans liked something they could stand a lot of it. Over and over. Again and again. Then forget about it because in five years, Hollywood would just reboot a successful series and make even more money. Hollywood liked two things: crappy movies and a crapload of money.

That's because we Americans are a pretty nostalgic bunch.

There's never too much of a good thing in the United States of America.

And nothing is sacred to Americans like their childhood. Nothing can compare to being a kid growing up in America.

Kids get spoiled rotten in this country.

There is no contest. We win hands down for spoiled kids.

Once a year you had a birthday and you got gifts and cake and everyone was nice to you.

Then all you had to do was wait.

And it would be Christmas.

That was when we really raked it in.

And Christmas was the best day to be a kid in America.

It might be Jesus' birthday but we kids got all the gifts.

Yeah, we were told that Christmas was about tidings of comfort and joy and peace on earth and goodwill to men.

But we knew the truth.

It was for kids.

As kids, we spent the entire year dreaming of what new stuff we should get. We expected to get everything that entered our head. America is the land of plenty and we all want plenty of stuff. So, it's a good fit.

The entire year revolved around Christmas.

Every retail store in the country and every manufacturer planned their whole year around this one day. Christmas would either make or break them. Every year, they hoped to make even more money. The inventory was made in the waning months of winter. It was bought in the spring. The marketing finished in summer. And it all rolled out the day after Halloween. Ads. Commercials. Displays. Merchandise. And the songs. Non-stop Christmas songs. To brainwash you into thinking it was the most wonderful time of the year and saturate your soul with happy holidays. But the peak of the retail's income was the day after Thanksgiving: Black Friday. It was "black" because on the ledger sheets of lore, the credit, or "+" (plus) column was in black and the debit, or "-" (minus) was in red. "In the black" meant you had profit. "In the red meant you had lost buckets of money. And Americans did not like to lose. Losing was un-American.

Mom and Dad were expected to work extra hard. Or open new credit lines. Or get a store credit card. Either charge the swag and drop it in the bag or put it on lay away for another day.

There was no limit to the spending because there was no limit to what was being made.

More stuff was being made so that more stuff could be bought. More commercials aired to tell us what we needed. So we knew exactly what to tell Mom and Dad to buy us.

And Santa?

We kids owned him.

We had him over a barrel.

And he knew it.

He and all his elves at the North Pole and every single reindeer and even Mrs. Claus worked for us.

Anything we wanted, we got.

We didn't even have to ask. Instead everyone asked us, "What do you want for Christmas?"

Once they asked you and you told them what you wanted, they had to get it.

Santa wouldn't dare leave you high and dry.

He'd lose his job.

And the whole country would go broke.

And I had never met a kid who had been put on the naughty list. Not once. But I sure knew a sleigh-load of kids who probably should. Maybe that was part of Buddy C.'s problem.

We kids had no clue about how things worked. We just expected to get everything on our wish list. To wake up on Christmas morning and find our heart's desires wrapped up in colored paper and ribbons under a tree blinking with lights.

All because it was Jesus' birthday.

Hadn't He been the first Christmas gift?

Born in a Crescent Land manger with the animals. Not in America with a credit card in His hand.

Who in this country would listen to angels brining glad tidings of comfort and joy and peace on earth and good will to men because unto us a Savior is born? Who would take up their challenge to go visit the new born Savior-babe lying in a manger with the other animals when we had strip malls and layaway and free shipping and no interest until six months later and pre-lit Christmas trees?

Even if we had baby Jesus with His butt swaddled in an angelic blanket asleep in a basinet waiting for us on a Christmas morning, most of us would rush on by to see what gifts lay under the tree with our names attached, ignoring the greatest gift of all that was real.

Somebody once said that as a child we believe in Santa Claus. Then as an adult we become Santa Claus. It must have been the same person who said child is father to the man.

The movie credits played through and the disc ended. Still having the remote, Lizzy B. switched back over to the HDMI with streaming wifi. I don't know what channel she selected, but she found an old tv broadcast with a thin sickly old man with a light blue Mr. Rogers sweater answering the front door of his home. It was not a home but a tv studio set made up like a open plan home. A thin white Duke entered. A rakish young man with a mod hair cut, a blazer jacket, open shirt and dark slacks.

The two bantered a bit about music and it being Christmas and how they each celebrated it at home. For as long as this broadcast signal was cast abroad across the universe, it would be forever Christmas, 1977 on a London soundstage.

The sickly older man had a rich baritone.

The younger dapper man had a broad tenor.

It was a duet.

But they actually were singing two different songs at the same time.

The older man was an icon of Hollywood's Golden Years. American through and through. And the younger man was a Brit. And an icon, too, of glam and new wave.

"Who is that weirdo?" Lizzy B. demanded.

"It must be David Bowie," Jacque A. volunteered. "Don't know who's he singing with."

"It's Bing and Bowie!" Bud C. corrected them. "Bing Crosby and David Bowie."

By God, he was right. How could I not recognize the two of them? Maybe apart I would have. But the two of them singing together was beyond bizarre.

"Hello everyone," Nurse Rochelle announced herself. She must have come on duty during the movie because I didn't remember seeing Nurse Michelle leave.

She walked into the lounge and took the remote from Lizzy B.. "Enjoy your movie?"

Then she clicked off the tv. "Time for one last session before you all turn in for the night."

Bud C. tried to sneak off and Cathy D. feigned a coma. But Nurse Rochelle was having none of it. She simply asked us a question. "If you could give someone in need just one gift, what would it be?"

Bestowing gifts. It was a kind of power. Broken and empty and full of unanswered needs, suddenly, I had been given a great power. What was I going to do with it? Where would I start?

For my parents, I'd pay off their home.

For my brother, I'd finish his downstairs basement with tile and mirrors and wired for sound.

For my first ex, I'd give her back the years we wasted on each other so we'd both be free and clear.

And if my grandma was still alive, I'd do all her yard work without having to be asked.

And then my mind turned to Blair.

What could I possibly give her that she had not already tried to take from me?

And that feeling of power faded.

I could no longer imagine what it was to buy a gift for someone, the one thing that they wanted above all things but never in a million years could get for themselves. Quick as a light, my head clicked back to the old way of thinking. That people made themselves miserable or happy by their own hand. And nothing could be done about the past.

What good was thinking about what I would do to help others when I couldn't even help myself?

Wasn't I better off dead?

Nurse Rochelle went into the Nurses' Station and opened up the window for the night-meds.

I took my place in line and got my nightly ration. There were now two different pills in my disposable medicinal cup. It ranneth over.

The first one, which I had been introduced to earlier, still marked with the letters F and L separated by a longitudinal fissure: the Lexpro. The other, much smaller, round and white, with an equatorial line, the letters APO above, the numbers 150 below. I didn't know what the new pill was for.

I paused while everyone else dumped the cup into palm and popped pills into mouth.

"Everyone to their rooms. Lights out in twenty minutes," Nurse Rochelle commanded.

Everyone sloughed off down the hall. Leaving me standing at the window with my cup.

"Mister Justin," Nurse Rochelle said. "You got a new medication tonight."

"What is it?" I asked.

"Trazadone hyrdrocloride. It's small but it's mighty," she answered. "It should put you down within twenty minutes. You'll be able to sleep for a change."

I dumped the pills from the cup to my palm then popped them into my mouth and swallowed.

Walking down the hall, I entered my room and went straight into the toilet closet, sliding the door shut behind me so I could have a private place to change into my pajamas. It was small. It was secure. And I was alone.

I hadn't been in there long before there was a knock on the door.

"Mister Justin?" It was Nurse Rochelle, God love her. "You comin' out?"

There was no hiding place in Kelter Ward C. Closed doors made people nervous. But closed eyes were worse.

I pulled the door back and walked over to my single bed. I slid under the starched sheets and began to read the first page of *Catch-22* which I had smuggled out of the Patients' Lounge.

Waiting for the trazodone to kick in, I wondered what it would be like to fade away into blackness and nothingness. Because that's not what had happened when I had died. There hadn't been any sweet oblivion. There had a circus with different sideshow scenes.

The night became silent. But I don't know about holy.

I heard the tread of comfort shoes and the swish of scrubs. Nurse Rochelle came back into the room to make sure I was out of the bathroom. Then she asked me, "Why would you want to go and try to commit suicide for, Mister Justin? Don't you know life is a precious gift from God? Why would you want to throw it away?"

I had no answer for her.

I only felt a drowse.

All was calm.

All was night.

I was an infant child.

Tender and mild.

A baby possum in its mother possum's pouch.

A blanket of black birds filled the room.

My eyelids slid shut. And I slid into silence and darkness. Swallowed by the void.

There was nothing sweet about being oblivious.

Sometime later, I returned to myself again. I was still lying in bed on Ward C. The light in the hallway was still on. It was still night. Again, I could hear the tread of comfort shoes and the swish of scrubs.

The light was blocked out by a moving shadow.

Someone was at the threshold of my door.

Nurse Rochelle making her rounds. Checking on the sleeping suicides. Making sure no sheep went astray to venture out into the dark woods were the grey wolves laid in wait.

Sometime later, the hallway light was again blocked out.

Someone giggled.

At first, I thought it was Bud C.. He had snuck down to my room knowing I would be conked out from the trazadone. Now he was standing at my door and, after making sure I was asleep, he was going to go through all my stuff.

Someone giggled again.

I was able to open my eyes.

It wasn't Bud C. standing at my door.

It was a young boy.

Who in their right mind would have let a child onto the low security floor of a Mental Health Unit?

The little boy had dark brown hair cut with bowl bangs. Brown eyes wider than a window. He was six years old and wearing Miami Dolphins pajamas top and draw string pants. The white top had orange stripes on the sleeves and an out of the aqua dolphin wearing team's own football helmet on the front. He grinned at me from under a Kool-Aid moustache. He grinned at me. "It's Christmas Eve! Come on out! Grandma and Grandpa are here!"

I used to have a pair of pajamas just like that because the Miami Dolphins had been my favorite football team when I had been six years old.

The memory was vivid. And standing before me. Because the six year old boy in the Miami Dolphin pajamas with the Kool-Aid moustache was me, myself, and I.

My God, what kind of medication was I on?

6-My Best Christmas, My Worst Christmas

My six-year-old self was excited beyond belief.

He had never had a broken heart.

He had never wasted a minute feeling bitter.

Everything was seen through the shiny gloss of his brown eyes.

What reason did he have to be depressed?

His six-year-old world was full of only the possible.

His? Didn't I mean *my?*

What was not possible was his--my--being here on Kelter Ward C while I—as my thirty-four-year-old-self-- was also here at the same time. How could a six-year-old kid in Dolphin jammies just walk in off the street when the whole city was locked under ice and snow? How could he have gotten onto a Mental Health lockdown? Surely, Nurse Rochelle wouldn't have let him onto a secure floor filled with addicts and suicides?

From where had this six-year-old boy that I was now seeing sprung? Better yet, where he had been hiding these twenty-eight years? And just how could I be in two places at once when I was nowhere at all?

At first, I was stuptified. I thought I was dreaming. But Nurse Rochelle had just come to check on me and left and then my six-year-old self had appeared. Could I have fallen into such a deep state of dreaming in just a few seconds?

And hadn't my six-year-old self mentioned it was Christmas Eve? That was just not possible. Christmas was still three weeks away. Wasn't it?

Here I lay under starched bedsheets in a mental ward full of patients slumbering in their beds with visions of pharmaceutical fairies dancing in their heads. I had only been admitted for one whole day and a night.

None of that mattered anymore.

Not the memory of what I had for breakfast: grits and a fried egg. Not the new meds Dr. Frost had put me on: Lexapro and trazadone. Not the cuts on my wrists. Or the stitched up wounds under bandaged bracelets.

Maybe those things hadn't happened.

The six-year-old boy in the Miami Dolphins pajamas giggled and beckoned me. The digesting breakfast, the meds' chemical traces, and the stitched up wounds on my wrists hadn't even happened to him.

To him, it was still 1976. Bing and Bowie hadn't even duetted yet.

He waited for me to get out of bed and go downstairs to see the gifts under the Christmas tree.

So I did.

I slipped out of bed and stood on the cold floor in my bare feet.

Then I stepped out into the hallway and onto a fuzzy orange carpet. It was at least ten degrees warmer. And the long ballast lamps of the overhead hospital lights were gone. Instead there was a square light fixture overhead. The walls were no longer painted with cruel antiseptic white. They were blue.

I was in a small hallway. Surrounded by wood paneled walls. A heat register behind me was blowing sweet warm air.

Ahead of me was a flight of steps to a landing where a front door waited to be opened to greet my favorite relatives to help celebrate Christmas Eve.

I was home.

13 Joseph Drive.

Home was a split level house with three bedrooms, kitchen, living room, family room, a bath and a half, and almost no closet space. The first home I had ever lived in. With my two parents and older brother.

I looked down and saw that I become childlike and evergreen. And wearing Miami Dolphins pajamas that I had put on after lunch. I was ready for bed so it could be Christmas morning.

Then all I had to was wake up, run downstairs, see all the gifts laid out under the tree, and it would be time to divide and conquer. Next, I would take down the stocking, a long white stocking with red and green stripes with my name stitched on it and empty it.

It hung there now next three others on the banister. One for me, one for my brother, one for Mom, and one for Dad. All stitched with names. All now empty but tomorrow morning they would be full of candies and little gifts.

And after we had opened our gifts and had emptied our stockings, we would go to Grandma's and Grandpa's for Christmas lunch, which would be turkey and dressing and cranberry jelly and turnips and my two favorites: mashed potatoes with gravy.

But before Christmas morning and Christmas lunch there would be Christmas Eve.

But there had been a knock at the front door. Grandpa and Grandma had arrived! Now we could start! That was why I was racing my brother down the stairs to the landing. Oh, comfort and joy!

As always, I lost. And my brother was the first to open the door and greet our grandparents.

"Merry Christmas, boys!" Grandma smiled. She was a petite lady and always neatly dressed with broaches and pendants on her blouses.

We shouted "Merry Christmas!" back to her.

First, she kissed my brother's forehead. Then she kissed me. As she bent down, I thought she smelled like pizza.

The reason why Grandma smelled like pizza was because she was holding two carryout boxes.

"That pizza?" I asked in expectation.

"Sausage and pepperoni," she said.

How could tonight get any better than this?

"Ho, ho, ho!" chanted Grandpa standing behind Grandma bearing paper grocery sacks laden with wrapped gifts.

Having them come was better than Santa Claus showing up with all his reindeer and a sleigh laden down with presents. They had brought gifts and cookies and best of all, F. U. D. G. E.

Mom came down to the landing and took the sweets platter back upstairs to the kitchen. Dad went outside to my grandparent's grey Buick Century to open trunk and retrieve the extra bags of gifts. I was amazed that there were even more gifts to bring inside.

"God bless everyone!" I wanted to shout.

My brother and I went ran outside in our pajamas to see inside the trunk. My grandfather had already gone inside with one sack but no less than three more waited in the trunk of his Buick. Each full of gifts. Some wrapped with gold, red, white, blue, and green paper and some tied up with ribbons and bows.

My dad let my brother take one sack while he scooped up the other two. Me, he shooed back inside since I didn't have any shoes on. He didn't want me to get sick and spend my Christmas vacation in bed.

I ran back inside and down stairs weaving between my sack bearing grandpa and dad. One by one the sacks were emptied and the gifts were piled under the Christmas tree. The green plastic shrine with spongy soft needles.

I had watched dad put it up. Section by section. Metal tube fitting into metal tube with triangular bolt tighteners to lock them in place. Then each plastic labeled branch was slotted into the corresponding tube. The large A ones on the bottom. The medium B ones on the second tier. The thinner C ones on the third. The smallest D ones on the top tier. And the very last branch, the shortest of all, was stuck at the very top straight up to the ceiling.

Next, dad tested each string of lights before he had strung them. He always started at the top of the tree. First, he had wrapped it with a string of white lights. Then, the next of gold. And then, my favorite, a string of multi-colored lights that blinked in patterns like crazy stop-lights.

After the lights had all been plugged in, Mom and Dad had put on the ornaments. They even let my brother and I put on a few by ourselves. There were silver bells. Small blue spheres. And large red bulbs. Four pointed golden stars. And ceramic angels, shepherds, wise men on camels, a pregnant lady on a donkey, and a baby in a manger.

One of the large red bulbs had slipped out of my hands and fallen to the floor, to break like the side of an egg. I was amazed to find it was hollow inside. Then Dad had demoted me to only putting the hooks on the branches and making sure that I turned the end of the branches up or gave them a little twist so that the hooks wouldn't slip off.

Mom applied a layer of gold and silver tinsel as Dad brought down a step ladder. He climbed up to reach the top of the tree to put on the final touch. A humble angel with ruddy cheeks and praying hands and folded wings played the herald from atop of our tree. The tree topper.

"'Glory to God in the highest, And on earth peace, goodwill toward men,'" Dad quoted.

"Why just to men?" Mom smirked.

"Now, hon, 'men' can also mean 'mankind' and in that case, the 'man,' or 'men', is short human. So, the angel meant 'humankind.' Look it up in the dictionary," Dad challenged. We never bothered. Because he was always right. Always. Like I told you earlier, there was HIS way or NO way.

Every year in Sunday School, we had learned the Christmas Story. And my mom even had a pop-up book called *The First Christmas* where we could move the Star of Bethlehem or the animals in the manger and the three wise men on their camels or the angel in the sky above the shepherds across the page. Except that the Three Wise men, who I later learned had been magi, hadn't been at the manger scene: they had brought the first Christmas gifts--gold (for a king), myrrh (for a priest), and frankincense (for burial)--much later. And the shepherds wouldn't have been outside at night in the middle of winter with their flocks.

The first Christmas had been probably been in August just before school started. But you can't have Christmas Break at the end of summer break just before school has to start and not have a winter break at the mid-way point. So, putting Christmas in December worked out well for teachers and students.

I wasn't thinking about the fact that there had been no decorated plastic evergreen coniferous tree in that Crescent Land substrata cave below the building foundation two thousand years ago to celebrate the birth of the king of the universe.

Instead, we watched the swag grow exponentially in mass under our fake plastic lighted Christmas tree. Retail shaped boxes. Shoe boxes. Round tin drums. Ring boxes. Flat boxes. Big boxes. And even bigger boxes. One was longer than me and skinner than my brother. And another so big and bulky, Dad leaned it against the wood paneled wall.

It would be impossible for my brother and me to count them all in our excitable state of minds.

It was my brother who came up with a brilliant solution to our thorny Gordian problem: just count how many presents had each of our names on it and see who had more.

Simple. Pure genius. But that was my brother for you. So my brother and I did what was easier. Count how many of them had our own names on them. I lost count past ten.

Ten gifts! Just for me!

And it wasn't even Christmas morning!

Then my brother let me know he had counted fourteen. I always lost out to him.

Dad and Grandpa told us to leave the gifts alone. Not to lay a hand or finger on them. Not to jostle them or shake them up.

But it was hard not to disturb a bow or taped corner that was just begging to be torn off.

Mom and Grandma called us all upstairs for dinner. Which was where that sharp sharp aroma of sausage and the well cooked pepperoni wafted. Hot, fresh pizzas.

We sailed upstairs, took a wobbling seat, stilled long enough for a prayer, grabbed a paper plate, held it out for a piece of pizza which we barely ate and pleaded to go downstairs now and start opening our gifts.

But no, we had to wait for everyone else to finish eating first.

After everyone had their fill of pizza and rootbeer, Grandpa announced, "This is what I look forward to every year—your grandma's fudge. Let's take the fudge plate downstairs and divvy up the gifts!"

Grandpa wasn't the only one who lived for Grandma's fudge. It was a once a year delicacy. And every year, Grandma would worry that it didn't turn out too well and every year Grandpa would declare it the best fudge ever.

"You say that every year, dear," Grandma chided him.

"I don't know how you do it, but you outdid yourself once again," Grandpa said.

"What if we had it every day, Grandpa? Would you ever get tired of it?" my brother asked.

"I don't think I could ever get tired of it," Grandpa confessed.

Grandma picked up the fudge plate. My brother and I raced downstairs in another heat. He won again.

By the time my parents and grandparents had come downstairs we were already divvying up the gifts. We figured if we had everyone's gifts sorted out then we could open our own that much faster. Figuring out who got what was simple. Each gift had a TO and a FROM so my brother and I knew who should get which present.

It took a while to get every package to the right person. Longer than my six-year-old patience could stand. Santa would have been proud.

Now everyone had a respectable pile of presents at their feet and when I sat down behind mine, I could barely see over it.

Then Grandma threw a wrench into our plan, "Everyone open one at a time and tell us who's it from."

I just wanted to open all my gifts at once. Free the toys of all that paper bondage. Then take inventory of Santa's swag. And start playing with the best of what I had gotten.

Action figures rated high. Also, hot wheel cars. But the number one Christmas item I most desired would be a toy gun or an army of green army men for me to command at my leisure.

It was pure torture to have to wait for everyone to open a gift and thank the giver one by one. But a fascination began to take place. I saw the astonishment on my parents' faces as they each gave and received gifts they didn't think that the other could afford and therefore hadn't expected. And I saw the gratitude on my grandparents' faces for the thoughtful things they received.

I had about twelve gifts. My brother may have had fourteen. I had just lost another contest. But as I opened them all, I was disappointed to find about five of them were clothes. *Clothes.* I couldn't understand why anyone would think I would want clothes for Christmas. I hadn't put one clothes item on my Christmas list. I already had drawers full of clothes. They thought I had wanted *clothes.* I had only put toys on my Christmas wish list. Each present of clothes was one less toy that I didn't get was the way I saw it.

Until I opened one package and saw that it was a Miami Dolphins bedspread. Then I cheered for clothes.

Now I could be wrapped up in the Miami Dolphin logo every night! And I scored even more with the next gift: a Miami Dolphin pennant I could put on my wall and a Miami Dolphin helmet! It was a tight fit but it was all mine!

My brother cleaned up, too. He got some *Superman* toys and a new *G.I. Joe* doll. All of which I coveted.

Grandpa got a new bolo tie and ate more fudge than both my brother and I combined.

Grey edges closed in around the downstairs room.

The downstairs dissolved: the lights turned dark; the tree receded; the family vanished; the fudge was swallowed by shadow.

The air grew cold.

The walls pulled away and I was exposed.

Outside.

Flying.

Over cold earth and through winter air.

Scores of roofs outlined by Christmas lights. Wreaths of smoke exhaling out of vents. Lawns crowded with inflatable, waving Santas and all his reindeer.

Empty streets.

Parked cars.

Families inside cubic warmed living rooms gathered around large mounted screens that streamed yuletide Christmas logs.

I could hear Christmas carolers singing outside the locked front doors of a hundred Ebeneezers. I could hear choirs of herald angels serenading to a whole countryside of shepherds. I could hear the bells of the reindeer from Santa's sleigh. I saw Rudolph's red nose so bright. I saw Frosty the Snow Man jaywalk in front of a traffic cop. I saw Jack Frost nipping at someone's nose. I saw people rocking around the Christmas tree. I saw people hopping as bells jingled. I saw grandmothers lining up Christmas card after card on their countertops. I saw little girls wait under the Christmas tree with mistletoe. I saw mothers in their night gowns kissing men dressed up as Santa Claus. I saw orphans being brought their figgy pudding. I saw three ships sailing. I saw a partridge, two turtle doves, three French hens, and four calling birds, all in a pear tree.

Then the music changed.

The winter sky was sewn shut. The air became somber. And the wind blew harsh.

Clouds resounded with the vibrations of a classical guitar. Thunderclaps hammered the strings of a baroque harpsichord.

Then a bell tolled.

A solemn tone. Followed by another half tone. And another one descending another step.

Tiny bells chimed in a four note ostinato in a cross rhythm against the tones.   They rang those bells, they merrily rang, to tell all the world, to loudly proclaim in one tone, a somber tone, a welcome home, they rang far and near, something was coming here, the same to young and old, something every tongue should be told, the bell tolled long, pealing prolonged.

Over and over, those same four notes.

From a whisper to a moan.

I sought refuge from the bitter cold.

A haze grew out of a vapor. In the middle of the air, it took shape and became light and warmth.

It sharpened until it hurt.

I realized my eyes had been closed and a bright light was pulsing over my eyelids.

I opened my eyes.

The light was coming from a standing lamp beside an empty recliner in the corner. My brother sat on a couch, quiet and not smiling. Except he was no longer ten, but seventeen and about to graduate.

And I wasn't six years old anymore. I was thirteen. And would start high school the next year.

We were in my grandparents' home at 13 Meriwether Lewis instead of at 2112 Joseph Drive. It was

Christmas Eve, but now we gathered together at their home. Grandpa couldn't get around too well anymore.

There had been a heart attack. Then a diagnosis of heart disease. Anemia. Poor circulation.

A cycle of hospital visits had started. Along with restrictions of diet and movement. Soon, Grandpa was spending more time in the hospital than out of it.

He'd been in a decline after a heart attack and his legs growing weaker and his breath becoming shallower.

It was only after we all had come into the living room that Grandpa finally made it from his bed to his favorite recliner beside the Christmas tree. He had his robe on and his slippers. His lips were pursed and I thought he was trying to smile but he was grimacing as he put a hand to his chest. Grandpa tried to be gracious, but often he would close his eyes and swallow like his throat hurt.

Tonight we hadn't eaten pizza together and told jokes. We'd eaten half warmed Kentucky Fried Chicken. It had been the only place my dad had found to still be open this late on Christmas Eve.

We ate the rubbery chicken coated in Extra Crispy recipe and the stiff mashed potatoes in silence. At the table sat Grandma, Mom, Dad, my brother, and me. From time to time, Grandma would call out to Grandpa who promised he would be there shortly and not to wait for him.

It was a strange Christmas Eve.

There was a tree. It was trimmed and decorated. But it wasn't on.

There was a tv playing *It's a Wonderful Life* but the sound was turned down.

There were no Christmas songs playing.

There was one chair empty at the table.

My brother and I grazed over the cookie plate but since no one was indulging, we feigned stacking any cookies on our plate. Instead of bragging on how many cookies we could eat apiece, we chomped in silence.

The fudge plate still was still covered in cellophane. Grandpa hadn't touched a one. He had been in bed most of the day and hadn't even tried to snag himself a sugar cookie.

The food was palatable but not enjoyed.

Things were changing. And I didn't know what was going to happen next. No one was even interested in opening gifts.

What was there to do? Except to go on with our Christmas Eve tradition.

Except that it would never be the same.

My grandpa sat in his recliner, pain etched on his face. My brother and I came into the living room to sit on the couch so we could keep Grandpa company, or out of habit, as we expected the next order of business to be tearing open Christmas gifts.

Grandma and Mom and Dad stayed in the kitchen. Holding a family conference.

A decision was arrived at. And a call was made on the old rotary phone.

Soon, a van plodded down Meriweather Lane. The headlights searching out the naughty and the nice. The emergency strobe lights flooding Christmas, red and blue over the neighborhood. Announcing the arrival of the ambulance.

I was helpless going on hopeless. Becoming cold. Numb. A solemn bell ringing in my heart.

The ambulance pulled up the long driveway to the front of the house. A paramedic walked by the large picture window where an unlit Christmas tree stood.

My brother answered the door. The paramedic was a young blonde haired man.

"I'm okay, you didn't have to call an ambulance," Grandpa whispered.

My mom approached with the young paramedic following. "You're in pain and we don't know what to do for you."

Grandpa shut his eyes and a tear dropped down his cheek. "But I don't want to ruin Christmas for everyone."

"You haven't ruined Christmas for anyone. We were all able to be together for awhile tonight. We can always open gifts together later. We love you," she said. Then she hugged and kissed him.

The young paramedic bent over Grandpa. "Hello. We've come to help. Can you tell me where it hurts? In your chest? When you breath?"

Grandpa shook his head. "It feels like I've had a bad case of heart burn all day long. And my arm feels like it got a cold."

The young blonde haired paramedic nodded. "We'll get you taken care of, don't you worry."

Another paramedic came in pulling a gurney behind him. His face was grizzled, his white hair cropped short. "Can we sit him, Mel?"

"Should be able to, Bart," the younger one replied. "Nothing broken."

Bart moved the gurney parallel to the recliner and ratched it up. Mel stood behind the recliner and pushed it. Grandpa slumped out of the chair and into Bart's arms. Then Mel stepped over and the two of them helped

Grandpa lay down on the gurney and get covered with a blanket.

"Who's his doctor and which hospital do you want us to take him to?" Bart asked.

Grandma told them and then asked, "How long will it take you to get there?"

"With Jasper driving, we should get there within twenty minutes. Shouldn't be a lot of traffic out tonight," Bart said.

Grandma was already getting on her coat. She wanted to ride with the ambulance. But my mom volunteered to take her.

Christmas Eve got cut short that night.

After that night, I never ate Christmas fudge again.

THIRD VERSE--The Ghost Of Christmas Presents

1-Warm Grits and a Cold Routine

> ***By the second day I had the
> routine down pat.***

The exact second Nurse Rochelle came by my door full of extra morning cheer announcing it was "wakey-wakey-eggs-and-bakey" time, I was full-on awake.

That would be between six and six thirty.

Then I was out of bed and grabbing a change of clothes and headed down the hall.

I was determined to be the first into the shower booth so I could get a fresh towel.

I was buzzed in. Then I disrobed and lathered up dry before I pulled the chain that started the shower's two minute buzzer.

I rinsed off and shampooed and then rinsed again all before the two minutes were up.

The water never got warm.

And I was as cold on the outside as I felt on the inside.

While I dressed the breakfast rack was rolled in— maybe by some of Santa's white gowned elf-orderlies. By the time I walked back to my room with no door, the rack waited at the top of the hall in full view of the Nurses' Station so they could keep watch on it.

That would usually be between six thirty and six forty-five.

So, I would detour to the rack and take my breakfast tray back to my room.

Usually, it was grits, toast, a fried egg, and orange juice.

Once I got adventurous and ordered French Toast. Big mistake.

This was hospital fodder. Meant to keep you alive for the next round of testing. Not meant to satisfy like Denny's fare or award winning IHOP or, hope against hope, a Waffle House.

So, I stuck with what I knew I could get to stay down.

By the time I had finished and put my tray back on the rack, most of the other patients had risen and grabbed theirs. The goal for most of us was to get our trays before Bud C. came sniffing around.

His six foot four frame had once upon a time held two hundred and fifty glorious pounds when he'd been healthy and so he'd had to eat the necessary carbs to keep those calories sticking on him. But the meth and speed had atrophied him away to one hundred and seventy pounds. And now that he'd gone cold turkey, his metabolism was back on the job and expecting the caloric intake of days gone by.

Nurse Michelle would usually bust him as he tried to pinch extra toast and butter pats and stuff them into his pockets. He knew she was watching him, but still he would try. She knew that he knew she was watching him and that she would catch him, too. He just couldn't help himself. He wasn't in charge of his body right now. His addiction was screaming for something to burn up.

Then Nurse Michelle would make the rounds past every doorless room. Make sure everyone on the ward was up. Showered and breakfasted.

That would be between seven and seven thirty.

I never went out into the Patients' Lounge first.

I always waited until someone else was there.

Usually, it was Jacque A. or Lizzy B..

If it was Jacque A., she would be forever shuffling a deck of well-thumbed cards which had a hole punched in the top right corner of each card.

And if it was Lizzy B., she would sit before the flat screen tv. Close as close could be. Esconced in her tunnel vision, soaking up one commercialized product message after another. Capitalism, Communism, Socialism, or any other that-ism or this–ism, what didn't change was the brainwashing-conscience-waking-soul-baking-propaganda. Over the years, those in charge had learned this never changing truth—people weren't that smart and liked to believe in what they were told. In short, we were and always will be and always had been: sheeple.

Case in point: Lizzy B.'s eyes soaked up a wild commercial for an electronic wrist watch that could gauge calorie intake and burn-off ratio and count your heartbeat and take your pulse as various people of various body types living various lifestyles with the theme/message, and words of LISTEN TO YOUR BODY repeated over and over to the rhythm and blues beat of a bad casio keyboard version of a funky organ.

Listen to your body. Right. Weren't we all here in Kelter Ward C because we had *listened to our bodies'* suggestions for far too long? By *body*, I surmised the advertisers meant *mind*. Sure, we could all count on our minds to tell us the truth. Always.

Which was more powerful? The mind or the body? Didn't the body exist to serve the mind?

Did our bodies always tell us the truth about what we needed? Or were our bodies also feeding us some sugar coated lies to get us do what it wanted? Which could get poisoned faster? The body or the mind? Because of listening to which one?

And what about our organs who suffered from our binging and addictions? Why didn't anyone ever listen to their organs' cries for help?

So much for listening to our bodies then. And our hearts were even worse off.

Just who could we listen to? If our hearts were sick, could we even trust our own hearts? And if our minds were poisoned, who was going to tell us the truth about ourselves without some sugar coated lie wrapped around a bitter political message? And were we even going to listen to the truth, even if we heard it while we writhed in addiction fed pain?

It seemed to me the last thing we should even think about trusting would be advertisements and messages across public airwaves and broadcasts.

Lauren, my first wife, said I thought too much and all my questions would just give her a headache. That was because she didn't want to think. Once she got an idea about how things were, she stuck with it. There was no changing her mind about anything. That's because that was who she was.

Maybe I did think about things too much. Maybe that was my problem. But, then again, maybe thinking about things was who I am. It's called being introspective or self-reflective, folks

I just wasn't too good of thinking myself out of a problem once I had thought myself into it.

I was going to need to some extra special help from someone somewhere with the power to restore me in mind, body, heart, and soul in order to lick this problem.

Even with Nurse Michelle watching, Bud C. was hovering around the breakfast tray rack like a buzzard. When Cathy D. would be the last to get her tray, she would be short a piece of toast and a few pats of butter. Nurse Michelle would pat Cathy D. on her sleepy head and give her one or two more butter pats.

Then at eight, Nurse Michelle would line us up for our morning meds.

And being good wards of the state sanctioned service, we would line up for them. This was when the orderlies would appear. To make sure that we would all take our medicine and once that bitter tasting medicine had gone down the hatch without any spoonful of sugar, the orderlies would disappear back into their secret lairs, which was only accessible through an invisible portal in the wall.

After that, we'd sit around the lounge comparing the side effects of our individual meds and then trying to outdo one another with sob stories of how cruel and miserable we'd been treated by everyone since the day we had been born.

Then at eight-thirty, Nurse Michelle would call the first group session of the day.

I had the routine down cold.

And soon I was craving a change.

I was ready to leave the hallowed halls of Kelter Ward C and get out of Dodge City.

2-The Revenge Of Jayne V.

"This is just for our daily intake, Justin," Jayne V. said after we were in the tiny interview room together. "How are you feeling today?"

"With my hands," I said.

She looked up from under her jagged bangs. I noticed it was a new haircut. Her rich auburn hair was spiky. She noticed me noticing and her dimples came out to wink at me.

"I was hoping for things like happy, sad, glad, mad, excited, or tired," Jayne V. said. She smoothed out the sleeve of her turtle neck shirt. The delivery of her questions was in an unaffected monotone. Her fingers tapping in my responses on her ipad as she created my narrative: pure professionalism.

"Excited to be here but tired of the food. Happy to talk with you now," I summarized. "What day is it?"

"Friday," she said.

"Then I'm glad it's Friday," I finished. Although, I had been seduced by the rhythm of the ward and sucked into the blur of routine, today didn't feel any different than yesterday. And if today was Friday then it was going to be exactly the same as Thursday: wake, shower, breakfast, meds, group therapy, intake, lunch, down time, dinner, group therapy, down time, meds, sleep.

"Is there any history of mental illness in your family?" she asked next.

"My grandmother used to threaten to shoot the governor because he was a Republican," I confessed. "But then he went to jail. I've noticed that here in Illinois both Republican and Democratic governors serve two terms: one in office and one in jail."

Jayne V. smirked. The dimples came out again. "I don't think that means she was crazy. High strung maybe. Was she your maternal or paternal grandmother?"

"Paternal," I said.

"Have you ever heard voices before the other day?" she asked next.

I felt my face turn sour. Did she think I'd gone crazy or something?

Well, let's see. On the crazy side of the ledger: two days ago—or had it been three--I had just died from an attempted suicide. Then I'd seen my dead grandpa. Followed by my six year old self.

And hadn't I committed myself into a low security mental health facility?

If it had been anyone else—say a close friend— wait, I didn't have a close friend—say a co-worker then— I spent more time with them than my own family—and my co-worker had told me they'd tried to slit their wrists and had OD'd on their ex-wife's pain killers and then watched their dead grandfather walk into their room after they'd been resuscitated, I'd've thought they'd completely lost it.

Become unglued.

Wigged out.
Blown a fuse.
Out to lunch.
Lost their marbles.
Gone soft in the head.
Wasn't playing with a full deck.
Didn't have the elevator going all the way to the top.
The lights were on but no one was home.
One fry short of a Happy Meal.
Cheese slipped off the cracker.
Driving on three wheels.
Gone stark raving mad.
A nut job.
Plain crazy.
Whacko.
Psycho.
Mental.
Insane.
I felt I could trust Jayne V.
I wanted to trust Jayne V.
Her crystal blue eyes seemed genuine, not cold. Her demeanor was more nice than professional.
She was cute.
If I wanted to get out of here, I had to talk to someone didn't I?
Then I told her something that I hadn't told another soul. "A few weeks ago, I woke up and thought I heard a woman crying. In total despair."
"Was your second ex, Blair, there?" Jayne V. asked.
"No. We hadn't gotten back together yet. It couldn't have been her. The locks had been changed and I was alone in the house," I said. Lying on the couch where I'd fallen asleep, watching *Cool Hand Luke* in the

back room addition, the loud crying had awoken me. The sound was so real and so sad and so broken. It chilled the bone and disturbed the bottom of my heart. It was more than a moaning. It was a wailing. The kind made by a banshee.

Jayne V. reflected. And then she asked, "Are you sure you've never had hallucinations before you were brought to the hospital?"

"Only when I've been stoned," I said.

On occasion I had partaken in eating Alice B. Tolkas or pot brownies. When the pot is heated the THC becomes psychoactive. If you smoke it, it goes from the lungs to the blood and to the brain. But it is weak and diluted. But if you ingest it into your stomach, it will get into your blood from there and go to your brain with quite a pronounced effect. It always a very intense trip. I tended to hallucinate and become paranoid.

One time, I thought my hands were two lead zeppelins and the universe was coming through in waves. But there was another time when I sat on a recliner in a friend's living room listening to some music, a hairless three foot tall green demon stepped out of the speaker to touch me on the side of my abdomen with his hand. The demon leered and popped his tongue in and out as he did so. I began to feel heat and gurgling in my bowels the moment he touched me. My belly bloated and I had heart burn that lasted for days. It got so bad I couldn't lie down at night.

Eventually, I was diagnosed with reflux.

My stomach had turned on me. Why, oh, why, did I not listen to my organs?

"When was the last time you used marijuana?" Jayne V. asked.

"About a year and a half ago," I said. "It was a bad trip."

"Alcohol?" she asked.

"Two months ago," I said. "I can go a long time without drinking. Then I'll get stressed, have a drink, and then another. I can't stop after just one or two or three. Then that becomes my new habit, again."

"Were you using when you were married to Blair?" Jayne V. asked.

I shook my head. "I quit right after I met her. I had been partying for years before I met her. She doesn't drink much and she didn't want me drinking at all. So, I after I met her, I pretty much quit. Then we got married."

"How long were you dating before you got married?" Jayne V. asked.

"About two months," I said.

"And this is your second marriage?" Jayne V. asked.

"Yes," I said. "I was married for about four and a half years the first time. Then I was divorced about a year and a half before I met Blair. And we lasted just a year."

I had just rattled off the last seven years of my life with ease. Seven years of spinning my wheels. Seven years of a roller coaster ride that I felt was starting to make another climb up a heartbreak hill.

The romance with Blair had been a rocket ride. A go for launch, ignition, and then lift off.

I'd been so proud to walk away from drugging. And for letting Blair be my accountability. I had placed all my love and faith and trust in her. She had proved her faithfulness in bed over and over, time and again.

See? I did listen to my organs once in a while.

Then the rocket of romance had turned into a runaway train and had exploded in mid-flight just like the Challenger.

My first year of sobriety—spent married to a bi-polar manic depressive--had come crashing down in pieces. Hardly a master plan.

"I know, I know," I admitted. "It just reeks of co-dependency."

Jayne V. had to look at me twice. "Who told you that you were co-dependent?"

"Isn't it obvious?" I asked. The truth was a hairless three foot tall green demon staring at me in the face.

She said nothing. Instead she continued tapping her reflection on my narrative into her ipad, clickety clack, with her press-on nails. Without warning, Jayne V. asked me, "Why did you cut on yourself?"

"I was mad," I shrugged. "I felt guilty. I'd made a mistake and couldn't take it back."

"What mistake was that?" she asked.

"First, marrying Blair. Then divorcing her. Then getting back together when her. My family is going to flip out when I tell them," I said.

"Does it matter to you what they think of her?" Jayne V. asked.

"They won't forgive her. They won't accept her back. They'll probably cut me off," I said.

"Maybe if you give them time--" she began.

I was already shaking my head. "With my dad, there's his way or no way. He won't budge."

"Is this the first time you have cut on yourself?" Jayne V. asked.

I paused.

How far did I want this to go? How much was I willing to reveal about myself? The first time I'd ever gone to a counselor, he had prefaced our first session with a warning: He could only help me with whatever I was willing to talk about; if I wasn't willing to talk about it, he couldn't help with it.

All this time, I'd been going from one bad choice to another. Leaving behind what I knew to be real in order to follow my "heart." What did my heart know? I had been baptized at age nine and age thirteen I was dead set on becoming a rock star. Death or glory, babe.

You cannot serve two masters. One master had given up His glory to die for me. The other wanted me to die in order to feed the fire. Yes, I had a Bible in the house, but if I didn't read it then it was nobody's fault but mine as the old blues song went.

I had been twenty-one when I'd cut on myself the first time. I was in my third year of college, had an A average, I was in a local rock group down the street trying hard to learn a song, I was working part time, and I was involved with a girl who didn't have any inhibitions. My parents didn't want me to be in the band. They thought the girl was too young for me. I was burned out on college, skipping classes, not sure about why I was even there anymore and the only thing that made me happy was playing with the band and the party scene afterwards. We rented a space above an old warehouse. We called it our party-pad. Every weekend, people would come watch us practice and we'd have to buy more beer than usual and it became a party. But the focus of the after party was this running game of Truth or Dare. Most people wanted to do the dares even if the questions were easy and so the dares just got more and more degrading. The girl I was dating became a focus of the dares. More like an easy target because she'd squeal with delight at the attention.

Then, come to find out, the girl was messing around with my band-mate behind my back. I had suspected them but both the girl and my friend denied it, but after somebody else told me it was true, I felt like the biggest idiot in the world. That night I took a razor and cut up and down both my arms. I could remember feeling each cut. The sting. The blood. And thinking it wasn't deep enough. That I needed to feel more pain. So I'd cut again. I lost track of the cuts past twenty. I was working at a pizza joint so I called them that morning and quit. Then I slept all that day. Then I quit the band. Then I quit going to school for a while.

I ruined my A average. Got put on scholastic probation. Slept all the time. Just had what kept me going those years in college? It's like that old cliché: sex, drugs, and rock and roll. It had become a list of priorities and the music was last. Except there was something else that was absolute dead last. Me, if I wasn't careful.

I turned my senior year into a dropping classes and getting incompletes. I managed to pass a few classes, but graduating from college was like flogging a dead horse. I'd go to bars and share pitchers of beer. When the pitcher was empty, except for the sliding suds, I'd wonder what the big deal was. After a while, I'd feel the same and in the morning, I'd feel worse. My parents threatened to throw me out and make me pay my own insurance. I got a full time job running stock at a shoe store and agreed to pay for my own insurance and gas money.

Then I had met ex number one: Lauren. She was a wallflower. A quiet church girl. A shoe gazer who kept her head down all the time and her eyes hidden behind long hair. Wanting to get married gave me something I hadn't had before: a reason to finish. I had to swallow my bad taste for the college busywork so it took me a year and a half to finish taking the last few credits I needed to graduate which I did at my own expense while I worked full time.

My dad and I had fought like a married couple over my future. I had wanted to become a teacher and he wanted me to work at a bank. He'd tried teaching when I was younger then he got a job working at one of the biggest banks around: Merchants' Bank. He said I should teach college because I couldn't handle disciplining kids who didn't want to be there. And so, I believed him and got a job at America's Bank down in the mail room, which I hated.

I took off on a Saturday so I could graduate college. I ran into my old band-mates at a mall when I was out shopping with my fiancé. We buried the hatchet and cranked the amps up to eleven.

And the whole cycle of madness started up again. Only this time, instead of Truth and Dare, we got more sophisticated and we left our wives at home and went to cigar clubs and then strip joints. There was always a party going on somewhere where people would pay money for exhibitionism.

I smoked more, I drank more, I rocked the night away. And in the morning, I'd be sicker and feel worse than before.

It had been at a reunited band party I had seen the reflux-causing demon while tripping on pot brownies.

I hadn't talked about these things in some time. Hadn't even wanted to think about them. All these memories were too fresh. Like pieces of a puzzle stuck to my fingers that I couldn't shake off. I knew the puzzle was incomplete, that pieces were missing, and that I was hurting. But I thought I could just go on like that forever.

Well, the stitches pulling at my cuts and itching on top my wounds told another story.

They told the truth.

If I was never going to name my hurts or talk about them how could I ever be healed? Did I even want to change?

All these memories had come flooding out of order at me. As I tried to process all these flooding memories, Jayne was waiting to tap in my response. "I was twenty-one the first time I cut on myself," I said.

"Do you remember why?" she asked.

"I felt guilty over doing something stupid that I shouldn't have. I had crossed a line," I said.

I hadn't talked about these things in a long time. My parents had never suspected. I hadn't even told Blair.

And certainly not ex number one. After being together for eight years and so much hadn't been said.

I felt exhausted. To the bone. I was tired of this game. "When can I leave?"

"When Dr. Frost thinks that you're no longer a danger to yourself or to others," Jayne V. said.

"Couldn't I just leave if I wanted to?" I asked. Then I pointed to the door behind her. "What's to stop me from just walking out that door."

"That door? Nothing. But the door beyond is a secure door. You can't buzz yourself out. You volunteered to come in here for treatment. And if any of the staff--the nurses or the orderlies, myself or Dr. Frost-- think that you are a danger to yourself or plan to harm anyone else, then you're not getting out of here," she said.

If I kept on seeing dead people or having my life flash before my eyes while I was awake maybe I was better off keeping it to myself.

3—Merry Christmas To the Merry Prankster

Jayne V. signaled that the session was over by closing out her app and curling her wrist around the ipad like it was a holy book. She was out the door before me.

I walked down the main hallway and stood between the Nurses' Station where the orderlies stood like gargoyle sentinels and the lounge where the other patients were gathered.

Lizzy B. sat in the recliner in sweat pants totally absorbed in another broadcast of "Good Morning, America" and totally alone. Jacque A. sat at the end of the lounge deep in an intimate conversation with a visitor. A dark haired girl with mascara running rings around her moony eyes. She was dressed much the same as Jacque A.. Black jeans fading to grey and a dark sweatshirt. The visitor was leaning in to whisper to Jacque A. while the other kept her eyes down.

Cathy D. was nowhere in sight.

I noticed two more people.

Either they were visitors or new patients.

Both were male.

Both completely opposite in manner and dress.

One sat sideways in his seat. One leg crossing the other, just above the knee in a gentlemanly fashion. He wore old style breeches, a vest, a waist coat, and a starched shirt. All with old buttons and eyelets. This one had curly chestnut hair parted to one side and warm brown eyes.

The second stood in old work jeans and worn construction boots. He had on a jacket frayed at the elbows and a dirty old mac over tousled red hair. His blue eyes crackled.

If they were visitors, then I don't know who they had come to see. Though they seemed to have arrived together. And if they were both patients, then they had become fast and close friends.

"Merry Christmas!" the chestnut haired one called out.

No one in the lounge gave any indication of having heard him. So I assumed he meant me.

"Come here and get to know us better, man!" he invited.

"Like man, bring us our friggin' puddin' and bring it right here," the red haired man with the mac said.

I came over empty handed. "Sorry. No pudding. Hospital food isn't the best."

The chestnut haired man nodded. "My name is rather cumbersome so I am called Boz by all who greet me."

The red haired man tipped the end of his mac to me. "And I'm the Merry Prankster. Always making some merry for others to enjoy."

"Do not let him fool you," Boz said. "His name is Randy T. McMurtry. And what might you call yourself?"

"A loser," I said.

Jacque A.'s visitor had heard me and looked over to me. Then she went back to her intimacy.

Boz cocked his head and Randy pushed his mac further back on his head.

"Were you born that way?" Randy asked.

I shook my head. "I've lost something."

"And what is it that has become lost?" Boz asked.

"I used to be happy. I was happier when I was a kid," I said.

"I wasn't," Lizzy B. said over her shoulder. "I've never been happy my whole miserable life."

Both Boz and Randy ignored her.

"Man, that's so true," Randy encouraged. "A child should be outside in the great wide open. Fishing, swimming, hunting, turning over every rock. Sleep out under the stars. Total freedom."

"I'm afraid my childhood was spent doing the exact opposite of that. I spent sixteen hours a day in a shoe factory, eating where I stood and often sleeping there, too. All to pay off my father's debts," Boz said.

"You never told me that, Boz," Randy said.

"You never asked me, Randy," Boz said.

"Well, in this country, we don't have compulsory work for children. There are child labor laws. Children are the apple of our eye. Our prosperity. Our reason for living. They get well fed and they have sports. No corporeal discipline. Smack a kid and the state should take them away from the parents," Randy said.

"I have toured this country coast to coast twice. I've seen for myself the emphasis put on sports and play and the coddling of every child from New York City to San Francisco. Every child in America has been taught they are to be cared for. But are we teaching them that they are responsible for their fellow man?" Boz asked. Then he nodded to me. "And now, if you will, it would give me great pleasure to know your true name. Every human is part of the Soul of Mankind. And each is known by a singular name by that greater soul. One should never give their true name lightly. A true friend will only call your name in need. But another might be selfish and maligned and if they were to say your name three times in a row, that other could enslave you. That's magic."

"That's bologna," Randy returned fire at the next breath. "I've got tons of names. I got the one on my birth certificate—the one my mom gave me—Randy T. McMurtry. There's the nickname my dad give me-- Murgatroid. Then the name my fraternity brothers give me--Juvenal. Then what my wife sometimes calls me when we're…you know…except she don't call me Randy and she don't call me Murgatroid and Lord knows she don't call me no Juneval, she calls me Mac. So, I got four names, at least. Whenever someone uses your real name, it's either the law or a spam call."

"My friend Mr. McMurtry is not one to speak in metaphor. He calls such language 'beating around the bush.' He is a proponent for plain speaking and plain dealing," Boz explained.

"Either you're a straight shooter or you're a crap slinger," Randy further illuminated. Then he indicated Jacque A. and her visitor. "Take her. She looks like a straight shooter. But sometimes not telling the truth and keeping it locked up inside can kill you. Now that big guy, Bud C., the who went into the small room with that very cute redhead. He's a crap slinger. He throws so much so fast some of it's bond to stick."

"Well done, Randy. You just used a metaphor," Boz said and clapped his cupped palms politely.

"Hells' bells, Boz. Been hangin' with you too long, I guess. Wish more of me would rub off on you," Randy said. "Anyway, kid, remember. The best lie is sandwiched between two truths."

"This isn't quite the place to start spinning lies," I told him.

"If you truly desire your freedom, you may want to reconsider," Boz said. "My own was won by keeping a terrible secret in my domestic affairs. Everyone need not know everything about you."

"See?" Randy cried. "There you are! Plain speaking out of the Victorian bard!"

"Well, if you're gonna lie, better make it a good one," Lizzy B. said over a booming commercial.

Randy laughed good-naturedly. "The skank's right."

"Can she not hear you two?" I asked the two men.

Randy looked up to the ceiling.

Boz shrugged. "Ahem, there is a slight peculiarity to this situation. Here we two are. And here you are. And there is that good woman watching those moving pictures and there are those two lesbians."

"Yeah, I see them and I see you," I argued. "The others all see me. Do they not see you?"

"It isn't like we're totally invisible, man," Randy said. "I mean, you can see us."

"Sweet Lord," I said. "You're not real."

"You okay, Justin?" Jacque A. asked.

I felt dizzy and weak. "I think I need to sit down."

So I sat down in a chair against the back wall. The one in which Boz had just been sitting.

Lizzy B. gave me the once over. "It's the meds. Doc ain't got the dosage right, yet. Better tell him to cut it back a tad."

4—A Hand For Dr. Frost

Boz nodded as he stood next to me and McMurtry tipped his mac. Worker's jeans followed woolen breeches and both men walked out of the lounge. Lizzy B. snuggled up in her dirty sweats on the recliner paying them no mind and Jacque A. was too wrapped up in intimate tones with her raven haired visitor to notice the pair's passing.

Was I the only that had seen them? The only one to hear them speak? They had spoken to each other and both had spoken to me.

When I had seen the hairless green demon, it had been both there and not there. There in a blink of an eye, solid but not solid, and dissolving away back into the speaker in the next instant.

That had been a hallucination. I knew that couldn't have been real. No matter how telling it was.

This was something completely different.

I could still see the pair walking right past the Nurses' Station. Both, being the gentleman, nodded to Nurse Michelle as she used her degree and training to click endless boxes for on-line forms. They didn't work through a wall like the orderlies or dissolve away like my pot brownie demon. They kept straight on down the hall and entered an open room. A patients' room. Maybe it was their room. Maybe they were roommates.

Maybe there were just more hallucinations.

I could explain away seeing my dead grandfather and even my six year old self from the trauma I'd been under the past few days—suicide, near death, deep depression, new meds. I was in some kind of shock and every time that I fell asleep, I dreamed up something even more strange and wonderful.

But now I was having dreams that walked and talked in broad daylight.

That wasn't shock.

That wasn't trauma.

That was a classic textbook definition of insane.

The main door buzzed open.

And in came dour faced Dr. Frost. In coudouroy slacks and rolled up sleeves. Dr. Martens comfort shoes on his feet.

He saw me then noted the time on his gold wrist watch, "Justin, I've got some time for you."

Now wasn't the time to thread the unraveling of my mind. Or pick up the marbles that I was losing. Or chase white rabbits down their holes.

I stood to attention. Hoping to God that all my buttons were aligned, my shoelaces tied, and my zipper was up.

"Ready?" the good doctor prompted.

What was I going to do, refuse a session? How bad did I want out of here? "Sure," I shrugged.

He led me to the other end of the ward. To the suite of offices. We found a deserted conference room and set up shop.

I sat on one side of the big table and the good Dr. Frost sat down at the end adjacent to me. He took off his gold watch and set it down next to a yellow legal tab. He held a black felt pen in hand.

"How are you today?" he asked. I noticed he hadn't asked 'how are you *feeling* today?' Probably had been taught that one in Psych 101. Probably would up my dosage if I tried it out on him.

Dr. Frost had exiled humor from his routine. His façade was a sheer wall and his demeanor a moat which kept me, the patient and the doctor himself away from his own personality kept safe behind the castle wall. Only I suspected that his personality had been locked away in the highest tower by the well-dressed ogre before me.

The good Dr. Frost was here for business. Shrinking heads was his business. And business was booming.

"Everything's well," I said. Except it came out as *swell.*

I winced at that. His job was to note my every word and tone and gesture. He could probably tell from the way my pupils were contracting how much the Lexapro was affecting my brain and could count my breaths in a minute to determine my heart rate.

I couldn't show him that I was nervous. I had to relax and not talk so fast. Keep my answers simple and to the point.

And not say anything stupid like *swell.*

I straightened up. Kept my head still. Kept my eyes locked onto his face.

I had to show him I was conscious and coherent.

Safe and sane.

Right as rain.

Harmless.

Wouldn't hurt a fly.

Or even eat one.

"That is good," he said pretending he hadn't heard my *swell* be it a slur or slip. He took out two pieces of technology from the twentieth century—pad and pen—to scribble a note. Maybe he was tracking my response time which meant I still got points screw up or no screw up.

All I had to do was keep up the appearance for another twenty minutes or more.

I could do this!

But what should I do with my hands?

Should I keep them in my lap? I put them in my lap.

"Is the trazodone helping you to sleep?" Dr. Frost asked next.

I paused.

I couldn't hesitate! In hesitation was death. He'd know I was pausing only to think up some story.

Was having my hands in my lap showing I was being indecisive? Should I put them on the table?

So I pulled my hands out of my lap and put them on the table.

"Yeah. I'm sleeping better," I said.

It was a half lie. I wasn't sleeping better, I was sleeping longer. Not waking up with panic attacks. Or sleep paralysis where the dark hag or black spiders were coming for me. Or having nightmares in the only hour and half of straight sleep I had been getting.

My fingers twitched. What if I started fidgeting with them? Twiddled my thumbs? Picked at my hangnails?

Wouldn't Dr. Frost know I was lying?

So I folded up my hands in the gesture of supplication.

Dr. Frost had watched me move and shift my hands. Then he squeaked a note on his yellow pad.

Were my hands betraying me? Did it matter where I put them?

"How do you think the Lexapro is working for you?" he asked.

I knew I couldn't hesitate so my mouth started talking before I could start thinking. "Great. I feel fine. Much better. I feel like it's helping. I've been in a good mood."

Dr. Frost put down his pen and looked at me while I talked. Then he looked at my hands.

My thumbs were pushing against each other. I unfolded up my hands and put my palms flat on the table top. Why were my hands fighting against me?

"That's a little fast for the medication to take effect. I didn't prescribe you a very a high dosage," Dr. Frost commented.

Something was affecting me. Grandpa, my Miami Dolphin pajama'ed six year old self, and Boz and McMurtry would all swear to that. But there was no way I was going to tell Dr. Frost that. "Just what is this Lexapro supposed to do?"

"It is a serotonin reuptake inhibitor. Serotonin is one of the brain's neurotransmitters. It affects your mood, your appetite, and memory. Among other things. When the brain has low serotonin or a lack of receptor sites on cells, depression occurs. Lexapro is a SSRI. So are Prozac, Paxil, and Zoloft. These make your brain produce new cells and more serotonin. Serotonin combines with tryptophan," Dr. Frost said.

I knew what tryptophan was. "Coma by turkey," I said.

Dr. Frost looked askance as he processed the comment. Then something weird happened. Something rare and wonderful. He gave the barest hint of a smirk. "Yeah. That's one source of it."

I had just won a point.

Somehow my hands had dropped into my lap. What was I going to do with them now? They weren't behaving. They were trying to betray me.

What was Dr. Frost doing with his hands? They held a pen and a pad. At least they had a job. Something to do.

Our hands lived a life of their own. Separate and outside of our brains. They picked up things that were shiny and new or old and alien. Things that didn't belong to them. They picked up cups before we knew we were thirsty. Forks and spoons before our stomachs rumbled. Phones when we wanted to text someone. Remotes when we needed to watch something.

Who was in control here?

Again, I pulled my hands out of my lap and put them on the table and interlaced them so they couldn't move.

Wasn't I in control of them? Weren't the bandages proof that I was still in charge? They had to suffer along with the rest of me.

The bandages were beginning to fray and become unraveled. The dirt of days had smudged them. The stitches were itching most of the time now. What did my wounds look like?

Dr. Frost must have watched my eyes drop down to my interlaced hands and then to my wrists. Since I rolled them over to where the wounds would be. I might as well have pointed to my wounds and say, "See?"

"Do you think you're still a danger to yourself?" he asked.

"No way," I said. The question was now *Was I in any kind of danger?*

"Do you know why you harmed yourself?" he asked.

"I felt guilty," I said.

Dr. Frost so noted it with his pen. Then the pen waited for more. "About what?"

"That I'm a failure. I haven't done what I dreamed about and when I try I get nowhere. I'm thirty-four and I've been married and divorced twice. I've had problems with drugs. I want to be a writer or a teacher but I've worked at a bank for almost ten years. I'm behind on the mortgage and got enough unsecured debt to choke a horse. In college, I was on the Dean's List for the first two years. I'd never done that well in school. Ever. Then I got burned out. I couldn't see what good it was doing me. Couldn't see the forest for the trees so I burned down the forest," I said.

"So, you do you think that self mutilation is a good way to solve your problems?" he asked.

"I meant it to be the last solution," I shrugged.

"What would you do to yourself if I were to release you today? Would you be able to the everyday pressures of work? Or your relationship with Blair?" Dr. Frost asked.

I pictured a typical day in my life. Work. Being at home with Blair. Talking to my parents.

"Work I can handle. I've been there almost ten years. And they haven't fired me yet. You have to want to get fired. Not care at all," I said. "My problem is that I care too much. Or worry too much."

"You can only do one thing at a time and live one day at a time," Dr. Frost said. "Same as the rest of us."

That was to be the most profound thing Dr. Frost would ever say to me.

He continued, "If I released you, what would you do to get help? Would you be willing to go to outpatient therapy?"

I didn't know what outpatient therapy was. But I was willing to try it out. "Yes," I said.

"What about Blair? And your parents?" Dr. Frost asked.

"Bottom line: my parents hate Blair and will not accept her back," I said. "Because she racked up one credit card after another. She can't hold a job. She cusses in her sleep. She fights with her mother who is keeping her son. I didn't know anything about bipolar manic depression. Then I met her. How much does it affect her?"

Dr. Frost paused and put down his marker and tried to smooth out the crinkles in his coudorouy pants. "Blair is very sick. It effects everyone different, of course. Some slight. Some more severe. Blair has a more severe form. I'm not sure if she realizes right from wrong. She makes justifications when she breaks the law."

"Well, she can get jobs. She can talk the talk. She'd make a good salesman. But she doesn't live up to her promises," I said. "She can get jobs. But she starts complaining she's better than everyone. Then she stops showing up. Then she needs money fast so she spins some new plan for a whole new career change. The trouble is, talk is cheap. Then work will try to fire her for no-shows. And then she's crying everyone's against her. I've seen her try to blackmail an old boss."

Dr. Frost winced. "If someone wants to be in a relationship with her then that person will have to be very sympathetic to all her needs and will have to able to take care of her. Do you think you're the one?"

What he was describing was a saint. Someone who had enough money, maybe enough not to work, someone who was mature enough not to put their own dreams and goals first, someone who had already accomplished what they had set out to do in life. Someone who had infinite amounts of patience. Slow to anger. Not easily offended.

However much I wanted to be that person, however much I wanted to love and care for Blair, that someone being described was not me. I wasn't there yet. Not by a long shot.

"I want to be that man. I want to get back to my life. Back to my job. My house," I said.

"We'll see," Dr. Frost said. "I want to make sure the Lexapro is helping. And I'll have the nurse change your bandages and check on your stitches. Make sure they are healing fine."

"Gotta hand it to ya, doc," I said. "I'm much better off since I came here."

Dr. Frost's hands clicked his pen to retract it and tore off the pages of notes from his yellow pad. He folded them and stuffed them in a flat leather portfolio. "Good," he said as rose out of the chair.

Time was up.

The session was over.

5—Bud C. Explains It All

I left the conference room as Dr. Frost called out for Lizzy B.. We all might be patients of the good doctor for all I knew. All our secrets kept and all our meds scripted by that one man.

I hadn't thought much of the outside world. Blair and the nurses had talked of there being close to eighteen inches of snow on the ground and more coming. With all that snow piled up against their doors everyone might be locked secure inside their own ward.

Outside was a winterland. Snow blinding and ice freezing. The wind breath's chilling.

Winter solstice was less than two weeks away. The candle of daylight would be trimmed back and the shadow of night would grow that much longer. With the sun so far away, the cold would be that much stronger.

Inside Kelter Ward C, every moment was the same. There were no windows and the only way to track the passage of time was by the rhythm of the nurses: feedings, medications, and group sessions. The lights were always on.

We were supposed to be awake for fifteen hours.

And we were supposed to be asleep for nine.

Somewhere in between we were supposed to be conscious.

The air was always brisk. I wore pullovers with long sleeves and an undershirt when I was up. And two blankets plus the bedspread pulled over me, along with socks on my feet when I lay down.

I heard it was colder in the morgue.

After I wok,e I would do some stretches before my morning walk to the shower. And before lunch, I would walk the hall, trying to raise my metabolism and my appetite. Lizzy B. told me that Lexapro gave you constipation and put weight on you.

Lizzy B. preferred her wife beater tees and sweat pants with her legs tucked under while she sat in the recliner. Jacque A. wore untucked wool plaid shirts and heavy lug sole shoes. And whenever they could get Cathy

D. out of be, she would wrap herself in a blanket using an end of it for a cowl.

And Bud C. wore a t-shirt that was fraying at the neck line with holes in the underarms and at the bottom and jeans with thinning patches on his knees. He kept himself warm by his constant walking. Moving up and down the hallway. Back and forth in front of the Nurses' Station and the Patients' Lounge.

They had been keeping him away from taking seconds and thirds from the breakfast trays. Weight wasn't sticking to him. He was an empty pit of metabolism. Always hungry. Always vacillating between smiling and barking.

But now he was becoming a grouch. He no longer smiled after his rude comments. Now he just growled before and after he made them. Both Nurse Michelle and Rochelle would make him stand in front of them and swallow his meds. Then he'd have to open his mouth, pull back his lips, and stick out his tongue.

Lizzy B. said out of the side of her mouth that still had some teeth, that Bud C. wasn't taking his meds so could stock pile them and sell them on the street once his time was up. Medicare SSI would only pay for so many free days. And that the orderlies half-expected him to break into the med cabinet. She prophesized three fates for Buddy: he would OD; he would end up in jail; or both at the same time.

It happened right after the lunch carousel had been brought in. Instead of buzzing the aide out, Nurse Michelle hit an alarm and came running out of the Nurses' Station with two orderlies rolling out of their rabbit holes in hot pursuit. Nurse Michelle called Bud

C.'s name and the orderlies overpowered him and brought him to the floor.

Bud C. had used the aide's coming and going as a chance to break into the dispensary closet and add to his cache. Face down on the floor, in front of the open closet with an orderly pinning his arms behind his back and a knee in the middle of it, the big guy howled and cried for mercy. Then he cussed out everyone in sight and gave a list of everyone who had been in a conspiracy against him since the day he was born. That included God, Santa Claus, and the last four presidents of the United States.

Bud C. had lost it.

His hands were zip locked behind him, and the orderlies dragged him down the hall by his upper arms with his feet dragging behind.

"I didn't do nothin'! I ain't done nothin' wrong! Don't let them take me! Don't let them take me upstairs! Don't let them take to Kelter A! They're gonna Helter Skelter my brain! Tie me down and shock me! Please God, no! Don't let them scramble my brains!" Bud C. begged and pleaded.

The door buzzed open and in came two more orderlies with a gurney. They picked up a wiggling Bud C. and plopped him onto the gurney. Then they strapped him down as he howled and thrashed, his face red and contorted.

That was when I saw Boz and McMurtry again.

Standing on the other side of the security door.

Looking at me as Bud C. was wheeled past them, giving the orderlies a good cussing.

Bud C. got only a part of his Christmas wish.

He was taken off the ward. But not out of the building.

6—Bandages Off

I was tired of life in Kelter Ward C.

I wanted to get buzzed out.

I longed to be on the other side of that security door. Even if it did keep out my problems: dealing with Blair and squaring up with my parents. It couldn't keep out my fears. They had been locked in here with me.

At least on the outside, things would be different.

There might be security cameras, but there would be no room checks or group sessions.

I could close a door and not have someone ask me to open it.

I could shave with no one watching me and not to have hand back the razor.

I had a house that I still owned; it said so in the divorce decree.

And the ex-wife that I had kicked out of my life and had taken back into that same house. Was she, too, awaiting for my return with unconditional love?

Maybe I was the one who deserved to be hauled up to Kelter A and get my brains scrambled instead of Bud C.

While I was here behind a locked security door, just what was Blair up to? She hadn't come by yesterday. Or even called. I could only trust that Blair was taking care of things on the homefront.

What did she have to do? Blair didn't work. Instead, she had applied for SSI disability but wasn't likely to get it anytime soon. After we'd divorced, the only money she had made was by selling what she had taken out of the house on eBay or by pawning them off.

But what money did she have now? She was no longer on my bank accounts and I had my debit card here with me and I hadn't left any cash in the house. Blair had been to see me at the hospital a few times now. Driving in my car which she was no longer insured on.

She was creeping back into my life. And by coming here I had ceded a little more power to her. During the divorce proceedings, Blair had wanted the house. Even though she'd never been on the title. But there was no way any bank would put her on the title when she didn't have any income. The bank, being the lien holder, had the final say. Blair had tried to get around this by begging to quick deed the house to her, which would leave me with the mortgage loan which would put me in an insane situation.

Kind of like now.

Because with a house came a mortgage, a mortgage that I was now behind on because I was in lockdown.

I began to feel like my life was running in circles that continued to shrink into a collapsing vaccum.

And why was I behind? I had let myself get talked into opening credit card after credit card with Blair's prompting as she lost job after job and we fell further and further behind on bills. It had come to the point where I could either make the house payment or the minimum payment on the credit card balance every month since I was the only one with a steady job and income.

So, between the choice of getting behind on the house or getting behind on all the credit cards, I chose getting behind on the unsecured debt.

One day while we had still been married, Blair had called me at work with yet another credit card representative on the other line, who was ready to give me another thousand dollar credit limit at twenty-four APR if I gave my verbal consent. But this time, I had said no. Blair started cussing me out over the phone with the credit card rep still on the line so I hung up on all of them.

At that point, I was ready to do the same with my second marriage. Just pull the plug. Make the insanity go away.

This second marriage had become a bigger and worse mess than my first. I felt so helpless and powerless that I was embarrassed and beyond miserable.

So, I paid a retainer to a breezy divorce lawyer, who laid out a quick path to freedom—give Blair what she wanted in trade for getting the house, and after the divorce, declare bankruptcy and forfeit the house. He promised me within a year, I'd have all my lost money back easy-peasy-lemon-squeezy-nice-and breezy. I told him the first divorce had broken my heart and this once had broken my pride.

I had not followed the plan to the letter. I divorced Blair, but had kept the house instead of letting it go into foreclosure. After possessing it for only a year, if I was to sell it I'd have to pony up more money to help pay off the mortgage after the sale. I was still stuck with either paying on the credit card debt or paying the mortgage.

Pride, again.

And now, by bringing Blair back into my life and back into the house, I was recreating the insanity all over again.

Taking myself back to the beginning.

Do not pass go or collect $200.

Instead, go straight to jail.

If I was to re-marry Blair, I would come full circle.

A smaller and smaller circle that was tightening like a chain around my heart.

I hadn't stood a chance by marrying Blair. I had stepped out of the party scene, which I had stepped into after my first , and had spent the last year stone cold sober married to a bi-polar manic depressive.

There was nothing more romantic than getting married. And expecting to live happily ever after. Yes, I knew I had problems and I could see, but not understand, that Blair had problems. Together, I thought we could help each other with our problems.

Who knows? Maybe solve them.

That wasn't a healthy interdependency. That was a formula for codependency.

The whole thing—meeting Blair, moving into a house with Blair, and marrying Blair—had been a romance that had taken off like a rocket and then exploded like the Challenger in mid-air.

Except now I was standing underneath the falling debris. Fiery shrapnel that was destroying everything it landed on.

My credit report.

My bank account.

My job.

My reputation.

My character.

My future.

My soul.

What had I been thinking?

I hadn't been.

Clear and simple.

Sitting here inside Kelter Ward C with Nurse Rochelle watching me shave and Jayne V. tyring to coax out my secrets and Dr. Frost tinkering with my medication wasn't helping me one bit.

My problems were still out there.

Waiting for me to get buzzed out and jump me.

Poor Bud C.. Like him, I wanted out, too. But I wasn't going to be carried out like a mad tranquilized bull. I had walked into Kelter Ward C on my own two feet. And I intended to leave the same way. Walking out on my own two feet.

After Bud C. had blown a fuse, it grew quiet.

Too quiet.

Bud C. had provided spice.

Now even the air tasted the same as the food.

Flat.

Bland.

Unappealing.

But without Bud C. there to disrupt the routine, the rest of us grew safe and bold enough to ask each other questions. About our feelings. And our problems. So, we could learn how to handle our own.

Lizzy B. was the oldest of us. And after half a dozen visits to Kelter Ward C—though, I suspected she'd been to others—she knew the whole process by heart. Knew the system inside and out. Knew how to play the left hand against the right hand. She talked in short halting sentences. Too many words and her tongue would spray out through the gap of her missing teeth and slur her speech.

Jacque A. appeared to be the youngest. Mid-twenties. No kids. Never married. Smart as a whip. Still finishing college. With enough time ahead of her to make a clean slate.

Or Cathy D. might have been the youngest. It was hard to tell her exact age with sleep wrinkles on her face and half slit eyes. With a blanket over her head like a cowl, she looked like a lost frazzled mother cat who had abandoned her litter. Sometimes her husbands or kids would call on the landline, but Cathy D. wouldn't take their calls. They never came to visit, but later, I learned Cathy D. refused any visitors.

Cathy D. didn't want to be friends. She didn't even want to talk. It was all she could do to plod out of her room with dirty slippers and plop onto a lounge seat to cocoon herself in a frayed blanket.

Not so long ago, I had been married to someone exactly like that. And afterwards, I'd started going out every night. And then I'd met Blair.

"I feel like I'm just now finding myself," Jacque A. said. "Like I've been sleep walking this whole time."

She showed me the sign of her awakening. A tattoo on her bicep. Her first. Inked in blue and green and red. A five pointed star set within a circle. The circle was green and each interlocking tip of the star was either blue or red.

"Most people think it's a pentagram," she said. "But it's also the sign of Venus. A goddess. The sacred feminine. You ever think of getting a tattoo?"

I shrugged. "Used to. I thought about getting an eight on its side."

Jacque A.'s eyes brightened. "Infinity. The sign of forever. Why didn't you?"

"Two reasons," I said. "One is that I'd have to hide it at the bank. Bankers are a pretty conservative bunch."

I had worked among them for almost ten years. But I was not one of them. I dreamed of people. Not figures. I crunched words. Not numbers.

"The second is why pay for a tattoo when I've got scars." I raised both my wrists. "I didn't ask for the scars. I earned them."

Jacque A. smiled. "Now that I've got my first one, I'm already thinking about my next one."

"Is that your girlfriend who's been coming to visit you?" Lizzie B. asked.

Jacque A. nodded. "She says she'll support me in anything I choose to do. But my parents' want me to move back with them. Except if I do that, I can't be with her."

"You better look to your own happiness. Don't let your parents run your life," Lizzie T. said.

"They think she's trouble. Yeah, she's got charged for doing meth. One time. Well, she overcame it. She might drink and smoke but she's not a tweaker anymore. And she's the only one who gets me. She knows my heart. She's my world," Jacque A. said.

Even though Jacque A. was in a different part of the world and separated from that part of her heart, she spoke with a hopeful light in her eyes that promised to burn away the snow outside the door. Or just burn her bruised heart.

"My family just doesn't understand. It's a different world now," Jacque A. said.

Jacque A. seemed intent on following her heart, bruised as it was. Even in her willingness to share her world with the one person, their shared world would be built on their shared hurts. How long would it last?

I could have envied her. Jacque A. was certain all her problems would soon be over once she walked out that locked door.

What about me? Had I finally found someone I could trust through thick and thin? Someone who would be my rock? That one person who would be my world? How small that world was becoming.

Because if I stayed with this person, my parents were done with me. I was going to have to choose and no matter who I chose, the other would be none too happy. Meanwhile, I was the one who was miserable. Just filling in more stones in my heart.

"Your wife is very pretty," Jacque A. confided.

I spat out a bitter stone. "She's my ex."

"Your ex? As in your ex-wife? So, you're getting back together?" Jacque A. asked. I didn't know if that sounded romantic or co-dependent to her.

I hated yes or no questions. I couldn't give straight answers. Which annoyed my dad to no end. Maybe the reason that I couldn't give straight answers was because the truth was bitter and embarrassed me. Another stone turned over in my heart.

"I haven't told my family yet. They'll be less than thrilled," I said.

"Better look to your own happiness, then. Your parents don't run your life," Jacque A. said.

Seems that advice was making the rounds. But was anyone going to listen to it? Was it going to help anyone?

So, I let the advice just hang there like frost in the air.

Then Jacque A. put her bandaged wrist atop mine. "I got six stitches. How many did you get?"

I one-upped her by putting my second wrist on top of hers. "Ten. Five in each."

"Were you really died?" she asked. She would never would have asked if Bud C. had been around. I wonder how long she had wanted to ask me.

I shrugged. "They say I was."

"Do you mind me telling me what it was like?" she asked.

"Not like being asleep," I said. "I was aware of everyone and everything around me. I was in the present. Then the past. Then in places I couldn't tell were real or not."

"So you're not scared of dying?" Jacque A. asked.

I shook my head. "Not of dying. Having to face what's in here." Then I tapped my heart.

Before dinner arrived, Nurse Michelle came to take off my bandages. Jacque A. scooted back as the nurse bent over me and slowly unwrapped one wrist and then the other.

The wounds had closed in places. Dots and dashes of healed skin and scabs. There was still bruising underneath. A fading shade of green. The color of spoiled meat.

"I can't promise you won't have scars," Nurse Michelle said as she swabbed down the wounds with rubbing alcohol.

There was a sting. The outside flesh had healed. But it was still weak.

Deeper down, inside, the healing stopped around my heart.

Was it so stony that it no longer mattered what I did to it?

7—Christmas Cheer

I was eating supper—baked ham and mac and cheese—in the Patients' Lounge at a table by myself. Lizzy B. picked at the tray in her lap while she sat in the chair rapt with the five o'clock news on the tv. Jacque A. played solitaire beside her unfinished tray. Cathy D.'s tray was still in the carrousel. She was still in bed. With the blankets pulled over her head.

Boz and the Merry Prankster walked into the Patients' Lounge and pulled up chairs beside me. Boz sat with legs crossed high to the side and his fingers tucked into the waist pocket of his vest. McMurtry sat leaning forward with beefy hands on his thighs.

"Looks like baked ham with mac and cheese," he said. "Smells like baked ham with mac and cheese. But is it really baked ham with mac and cheese?"

I cut a piece of ham and stuck in my mouth. No one else in the lounge had responded to the pair's presence. So, I chose not to reply.

"Good evening, Justin R.," Boz greeted. "I trust that hospital fare is better than what gets served in the poor house. One would rather die than go there."

"Look around," McMurtry said and then gestured with his hand. "This ain't exactly Buckingham Palace."

"Nor is it the Tower of London, Mr. McMurtry," Boz added.

"How they treatin' you, Jimmy?" McMurtry asked. "You okay?"

I scooped up a sporkful of mac and cheese.

"Is it that you do not wish to speak to us or is it your manners that prevents you from speaking with your mouth full?" Boz asked.

"He doesn't think we're real, Boz," McMurtry said. "Thinks he's going crazy because we keep showing up. And if he talks back the others will think he's crazy. Don't you think we're real, Jimmy?"

I shrugged.

"I suppose it is easy to doubt one's senses," Boz said. "Consider what you are eating. If that ham is undercooked it may poison your stomach. It will cheat the whole of you."

"It's all perception, Boz," McMurtry argued with eloquence and arrogance. "We believe what we see and we see what we believe."

"So, we can't believe what we can't see?" Boz asked. "That hardly disproves something's existence, Mr. McMurtry. What if the earth was covered with fog every day and night? Could we say the sun doesn't exist if we couldn't see it shine?"

McMurtry waved off the argument, "Outta sight, outta mind. Like both of Jimmy's exes. Or his poor mom and dad."

Again I shrugged.

"Relax, Jimmy. If you was crazy, and I mean really rat-bat crazy. Non compos mentis. They'd have you up on Ward A. With Bud C.. Turning your brain into jelly with all them electrode gizmos. Wanna go up there right now and wish him a merry Christmas?" McMurtry asked.

I shook my head.

"It is required of every man to walk among his fellow man," Boz said. "Also, we are to love our neighbor as ourselves."

"Straight out of the good book!" McMurtry clapped his hands. Then he started nodding and pointing at me with a fat forefinger. "I know what ya need. Ya need to walk a mile in someone else's shoes. Step outside yer own head for awhile. Changes in latitude, changes in attitude."

"There must be someone that you care about enough to want to know what is happening to them right now while you've been ensconced here," Boz suggested.

Again I shrugged.

"What about ex number two?" McMurtry asked. "After all that bad blood. All that fussin' and fightin' over money. The washer and dryer. She must be the love of yer life to let her back in the house--yer house accordin' to the divorce decree--while yer here playin' footsies with one of the head shrinkers."

I had done my very best not to think about it.

"What about family, kith and kin? How do you think they fare at this time of year?" Boz asked.

"You don't send Christmas cards do you?" McMurtry asked.

I shook my head at that.

Jacque A. noticed me shaking my head a lot. So I scratched my temples. Then I jabbed my spork into the last bit of mac and cheese until it stood straight up.

Then Boz held up his forefinger at McMurtry and leaned in closer to me. "What about your first ex- wife? Think she's been healthy, wealthy, and wise since you two parted?"

Slamming both hands on the tiny table, I demanded out loud, "Show me."

"Merry Christmas!" Boz said and snapped his fingers.

Just like that we were in another part of the hospital.

Both Boz and McMurtry were walking ahead of me. Boz sauntered in white lace shoes, creased white slacks, and a long sleeve button tunic that had no collar. McMurtry strolled in white pants tucked into black loggers' boots and held up by white suspenders, a white button shirt tucked in the belt line, girded with a white cricket codpiece, and topped with one fake eyelash, a black bowler hat and a cane across his shoulders.

I padded behind them barefoot, wearing an orderly's uniform.

We passed patients in open back hospital gowns with dirty back sides, with long nails caked with black detritus underneath, and matted hair. We passed patients in stained robes and pajamas. Some with calloused bare feet and long brown toe nails. Some with worn slippers. All of them were caught up in a shuffle of the living dead. With blank stares. Slack mouths. Dilated pupils.

Somewhere up ahead a woman was moaning.

It was coming out of the walls. Pouring out of the air vents. The sound of her soul was broken down. Hope abandoned. Cast away from the face of God. Left out in the darkness to wail and gnash her teeth.

It was the same crying I had heard last month when I had been alone in the house before I had let Blair come back.

I knew where we were. I'd never been here before but Buddy C. and Lizzie B. had talked about it often. It was the place we were afraid to go.

I was up on Kelter Ward A. Where the catatonics walked their eternal last mile. Where the vegetables lay planted in their beds behind locked doors. And where the deranged and the disturbed thrashed against padded rooms having no rest and getting no peace.

Was that tortured woman here?

Was that whom we were going to see now?

Who was the tortured woman?

We came to the last room at the end of the hall. There was no noise from this end. All was still.

There was a small observation panel in the door. McMurtry indicated that I should look through it and into the room beyond.

I looked through.

They were using bait and switch.

It wasn't my first ex-wife.

It was Bud C.. Lying strapped to a metal table in a hospital gown too short for his frame. Straps held down his wrists and ankles and waist and his head.

There was an IV drip in his vein. A metal bit in his mouth. And electrodes hooked up to various muscles leading back to a fat piece of machinery with a high voltage read out.

They had made him ride the lightening.

They were breaking him like a stallion.

In a few days, after his overloaded synapses would come back on line and the static had cleared up and his mind could tune into the wifi server, Bud C. would get his wish.

They would dump back onto the street
Back on his bare feet.
Put him right back where they had found hm.
A dog without a bone.
A man without a home.
Left alone to his own devices.
Who would remember him on Christmas morning?

"Not much we can do here. Next stop, if you please," McMurtry said.

Boz raised his fingers, "A very merry Christmas!" and snapped them.

In a blink of an eye we were off Kelter Ward A and out of Our Lady's Hospital.

And somewhere else.

It was a home.

A modular home.

One level.

Double wide.

The kitchen was framed with Coca-Cola curtains and a framed Mary Englebrite picture. The rest of the walls and every available square inch of table top were filled with pictures. There was a linear story to them. Single photos of a brown haired young woman and a tall athletic boy. Then one of them together, newly married. Then the two of them with a little baby, now parents. Then the young woman, now pregnant, holding another baby with a little child beside her. And then one of four children together.

None of the furniture matched. It could have been taken off someone's curb before trash day.

The four children were playing and running around the family room. Each a year apart in age and build and need. Boy, girl, boy, girl dressed in hand-me-downs, the youngest in diapers.

There was a shrunken plastic tree barely taller than the oldest child. Garnished with tinsel and white lights. Atop the tree was a plastic star with a picture inserted inside.

It was the young woman. Probably a senior high picture taken by a professional photographer. She was dressed in dark jeans and a long sleeve plaid shirt. A gold necklace under a bright fresh face. Her hair combed, parted down the middle, and layered to the side. Her face rouged. Her eyes penciled.

I looked again. It was someone I knew. It was Cathy D..

This was her home. Her family.

A tall unshaven man with receding blonde hair bent over to pick up the second from youngest child while he held an old cordless phone--also a yard sale item—his bulging stomach pulling at his waist band and exposing the crack of his buttocks.

"Whazza matter, honey?" he shushed the second youngest, which was his youngest boy. Then he continued the conversation with the person at the other end of the line. "I haven't spoken with her in two days. No, she still won't take my calls. Did you try to see her? She wouldn't let you?

"The last thing she said to me was she'd had enough. Couldn't take it anymore. It's like she's just giving up. No, I don't know if she wants a divorce. Yeah, I'm startin' my new job tomorrow."

He gently rocked the young boy who straddled his thigh. The oldest boy was pulling the hair of the next older girl.

The youngest toddler sat still in his soaking pampers, taking in the pandemonium around him. This would be one of his strongest memories of family. Of Christmas time.

As I took all this in, I was aware of Boz, again in his woolen breeches and tunic sitting alone on the sofa smiling at the children in horseplay. While McMurtry in his white pants and suspenders tipped his bowler hat at the toddler and held out his finger to her. She grabbed it and looked up at his ruddy face to give him a smile.

"When you talked to her last, just what did she say? Silence? More than anything she just wanted a day of silence? Well, she's been there five days now. Don't you think if I could take her somewhere I would?" the husband asked. "She's forgotten that it's not about her. It's about us."

The oldest girl pulled hard on her father's belt loop. "Is mommie coming home tomorrow?"

The husband bent his head toward her. "No, mee-mah is coming over." Then into the phone he said, "You will, won't you? I've got to be at work tomorrow night. There's no way I can afford a baby sitter. The little ones will be good for you. And the big kids I can take to school myself."

"Yeah! Mee-maw is coming over!"cheered the oldest boy.

Taking the cue from their oldest sibling, most of the other kids echoed it.

The father had to lean into his phone to screen out the noise. "Pee-paw got the kids what? He's wanting me to go in on that?" He became crestfallen. "I couldn't afford that right now. Okay, we'll talk again tomorrow. Thanks for helping us out right now."

As soon as the father ended the call, the youngest boy squirmed in his father's arms. "I want momma."

"So do I kiddo," the father told him.

I turned to Boz who said, "Most people just want one thing for Christams. And only that one thing can make them truly happy."

"Making people happy is easier than it looks. All you gotta do is listen," McMurtry said.

"Sometimes it's written on their faces," Boz said. Then he pressed his thumb to his first two fingers. "God bless us everyone!

And then snapped his fingers.

And the three of us were in another home.

A small apartment.

With a loveseat and a recliner and a small plastic Christmas tree on a night stand that had been moved in front of the window. The couch was empty save for a purring black tom, the tree was not lit, and the recliner held a dark haired woman with glasses. She sat snug in front a large tv screen, with an ash tray full of cigarette stubs balanced on her lap and a lit cigarette between her knuckles burning down to ash. The tv streamed *It's A Wonderful Life* as George Bailey looked through his vest pocket for Zu-Zu's petals. The young woman's fingers clutched a warm beer bottle.

I had seen the young woman before. In the lounge at Kelter Ward C. Talking to Jacque A.

And I wondered what would be different if Jacque A. were here now. Would she be on the couch with only the cat to talk with?

"Sharing burdens is better than being alone," McMurtry said.

"How is sharing codependence any better than being alone?" I asked.

But then Boz raised his fingers again, "We wish you--!"

He snapped his fingers and I was alone in another home. A duplex. With the lights off.

The front door opened. In came an older woman loaded with bags of gifts bearing the names of various department store chains.

It was my mother.

She turned on the lights, set the bags down on the kitchen table, and took out newly purchased cds. My mother unwrapped them, threw the cellophane packaging away, and stuck the two cds into a clip which was inserted into a cd soundbar player. At the touch of a button, some of her favorite Christmas music—originally found on the thirty three and a third wax albums she once stacked on her turntable to pump out their analog soundwaves—sent its now digital signals throughout the house.

Then my mother labeled some of bags with the person's name that they had been bought for. A few others she took out of the bags and set down on the table. The rest of the bags, my mother took into a spare bedroom and put them inside a closet. And from out of that same closet, she took a tub of wrapping paper and bows, tape and scissors, name tags and pens. Taking this back to the kitchen table, she wrapped a few of the gifts she meant to give out ahead of Christmas to co-workers and friends.

"—a merry--" Boz continued.

I heard his fingers snap again.

And in the blink of an eye I was inside a church.

I had grown up in one. Spending half the week there. Twice on Sundays and Wednesday nights. One of my precious summer vacation weeks spent making a macaroni ark in VBS. And if there was a revival, then every night of the week.

But then I had grown up and I thought I no longer needed church.

It was for the weak.

Things never changed at church.

Always the same words and the same songs.

Ex number one had insisted we'd go to church. So, I had gone back. We had played our courtship by the rules of the good book. Do not open until Xmas.

Only waiting had put off another problem.

Intimacy.

I craved it.

And she feared it.

Instead of growing together, we had grown apart. And I felt cheated. Mad at God.

It had taught me a hard won truth: people do not change. I had married for expectations. I expected my first ex-wife to come out of her shell, get through college, get a stimulating career, learn to love and appreciate me. As I put the wedding ring on her finger, I thought to myself: now she'll change; except as she put the wedding ring on my finger she was thinking to herself: now I don't have to change.

You cannot make someone change and the harder you try they will just resent you.

It was another stone in my heart.

After the divorce, I spent years partying in a tail-dive straight down an elevator shaft. I tried to come up for a breath and clear my head. I took myself to a counselor, who just happened to be a Christian counselor. He told me two things I will never forget: one, that he could not help me with anything that I refused to talk about and two, I didn't have to get married, I had chosen to get married.

The truth hurt. How could that be God's fault? God didn't tell me to marry my first ex any more than He made me do anything I had ever chosen to do. I thought up getting married all by myself.

So, what had I done? I thought myself brave enough to go sober, but I soon learned I couldn't do it alone. I had met Blair soon after. Blair, with her bi-polar manic depressive ways that required nineteen pills just for her to function, if one could call narcissism and pathological lying the new normal functionality.

I knew nothing of bi-polar manic depression or borderline

So, that was how my second marriage went down the tubes. A classic case of being on the rebound. But the assist was bad and the point was denied.

The blame lay with me.

The double fault was all mine.

And the guilt was another stone in my heart.

A group of Christmas carolers sat in the choir loft with their grateful hearts, tuned to the season. Their joyful glad tidings gave me some cheer. It warmed my heart.

They practiced a medley of old church carols and then some of those classic secular tunes my mother had just re-bought on digital discs.

They laughed and chided in between the songs.

And gave their attention to the music leader who laughed and chided with them.

The music leader was my dad. Arrived at church straight from work to lead the charolers' practice. He reminded them of their weekend itinerary: the several nursing homes they were due to visit and spread Christmas cheer to, the houses they planned to carole outside to exchange a carol for cookies, hot chocolate, fudge, and eggnog in that succession.

"—Christmas, one—" Boz continued on.

I heard a finger snap over the carolers.

And I was in an older home that had been rehabbed.

I was in a living room. Full of older formal furniture stacked with moving tubs. Some were open and junk was strewn about everywhere.

It was the throne room of a hoarder.

There was one open space on the frayed couch.

And one open spot on a glass table.

I recognized both pieces of furniture.

The couch was Blair's.

The table was mine.

Blair sat in her old granny nighty on the couch with her laptop before her on the couch. She was clicking through on-line store catalogs. Not for her family. Not for my parents. And not for me.

She was dreaming of all the goodies she wanted to put on her wish list.

Next to her were bills. Credit card statements. Showing maxed out balances. And growing interest payments for being behind past three months.

If there was a way to squeeze blood out of the stone, then Blair would find it. Except my heart was the stone. And that stone was out of blood.

"I'm going to have a merry Christmas if it kills me," she said out loud.

Her laptop chimed. And an IM box popped up.

MRMAJICSTICK: DO YOU WANT TO PLAY?

"—and all!" Boz finished.

He snapped his fingers a final time.

And I was sitting by myself at the table in the Patients' Lounge.

Jacque A. was still playing solitaire.

Liz B. was still in her recliner—throne.

And Cathy D. who had been coaxed out of her bedroom was picking the green beans off of her tray. Her every movement languid. Her eyes squinting against the glare of the lights.

Nurse Rochelle had been standing over her making sure she was eating something. But now she was engrossed in my vacant look and the last bit of my mac cheese that had gone cold.

How long had I been just sitting there?

"If you're finished Mr. Justin, please put up your tray," the nurse instructed.

"You left some," Lizzy B. said. "Bud C. would've cleaned that tray right off while you were day dreaming."

8—Good Tidings

My heart was racing.

My eyes danced back and forth.

My hands clenched tight.

I was in the Patients' Lounge—

--but before that I had just been back at home watching Blair--

--and before that I had been at my Dad's church--

--then my parent's duplex--

--what I assumed was Jacque A.'s apartment--

--Kelter Ward A.

I had been everywhere at once.

And nowhere at all except right here.

I had accompanied Boz and McMurtry on some grand tour.

Now they were gone and I was back where they had found me.

Was I losing my mind?

I couldn't have been in any of those places. Not really. I must have been sitting here all along, even though, each of those places had seemed as real as the lounge.

Could it have been lucid dreaming?

I snapped my fingers.

And then I blinked.

I was still in the lounge.

It seemed real enough. So did the table. And my tray. And my spork which I pulled out of the last bit of cold mac and cheese.

"Everything ok, Mr. Justin?" Nurse Rochelle asked.

"Yep," I nodded. What else was I going to say? What else was I going to do? Stab myself in my heart of stone with a spork?

The security door was buzzed open by one of the orderlies from the Nurses' Station.

In came Jayne V. bearing good tidings with a smile.

I sat upright and collected my senses.

"Good evening everyone," she said as she came into the lounge. A thick manila folder was tucked in the crook of her elbow.

"Someone goin' home?" Lizzy B. asked. "Well, it better not be me. Medicare should be giving me two more days."

"No, not you Lizzy B.," Jayne V. said. "Justin, I need to see you."

I got up and followed her into the small interview room. We took up positions facing each other over the desk. Jayne V. smiled as she thumbed up my patient portal on her tablet.

"Dr. Frost thinks you are well enough to be released, Justin," Jayne V. said. "How is the medication working? Have you had any problems sleeping? Or anything else?"

"You mean have I had any after effects from dying?" I asked.

To a medical clinician, my being dead a short while had been just a clinical event. The stopping of my heart. The cessation of my breathing. The beginning of brain death. Irrefutable physical details. But at some point— around the five minute range—the brain starts to experience damage without oxygen.

So, I took it to mean she was probing to see if I was suffering from symptoms of brain damage. Like being confused in speech or aware of time and place. Like having hallucinations.

"Kind of hard to top that," I said.

Although, the episodes I'd been having—visiting different people and locales at the snap of a finger—were coming close.

Jayne V. smiled. For the moment, she was the audience. A mirror. "We don't believe that you are a danger to anyone else," she said.

I gave a slow nod in agreement.

"Have you had any thoughts of suicide lately?" Jayne asked.

I shook my head.   I'd been too busy wondering if I was losing my mind.

"Dr. Frost wants you to keep taking your Lexapro and trazodone as prescribed. Tomorrow is Friday. You can be released provided you agree to begin attending intensive outpatient therapy," she said.

"What does that mean?" I asked.

"You will be released to re-integrate yourself into society: your home, your family, and your work. Also, you are required to complete thirty-five hours of intensive out-group therapy. It will be conducted by Hope Counselors, Inc at our offices here. We will meet for three hour sessions, five days a week. Monday through Friday. There will be an additional two hour one-on-one meetings with your counselor each week," Jayne explained.

"That's only thirty-two hours. What about the other three hours?" I asked.

"You are to attend two twelve-step meetings, one a week. Your counselor will provide you with a list from which you can choose to attend based on your schedule and proximity," Jayne V. said.

"Who would my counselor be?" I asked.

"Me, if you wanted," Jayne said. "I work for Hope Counselors, Inc. and we specialize in drug addiction recovery and co-dependent behavior. You do realize that you have a drug personality and patterns of addiction?"

I shrugged. "I get depressed. I just don't know why. I can go a while without using drugs. I was a year and a half without a drink before I came here. But then I got stressed out."

"And you turned to psychotropics and suicide ideation which got you in here. So, in addition to the group sessions and the twelve-step meetings, you will have to see Dr. Frost once a month. Hope Counselors offers freedom from drug dependency. We offer to help you form a new community of support. This is your opportunity. But at any time you feel your medicine isn't helping, or if you begin to have feelings about suicide, or if you show signs of severe depression, or threaten anyone, you will be right back in here for further observation," Jayne V. said.

She turned the tablet around thumbed through form after form for me to scrawl my signature in a capture box with a finger. Confidentiality releases. A contract for Hope Counselors. Government subsidy insurance waivers. With all the dates populated.

Jayne V. nodded and took back the tablet. "It is hospital policy that a patient may not be discharged without being accompanied by family or friend. We cannot supply you with transportation. Do you have someone who come and pick you up?" she asked.

Of course, I had.

The love of my life.

My second ex-wife.

Who hadn't even called me today.

I nodded and left to go to the lounge to call Blair. If I couldn't get a hold of her, I'd have to call my parents and fill them in on my latest adventures.

It rang five times before she answered.

"Hell-oh," she said through a mouthful of sleep.

"Why didn't you call me today?" I asked.

"Oh, honey. What time is it?" she asked. I heard her knock things around on her dresser. "Five-thirty? Crap. I've been sleeping all day. Dr. Frost's got me on way too much klonopin."

"Can you be here tomorrow at eight with my car to pick me up? Dr. Frost is letting me go home," I said.

"That's fantastic, honey!" she declared. "We are going to be so happy! Everything will be different! We'll have the best Christmas ever! We don't need your parents!"

FOURTH VERSE--The
Ghost Of a Christmas Chance

1—The Door Into Winter

There were no more visitors that night.

The trazadone did its job. It put me straight under. And kept me there 'til morning.

Snug as a bug in a rug.

When I woke all was still on the ward. Not a creature was stirring. Not even a catatonic on Ward A.

My mouth was dry and my tongue was swollen and my mind was blank except for a single thought.

I was gonna be outta here. Today. This morning.

Free from doors being kept open and prying eyes.

Free from searching questions and security cams.

Free from orderlies in white tunics and nurses in scrubs pushing medication in plastic cups.

Free from stiff starched sheets and bland meals.

I was just one bowl of grits away from eating a toasted peanut butter and jelly sandwich with chocolate milk in my own house this very day.

Now I had a reason to get out of bed.

Nurse Rochelle had yet to make her last rounds of the night when she did her morning wake up call. So, I beat her to the punch and put my feet to the floor.

I showered.

I shaved.

I packed.

I waited for Blair.

I walked back and forth down the hall.

I sat in the lounge until Lizzy B. and Jacque A. came out.

"She's coming to pick you up, Justin? You really gonna to take her back?" Jacque A. asked.

I shrugged. Who else would want me? Blair was the best I could do.

She gave me a bear hug. "I hope Rachael's waiting for me. I should be out of here soon."

"I had a dream about it," I said.

Jacque A. gave me another bear hug and smiled from ear to ear. For a moment, I wondered if we weren't going to get exactly what we both asked for. But nowhere near what we needed. Somehow, I feared that by walking out of here--which had been some kind of protective womb or eye of the storm--that both of us were walking back into the full force of the hurricane's gale wind.

Hurricane Blair, for me. Hurricane Rachael for her.

Maybe Lizzy B. knew the score. Staying off the street for a few days with a roof over her head, a starched bed, and three bland meals a day was Heaven compared to the everyday Hell of life on the street.

But she surprised me by getting out of her recliner and coming over to lay her bare sagging arms across my shoulders. She wrapped her turkey neck around mine. Then she puckered up and gave me a sloppy kiss on the forehead.

"Luck," she mumbled through her front gums as I gave her a bear hug.

I wasn't so sure "luck" had anything to do with my life anymore. "I hope you're out of here soon."

"Hon, I don't wanna leave. Ain't nothin' waitin' for me out there but one more hit," she whistled through her back teeth. Then she returned to her throne of exile and court of petitioners: a slick recliner and the plastic smiles of the morning newscasters who pretended all was right in their little broadcast world.

It was ten to nine. I tried to sit still and wait.

At five past, the security door buzzed.

Jayne V. came in to see Jacque A. in the Patient Interview Room. I was both happy that she might get released this afternoon and sad that it wasn't Blair, because I was supposed to have been released by 9.

I went back into my room and made sure the drawers were empty and all my clothes were packed. They were.

I turned around twice to make sure I hadn't missed a thing. I hadn't.

When I came out it was now nine fifteen.

The door wasn't buzzing open.

So, I went back into the patients' lounge and asked to use my cell to call the house. No one answer.

Either Blair was driving here in my car right now or she was digging deeper under the blankets.

Blair did her best to ignore time. She thought could bend or slow it down at her will, when all it did was bury her under the wave of each moment.

With nothing else to do but wait, the questions started in my mind:

What had she been up to since I'd been stuck in here? Had I already forgotten the vision Boz and McMurtry had brought? Or Grandpa's warning?

Had she just taken her meds and was going to sleep all day?

Was she going to stay at 2112 Springhill Drive?

Was she planning to move out and move in with someone else?

Had she met someone with whom to plan out such a move?

Was she prepared to give up her family for me?

Was I willing to give up my family for her?

Did she love me? And how far would that get me?

Did I love her? And what good would that do me?

Could she help me? How could she help me?

Could I really help her? Did I even want to help her?

Had she even missed me? Or had she used the last few days to get the locks changed on the doors? Where would she get the money?

She had none. No job. And she'd gone through her divorce settlement.

I was still her meal ticket. The divorce decree had given me the house. Blair had taken the contents.

She had no running car but she was driving mine as an uninsured driver across a snow covered town.

The door buzzed.

In walked Blair.

The woman that I wanted to spend forever with. Well, not forever. Just for now.

Her long brown greasy hair had been combed to one side. She wore the same Gap pullover that she had on her last visit. The bottom of her sweat pants were caked with snow and her Nike running shoes squeaked.

Her face was pale and unmade except for two red spots on her cheeks. Hallmarks from trying to burn winter from her body. Nurse Michelle came out of the

Nurses' Station to intercept her as I walked out of the lounge.

"Honey!" she cooed and kissed my forehead.

"Justin is ready to go and we've taken good care of him," Nurse Michelle reported.

"So, you didn't have to put him on Ward A," Blair joked. "You still shock people up there?"

Nurse Michelle didn't even flinch. She wasn't the type to humor a fool.

I remembered my visit up there with Boz and McMurtry. The lost souls with slack faces. And Bud C. strapped down to a table.

Maybe it had been just a daydream. Maybe Bud C. hadn't even been put on Ward A. But the place was real. It was up there. It was a dumping ground. It was hell on earth.

And yet, Blair knew enough about Ward A to crack wise. Just another one of her bluffs? Blair thought she knew everything better than everyone else.

"Justin didn't give us any trouble," Nurse Michelle said.

The swollen pink scars on my wrists said it loud and clear enough. I was more apt to hurt myself than somebody else.

I wasn't paying attention anymore to the farewell formalities. The security door was standing open. I wanted to go through it.

One of the orderlies brought my overnight bag. Shook my hand. And then camoufagedhimself back into the white wall.

"You're all signed for and packed," Nurse Michelle continued. "Dr. Frost has got your prescription called in.

You can pick that up after three. And your first group session will be next Monday at 6 pm."

"He'll be here at 5:50. I'll make sure he won't miss a single session," Blair vowed.

She could promise the moon. But the moon wasn't hers to promise. She could smile with all the selenite glow of the moon's face. But she wasn't the moon.

I was leaving the professional hands of the Mental Health Unit and Hope Counselors, Inc. I was just so happy to be out of Kelter Ward C. I hadn't thought out much beyond getting past that open door.

There was another urge.

Not in my feet.

But in my tongue.

My mouth began to water with the ghost of a taste. Something sweet, sticky, and bitter.

Blair had captured Nurse Michelle's attention and was talking about Christmas preparations for her family. Often her own family didn't invite her over to Christmas. Often in the past there had been some big fight at which Blair had been at the center in some shape or fashion.

Nurse Michelle was doing her best to be polite to Blair and perform her duties. "Bye, Justin! Stay blessed!" she called.

That was my cue.

I picked up my overnight bag and walked through that open security door.

I felt a curling in my stomach. Something pulled down on my intestines and gave me a cold tickle. Like I was stepping into a roller coaster that was about to climb heartbreak hill for the first big dip.

Anticipation.

I was leaving!

Only when I was safe on the other side of the door did I remember to turn and say, "You, too!"

Blair was in the midst of a conversation with her newfound best friend, Nurse Michelle. One of the orderlies gave a behaviorist's learned cue by buzzing the door, causing Blair to pick up on the learned cue and break off her conversation to escape being locked in Ward C. I would have been just as happy if they had.

I traipsed through the waiting lounge and had to squint against the morning glare coming through glass and shining off scrubbed floors. To my right was the junction of the long corridor that led back to the emergency room. Our Lady's hospital was nothing but one long corridor, honeycombed with lounges and security doors.

Blair's Nike runners squeaked over the floor of tracked in snow and ice. "Honey! Wait up! I've got the keys!"

Behind me a screen door rolled back.

"Mr.R.!" an administrative assistant called me back. Was anyone ever free of medical bureaucracy?

I turned to the admitting window that served both Hope Counselors, Inc. and the Mental Health Unit. A middle aged woman with too much make up and colored hair held out an appointment card.

I walked back to the window and took the card. It had two times marked on it.

"Your group session runs Monday to Tuesday and Thursday to Friday six to eight pm. You will need to come here for one individual session for the next two weeks. The offices for Hope Counselors, Inc are further down the hall to your right. You park at the back of the building and use the entrance doors there," she instructed.

I'd have to come back to Our Lady. And that was okay. As long as I didn't have to walk through the security door again.

Blair waited by the front doors. "At least you got the weekend before you have to come back."

She took the lead and even held the door open for me. We were at the top of that first hill on the roller coaster. I took a breath and stepped across the threshold and out of the hospital for the first time since I had died.

And it was all downhill from there.

The world had been turned white. Into a frozen winterland. It was blinding.

I closed my eyelids but the brightness seared through.

Ice hung in the air and chilled my every breath.

Everything had changed.

The parking lot was gone. Snow sat atop of it. Piled up waist high between parking row aisles constricting the lanes and hardening the veins of the traffic flow.

Signs were buried up to their neck.

Curbs replaced by dirty fjords.

All of the evergreen trees along the berm bore white cloaks and chaperons.

My red Dodge Stratus sat parked and running with the driver's door open under the carport.   Next to a sign that read PATIENT PICK UP ONLY. Though, there no longer was any clear delineation for any such place.

"You left it running?" I asked.

From the open driver's door I could hear the heater blowing on full blast and the strains of "Sleigh Ride" by Steve and Eddie. That was one thing Blair and I shared: similar tastes in music.

Blair scrunched across the packed snow to slide into the driver's side.

"Don't worry, honey," she said. Everything she did had a reason that suited her. Everything she did was right in her own eyes. "This is for patient pick up. You're the patient. And I'm picking you up."

"Someone could've carjacked us," I said. Exhaust vapors clung to the undercarriage and tires. Tiny icicles like barnacles crusted the tailpipe and wheel rims.

I opened the back passenger door to put my overnight bag behind my seat and waves of heat rolled out at me. Melted snow was running in rivulets from the roof that she hadn't bothered to clear off.

The heat began to smother me. "I think I'd like to drive."

Blair had already slipped behind the wheel. "Honey. You're getting over a shock. You're still got to take it easy. I wanted to make things easy on you and treat you on your first day out. I'll be your chauffer."

I surrendered and climbed into my own car as a passenger. I buckled up and felt the roasting air begin to dry out my face and scalp. Every single dead skin cell on my body, from head to toe, needed to be sloughed off soon or I would start scratching.

Blair put the Stratus into drive and the wheels spun against the snow. "What's first on your list?"

I pushed the sleeve of my jacket up to scratch at my wrist. "I want to take a long hot shower."

"Then we can go Christmas shopping. Pick up your prescription. And go to Antonio's for dinner," she said.

"I see you've got a plan," I said.

"Honey, I always got a plan," she said. Her hand lifted up to her temple and a finger made circles. "The wheels are always turning up here. You'd better keep up."

But the motion was also a visual sign for something else. For being crazy. Bonkers. Cracked-up. Batty. Loco. Way-cray. Nutty. Whacky whacked-out whack-job. Non compos mentis.

She was giving herself away.

I stifled a laugh in my throat. If I was to laugh now, I'd lose it and never get it back together. I had just left the madhouse and was about to lose it. Because I had exchanged one madhouse for another.

Blair blinked at me without understanding. She was not omniscient after all. Merely human.

The Stratus ground in low gear as it crept through a devastated parking lot. Every parking line obliterated. Every space cut out with a plow. Every car parked askew and hulked with snow topped hoods and hoods and icicles plastered to undercarriages.

Old Man Winter was here.

With a vengeance.

With lashes of snow and bindings of ice and a heartless wind chill.

I'd not seen this much snow since the blizzard that had buried the metropolitan area back in the winter of 1979. Eighteen inches over two days. And then almost double that the next week. Power lines had snapped. Water lines had frozen. School had been cancelled.

There had been no heat, no water for days.

We took refuge in our grandparents' basement. There they had a cast iron wood burning stove. We had gathered in a circle of family warmth and safety and used a portable gas stove to boil water and do our cooking in cast iron pots.

"How does dinner at Antonio's sound?" she asked.

Being out in this winter maze and going to the madhouse of Best-Mart did not sound fun at all. But the promise of a good dinner…Antonio's Dolce Vita's…

"Tonight's Friday. That means prime rib," she reminded me.

My mouth watered. I hadn't had a decent meal in days. My taste buds had fallen asleep.

"That does indeed sound like a plan," I said. Antonio's might indeed be the dolce vita but it wasn't a cheap affair. Blair had never been concerned with the fact living the sweet life was not cheap. I hadn't looked at my bank account to check on my balance.

If I didn't want her driving my car then why had I brought her back into my life? I wasn't going to let her have access to my money. I thought we could try this living together where each party was in charge of their own responsibilities.

If that was the case: living together on a trial basis, then why had I picked her again for my partner?

Because I didn't want to come home to an empty house.

With just myself in it, it was a house and not a home.

And there was another problem. I blinked. I breathed. The meds kept me in a numbly comfortable place where things came at me in waves and I could only think in drowsy snatches.

I was barely reacting so just how much thinking was going on I couldn't be sure right now.

I needed to focus.

From the parking lot to the exit ramp back to Highway 15, the snow had hardly been touched. And the

highway wasn't much better. The lanes reduced.
Bookended by snow and ice taking the place of the white
and yellow lanes.

Traffic was sparse. Blair stayed in the slow lane
and kept the car in second gear. Even the wheels of the
most cautious drivers sprayed out salt rock and slush.
Not quite a sleigh ride for anyone.

And the person driving my sleigh was the woman
who had caused me a lot of misery and grief. A woman I
had petitioned to be divorced from just three months ago.
But this is what I had chosen for myself.

Blair turned up the oldie songs on a Christmas
music station to drown out the hum of tires churning the
snow and the heater blowing at full gale. When she
braked for our exit onto Dutch Hollow Lane, the Stratus
slipped a bit as the tires cut through the accumulated
patches left by the snow plows.

Most of the houses had been built in the 1940's or
1950's on a two bedroom, one bath, living room, kitchen,
and carport plan. But the blizzard' had spun out its riches
all across the neighborhood, turning everything into more
of the same: a sheet of ice.

It obliterated the lay of the land.

Erasing streets and curb.

Submerging yards and driveways to mounds of
crystallization.

Turning parked cars into snow mounds save for
grey tire treads that poked out.

Snow clung to crevices and cornices and drifted off
window ledges.

Enveloping trees into snowman sentinels.

Sagging electrical lines like weighed down
spiderweb.

The plow might have come by once but the snow had just drifted back and refroze. She drove through rutted tracks that had been mashed down by tries. Not a single driveway had been cleared off. They all held tire tracks of people coming and going on their merry way to work with about an hour of travel time added on.

If Blair hadn't been driving, I might have not been able to recognize the house from all the others.

Our house had been a rehabbed foreclosure. Along with the standard house layout, the rehabber had built on an extra two room addition.

We had moved in September of last year and by September of this year, we were divorced.

A record for me.

But not one to brag about.

I pick our house out, my house according to the divorce decree, by the three tall oaks that dwarfed the house. Two stood entish watch over the front yard while wisest towered over the house in the backyard. With one stomp, this sylvan giant could crush our house. Judging by its girth and height, it had kept its storehouse of knowledge and acorns for hundreds of years.

But even under this blizzard, birds kept their heads close to their wings and squirrels hunkered down in their nests. Iced over berries and frozen nuts would have to wait for another day.

Blair had to gun the Stratus up the slope of the driveway. We had no garage. She could only get it halfway up before a tire got stuck in a rut.

Time to get out and cross the threshold back into domestic bliss.

This was the house.

2112 Springhill Drive.

We were home.

2-Home for the Holidays

Blair shut the car off with the vents on high and the radio blaring out the first ship of "I Saw Three Ships." She yanked the keys of the ignition and stuffed them into the kangaroo pocket of her GAP hoodie, which bulged out from her pooch.

Blair had a bit of a pudge.

I held out my hand. "Keys."

There was a hint of a scowl. "Why?"

"Because it's my car," I reminded her.

Her eyes flashed. She pulled the keys out but kept them locked in her fist.

"I want to see them, first," she said.

"See what?" I asked.

She mimed slitting her wrist with the fist full of keys.

I held one hand up at a time and pulled my coat sleeve down.

She got a gander at the marks. There weren't any scabs. The bruising around the wound was fading to the color of burned skin. It had closed quickly and might turn to a whitish upraised crescent. A braided new moon of scar tissue.

Blair held out the hand with the keys. She bared her wrist with the other hand. Just beneath the butt of the palm and off center of the cephalic vein was a mark. A sideways white X. An old scar.

So, we had another thing in common: self-harm.

Just two cutters.

Two ex-suicides.

Nurse Rochelle's voice was in my head, *"Why would you want to go and try to commit suicide for, Mister Justin? Don't you know life is a precious gift from God? Why would you want to throw it away?"*

How many people no longer believed in peace on earth and good will to each other or even themselves? Did buying gifts and wrapping gifts and giving gifts and getting gifts and unwrapping gifts put off answering Nurse Rochelle's question?

Did they know they had stones in their heart? How bad did they want a fleshy heart? How many people thought about giving up and committing self-harm?

I still had no answer for Nurse Rochelle. While I bore the mark of my argument against her question, I had failed to kill myself. Perhaps, my argument was wrong.

Maybe I needed a new answer. A better answer.

Blair flipped her wrist over to surrender the keys in my open palm. Then she pushed the driver's door open with a rusty squeak. "I hope you can find the time to shovel the driveway. I don't want to slip and hurt my knee again."

I hadn't known she'd fallen. "When did you fall?"

She waddled through the snow with a pronounced limp. "Coming out of the house to drive to the hospital this morning. I almost couldn't walk."

Yet, her knee hadn't stiffened so bad that she couldn't drive or even complain about having to drive.

Hmm.

My excitement about getting sprung from the booby hatch, my hope of a new morning, my expectation of coming home was starting to fade. It had been blanketed by lexapro and buried by snow. But now I stood before my house. I hadn't given it up according to

the divorce decree. It could be my home. I didn't want
to lose that chance.

So, I walked into 2112 Springhill Drive.

It was full of storage tubs and banker's boxes
stacked to the ceiling. Leaning sideways because lids were
missing or sides were cracked from having too much
weight placed on them. Several bankers' boxes had word
after word written and crossed out on their labels--only
God knew what was in them now.

Years of possessions Blair had collected or
snatched up and now clung to. Things she still wanted
whether or not she still needed them. Arranged in a maze
between the living room and the kitchen.

Blair had returned.

My love had come back to me.

With all her junk. Some of which had once been
mine or my family's.

I had taken in a hoarder.

3-A House Is Not A Motel

*2112 Springhill Drive had become
a merry-go-round-broken-down.*

It was just a house.

A piece of property.

A retail listing.

Surveyed and laid out for property taxes.

Thirteen hundred square feet. Including the
original four rooms and the two room addition.

It had seen a whirl-wind of activity over the past
few years: arrest, eviction, foreclosure, rehabbing, and
flipping.

The previous owner busted on a DUI. The unemployed girlfriend evicted. The house foreclosed on. But before the bank could sell it off, the sewer had backed up inside the whole house--the culvert that swallowed all the neighborhood run-off sludge squatted under the front curb.

The rehabber had pumped out the house. Tore out the rugs. Dried the walls and painted them over. Had some new bushes planted for curb appeal and a contract placed with a realtor, who planted a for sale sign before we came a-calling last August.

But it wasn't all a buyer's dream. It had a slab foundation with pipes and gas lines set in concrete. The stove was gas. The heater and water tank were as old as the house. The air conditioning unit was as big as our kitchen table and set on a pile of flat garden slabs, like some kind of cairn. And the slope of the roof addition seemed flat to me but had passed the assessor's inspection.

Blair and I had only added to the whirlwind with moving in, separating, moving out, and now moving back in.

I had just turned thirty-five and Blair would be thirty-one this coming Spring. We were getting too old to play house.

Before I stepped into my marriage with Blair, I had stepped off the party train after a year and a half. And I had gotten onto the party train because my first marriage had abruptly ended in divorce. It had not been a happy marriage. Because I married for expectations. I thought my first wife would change. By that I meant, finish college, get a stimulating career and want to grow together.

But I had to learn the hard way when people are exchanging wedding vows, one person is slipping the ring thinking, "Now they will want to change" while the other person is thinking, "Now I don't have to change."

Usually, people do not change and if you try to make them change, they will resent you. What you see is what you get.

If I had simply told my first finance that we would wait to get married when she got out of college and got a job that made as much as me, so that we could build our home and financial budget together, I would still be waiting.   And I probably wouldn't have married her.

We dated for three years while I finished school and got a job at America's Bank while she changed majors and kept a part-time job. After four years of marriage, I told her one January she had enough credits to graduate college and needed to step up. She said I was against her like everyone else and we divorced six months later.

Eight years together. It was my longest relationship up to then. And my biggest failure.

On our last night together, my first wife said that she felt like an idiot because we were ending in divorce. To which I replied I felt cheated and I wished I could get back the last eight years of my life.

The last thing I wanted to do was lick my wounds like a sick dog, so, I jumped on the party train and acted like a mad dog. My mantra, my life verse became Revelations 12:12 "*…because he knows his time is short.*" If I wasn't going to be here for a long time then I was going to be here for a good time.

It wasn't time to think; it was time to drink.

It became party time.

All the time.

My typical drug diet started with a shot of tequila followed by a beer chaser. After several rounds of that combination someone would offer a few lines of coke. Now, I should point out that alcohol is one the cheapest drugs available to consumers, so it makes it easier to share since most people don't like to drink alone. In fact, when asked what my favorite alcoholic drink was, I never hesitated in responding, "Free."

But the coke is not shared out of the goodness of a cokehead's heart of stone, but dispensed as status symbols being it is not cheap. Now coke is from a whole other family of drugs and does the exact opposite of alcohol. It's what I called "switching gears" and it would make me edgy. So, to take the sting out of mixing those two drugs, I would puff on a marijuana joint and if I wanted to push the envelope further, I would swallow the roach which always made me hallucinate and most often turn into a bad trip. At some point, I would have to find a bar that would stay open longer than the one that was just shutting down. And by early morning, I'd find myself switching over to a mix of alcohol and energy drinks to see me until the last bar would shut down at five a.m.

Homeward bound I would rush. Chasing the coat tails of night. Racing the rising sun.

But what I found even more dangerous than driving under the influence of various drugs was driving behind the wheel sleepy. Sometimes I'd fall asleep on the way home. I'd nod off on an exit ramp and feel like I was sinking in to a comfortable pillow all snug like a bug in a rug who'd just popped out of a jug.

I treat the whole experience like being at an ice cream store with the drugs being all the different flavors that I could try out and combine.

Drugs were like an elevator. They took me straight up and everything was a laugh. Then they would drop me straight down. And I would come down hard.

With the sun shining through the window on my face, there was no way I could sleep. I'd have to get up to vomit and spin to the rhythm of my hangover. Then, I'd start crying and feeling so guilty over not just wasting my whole night partying and now the whole day recovering. Before I'd know it, I had my wrist stretched over the kitchen sink with a knife against it daring myself to cut away and bleed my troubles off.

I thought finding someone who would love me for me would make me happy. I was putting my faith in the wrong place. Either people would let me down or I would let them down. I didn't think that there was a Higher Power that could restore me to sanity and begin to heal me or even forgive me. I thought I had to get some things straight in my life first, before God would ever deign to help me.

I met Blair on-line through i-Hearts. After a few emails, we exchanged numbers. I came over to her townhouse to meet her. Her townhouse seemed well-ordered next to my mouse proud townhouse. Her neighborhood peaceful compared to my backwater refugee station. She didn't go out much and she was forthright in being bi-polar manic depressive. Which I was ignorant of. She even confessed that she was a sexual abuse victim. Which I thought only happened to other people somewhere else rather in my own backyard. I didn't know much about the fallout of these issues, but I was willing to learn.

I went home and justified dating her this way: I had problems; she had problems. Maybe we could help each other with our problems.

After the next night, we were inseparable.

Two magnets drawn together by the attraction of need and expectations.

And that ignited our space shuttle climb off the launch pad to mid-air disaster.

We married two months later in the St. Louis city courthouse. As part of their pre-marital interview, they asked if we were blood kin. A judge then proclaimed us husband and wife by the power vested in him.

Then we had closed on 2112 Springhill Drive.

Our first move-in took over sixteen hours. My dad and I started at six in the morning at my old mouse infested townhouse. Blair didn't show up to help. The movers came to pick up my meager belongings—all hand-me downs from various family members—and our next stop was Blair's townhouse where I found her still in bed and un-ready and unwilling to help. My dad and I cleaned out her closet full of cast away shoes and the basement full of tubs from her move into this townhouse, not six months before.

We packed her stuff all day while Blair cried and fretted. The load-in into 2112 Springhill Dive was faster. My dad had to leave at five p.m., but before he left, we assembled the bed so Blair could collapse and sleep her headache away.

Sometimes Blair acted like she was the only one in the world.

As if everyone in the world existed only to serve her.

She could be a bit of a narcissist.

I kept thinking things would get better. Things would settle down. She would change because I would be an influence on her and then God would bless our union. Surely.

Within the next twelve months, I received a crash course in the world of Blair. Living with a bi-polar manic depressive in all its mad dog glory and crazy beauty was like living inside a whirlwind where my voice and my hope got sucked into the vortex spinning around me. My world start to mirror the stones in my heart: throwing my fears and hurts back in my face from out of the raging storm.

I left and had Blair served with divorce papers by the time of our first anniversary. By the end of that same month, we were divorced.

We met for the dissolution of our marriage at the side chamber in the courthouse.

My lawyer with me while Blair represented herself.

Her first ploy was a plea to rescind the divorce filing or she would demand more money she felt due her, to which my lawyer said no judge would ever grant. Her last ditch attempt was to have me quitclaim the house to her. I would sign over the deed to the property to her while I kept the mortgage loan with the house as collateral. I told her no bank would allow her to have the property when they had a lien on it, no matter what a judge decreed.

That was how Blair thought. Do what thou wilt and who cares who gets harmed as long as thou get what thou wilt.

Blair signed the divorce decree, giving her a small settlement in place of some property value and entitling her to what contents we had divided up between ourselves and directing her to vacate the property within two weeks, leaving me with the property, the mortgage, and all of the unsecured credit card debt.

My lawyer left to swing by the judge's chambers to get his signature and then by the clerk's window to get it notarized. As I sat a desk opposite Blair to cut her the settlement check, Blair threatened not to accept it and to contest the divorce if I didn't add more zeroes to the amount. I counter-threatened with not giving her a check at all, having a judge decide who gets what which may work out worse for her.

My lawyer intervened with this advice: for me to cut Blair a check for the amount specified in the decree and for Blair to take the check because that was all she would be getting.

He handed us each copies and reminded us to go our separate ways and stay out of each other's business.

The lawyer then went on his merry way.

Blair took her copy of the divorce decree and her check and exited the scene, but not my life.

As I left the courthouse to get into my car, I raised my hands high, "Free at last! Thank God Almighty, I'm free at last!"

A car sped by me as the driver laid on the horn. It was Blair, yelling some parting threats through the driver's side window in a car that she must have borrowed from her family.

I waited out the specified time for Blair to vacate the premises at my parents' townhouse. After the time for her to leave, I waited another week before my mother and I returned to 2112 Springhill Drive to do a cursory check.

Blair had not only vacated the property, but had emptied it.

There was a clause in the divorce decree that stated we had divided up our belongings on the day of our divorce. To her that meant: I got the house and she got the contents inside the house.

Everything: her collections of moving tubs and shoes.

My hand-me down pre-marital furniture.

And the appliances: the stove, the refrigerator, and the washer and dryer set. The ones my parents had gotten us a house-warming gift.

When she took those appliances, she cut the hoses.

When she cut the hoses, water leaked out.

From the kitchen into the living room and through the back wall of the kitchen into the master bedroom.

Our cursory found not only the appliances missing, but the rugs were soggy and the walls of the kitchen and bedroom had dark wet spots.

Before I could move back in, the carpet needed to be cleaned and dried. I'd have to get a space heater for the kitchen wall and bedroom.

I couldn't help but think 2112 Springhill Drive didn't flinch. It had seen worse. Maybe the rehabber should had installed a revolving door.

That was more akin to the reality of the situation of our playing house.

We had been fighting over junk. Clutching at the hoard in our nest. Like it was our junk that defined us. Only our junk could make us feel safe.

I barely had enough junk to fill up one room, let alone six. My parents helped me get a single bed, a small refrigerator, stove, and a cheap washer/dryer set.

Christmas was coming on. The supreme day of getting more junk. And I expected to revel in the yuletide by myself.

Except, I didn't feel alone in the house anymore. I felt like someone was watching me all the time. Especially, when I was in the master bedroom.

I would rather asleep on my Grandpa's old recliner in the back room addition and that was where I heard the weeping woman.

After that came the barrage of calls and visits from Blair. She was intent on me reconciling with her within that thirty day window of the divorce having been filed.

I was stupid enough to visit her in her new digs: a three room apartment that was stacked to the gills with her not only her stuff but my belongings I couldn't take with me to my parents' storage.

I had been given a whiff of freedom. A shot at starting over. A chance to for a re-do.

And I was blowing it.

My reason for holding onto the house was if I bankrupted, I was afraid I'd lose my job at the bank. It wouldn't look good for me to come up on a Special Assets list for charging off my credit card through the bank. I would be beyond embarrassed.

My divorce lawyer had been shocked I hadn't wanted to bankrupt and get away clean. To him that probably smacked of more pride. I couldn't hold onto the house and make payments on my unsecured debt. Holding onto to my first house was proving to be a stone around my neck.

Maybe I was just kicking against the goads.

Crawling over broken glass after breaking glass in case of an emergency.

I was barely keeping my head above water.

Swirling around a vortex with the weight of the stones in my heart threatening to pull me under.

How much worse could I make it for myself?

All I had to do was look at the pink winks on my wrists.

Instead of going over to Blair's new apartment, I should have heeded the advice of the divorce decree: stay out of each other's business. But my first marriage had ended with such acrimony we never spoke to each other again. I didn't want any more guilt to plant stones in my heart.

So, I went over.

Every square inch of space and volume of Blair's apartment was full of tubs and baskets. Her junk, my junk. Board games I had played as a child. Pieces of my mom's first Ethan Allen colonial furniture set.

It hit me in the gut to see memorabilia mounded together like trash in some mad hoarders' nest. Because that was what Blair had made. A rat nest stuffed so full there was no room for the rat.

Blair still had no job and had to use the divorce settlement to pay first and last month's rent—which is the same situation she'd been in when she'd first contacted me through i-Hearts. Her main focus, she said, was trying to sell as much of our old junk on ebay to pay for her rent and expenses. She declared she was doing great, and making big sales, and making more money than I did at the bank while she stuffed USPS mail boxes to go out across the nation of fellow hoarders.

But it was just another narcissistic claim. Nothing bad ever happened that she couldn't control. Until she reached out to pull the life-guard down with her.

I heard a familiar still, small voice that meant to set me straight. *She's taken all this stuff to hurt you. There is no way she is going to be able to keep it.* It might have been the voice of Grandpa. Or Boz or Randy McMurtry.

The whole thing was sick. A symptom of her sickness. A sampling of her madness.

And on top of that, the still, small voice added, *It's just stuff.*

Why do we want stuff so bad we are willing to work long hours for stuff, buy more stuff, and stuff that stuff into our closets?

Again, I realized I was free. Free from stuff. Free from Blair. I had the paperwork to prove it. I had paid for my freedom with the settlement.

She was making herself sick in trying to hold onto the stuff like a mad spider with a clogged web.

What was I doing back in her apartment? Getting ready for round two? My window of freedom was closing.

The chains of co-dependence fastening again around my ankles, like tendrils of misery seeking warm hope to feed off. I hadn't seemed to care, this time. They used mosquito spit, so that I felt less pain as they tightened their grip and started to draw out my blood.

I was numb.

A child deaf, blind, and dumb.

Blood pricked from my thumb.

Drawn back to the flame, a moth.

Over red hot coals, my feet to walk.

I went back home that night to my sparsely decorated 2112 Springhill Drive and fell asleep on my Grandpa's old recliner back in the new room addition. The only other piece of furniture was my great-grandpa's radio cabinet I used to put my small twenty inch tv on.

It was hard to sleep on my single bed in the huge master bedroom. I had the bed up against the window where it could catch the neighbor's yard light. So, I had retreated to the other end of the house.

Everytime I was in the bedroom, it felt like someone's eyes were boring into my spine. Someone who was not altogether happy over what had happened in this house. Someone who might very well thought it was still *their* house.

I had fallen asleep watching *Cool Hand Luke* on my DVD player. Most people know about the "the failure to communicate" line. But most don't know later on in the story, the warden gives Luke a second set of chains with this admonishment: run once, get one set of chains; run twice, get two sets; there won't be a third set because Luke was invited to "get his mind right."

The tv should have just gone to a blank screen after timing out once the movie was over. But somehow, the tv switched back to cable and was blaring a loud commercial about a product to defeat insomnia. The insomniac looked a lot like a Romantic poet and short-story writer with black jacket and a black gravottetie. The familiar who haunted his sleepless night was a ebony raven, who spoke only one word: Som-lace, the name of the product guaranteed to give respite and surcease of sorrow.

Even though, there the commercial was three times as loud as human comfort could stand, another sound had awoken me.

Someone crying.

In the back room addition with me.

A heart-broken wailing.

A banshee weeping.

A set of teeth gnashing.

Out of the depth from a hurt soul came profuse pain.

The volume was real and sadness pervaded the room.

It was not a dream and it was not from a stupid commercial on the tv.

I did not want to open my eyes to behold my visitor.

I did not want to sit up for a meet and greet.

It wasn't Grandpa or Boz or McMurtry.

Instead, I pulled the throw over my head and wished whatever it was—be it a dollop of undercooked hamburger, a smidge of mustard, a crumble of cheese, or a drab of ghostyard gravy--away without the help of a monkey's paw.

That morning I awoke to no sign of the presence or feeling of being watched. But whatever it was had been a harbinger. For there was a knock at front door and when I opened it I should have not been surprised to see Blair standing there.

I invited in her and we sat at my grandma's old formica table.

We made amends.

I forgave her before God and mistook what I thought was fleeing guilt for another clink of the codependent chain around my ankles, I had invited her back in.

On a trial basis. The divorce was final. So, I thought we would just try to live together and see how that went. I was hoping for no more drama or trauma.

Now she was back in the house, without my parents' knowledge.

With all her stuff.

The same old belongings in the same old cracked storage tubs and bent baskets were back in their stacks.

Almost in the same place where they had stood just over a year ago. As if nothing had changed.

Had I divorced Blair and forced her to leave the house just to bring her back in? Was I that afraid of being alone?

Whatever sense of expectation or hope or newfound freedom I'd had upon waking up this morning in my single bed in Kelter Ward C had disappeared the moment I walked back into 2112 Springhill Drive.

I stepped back into the house that I owned.

But it wasn't a home.

There weren't any Christmas decorations up. No tree or lights. No smell of holiday desserts being cooked up in the kitchen.

The only thing waiting for me was that old helpless feeling.

I was lost in the stacks of stuff.

Smothered.

Buried.

Closed up in a tight space full of junk.

And if I was going to have feel all that, then I didn't want to feel anything at all.

4-Deck the Halls

> ***Blair squeezed past me into the kitchen where we had pushed tubs aside to have space in the living room. "Let's go shopping."***

"For what?" I asked.

"It's Christmas, you dork. I want to spend it with you," she said.

It might just very well be just the two of us Christmassing with each other this time around.

"What's at the store that we could possibly need?" I asked pointing to the stacks of tubs.

"I want a Christmas tree. A pre-lit tree. A nice pre-lit Christmas tree. Not the cheap piece of crap that my mom and step-dad gave us last year," she said. "It was old and nasty. So they gave it to us. Then they went out and bought themselves a new one. I was insulted."

Yet, last Christmas, I had helped Blair put that cheap tree up in the living room. Then we had decorated that same nasty tree. It hadn't been an insult then.

But now it was.

"So I gave that piece of crap tree to Goodwill, so, now we need a new one," she continued.

"I've got money for groceries, the mortgage, and utilities. Maybe a few gifts. That's all," I said. "Which is it going to be then? Groceries or a pre-lit Christmas tree?"

"I've got my WIC card and unemployment money for another month," she said changing the choices. "I'll buy the groceries. You pay the mortgage and utilities. I can buy the tree with my unemployment. Save your money to buy gifts for your mom and dad."

Blair had barely worked long enough during the last year to even qualify for unemployment insurance. And the Department of Human Services only gave out a WIC card to women with dependent children. Bair had surrendered custody of her only son years ago, and the child had had little to do with her ever since.

"So, you're telling me that you're going to spend money on me that was given to you by the state for you and your son who doesn't even live with you?" I was stupid enough to ask.

"As soon as it hits my account, it's mine," she said. "They don't know what I do with it."

For Blair, the ends justified the means. The end was whatever she wanted, when she wanted it and no one could convince her otherwise. Everyone and everything was just a means. Before we married, she tried to blackmail her last boss for hush money over harassment.

I couldn't keep up with what lies went with who. I could only state the obvious. The truth.

"If you really want to pay for something you could help me pay down the credit car debt," I said. "That would help convince my parents to forgive you."

She scowled, "If they say they're Christians then they should just forgive me already."

"If we stay together, will you help me pay off the debt?" I asked.

"Better than that. I'm telling you I can apply for disability. Get a back check for the entire time we've been married. That would take care of the debt at once," she promised. For her, if she said it then it was real. Better than a promise. "Your meds won't be ready until after three. We've got to till ten tonight to pick them before Best-Meds closes. We could go out to dinner at Anthony's."

I gave her a look down my nose at eating out at a sit down restaurant. Doing that every night was no longer in my budget.

Not to be undeterred, Blair called the number on the back of her Unemployment Insurance debit card. As I heard the computer generated male voice stating a balance, Blair shook the card in her wrist. "It's there. I'm paying. It's Friday. That means prime rib night. And I want to see their gingerbread houses."

Anthony's Dolce Vita. Friday night. Prime rib, baked potato, and ground horseradish sauce. I had to admit, that sounded better than a toasted peanut butter and jelly sandwhich.

"Gingerbread houses?" I asked. Why weren't we unpacking the tubs? Putting our house in order?

"Yeah," Blair said. "All the employees make a gingerbread house. It's a tradition at Anthony's. They make a contest out of it. The winner gets a nice big holiday bonus."

"Prime rib sounds good," I admitted. "Not sure about the gingerbread house."

"You just look at them. They're not for eating, you dork," Blair scolded as we if were besties sitting next to each other in elementary recess.

She had to squeeze sideways down the narrow tubs before reaching the small hallway to the bath and bedrooms.

With her out of the room, I felt a sudden urge. Better check the balance in my bank account since I had an auto-deposit on the day I'd been admitted. And to make sure the password I'd set up to keep her out was still good.

Blair's laptop lay on the only clear spot on her formal couch.

I picked it up and sat down between boxes and tubs. I got on-line and accessed my bank account. The password screen had been locked.

So, someone had been trying to gain access while I'd been convalescing in Kelter Ward C, after all.

I unlocked my password and reset it by having to change it again. The most recent auto-deposit reflected last month's check from America's Bank. The only pending debit was from the emergency room of Our Lady's.

All was as it should be.

But there I sat with her laptop. With an open IM box for her user account. All I had to do was access MESSAGES. Then click on HISTORY.

And then we would see what we would see.

I felt a chill. A sense of power. A moment of strength. A chance at self-determination.

Two could play this game.

I could do it.

But should I?

We still had a chance at happiness. She might actually do what she would say she would do: apply and be awarded disability and receive a back check.   And that would be a great weight off both of us.

Twenty days until Christmas.

Wasn't that what I most wanted? A home? Built on trust and happiness?

Blair came out of the bedroom with dark red cordorouy jeans and a light pink sweater pullover that zipped up to her neck. It caught the curves of her hips and the majesty of her neck.

Her hair was relaxed and still damp. The dark curls contrasted against the glow of her cheeks and lips. Amid the stacks of tubs and bursting boxes, she sparkled.

"You clean up nice," I said holding her laptop on my thighs.

"Watcha doin' on-line?" she asked.

"Just checking the balance of my account," I said.

She fished through her purse and held up two cards given to her by Family Services. "We can check my WIC card when we get to Best-Mart. Let's go there first for some Christmas decorations. We're a little late putting anything up but it's all about having Christmas in your heart, right? After that we'll go to the grocery store. Then check on your prescriptions. And then go to dinner."

Blair had just planned the rest of the day. She started for the front door and I made sure to grab my car keys and we left 2112 Springhill Drive for the nearest Best-Mart.

Just like any other normal couple.

I had the Stratus in low gear most of the way as it trundled over packed snow and slushy tire ruts that would only refreeze as the sun began to set. Best-mart had plowed the parking lot but hadn't hauled the snow. It had to go somewhere so the plows had make bulwarks to hedge in the cars and make each light pole an ice fortress.

I swung around a deep pothole full of dark slush water to let Blair out near the front door because she kept on about her knee hurting. The managers had portable space heaters blowing on the sidewalks as associates salted, swept, and scraped off the chunks of ice and snow. As I pulled away, the car rolled over the pothole and bottomed out.

Blair limped over to wait for me next to a Salvation Army bellringer. A mainstay of Christmas. A reminder of angels first-class still earning their wings while keeping a first edition of *The Adventures of Tom Sawyer* in the pocket of their overcoats.

But this weathered man had on a skull cap and a coat zippered to his weathered cheeks. Other than jerking the bell, he kept silent. His method encouraged no one to break loose with the geetas.

I parked the car and the walk back up to the store entrance winded me. I was out of shape.

Blair had a list out. I reminded her we were here only for a Christmas tree. A pre-lit tree. A cheap pre-lit Christmas tree.

She nodded and was already looking for glittering sale signs and bargains.

Anything that glittered was gold to Blair.

And everything seemed to glitter in her eyes.

It was the height of Christmas shopping. Less than three weeks before Christmas. The heart of the season. Although, we had forgotten the reason.

Retailers had their own reason: they lived for the Christmas season. Their entire next year's budget would be built on the real profit returns of this season.

Yet, when we walked into the store, there was no holiday greetings from any store associates.

There were no decorations.

There was no hint of seasonal color. No extra splash beyond their corporate brand.

There were announcements but without any seasonal tags.

There was music, but it wasn't anything Christmasy. It was just a programmed selection of their best selling music cds.

There was nothing but the usual, every day guaranteed low prices.

Best-Mart had gone secular.

"I can't believe the workers aren't allowed to say 'Merry Christmas' here anymore. This is freakin' Best-Mart," Blair complained.

"Freedom of religion," I said playing the devil's advocate. "Separation of church and state."

"You mean 'freedom from religion.' How is not talking about Christmas exercising religious freedom?" Blair asked.

"Because we when say 'Merry Christmas' we may be offending someone else's religious freedom who doesn't believe in Christmas or want to be merry about it," I explained.

"Let them be offended!" Blair said. "That's what we do here! We celebrate Christmas! And we buy a butt-load of gifts to prove how much we love each other. If Christmas offends people how come they don't get offended when they receive gifts? Can you imagine some kid climbing into Santa's lap and saying, 'Gee, Santa, I don't believe in you so I can't accept a gift from you because that would be trespassing on my right not to believe?' What about all the trees and lights and inflatables? How come they haven't been banned?

"What would retailers do without Black Friday? The stores are open all day long on Thanksgiving, so the pre-sales have to start on Wednesday night and even go to Monday with on-line sales. Spending money for Christmas is wrapped up in the DNA of America! What do they expect us to do instead? Keep everyone locked inside their home and just give them on-line credit to spend and send groceries to their house every week? Talk about an almighty humbug!" Blair finished her tirade by balling up her fists and swinging them around her limp. Two rosy spots burned through her frosty cheeks.

"Let's find the freakin' Christmas stuff," she huffed, leaving me behind in her wake. Blair fought upstream at full speed between both lanes of shoppers on Deals Galore Boulevard.

Absent the Christmas decorations or music, the stress of the season still put the hustle in the shoppers' bustle. To and fro went moms and grandmas as they thumbed through sales ads on their phones, pushing carts full of kids too grown to accommodate their bony legs, while they put their say-so to the list in hopes of an omnibus spending package. Dads trudged behind as the caboose without a ramrod, just a helpless conductor onboard a runaway train.

Blair bid "Merry freakin' Christmas!" to a conscientious mom and dad as they passed by, debating the pros and cons of getting a Red Ryder BB gun, with the dad ready to proclaim victory until the mom reminded him of his latest sweepstakes win: a laced go-go dancer's leg lamp which re-ignited the debate over gallery art and tacky man-cave trash.

Then Blair threw out a "Gee, wish we had some Christmas music to set the mood!" to an older man coming at us in the other direction of Action Alley with a ring of puffed-up white curls like a hedge around his bald pate and spectacles slipping down his aquiline nose with cheeks redder than a reindeer's nose while carrying stacks of clothing boxes. A young boy in tow pushed a shopping cart full of ever bigger gifts, including a frozen turkey, while the older man whistled "Joy to the World" back to her and promised that the delivery of all these gifts would put his much-maligned employee into arrhythmia—the turkey alone was bigger than the man's youngest disabled son.

When we came to the Health and Beauty Aids, Blair accosted a middle-aged, blue-streaked hair store associate with piercings and tats with a tawdry "When can

I get my picture done with Santa? I so want to sit in his lap!"

The associate blinked a phlegmy eye and retorted with "Maybe he's too busy with his North Pole Dance" before sticking out a pierced tongue.

Blair was awestruck and had to blink while processing the reply. "Did Santa even bring any decorations with him for Best-Mart to sell?"

The intrepid associate pointed to the far wall where there stood a portal to an alternate world within the enclosed Best-Mart universe. "Try Lawn and Garden."

Blair was exasperated. "'Lawn and Garden?' Why 'Lawn and Garden?' If it's making your company profit why put it in the back like some ugly red-headed step-child from Missourah?"

But that was exactly what Best-Mart had done. Exiled all of the possibly offending Christmas merchandise to the farthest corner of the store, where its presence was negligible, while still having profitability squeezed out of deeds done in a corner.

Here, in this antechamber with ceiling to wall racks for lawn and care items, Christmas still held court. As long as those wishing to celebrate their religious freedom did so in a non-threatening and respectful manner. However, the question of good taste was not in consideration as inflatable Christmas icons waved and swayed as their air-pumping machines ran cubic inches of noble gases through the fabric.

Strains of spry Christmas songs and old carols echoed down the aisles and over the endcaps and across the tables and under the stands, being sung by mounted bass, shaking Santas, Sinatra-sound alike lightpoles, animated reindeer, ruddy-cheeked elves, and grateful snowmen.

Here, Christmas still ruled supreme.

Among this treasure trove of decorations.

Mother lode of ornaments.

Nexus of Christmas wrapping paper.

Complete with a primeval forest of plastic Christmas trees.

With shelves stacked full of boxed ornaments: stars and spheres and anamorphic Christmas shapes. Pegs loaded down with stockings and wreaths and holly-hocked door knockers. Selections of Russian baubles. Interchangeable wooden pieces for manger scenes. Old-fashioned village buildings pre-lit with tidings of joy. Even Christmas themed birdhouses.

There were rolls of wrapping paper. Packages of name tags. Bags of bows. Spools of ribbons. In all kinds of colors and patterns.

There were reindeers for the walls, halls, and windows.

There were pictures of Santa Claus throughout the ages. Saint Nicholaus in his red bishop's hat. Kris Kringle as a woodsy deity in a long green cloak and gnarled wood staff. Sinterklaas as a jolly old elf. Pere Noel in his white fur trim robe. A Dickensian Father Christmas in stove top pipe and coat tails. An obese American Santa Claus in red coat, pants and hat with white fluffy trim about to put himself into a diabetic coma with a plate of chocolate chip cookies and a bottle of Coca Cola.

And angels, angels, angels, everywhere.

They glowed. They shone. They glittered. They sang. They spread their wings. They held long trumpets. They did everything but what angels did do: tell someone

"Don't be afraid" and proclaim "On earth peace and goodwill towards men."

They had come down from the realms of glory to become tree toppers here on earth. Or Lamps. Candles. Stickers. Plush dolls. Paintings. Carvings. Statuettes. Even keychains and car deodorizers.

Underneath it all and all around us were the soft refrains of Christmas songs. "Let it Snow! Let it Snow! Let it Snow!", "Jingle Bells", "Baby, It's Cold Outside", and "Have Yourself a Merry Little Christmas" by the Rat Packers Sinatra and Martin. "Do You Hear What I Hear" and "The Christmas Song" by the old smooth crooners Bing and Cole. The big band version of "The Most Wonderful Time of the Year." A doo-wop version of "White Christmas." Elvis singing "Blue Christmas" and "Here Comes Santa Claus." And more modern selections: Bruce Springsteen and the E Street Band singing "Santa Claus is Coming to Town", The Eagles crooning "Please Be Home for Christmas."

And the orchestral folk of "I Believe in Father Christmas" by Emerson, Lake, and Palmer. Whose lyrics descried exactly what we were doing.

In this storehouse of wares, Blair stood amazed by the power of the commercialization and the mass of merchandise. While I was hiding behind a Floydian wall. It would take a lot of stimuli to get past that.

But Blair had been taken over by a mania she considered most wonderful and was far from true holiday cheer.

Up and down the aisles she went. "We came here for a Christmas tree," I reminded her. Blair's eyes went big. "We came here for a Christmas tree," I called to her through the time-space continuum. Her pupils dilated.

She was in a trance. Item after item, each under a dollar or two or three or four, found their way into her hands. Then, from there, into the bottom of the shopping basket. "We came here for a Christmas tree," I said from a far-away place.

I do believe she was ignoring me. Lost in her own marshmellowed world.

Then we came to the stands along the walls where the inflatable demigods held sway: A large comic Santa. A bloated sleigh. And an epileptic snowman thrashing his maniacal arms.

And below them on shallow shelves, I beheld the variations of how to deck the halls and walls inside and out: boxes of lights by feet 25 or 50 or 100 in assorted Christmas color and winterized shapes: white, gold, blue, red, and green; straight, mini, tear-like bulbs, or icicles; accessorized extension cords, gutter hooks, and individual bulb replacements.

I began to wonder how many strings of lights I would need to buy to make the outside of our house a runway for Santa's sleigh? Just looking at the depicted scenes on the outside of the boxes convinced me that I could arrange the lights in the same tasteful manner and turn our silent night, holy night into a drive-by attraction like we used to have in our old neighborhood, where people could drive through in the warm safety of their cars to admire the cheery Christmas lights.

Next to the rows of lights stood fiber optic infused creatures with tuberous and veinous strands wrapped around metal forms of reindeers and trees and angels, giving them a sympathetic system that ebbed from white to blue to red up and down the network of wire.

And Audio-animatronics. Life-like representations of Santas and angels. Moving their hands up and down.

In and out. Titling their heads from side to side. Trapped in their servitude and patterns of kindness. Showing a robotic modicum of generosity.

Last of all, we came upon the Christmas tree models on display. Firs, evergreens, and pencil trees. Frosted, bare, and pre-lit. In the bins above the models the appropriate boxes were stashed.

Blair took her time. Perusing the possible merits— excluding price or height-- of each tree. Why change her modus operandi now?

We had been there long enough for the songs to cycle through three times.

She settled on a frosted fir tree that was pre-lit and that stood six feet tall. It cost nothing less than one hundred and ninety-nine dollars. Plus tax. There were others more expensive she took the time to consider, but I was able to redirect her to the frosted fir. And others far less expensive that I wanted her to consider that she just shook her nose at.

I convinced her to forego some of the little baubles she put in the cart as frivolous—if anything Christmas could even be put in that category. Blair prepared to check with her unemployment debit card.

Next to the register were rows of popcorn tins with North Polar Bears and Christmas puppies and boxes of old fashioned assorted candies.

A Christmas memory of another desert flooded into my mind.

A certain taste.

Of happiness.

Sweetness.

Joy.

"See something you want? Get it. It's on me," Blair urged as the cashier scanned item after item.

I shook my head. "Homemade is better."

"Honey, I can make whatever you want. How about some chocolate chip cookies?" Blair offered and then got caught up in her own whimsy; either that or she was doling out more condescension under the assumption that a thirty-five year old man would eat it up like a six-year old child. "Mmm. Doesn't that sound wonderful? We can make them before we go out to eat at Anthony's and when we get home they'll've cooled off and we get eat them with a big glass of milk."

It was a picture perfect plan. No fuss, no muss. Easy-peasy, nice and breezy, even lemon-squeezy.

Except it turned to lemons fast when her transaction was declined.

First red flag of the day.

Blair was sure there was misunderstanding and had the cashier run it again, but the register kept spitting out the same "Zoltar Speaks" message: INSUFFICIENT FUNDS.

The second time, Blair got blushed and called the number on the back of her IDES county government debit card. When she got the menu she had to choose "English" then number one four times to navigate the menu. Finally, she listened to her balance. "Crap."

She frowned. "I've only got one-seventy left."

Her total was two-hundred and seventy-seven dollars and ninety-eight cents. She did the subtraction in a blink and then looked at me after deriving the sum. "Could we split. I do the one-seventy and you pay the one hundred and seven and the change?"

I shook my head.

"We need a Christmas tree," she said.

"No, we don't," I said.

And an argument ensued. It was stupid for her to spend all of her money. It was the tree she wanted most. And it was the tree that cost the most.

So, I bit the bullet. I thought I was doing the right thing by stepping up and buying the tree for her. I gave the cashier my debit card to swipe. The Best-Mart associate swiped it and handed back the card and the receipt. Both of which I put in my wallet.

Blair's countenance became cheery in a second. But I think true peace was beyond her. Having gotten what she wanted, she again made the offer to buy me refrigerated cookies by taking the time and trouble to warm up the stove and put those the pre-cut cookies on a sheet and put them into the oven for less than twenty minutes and expect to them to taste like a childhood memory of Christmas.

Except it hadn't been cookies that I was craving. It was something else unnamed. Something made by someone who had loved me unconditionally.

But now there was another red flag on the play.

Blair had made a promise.

Yet, another one. Given her recent history, it might go unfulfilled the same as all the others. Just more talk to make her sound good.

I chose to ignore the call and took possession of the ball with no added yardage.

But did I have control of the ball?

What, if anything, in the whole wide world of sports did I have control of?

Expectations. Like it or not, I was being affected by her choices and chained to her promises. And who was going to pay for all these unfulfilled promises made?

Me, that was who.

5-Gingerbread Houses Are For Gingerbread Families

Her burst of mania over, Blair
yawned on our way out the door.
"These new meds Dr. Frost has me
on are making me so groggy."

"I'm hungry. I need something on my stomach. You hungry?" she asked.

I sighed. "Need to get my meds. And we need to get some groceries to put down our necks."

"We can do that after we eat. Maybe I need to eat something with these meds. Maybe that'll wake me up. Let's get on over to Anthony's.   Otherwise they'll run out of prime rib," she said.

Anthony's Dolce Vita was a mom and pop place offering a wide fare of food--steak, chicken, seafood, some Italian and specialty sandwiches: French Dip and Ruebens. The waiting room was standing room only. Not because it was packed but because all of the chairs had been taken out to make room for the employees' gingerbread house displays.

There were all manner of miniature homes of gingerbread with sugar frosting trim and sour gum curb appeal. There were Elizabethean cottages. A Dickensian Fezziweg's warehouse. A Scrooge and Marley's counting house. An Italian square and fountain. A gothic cathedral. An Alpine skiing village. There was even a gingerbread North Pole with a Santa Claus village.

And among these four slices of gingerbread walls in this gingerbread world there were gingerbread people.

Gingerbread children, gingerbread parents, gingerbread dogs, gingerbread reindeer, gingerbread elves, a gingerbread Santa in a gingerbread sleigh, and gingerbread snowmen.

Friday was prime rib night and on Friday night Anthony's was overflowing by five and by seven Anthony's would often run of prime rib. All on a Friday's night. The main room was hazy from searing medium rare meat and the dripping of melting fat and the air salted and peppered and softened by butter and sour cream.

We were seated. We ordered. And out came the plates of prime rib.

The meat looked pink and juicy. The potato steaming and fluffy. But the taste did not match the look.

It didn't taste sweet or sour or salty or bitter. It tasted like there was a plastic coating over my tongue. It made everything taste like paste. And when I tried to wash the blandness away, even my water tasted oily and waxy.

I had my Lexapro to thank. It was working well. Working its wall of ice to protect me from any stimuli.

I could barely eat half my portion.

Blair gulped her food down in one breath while talking. It was the usual complaints. Blair's family hated her to the point they had formed a conspiracy to make her life miserable. The proof was they had successfully brainwashed her son against her.

The world was full of Blair haters.

Bosses who always gave her a bad review.

Jealous co-workers who did their best to get her fired.

All part of a plutocracy.

Meeting in secret to craft policies intended to keep Blair under their thumb.

Members sworn by a pledge unto death to deal life unfair to Blair.

During the separation and divorce, she had accused me of joining their club.

Of marking her for the Sanhedrin with a kiss.

Of stabbing her in the back during a session of the Roman Senate.

Of leading her to the guillotine.

Of being a turncoat and giving her over the enemy.

I had gone to the dark side.

But now that I had seen the light and repented, I had been welcomed back into my own house as a prodigal.

Tonight we had celebrated by killing the calf.

She paid the bill. At least, she had kept that promise. That was one for one.

Not that I should be keeping score. But I was. Why?

Because someone had been trying to get into my bank account the last seventy-two hours. And it hadn't been me.

We left and went through the drive through of Best-Meds. The female pharmacist behind the plate glass put my bag into the transaction drawer and asked if I had questions. So, I asked, "What's the one thing you most want for Christmas?" To which she answered, "A Wicked Plush Sherpa Throw Electric Blanket from Jingle Bell's."

Blair gave me the stink eye.

"It's a question we asked ourselves in Kelter. I guess to get our minds off our trouble," I said in my defense, even though I didn't need a defense because I didn't feel guilty, even if Blair wanted me to feel ignominious.

"The only trouble you got is how are you going to tell your parents we are back together," Blair said and snatched the folded over pharmacy bag, that was stapled at the top with a receipt and tag of care directions complete with side-effects. She tore it open with a petulant twist.

"Dr. Frost gave you Lexapro and trazadone. Something to keep up you during the day and something to put you down at night. Better follow the dosage and make sure you got food on your stomach when you take Lexapro," Blair said and then tossed the bag into my lap. "There."

Like it was going to do me any good nestled in my lap while I drove.

She was trying to pick a fight.

Amazingly, my gall didn't kick up and I didn't feel my cheeks start to burn.

All in all, I felt pretty cool. Just like ice. The Floydian wall held.

"You seem to know about Lexapro. Ever been on it?" I asked.

"Yes," she said.

"Will it whack me to the gills?" I asked.

She smiled. "It's pretty tame."

"Will it give me hallucinations?" I asked again. I really didn't want to open the fridge and grab the mustard and close it to find Grandpa or Boz or McMurtry standing next to me.

"No. It's not a psycho-tropic, you dork," she said.

"Will it make me gain weight?" I asked.

"Maybe. Anti-depressants tend to make you do that," she said. "Let's go home."

I shook my head.

"Why not?" she snapped and narrowed her eyes.

"Groceries," I reminded her and headed the Stratus towards the closest grocery store.

Blair sighed, "I'm tired."

I was, too. Of many things. But I had a wall of ice around me. Nothing could reach me.

The trip to the grocery store was just like the trip to Best-Mart. I clocked Blair's stay in one aisle at forty minutes as she checked over each can of beans like she was on a once in a lifetime visit to the Smithsonian.

We got home after nine and I took my dosage of Lexapro, but decided to wait and see if I would need the trazodone. For years, the moment I laid down my head my thoughts started to race. Followed by heart palpitations. Anxiety attacks. Worse, I would wake with bloodied cuticles around my fingernails and streaks of blood on the drywall at the head of the bed. Worse than that, I had episodes of sleep paralysis. I would wake up and couldn't move and there would be anamorphic shapes like spiders climbing the walls, taller shapes animating jackets and towels coming through the bedroom door or slipping out of my closet.

To relax ourselves, we watched a double helping of *Everybody Loves Raymond* while stretched out on my pre-marital couch Blair had returned.

At the point of pure peace, Blair broke it with: "Justin, you need to see your parents. You need to tell them we're together."

The thoughts began to race. And my heart kicked up its pace.

"I know," I said. If I didn't tell them what was up someone else would. They'd find out like it was some kind of dirty little secret. It was, wasn't it?

They wouldn't like it. They'd consider it shameful. But I'd better be the one to tell them.

"When are you going to tell them?" she demanded.

"Tomorrow," I said. It would be Saturday. And I'd have the rest of the weekend to get over it.

Maybe it wouldn't turn out as bad as I feared.

"I love you," she said and kissed me. "I've missed you."

That was my cue. It was getting on in the evening. Soft dim lighting. Two consenting adults. Glances out of the corner of her eye.

But I was behind a barricade of ice. The Floydian wall was too high. A backlog of feelings had been put into deep freeze and there wasn't enough heat to alleviate the blood constriction.

The flesh was weak, very weak, and the spirit wasn't even willing.

"It's okay. It's too soon," Blair whispered.

"If this is because of the meds, I'm gonna quit taking them," I vowed.

Blair kissed me and lay her check against mine. "It's because you're stressed still. Or in shock. Because of all you've been through. You'll feel better after talking to your parents. You'll see."

I would see, alright. But for now, I was getting sleepy. No need to bother with the trazodone.

"Justin," Blair whispered.

"Hmmm?" I queried from the doorway of sleep.

"What was it like?" she asked.

"What like? Being on Kelter C?" I asked.

"No. Been there. Done that," Blair said. "I meant being dead."

"Meh," I lied. "Nothing to it."

"So glad you didn't die. I'm so glad you're here. We're gonna have a great Christmas," she slurred.

She may have meant every word she said, but if she made good on her promise remained to be seen.

Was I just setting myself up for what had happened the last time—or even the first time around with Lauren? I kept thinking people would change. Except, I was learning people don't change.

It was easier to keep a stony heart because it was too scary to change it into a fleshy heart.

Did I even have the power to change my own heart? Or was I just setting myself up for failure again?

Before I'd met Blair, I knew absolutely zip about a bi-polar manic depressive.

Life with Blair was…

Riding a roller coaster with the cars put on backwards on a Double Ride Day.

Swimming out to help a drowning person and having them pull you under.

Either she was making me laugh at stupid jokes or crying about how worthless she was.

Either she cooed with lovey-dovey words of endearment or spat out curses with venomous words and a hateful tongue.

I was caught between sparks in the bedroom and dishes flying in the kitchen.

I was either in the best of all possible worlds and or had the four horsemen of the apocalypse riding me down.

It was either feast or famine with Blair.

I would have settled for just two days in a row of boredom.

No two days were the same.

The only thing that stayed the same was the drama.

And after a while it wore me down.

During my stay in Kelter Ward C, I had come to know quiet. There were times I could hear my heart beating while I lay in bed, without a thought in my head. The only thing blowing was the heat through the register.

But I found it was when I relaxed that thoughts came stealing, shapes came creeping, and past hurts came weeping.

Blair shut off the tv and went to bed.

I lay on the couch and said a silent prayer: I hoped I was doing the right thing by getting back with Blair. My parents would think I'd lost my everlovin' mind. So, I said an extra prayer that my parents would accept her back and that would be unto me a sign that only good things would come out of this.

But it was a prayer from a heart of stone.   It was the stone of the past. Something I didn't want to change.

Would God bother with that kind of prayer? He only listened when people were broken and cried out from the heart. I hadn't been broken enough.

Had I forgotten what I really wanted for Christmas?

6-"Beginning To Look a Lot Like..."

The next morning, a Saturday, I woke up on my pre-marital couch and made a promise to myself.

I was going to get my life all sorted out.

I would keep Blair. Because I needed someone to love.

I would keep the house. Because I needed a home.

I would pay off the debt. To show my family how responsible I was.

I would go to work and not complain. Because it was mind numbingly boring.

And I would go to group therapy. Because I needed to learn about my illness and how to get better.

Everything would work itself out. And, somehow, my Christmas would be freakin' merry.

Blair helped me sort out my life by giving me one of her old pill boxes. It was a simple seven day box. Seven compartments each stamped with "Monday", "Tuesday", etc.

She had graduated to a complex box. Hers had seven rows. Each with three compartments. "Monday morning," "Monday afternoon", "Monday evening", etc.

She dumped out some meds from both my prescription bottles and help me count out enough Lexapro and trazodone for an entire week. Two Lexapro a day and one trazodone at night—if needed. Plus Tylenol for every day aches and pains.

Then Blair got a shoe box from under her queen sized bed—the one we had shared in marriage and now sporadically shared. It was full of prescription bottles. Skinny and big and fat and orange. Over the counter and white. Tinfoil coated tab sheets.

All kinds of brands and flavors.

A cornucopia of pscyhotropia.

She checked the bottles for expiration dates. She shook them for contents. Then she spilled out a few meds from certain bottles.

Taking each into her palm, she named them one by one.

"Oxycotin." It was white and round, stamped with O C.

"Klonopin." It was round and pale blue. With an opening in the shape of a K in the middle. KLONOPIN was stamped on the front. And ROCHE on the back.

"Roxicet." It was white and round. The front stamped with 54/543.

"Now, Dr. Frost has me on Seroquel. And Zoloft, which I hate. And Luminal for sleeping. But this is my new fave. Darvocet. Got this from the emergency room when I strained my knee. Dr. Frost doesn't know I use it," Blair said. "You know what it does firsthand. Strange you knew to use this one when you tried to…"

From what little I knew of pharmacology, every family was represented. Sedatives and tranquilizers. Opiate pain relivers. Serotonin Re-uptake Inhibitors.

We counted out my pills per day.

Then we counted out hers per day.

I had four.

Nineteen for her.

I was in the minor leagues.

She was a true professional.

We had shared several things together since I'd been released: getting a Christmas tree, dinner, and now this.

Saturday wasted away. And Sunday was a blur of grey shadows. I spent them on my premarital couch in the back family room. And Blair spent it on her queen sized bed, sleeping under the blankets.

Sometimes she talked in her sleep. But she just didn't just talk. She screamed and cussed. Arguing with someone.   The boogeyman, maybe.

I put off seeing my mom and dad. I hadn't wanted to ruin their weekend. Or mine.

On Monday at 6:30 am, I kissed Blair goodbye, just like when we had been married and I drove the Stratus through slushy streets--white snow turning back to black and oily curbs--to the Metro station. Hordes of people waited there with me to ride the Metro to downtown St. Louis. I stalked the streets with the multitudes until I ducked into America's Bank Tower, to ride the elevator up to my dreamless job.

Almost ten years of service for the counting house. In that ten years, the bank had changed its name three times due to mergers. Whatever the name, it still amounted to the same. I served a counting house. What did it matter where their coffers were headquartered? St. Louis? Charlotte? San Francisco? Boston?

In ten years, I'd worked in four different departments due to layoffs and consolidations. Every year I was in a different building or on a different floor with a different job title.

Our most recent boss had warned us not to stay in a position more than year. That you were just asking to get fired if you did. Change was good. Change was not to be feared. Change was not getting a tight feeling in your gut. Change wasn't having your heart palpitate. Change was exciting. Whatever change was, it wasn't boring.

America's Bank was nothing but a counting house.

We counted change.

And just how much was a bank ever going to change?

You had addition, subtraction, multiplication, and division. Principal and interest (which really was boring). Tellers who never told you a thing. And a Trust department who chained down their pens.

But it was really all about addition.

In banking, there were only two rules.

Rule number one was "Never risk the bank's money."

Rule number two? "NEVER RISK THE BANK'S MONEY!"

I took the elevator to the thirteenth floor. Got out and pulled my sleeves down to my palms. Then walked to my cubicle and found it had been turned into a resting place for unfiled documents.

Someone else had done my work load. Now I had it back. I hadn't been missed.

I felt embarrassed about my wrists. I didn't know what to say in case anyone asked how my vacation had been. I felt like everyone knew everything anyway, but they didn't want to say anything to upset me. Because I might have lost it.

Other than that, I kept my head down until four o'clock. No one spoke to me and I didn't speak to anyone. Nothing had changed.

I left the same way I came. Took the Metro back to my stop and drove the Stratus back to 2112 Springhill.

At 5:25 pm, Blair kissed me goodbye and let me out under the carport of Our Lady's and took my vehicle to swing by the grocery store to get more groceries somehow we didn't get on Friday night.

And I walked into the darkened utility corridor. The lights behind the beveled glass check-in window were dark. The door to Kelter Ward C stood hermetically sealed, waiting for the secret password.

But I saw a light down a narrow hallway to my right. Heard voices coming from an open room. I walked into a conference room with two chairs set on either side of a moveable dry erase board on an easel and five chairs gathered around it in a semi-circle.

This was a front room for Hope Counselors, Inc.

There were four other people milling about the room. Three men and one woman. The men were both older and younger than me. The woman much younger.

We were all cautious in this new situation. Not sure of what to do or say. Or what would come next.

Two other people came in. A man and a woman. Both were middle-aged. Dressed in khakis and simple polo shirts. The woman was a bulldog—barrel-chested, paunchy and all jowls. The man was a long drink of water—bony and leathered skin, like an old west sheriff.

"Good evening, group," said the lady bulldog. "Everyone have a seat. Every night we will start promptly at five-thirty. If you are late you will have to explain to the group why and write an essay."

We all found a seat. I looked around the room.

"There will be three of us who will facilitate these sessions. Two of us will be here each night, taking over half of a session at a time. I am Sandy L. And this is Paul D.," Sandy L. said.

Paul D. had some copies in his hand which he began to pass out.

"The first thing we will do is go over the rules," Sandy L. said.

I took my copy and looked it over.

GROUP RULES

- **Respect confidentiality: What you hear here, stays here**
- **Respect this place: be on time and stay for the entire session**
- **Respect others: do not interrupt a speaker or cross talk**
- **Respect the focus: share your experience rather than advice or judgment**
- **Respect feelings: All feelings are encouraged, but not all behaviors are acceptable.**
- **Respectful language: Do not use foul language, threats, or violence**
- **Respect relationships: fraternizing or dating other group members is not permitted.**

"What does 'fraternizing' mean?" asked the youngest man next to me hiding beneath a hoodie.

"Don't hook-up out with anyone in the group," said a sturdy-built man.

The young woman, her skin porous and dark roots showing in her platinum hair, went wide eyed.

"Group, let's introduce ourselves," Sandy L. commanded and took charge. "I'm Sandy L."

"I'm Paul D.," said Paul D. with a whistle through his teeth.

"I'm Hannah S.," said the young dirty-blonde girl.

"I'm Ja-rod W.," said the sturdy built man.

"I'm Everett P.," said an older man.

The young man next to me wouldn't play the rules and refused to give the initial of his last name. He just shrugged and said, "Thad." He kept his hoodie up and his head down.

"Justin R.," I said.

"Let's go around and tell why we are here," Sandy L. L. said next.

"I've been through FINS, DHS, and foster care since I was five until I was emancipated at seventeen. But then I had my child last year and DHS got called on me. They drug tested me and it came back dirty," Hannah said. Then tears ran out of her dark circled eyes. She was much younger than I had thought. The sleep lines and the dark circles had put about ten years on her. "If I want to keep my child, I have to come here."

"I'm in a sorta similar situation," Everett P. said. "I got popped on a random test at work. I don't do much other than drink and blow some weed now and then. But if you want good money you gotta work at the steel mill. And if you wanna keep a job at the steel mill, you gotta work them crazy shifts. And if you wanna stay awake, then you gotta take something. Everyone does it but I'm the one who gets caught. Don't know why they're buggin' me about it. But if I want to keep my job, I've got to finish this group therapy thing. And if I lose my job I lose my wife and kids."

"I did this to myself," Ja-rod said. "This my first step to gettin' better. I was tweakin' and beat on my girlfriend cuz she didn't make what I want for supper. Sat in jail 'til I could make bail but one of the conditions was for to come here. I ain't proud of what I done but it ain't never gonna happen again. I ain't goin' back to druggin'. I will do whatever it takes to stay clean."

I decided it was my turn. "I'm here on my own. I was feeling real down so I tried to kill myself. Well, I kinda did kill myself. But my ex-wife was home and got an ambulance there in time to bring me back. So, I agreed to be admitted and just got out of Kelter Ward C."

Hannah beamed, "You too? When were you there?"

"Just got out on Friday," I said.

"Missed you by about three days," she said.

Sandy L. quieted us all and prompted the last one to speak with a nod.

"I know why I'm here," Thad said under his hoodie. "But it just won't do no good."

"And why not?" Sandy L. asked.

Thad shrugged. "Nothin's gonna change."

"I sure hope that ain't true," Ja-rod said.

Sandy L. passed out as second paper.

"THE DRUG PERSONALITY:

Mood swings

Unreliable

Unable to finish projects

Has unexpressed resentments and secret hatreds

Dishonest and lies to family, friends, and employers

Isolates and withdraws from family and friends

Chronically depressed

Engages in risky sexual behavior

Develops strong defensive mechanisms (denial, rationalization, minimization, projection, justification, blaming)

Monetary problems, doesn't or can't pay bills

Difficulty with interpersonal and professional relationships, unable to hold a job

Engages in illegal or immoral activities to obtain drugs"

We read them aloud and she asked us to give examples from our experience about each. There was no denying it. I had exhibited all these characteristics at one time or other.

And though I didn't think myself my as a criminal because I'd never stolen to get money to buy drugs, I had lied to loved ones so I could drug. The only difference between me and a felon was I had never been caught. But I had still broken laws and rules.

What stung me was I had lied to my first ex, and before that I had to my parents to slip away to do drugs. Just stepping out. From the boring family fire.

Every Sunday morning it was the same old hymns and same old sermons. Before I gave up the ghost there were still wild hairs to scratch. I'd slipped out the back door not knowing where I was headed. But the funny thing was my feet knew where to go.

I didn't want to be trustworthy. I didn't want to loaded down with responsibilities. I wanted to do what I wanted to do.

Which meant I became a jerk. Not some free spirit in tune with a higher form of consciousness painting white feathers and peace signs on everything around me as the moon came into the seventh house. I turned into a potty-mouth quick-talking self-seeking unreliable whiner who always made the time to get high.

First, I was a jerk to my first ex-wife. Then to my family. And anyone else around me. Including me, myself, and I.

We took a break.

Came back and Sandy L. went at us again with a handout. This time it was a questionnaire. With 7 questions.

"RECOVERY

Answer the following questions about your use of substances to help clarify whether you are in control of the substance use or whether it is control of you.

	YES	NO
1. Do you ever spend money on substances that was needed for rent, bills, or groceries?	______	______
2. Do you binge on substances?	______	______
3. Have you ever dealt substances?	______	______
4. Have you traded sex for substances?	______	______
5. Do you ever miss appointments because of use?	______	______
6. Have you made promises that you do not keep or miss appointments because of use?	______	______
7. Do you believe that you are addicted to drugs-alcohol?	______	______ "

I answered "YES" on all but #3 and #4. I hadn't sunk that low yet. But there was no denying #7.

Then Sandy L. L. asked us the final question of the night as a group: "Are you any of you ready to admit you're addicts?"

One by one we each answered.

Ja-rod W. was first. "Yes. And I want to stop. I'm going to stop."

Hannah S. next. "Who am I kidding? My dad was one. And now I'm one. My mom died from it. My dad lost me over it. But I don't wanna lose my kid over it and I certainly don't wanna die from it."

Then me. "I never thought of myself as one. But that's just a lie. I am an addict."

Everett P. was stubborn. "I don't think I am. Just for takin' a little speed. I don't belong here."

But Thad G. outright shocked us. "I am what I am. And I ain't gonna quit. I'm gonna die an addict."

Paul D. came up behind him and tapped the hoodie-caped young man on the shoulder. Then he led him outside. It was time to circle the wagons.

There was another set of handouts. This time it was two pages. The first one was a time sheet with some instructions at the top. And the second was a list of court approved substance abuse/support/recovery groups listing the organization's name, their addresses, and what days and time they met.

"Let me just lay it on you. This is serious business. You need a good support group around you twenty-four seven. I will remind you as a part of your intensive outpatient program, you need to complete twelve hours a week of therapy. Eight hours are done here when you come four nights a week for two hour sessions. You will need to schedule a two hour one-on-one session with one of our Hope counselors. You will also have to go to a twelve step program meeting of your choice for two hours this week. Look over the list I gave you and choose one that is closest to you. We are not meeting on Wednesday, so I would do a group that day. Otherwise, you will have to find a meeting that starts after eight or one that meets on the weekend. You need to pick one of these groups to attend, get it signed by a court approved counselor—that means they have are a clinical licensed social worker or a mental health paraprofessional or a licensed drug counselor—each group should have one type or the other and they will direct you to that person. They may not sign your timesheet until the session is over, so don't forget: It needs to be signed and dated and it needs to indicate that you were there for two hours.

"Remember, life runs twenty-four seven. If you want to make recovery a part of your life, you need to work your recovery twenty-four seven," Sandy L. said.

I never did see Paul D. come back in with Thad G.

The session was over.

Blair waited in the parking lot in my Stratus.

"How did it go?" she asked as I got into the passenger seat of my car.

I shrugged. I had lived through it. But it hadn't been comfortable—often, the truth isn't.

"I had to admit something I never have before," I said.

"What's that?" Blair asked.

"I'm an addict," I said.

"I wouldn't have thought so," she said.

"You knew that I partied a lot. Bars and bands and strip joints. I don't use or abuse when I'm around you. But I still get depressed," I said.

"Honey, I love you. I'm not going to let you use drugs. I'm here for you," Blair said.

"Are you sure?" I asked. "You can deal with me and my problems?"

Blair looked straight ahead along the road. "Yes. Can you accept me and all my baggage?"

And did Blair have baggage. A whole train load.

In my mind, I crossed my fingers. "Yes."

Hadn't I already paid enough for my decision?

"Good, then let's go tell your parents. Right now," she said.

Nope. There was still some more to pay.

I had lost a lot: belongings, friends, pride, self-respect, self-worth. I had gotten my house back but I still had a ton of unsecured debt to pay off.

And now I was in danger of losing my family. But there was only one thing left I could lose.

My life.

And I had even tried to throw that away.

Believe it or not, we pay for our decisions. There are certain consequences we can't escape. No matter how much we lie. And the first person we lie to is ourselves.

Maybe we lie to God at the same time. If He knows everything then He knows everything at once. Why does He let us lie to Him and ourselves? Until we come up with a different answer?

My problem was a conflict between what I wanted and what was going to happen, regardless of what I wanted. I had no one to blame for what was going to happen next except for me, myself, and I.

The duplex my parents had moved to was fifteen minutes from the hospital. My mom had already retired and my dad was set to. So, they sold their house to save up a down payment on a new house. Their retirement house. Now they would have an empty nest if I stopped bouncing back.

To get to their nest we took Highway 15 and turned at Hart's Orchards.

I made her park at the curb and not pull into the driveway.

"Stay here," I said and unbuckled. If there was ever a time she needed to listen it was now.

"This concerns me, too," Blair said. She had turned off the car but hadn't unbuckled.

"It's about you. It's also about me and my parents," I said. "You want me to talk to them then let me talk to them. Alone."

I took my last deep breath, got out, and shut the door behind me.

I walked up to the door on their side and rang the bell.

Mom answered the door. She let me in. Dad was in the kitchen.

"This is a pleasant surprise. We've been praying that you'd want to come and talk," she said.

The house was full of old and new belongings. They'd had to downsize for the move. Pack up some precious keepsakes. And sell off or give away what they no longer needed. Which included most of their furniture. The old set wouldn't have fit in the duplex. And the new set was temporary , meant to hold them over until they got settled in their retirement house.

I sat on a new sofa in front of their new tv. Mom took up the controller and turned it off.

She took a seat in a new recliner.

We waited for my dad before starting.

"Your father's cleaning up in the kitchen. He's such a big help. Willing to do so much even after I retired," Mom said.

I hadn't eaten. But I couldn't have eaten if I'd tried. My stomach was in knots and my mouth was dry.

"What you havin'?" I asked just to make small talk and keep myself from freezing up.

"The usual for Saturday night. Pizza," she said.

We waited a little longer. Dad wouldn't be rushed. I felt like a student cooling my heels in the principal's office until he was good and ready to talk to me. The whole idea of having to wait was for me to know who was in control and who wasn't.

Dad finished washing and drying off dishes and came out. He looked none the happier from a visit by his other prodigal son. I was the youngest and that meant I had been the most spoiled. I'll be the first to admit that my parents had spoiled me. The more they tried to help me, the more I seemed to have not learned my lesson.

Maybe it was time for them to cut bait. Kick me off the pot. Forget about tough love and turn a cold shoulder. Write me out of the will. Leave me to wallow in my pig pen until I got tired of smelling and wearing pig crap.

He gave me a "Hello, son" but his dour face said otherwise. Taking a seat in his new recliner, he began the conversation. "Do you have something to tell us?"

I inhaled. Deep. And used every bit of my breath to tell them. "Mom. Dad. I'm an addict."

I thought it was the worst thing that I could have possibly told them. I was sure that I had lost all their respect. I was down there with murderers, rapists, and pedophiles.

Dad paused. Mom's eyes went red. "Who told you were an addict?"

"Me myself. I've finally realized it. Along with all this depression," I said.

"Do you use needles? Are you a junkie?" Dad asked. Maybe that was his definition of what an addict should be.

The truth was that addicts came in as many flavors as there were drugs. How to self-administer the drug and how often determined the habit of the user. But the bottom line was the same. Addicts needed to get high and would use whatever it took—a syringe needle or a dirty bottle or near ashed-out cigarette butts, a can of beer or an out of date prescription pharmaceutical bottle or a punch out tab of amphetamine-souped-up-nasal decongestant. Investing the time in preparing to get and maintain that high while seeking out new thrills and sources was a lifestyle that robbed a life, not enriched it.

"No. Mostly it's alcohol," I said.

"From all that time with the rock and roll bands," he said intending to make me feel guilty over his mistake. They had never liked me being in bands. Then he went back to interrogating me. "Who told you were depressed?"

"I must be because I tried to kill myself," I said.

"Why did you try to kill yourself?" I thought the hardest thing would have been having to tell them I was an addict. But this was harder. I was being laid bare. All my faults were his faults. And in exchange: All his hurts, my hurts. Except the upbraided and swollen marks on my writs were mine, not his.

"Dad, I died. They had to bring me back," I said.

I hadn't wanted to tell them this. But it was like I had to prove myself to my Dad about how serious my depression was.

"You say you died, but here you are standing in front of me talking to us," Dad said. "How long were you dead for?"

"About five minutes," I said.

That brought fresh tears from my mom.

"Bah, that's not dead. Not even a minor miracle. What, did they juice you with the paddles? So, the coroner never proclaimed you dead. Now if they wheeled you down to the morgue and you'd sat up and asked for a glass of water, that would be coming back from the dead. Not holding your breath for five minutes," Dad said. "Did you go down a dark tunnel? See the light? See Jesus? Or did the devil and the Archangel Michael fight over your body?"

Mom admonished my dad. "Shh. You can tell he's got wounds."

"I don't know what to expect from you anymore. Your mother and I don't know what to do for you anymore. I really just want to remove my hedge of protection around you and let you go your own way and if you get blown away by the wind, so be it. Either you'll come to your senses or it'll kill you," Dad said.

"Sounds like you came pretty close," Mom said. "You still haven't told us why you tried to kill yourself."

"You couldn't even do that right. You've been making mistakes for awhile now. Least you're consistent," Dad said.

I spit a stone out from my heart. A true, cold stone. So, sharp along the edges that it would cut. "Would you have wanted me to get that right? Do you rather I'd've died?"

I wasn't so sure who that had been aimed. Me or him. Or both.

"No, of course not. What I want is for you get to your life right. Get on the straight and narrow. And you're never going to do that until you give it over to

God. Let Him guide you. Let Him work on you. I can you show how if you just listen to me. Why don't you trust me?" Dad asked.

"I didn't want you to worry," I said. "It's my problem and this is the best way I know how to deal with it."

"Well, when you call us and tell us you're in the hospital because of a suicide attempt, we're going to worry. We're your parents. Hello," Mom said.

"It doesn't just have to be your problem. God is bigger than any problem you have. You should have stayed in church. So what if you and Lauren didn't work out. You're the one putting yourself through this. Just look at your wrists. That's not how you handle problems. You still got your whole life ahead of you.

"God doesn't change. He loves you. He sent His Son to die for you. He's letting you keep on this way until you decided you've had enough. You don't want to tempt God, Justin. You've got hope as long as you're breathing. But when you stop breathing, you're gonna have to stand before Him and give an account of all you've done."

"Lauren's got more problems that she knows how to deal with. So, it was easier for her to blame someone else and just keep her head in the sand. She doesn't want to face the world. She's damaged goods. I didn't have to marry her. It was a mistake," I said.

"And you just got out of a second mistake," Mom said. "By marrying Blair. You need to let your life settle down. Your dad's right. It's like you're just blowing in the wind."

While Mom was being hopeful and helpful, Dad named the thing that must not be. He said aloud their worst fear. The absolute worst thing I could do short of murder. "Are you back with Blair?"

"Yes," I said.

Dad slapped the armrest of his new recliner. "Man alive! If it didn't work out the first time, what makes you think it's going to work this time?"

Mom's tears poured over the ducts. "She doesn't deserve you. You're settling for far less than God has in store for you."

"We can help each other with our problems. She understands me. Lauren wouldn't even try or even want to try," I said. "Blair and I have forgiven each other. Can't you find it in your hearts to forgive her?"

Dad shook his head. "No. She's caused us a lot of problems. I don't want to go down that road again."

"We might be able to forgive but not forget. She is trouble. Look at all the hurt she's caused you and the family. All that money you two wasted. She seems to live for it. She'll never be happy," Mom said.

"Did you marry her again?" Dad asked.

"No," I said. I hadn't thought that far ahead. Everything was blocked by ice.

"Are you going to marry her?" he asked.

"I don't know. We'll have to see how it goes. I'd like her to help me pay off the debt. What if she was to pay you back?" I asked.

Dad shrugged. "Do you really see her paying us back? Do you ever see her being able to help you with the responsibilities of making a home together let alone keeping one? How many times did you have to ask us for help? How are you going to handle any better it this time?"

"I'm going to group therapy now. As part of my rehab. To help fight my depression," I said. I didn't tell them that attendance was mandatory or the insurance wouldn't pay for my missed days at work.

"If I was married to Blair, I'd get depressed, too, Justin," Mom said. "She's like a spider that clutches at everything around her while getting sucked into a vacuum cleaner."

"Everyone gets depressed. Even I get down," Dad admitted. "But you don't have to always act on your feelings. You don't have to listen to them. Sometimes you shouldn't even trust them. Not everything is as bad as it seems. And likewise, not everything is as good as it appears. You want to get real help. Join a church. Come back to God. Only by serving God will you ever find true peace. I'm not saying you won't have troubles or bad days but your peace will be secure and outweigh anything this world can throw at you."

"I want to try and work things out with Blair," I said. "I don't want to be alone."

"Son, God would never leave you alone. And He doesn't bring confusion or pain. If you want to help Blair then pray that God would heal her and bring her the peace she needs and the help she deserves," Mom said.

I had felt like a failure so much and for so long while growing up, I thought that's what I must be. And after Lauren and I divorced, the feeling of failure only got worse and being alone was the kind of punishment I deserved. It was my fault I had blown a chance at happiness.

I thought you only got so many chances before you crapped out. I was already oh for two. And getting ready for my third roll when the table was far from hot.

How many chances could I possibly have left? Was it even luck that I was playing against? Or was I just kicking against the goads?

"If you won't listen to me, maybe you'll listen to your mom," Dad said. "We must seem like out of touch squares to you. We hear about these things through our friends who have kids that give them all sorts of trouble."

"I never would have thought of talking back to my parents," Mom said.

"People just didn't talk about their problems. They just focused on what they had to do to survive," Dad said.

"Your grandparents went through the Great Depression. They were blessed just to have jobs," Mom said.

"And we went through the sixties," Dad said. "We missed all that sex, drugs, and rock and roll. We didn't go to Woodstock."

"I was pregnant with you and trying to work as much as I could before I had to take off," Mom said.

"And I was teaching. But I wasn't making that much. It took me a while to find a job I liked that could provide for my family," Dad said..

"We were too busy working and trying to make a living," Mom said.

Dad went straight for the throat, "If you take her back you'll be showing your whole family you can't be trusted."

A flame popped up out of the wall of ice. A bit of it melted and ejected a stone. A fiery piece of brimstone.

If Dad was going to play judge and jury, my gut reaction was to run. I didn't have to play this game. How was it going to help me?

Before I knew it, I was up off the couch and headed towards the front door.

Dad sprang up from the recliner and in a flash beat me to the door.

"As long as you're with her we want our keys back," he said blocking the door.

"Keys?" I asked. I didn't know what he meant. The car was mine. So was the house.

"The keys to this duplex. And the keys to my truck," Dad said.

I was stung. He wasn't kidding. If Dad didn't trust me any longer then fine. What he wanted was easy enough to do.

All I did was reach into my pocket and take out my key ring and pull off the keys to their duplex and to his truck. I handed them over. But Dad wouldn't get out of my way.

"If you're going to take her back, then your family wants their things back," Dad said.

A surprise move. I hadn't seen that coming. The flame smoldering out of the ice wall was sparking into anxiety. It morphed into bestial fight or flight.

They were perfectly willing to let me go. But at a price. And they didn't think I could pay it.

It was just a game of bluff.

Stand and deliver.

A peeing contest.

First to flinch.

"What else?" I asked.

"All the furniture we let you borrow when you moved back. And all the money we gave you. We'll want it back," Dad commanded.

That wouldn't be so easy. I'd have to get a moving van. Use a dolly. Load it, drive it over here, and unload it. All by myself. Ain't no one was gonna help me.

And the money? We weren't talking twenty dollars. Or even a couple of hundred here. I was in deep with them. Not to mention being maxed out on my credit cards. And hounded by creditors.

"I'll get you your stuff back," I huffed.

"When? This weekend? Can you even afford a moving van? What about the money?" he demanded.

"I'll get the money back, too," I said.

"When?" Dad barked.

In my mind's eye, saying it was as good as doing it. Except saying it wasn't the same as doing it. Not even close.

For Dad, there was what you say and there was what you do.

Words meant something.

If you couldn't promise something, then you shouldn't say it.

You should keep your word.

You were only as good as your word.

And mine wasn't worth squat.

"You'll get it back. In time," I snarled.

Then we'd be square and I wouldn't owe them a thing. Then I could lift up my head and shout, "I'm free! Thank God, Almighty! I'm free at last!" Only, they had helped me in another situation to reach that point and here I was slipping the chains back on.

But time wasn't on my side. I didn't even have time to play b-sides. Time waited for no one.

And so, it was time to go.

"Justin, don't go," Mom said. "Not like this."

"Sit down, son. Let me talk some sense into you," Dad said. I guess he'd pushed it apart as far he'd been prepared.

They weren't going to do anything more to me.

But, boy, was I mad.

Burning white hot righteous anger wrath raining down from on high to smite the heathens mad.

I was mad at everyone and everything. Including babies and flowers. Ice cream and puppies. The entire world had been made just so I could be mad at it.

I was an adult.

I could make my own choices. Even if they were crappy ones. That might haunt me.

And I was going to make one right now.

They had the front door blocked, but not the back door.

So I retreated to the kitchen. "I'm leaving and I'm never coming back to this house again!"

It's amazing how anger helps my public speaking. Every syllable stressed. Every word coming out clear and pronounced.

"Justin!" Mom called. "Come back!"

"There goes a man ruled by his emotions!" Dad shouted as I left. "He's not even thinking!"

I was out the back door and around the corner of the duplex.

The front door didn't bust open.

No one chased after me. Proverbs 28:1 *The wicked flee when no one pursues.*

I walked around to the driver's side of the Stratus. Blair slid down the window.

"Why did you come out the back?" she asked.

The door was unlocked. I opened it.

"Move over!" I barked. If she didn't want to test how mad, I was then she'd get in the backseat.

"Why?" she barked back. Just mirroring the emotion I was giving to her.

"'Cause it's my car and I'm freakin' drivin' it!" I said. Hers had been repo'ed. Long ago.

She wisely slid over and I climbed into the seat. Jerked it back. Yanked the steering wheel down. Put it into drive and peeled out. It was the first step in never going back.

Blair didn't know better not to ask. "How bad was it? It couldn't have been that bad?"

"Worse," I fumed.

Never going back.

Never.

Going.

7-"Nibbling At My Nose..."

Back at 2112 Springhill Drive we walked in and smelled gas.

"I smell gas," Blair said.

Actually, she couldn't smell gas.

And neither could I.

No one can smell gas.

It's the mercaptan that it's mixed with natural gas you smell, so when a line ruptures, you will know the gas is leaking. And you will know the smell of mercapatan because it smells like rotten eggs. And when you smell the mercaptan, you need to vacate the premises before an explosion occurs.

"The gas is leaking!" Blair shouted. She scooped up her cell phone and said, "Google, find the number to the gas company." Once the faithful AI had brought up the company name information, overlaid on a grid map, Blair commanded, "call 'Just Gas'. Now!"

It was past nine at night on a Monday. I hoped the gas company had someone on call. The call went through. "Hello? We think we have a gas leak in the house. No, I can't hear it. I can smell it! Where? Mostly in the kitchen! That's where our gas line is!"

I followed her from the living room into the kitchen. The smell of mercaptan was prevalent here. It did smell like rotten eggs. Sprinkled with a touch of diesel. Burning and pungent.

"What? You have someone on call? Really? Okay! Could you give me the number?" Blair said making circles in the kitchen. She cradled the phone in her neck. "Honey, quick! Get something to write this down!"

Before I could get both a paper and pen she was relaying a number. I made her repeat it after she made the gas company representative repeat it to her. Then she through open the kitchen lattice.

"Thank you so much for your time and information!" Blair said on a gracious note that was out of character. She ended the call. "Help me get all the windows open! We've got to get out of here!"

But she was already a whirlwind of alarm and expectation. Next, the sash of the family room window squealed open. "Don't just stand there! Open the freakin' living room window!"

I squeezed around the Christmas tree, which still hadn't been plugged in after we'd put it up yesterday. I could only get the window up halfway before it jammed. Then Blair had me by the elbow and pulled me towards the front door, telling me not to look back or I would turn into sulphurous rotten eggs.

Out the front door we ran. Tracking through the mashed snow. Standing by the Stratus in no time.

"So, we just stand out here until all the gas clears out?" I demanded. The air began to cut through my thin layer of clothes and chill my skin.

Blair looked at me with disdain. "It's gas, stupid! The house could have exploded!"

"How long do we stand out here?" I asked.

People in gas houses should not throw matches.

Standing out in the snow, exposed in the winter night was the perfect time to regret living in a gas house.

"The gas company will send someone here to turn off the gas from the outside," Blair said.

"So, we'll have to keep the windows open for a while longer," I said.

Blair rolled her eyes. "It's gets better. The gas company said we'll have to have heating and cooling guy come and see where the rupture is and fix it."

"The gas company won't do it?" I asked. "It's their line."

"You'd think so," Blair concurred. "But no. They only install the gas and do outside maintenance. If it's inside you gotta get a heating and cooling guy."

We were prescient enough to wait in the Stratus. But the cold air cut through metal and glass with ease. I had to turn the engine on so we could use the heater to keep warm until the man from Just Gas got here.

A gas utility truck, with a diesel and chasis of compartments resting on a doulie cracked through the frozen snow behind us in the driveway. A man in Dickies duck insulated overalls got out with a shovel and crowbar. He went to the side of the house beside the kitchen window and dug down about a foot to uncover the metal plate housing for the gas valves before using the crowbar to take the metal plate off.

In less than three minutes, he signaled with a wave that he was done.

I slid down my window to hear him say, "You'll have to the gas line checked inside. Then call us and they'll send someone back out to turn your gas back on."

We went back inside and closed the windows.

The air had been scrubbed clean but robbed of any warmth.

It was fresh and frigid.

Blair called a heat and air guy that the gas company had recommended and harangued him into accepting the emergency of our plight. The man arrived within a half hour. It was ten-thirty o'clock by then.

Past my Cinderella hour. If I was going to be fresh for work, I liked to get to bed before ten. Of course, I also like to be warm and snug like a bug in a rug.

The things we take for granted: heat.

The heat and air guy helped us locate the gas line coming inside from under the kitchen window. We pushed the stove back and discovered the gas line coming out of the foundation. I could see the damage well-enough. Just below the shut off cap at floor level, the line had been pinched and cracked.

The heat and air guy said that was the worst place to get a break in the line. There wasn't enough space to put on a new cap. We had to pull back the linoleum as he fetched a jack hammer. He chipped out enough inches to clear more of the gas line before telling us that he did not have a spare gas cap. He gave us a choice: he could return tomorrow after securing the part or we could go to Lowe's and get the part. Either we could put the cap on ourselves or have him come back and do it for us.

We elected to get to Lowell's before they closed at twelve midnight: their Cinderella hour. He left us a bill and further instructions: to get a hammer and chisel and chip down about another inch to make sure there wasn't any further damage. That should be enough space to put a new gas cap on.

The last thing he did for us was to take wire cutters and take off the old cap and the pinched section of the line. By eleven-forty, we were back into the Dodge Stratus with the old gas cap as a model and made for Lowell's in the refrozen snow tracks. By eleven-fifty three, we were at Lowe's and had found a store employee to help us track down the equipment, along with their suggestion of a converter for the gas-line coming off the cap and going to the stove.

Just another hurdle in getting the job done.

It was twelve-thirty before we had the new gas cap on the line and a gas converter going to the stove.

The job was done. We had followed everyone's advice and had not blown ourselves up in the process. I was pretty proud of us. We had just worked through a minor emergency together without major fussing.

Blair had to leave a message with Just Gas to come back as soon as possible to turn the gas back on.

It was well past my bedtime. I hadn't turned into a pumpkin. But it was going to get awfully cold out in the pumpkin patch.

The thermometer on the wall read fifty.

We left the taps running on all the faucets. Dressed in pullovers and two pairs of pajama bottoms and socks. We covered up with two quilts and a fleece throw.

We rolled up into fetal positions and huddled close. Not for intimacy. Just to keep warm.

In the morning, the thermometer still registered fifty, this time with a small snow-flake icon. I could see my breath. It was way colder than fifty.

At least, with leaving the taps running our pipes hadn't burst. One emergency at a time, plese.

I took a quick sponge bath with a wash cloth in very cold water before leaving for work. Even with my business casual clothes on, my flesh was goosed. I would have to warm up in the car.

I was so ready for heat.

Just Gas had called back with a late morning turn-on time. It would take a couple of hours for the house to heat back up, so Blair was prepared to keep her kerchief on, gloves, too.

As I left Blair asked if there was anything special I wanted to eat.

"Fudge," I answered in hope.

She rolled her eyes in response. To her, it was tantamount to a curse word.

I could not get warm enough. The radiant heat in the Stratus unthawed my toes. The Metro cars were warm and chock full of bodies. And it was roasting at work— so dry that static electrical charges grew in each cubicle.

I was never so happy to be back at work.

Just for the warmth.

Coming from in cubic inch vent sized air.

Not from the smiles or hearts of my co-workers.

Even if it was numbing-mindfully boring.

Two days back and I was caught up with my back log of work.

Back in the groove of auto-pilot.

Back in the clutches of looking at people's credit scores, deciding whose line of credit got shut down.

Back in a routine of chained down predictability.

Looking at accounts on two different computer screens.

Looking at a snap-shot of people's lives through the credit lens.

I hurt my own feelings by looking up my personal FICO score. It was headed south to a "poor" rating. If I could look it up and sense a red flag, some bill collector working somewhere for the bank was probably doing the same. It wouldn't take much for a supervisor to call my supervisor and then the bank might encourage me to seek out a different situation for gainful employment.

I figured it was just a matter of time until the hammer came down.

The hum-drum of my unstimulating job did much better than any pharmaceutical cocktail. I had the fear of being found out for high debt lurking in the back of my mind. I made sure to keep my wrists hidden by pulling my sleeves down at all times, especially when someone walked by my cubicle to hand me yet another file of a client hoping to cruise through Christmas credit with bleeding credit.

It was a lesson I'd learned long ago at the bank: keep your head down and hold your breath.

Lexapro kept my synapses stable. What I feared hadn't come true. Yet.

The disruption came when Dad sent me an email, reminding me of my promise to return all borrowed furniture forthwith. And be even more forthwither about paying him back every cent I'd borrowed (or wasted) over the years. He even gave me an estimated balance, along with condemning mistakes from my past of everytime I had failed his parental advice and shown scorn to his care.

But his email only stoked the fires beyond the wall of ice. Why not give him what he wanted? Not of some filial obligation, but out of spite.

If he wanted to get mad, I could get mad right back and chuck some stones from out of my heart.

It would take a single 10x16 moving van to fit all their belongings. It would require a dolly (which was extra if I broke the tag to use it). I would either have to do it on a late evening or the weekend given my current schedule but, instead of caroling, I could roll up and deliver the furniture in their front yard on a cold winter's night.

As for the money, I could get a personal loan and write them a check and put it in the mail.

That would show him.

Shut him up for awhile.

Only thing was, after looking at my FICO score, getting approved for a personal loan was doubtful and if I could get money to pay back my dad then I also needed to pay the other creditors.

Just more stones around my neck.

What was the trade off of getting my dad off my back?

Losing my family forever so that things could work out for Blair and I?

Someone had once said that love was "friendship set on fire."

So far, mine and Blair's love had burned ourselves, my back account, my parents, and was now in danger of engulfing the house.

Someone, far wiser than the average bear, had also once said a love could become "a funeral pyre."

And what fed a funeral pyre? Dead bodies.

I was stupid enough and vain enough at this point to believe I still had control over this fire. But too many of us were getting too close to the flame. Too many were holding red hot coals to our chest as our skin smoldered away.

What I needed was peace.

To just give peace a chance.

But just like that song set on a Christmas morning during the Civil war when the author heard the bells on Christmas Day, there was "no peace on earth."

We didn't want peace. We wanted what we wanted. More gifts wrapped in pretty paper and bows, thinking that would change the stones in our heart to baby-soft new skin.

We were buying ourselves off with cheap and hollow gifts.

Now I knew what Bud C. meant by saying, "Goodwill to me."

He meant for himself and screw everyone else.

There was no "me" in Christmas.

Sometime in the afternoon stretch before four o'clock announced quitting time, my unchallenged brain had unconsciously scrawled out the word CHRISTMAS on a sticky-note. Then, it had written had anagrams.

Christ

Mass

Star

Harm

Rash

Chasm

Sham

Trash

It's always hard to look busy in the last forty-five minutes of the work day. Our minds were open ledger books to read and shut at will as we tidied and cleaned our cubicles. We had one eye on the clock. Watching the small hand getting closer to touching four. Ready to hit the door at the appointed time. Four o'clock.

The most daring souls slipped the chain at their desk and snuck out the door by three-fifty-five. Such impudence! Yet they had it all pre-arranged. They justified shaving off a few minutes at the end of the day with the promise of being there all the earlier the next morning.

Such ill-use of the boss' generosity!

I played the good employee and waited until the big hand touched the twelve straight up and the little hand scraped the four.

Then I made good my escape.

I left the Tower. Walked downtown to the underground Metro station. Rode it all the way to the station near Highway 15.

Got into the Stratus and drove it back to 2112 Springhill Drive.

The thermometer read seventy-eight.

It was boiling.

Blair still complained of being cold, but she said the Just Gas man had promised to move the turn-on fee to next month's bill.

Glad tidings of comfort and joy!

I had just enough time to swallow down a peanut butter and jelly sandwich and chase it with barely stirred chocolate milk before heading out the door to the Our Lady's ancillary entrance, where the next group session was to meet in less than thirty minutes.

Blair pestered me with having the car to driving to her mother's. She didn't like not having a car. It was a sore subject.

We weren't married, so I didn't owe her a better car than she had. If she wanted a car, it was up to her to get a car.

She pestered that she'd been inside all day. Yesterday, too. She wanted to go to her mother's and plan Christmas.

I suggested she could make some Christmas cookies to bring back to 2112 Springhill Drive. This week she and her mother were talking.   Come Christmas, it was anyone's guess.

Also, her son was over there and she wanted to spend some time with him and find out what he wanted for Christmas.

Where might any of us be come Christmas day?

Just from within my little Kelter Ward C group, I could think of a few that might be alone come Christmas Day—would Lizzie B. find warm shelter? Would Buddy C. have a jacket or be so tweaked he wouldn't feel the frostbite in his extremities? Would Cathy D. want to come out of her room to spend time with her family?

Christmas could bring a lot of stress.

Was that what Christmas was about? Stressing out to get peace? Or was it our expectations at work?

In the end, I let Blair drive me to the ancillary entrance to the Hope, Inc Counselors offices behind Kelter Ward C. I got out and she drove off in my car.

How quiet this side of the building was compared to the endless stream of trauma at the ER on the other side. How dark the face of the building was except for the parking lot lamp. Five floors of drawn windows. The sleepy utility corridor led to an after-hours front room with light beckoning from behind partially closed venenitan blinds.

In the twilight, in the evening, in the black and dark night, there was a light.

A glimmer of hope.

Somebody was waiting.

Like it or not. This was home for the next two hours.

Tonight was session number two.

There were still eleven days and over twenty-four hours left of therapy. Seven days with the main group. Two nights at a twelve step program. Wednesday being the suggested night. Tomorrow in fact.

After all those days were done and our logged hour sheets turned in, we would have one final eleventh meeting with the main support group before being released out of the program. Counting the four weekend days where we didn't meet, that put our last session on December 23rd.

That was cutting it very fine indeed.

Not a of lot time to schedule more shopping.

Not that I had a lot of disposable income for gifts this year anyway.

And not that everyone was expecting a gift from me anyway.

And just how many would I be getting from anyone else?

Just a few days ago, my own life had seemed disposable. I hadn't thought it very much as a gift. I hadn't had peace or even paraphrasing Buddy C., I sure didn't have much goodwill towards myself.

-8- "Oh, Bring Us Some Figgy Pudding, and Bring It Right Here"

And it was not lost on me that I had loaned Blair my car to visit her mother, who was the guardian of her son, who wanted little to do with Blair, while my own parents wanted nothing to do with me because I was in a relationship with Blair. And I was having this epiphany while taking meds to deal with my depression over being in a dysfunctional relationship while attending a meeting on how to cope with being dysfunctional.

It was easier to shove all those thoughts and feelings away behind the Floydian wall of ice. Even if that wall was beginning to sweat and shrink.

Grandpa's favorite phrase of "You better get your mind right" no longer had any meaning.

What needed examining was my heart.

Paul D. led the session tonight. He stood tall and lean with a graying pony tail. A drooping mustache and whistled through his bridgework.

"An addict is only going to give up when they've hit rock bottom," he said. "And that's different for every person. Now, how do you know when you've hit rock bottom? When you realize you've got nothing left to lose. Including your life. And in some cases addicts hit rock bottom but they don't get back up. They end up on a slab. 'Cause they lost the more important thing. Their life."

"Man, I've OD'd before. Just like sleepin'. I ain't scared of dying," croaked Thad G.

"I came out of my room one Christmas Eve to find my dad turning blue on the couch with a needle in his arm. He was OD'ing right in front me. So, I called the paramedics. They juiced him twice. But he kept flat-lining. So, they jabbed him with a shot of adrenaline straight to his heart. It was the only thing that brought him back. They said he probably died for a couple of minutes," Hannah said as the checks on her blanched face burned to red cheeks and her eyes weeped with the memory.

"Man, I was pronounced dead and taken down to the morgue of this very hospital. I scared the crap out of the attendant when I sat up and asked for a glass of water," Thad bragged.

That would have impressed my dad, given his threshold to meet in order to be declared a miracle. He probably would have even put ice in Thad's glass.

"That's cutting it too close," Ja-Rod said. "You must have seen or heard something."

"Man, there ain't nothing out there after you die," Thad argued.

"Then you really didn't die," Everett P. declared. "The brain doesn't shut down until about ten minutes after the heart. That's a proven fact."

"There's been people who come back from the dead after being dead all the time," Hannah said.

"Then what's the record? Cuz I beat it," Thad said.

"The American record is seventeen hours set just a few years ago. The woman was dead for thirty minutes. Put on life support for seventeen hours with no brain activity. But when they took it off, she resuscitated and went on home," Sandy L. said as she came into the room.

She might have been there but only as an observer as Paul D. had done last night. Perhaps he and Sandy took turns.

"But there's an even longer record. A woman skiing in Norway had an accident and fell through the ice while skiing on a frozen river. Only her feet and skis were above the ice. She was under it for over eighty minutes before they could get her out. She wasn't breathing and they couldn't resuscitate her. They recorded her body temperature at 56.7 Farhenheit. They had to take her blood out of her body and warm it back up before pumping it back in. After about ten hours, they got a heartbeat. They think that the prior CPR put enough oxygen in her brain to keep her going. She was on a breathing machine for thirty-five days and it took about a month to get her stomach and kidneys working right. At first, she was paralyzed but she regained complete movement," Sandy L. said.

Nobody said a word. To refute or rebut. Or redirect.

So I did, "That's not the record. The longest record was when Lazarus was dead for four days before Jesus called him out of the tomb. By name."

"Praise God," Ja-Rod said. "Jesus, the only One who raised Himself up from the dead. Said He'd do it and He did."

Thad G. raspberried, "Man, there ain't Jesus gonna come from the sky. I tell ya, I didn't see nothing. I didn't hear nothing. Cuz I was stone cold dead."

"Apparently not, Thad," Paul D. said. Like most counselors I had met, he was a good listener and often asked questions before giving any advice. But this time, he put the hammer down. "I think you missed the point. It's about how long you stay dead, not how many times you die. Sooner or later, you keep rolling the dice when trying to kill yourself and you're going to come up a winner. Only you'll be a loser because you've lost your life. We all got it backwards here. We keep pushing the envelope on death when we should be diving deeper into life. Death won't give meaning to your life. It'll be the end of it.

"Thank you Justin for bringing up the Lazarus example. Jesus proved a point by raising a man who been dead for four days. There was no way anyone could say that Lazarus was not completely dead. Now, would you to describe your own recent experience, Justin?"

Everyone looked at me. I felt a little embarrassed. But wasn't the point of these group sessions to admit the truth and learn how to deal with it?

"I took a handful of my ex-wife's Darvacet and tried to cut my wrists. But my ex-wife found me and called the EMTs. They brought me back in the ambulance. They said I had been dead for five minutes, at least, probably longer than that," I said with everyone watching me except for Thad G. "And I did see stuff. Strange stuff. And I kept seeing strange after I came back. But I haven't told anyone that. Not even my ex-wife. And I'd really not like to get into who I've be seeing."

"Amen! Amen!" Ja-Rod shook like a bowl of jelly and tapped his index finger at me while he laughed with joy. "You been touched, my man. You been touched."

"Nothin's touched you. There ain't nothin' after death to touch. And life has nothin' here that you can touch. What's the difference?" Thad dared to argue. He seemed past the point of wanting to be proved wrong. He seemed to biding his time until he would be proved right.

But we weren't "here to fix each other."

If Thad G. was right, then nothing would be waiting for me. It seemed an easy thing to do: to lie down and close my eyes and give up the ghost, or be gathered to my grandfather or Boz and Randle McMurtry or whoever would claim me. Yet, other stones had been kicked up in my heart.

Something was watching me when I was in the house.

Something that had given a banshee wail.

Something definite that I didn't want to face.

Something that had yet to step out of the shadows to be named.

Something powered by guilt that didn't want to forgive.

This time it was Sandy L. who approached Thad G. and drew him outside.

Paul D. continued, "The first step after hitting rock bottom is wantin' to let go of the addiction. And realize it's a disease. It what's been draggin' you down. Gettin' you nowhere. Slowly killin' you.

"'Cause you're no longer in control. The addiction is. And it doesn't care a thing about you. It's like a virus. A slow burn or a quick burn, depending upon the chemical abuse. It wants to live through you but in doing so, it uses up. In the end, it will burn you to ashes. Addiction equals death. It does not give life, it takes it

"Let's take a minute and go around the room and tell each other when our last high was. When was the last time you got high and what did you use," he said. "I'll start. The last time I was high, I got drunk from Kentucky Ten High. I got into a huge fight with my wife. Or at least so she says. I don't remember. I woke up in the drunk tank. She'd called the cops on me. Said I went after her with a knife. I don't remember a thing."

Hannah went next. "Well, the last time was today." All our heads turned at that.

Paul D. stepped in. "I should explain that I am the therapist for Hannah's family. Both her and her dad. Hannah, explain your addiction."

"I take Xanex. More than I should," she admitted.

"And the doctor said you just can't stop completely, right?" Paul D. said.

Hannah nodded. "It might kill me."

"Because it's so addictive. You have to gradually wean yourself off before you can start a clean detox," he said.

She nodded. "I'm down to four a day now. I don't feel right without."

"Wow," Paul D. said. "Four? What was your usual intake?"

"Six? Eight? I'd do a whole bar in a day if I could," she smiled sheepishly. "I am the Xanex queen."

"Well, I never done pills until I started this job," Everett said. "Nothing else can get me through. Can't drink or blow weed on the job. Or on lunch even if I sat out it the cars. If I got sleepy or my joints would start hurtin' I'd just pop a pill. We all did. Last time was two weeks ago. Then I got popped. Now I'm hurtin' and tired all the time. Don't know if I can keep up. Might be better just to get fired so I don't have to deal with this crap. But then they'd turn me in and I'd have a possession charge."

"I done told 'bout my last time. 'Xcept it's gonna be my last time ever," Ja-Rod said. "When I got back, my old lady had gathered up all my stuff—pipes and spoon and baggies. She'd found it all, every stash. Including some rocks that I had been savin'. She said, 'Do you want

this or do you want me? Better yet, do you want this to
be your future 'cuz I won't be in your future if you choose
this stuff. So, whatcha gonna do?'

"I went and got some charcoal lighter fluid and my
favorite lighter. It was silver chromed plated. With a
pull-back cap. It had a skull face wearing a top hat over
dreads and a bling necklace. It had sunglasses over the
left eye but the right was this sickly yellow. All its teeth
were gold but not well polished like it had lost its luster.
Now in the hat band was a hand of five cards. All the
aces: heart, clubs, diamond, and spades. But the last card
was a joker. That was the name on the lighter: 'Joker.'
That was my clubbin' name. My old gang name. 'Joker.'
Well, the joke had been on me the whole time and this
time I was done with it.

"I threw all that junk in the waste basket. Soaked it
good with the charcoal lighter. Then I put the joker
lighter to it. When the flames got big, the last thing I did
was keep the flame on the lighter and drop it in the waste
basket. There ain't no goin' back. I don't want to be
Joker no more. I wanna be me. Ja-Rod Devonye W. Jr.
And I want there to be a third but I don't want him to
have nothin' to do with drugs."

Since Thad had given us a good idea that tonight
might well be his last high, I was up next.

"The last time was…two weeks ago. A friend
invited me to go and see the Fixx. They were playing at a
small club in downtown St. Louis," I started. I saw blanks
looks in the circle. "They were an eighties' band. Big hit
was 'One Thing Leads to Another.'" That turned on
some lights. "Anyway, this club was one I used to play in
with my band. They knew me. I knew them. Which
meant I could drink for free.

"I remember getting there. The band started playing. And we started drinking. And I don't remember anything after that. I couldn't tell you one song they played that night or who I saw or what I said," I said. "The next thing I remembered I was driving up the wrong exit ramp on my way home."

Paul nodded. "Now the next question. How old were each of you when you started using?"

I went first this time, "Thirteen."

"Ten," Everett said.

"Same," Ja-Rod said.

"Seven? Maybe six?" Hannah queried herself. "I don't remember."

I wondered what age Thad had started.

"We can help you. But only if you want to be helped. And we can only help you with the problems that you are willing to admit you need help with. So, whatever you hold back won't get fixed," Paul D. said.

Sandy L. led Thad back in. His face was ashen. The bags under his eyes darker than before. Skin drawn tight over the skeleton of his face. He was sick. Very sick.

"Now in order to fix something, like changing a habit or behavior, we have to replace it with something else. We have to replace your addiction with recovery. All these habits you've developed over the years to deal with your addictions have to be replaced with positive growth if you want to recover," Paul D. said.

"But there's one thing extra. One ingredient more important than all the others. You gotta have a faith system. You gotta believe in something bigger than yourself. Because it's you that's got a problem and how can you help yourself get better and stay better? You can't. You can't do it alone."

Sandy L., who had been sitting back as an observer while letting Paul D. have a crack at the whip, spoke up. "It doesn't matter if you believe in a higher power or not. You will have a greater chance of success at recovery if you have some kind of belief system.

"Officially Hope Counselors, Inc. can't talk of faith. Even if Our Lady does own this building. This program is being funded by the government and they demand separation of church and state. Which means if we want to use their federal money stamped with 'In God We Trust' then we can't say 'In God We Trust' at any time during our sessions because that is a violation of inalienable genetic civil rights. Who made the inalienable rights inalienable? If they are genetic then why do we need the government to tell us our rights? These are things the government will not let be discussed under the geas of free speech."

I piped up, "James Madison said: 'But what is government itself but the greatest of all reflections on human nature? If men were angels, no government would be necessary.'"

The problem was not in our 'stars' or our 'bars' or in our 'utopian ideas.' Yes, all these are flawed. Because the problem is in our hearts. Our hearts are flawed and full of flawed stones from the start. And sooner or later, our actions will reflect that.

My higher power was the Godhead: Father, Son, and Holy Ghost. All three together at once and separate. Mind, body, and spirit. Water, ice, and steam. Light, life, and love.

When I was about three, I had my first God moment. I had grown up in a church were my dad was the music leader. It was an old white board chapel with stain glass windows and a balcony and a steeple with a bell.

I was up in the balcony while the congregation was singing and my Dad leading the music. The light came through the stain glass windows streaming. And I felt something outside of me. All around me. Making me aware of its reality. There was light, life, and love. There was peace.

Eternity was real. Heaven was real. It was just beyond my fingertips. All that separated me from it was a thin veil. I wanted to pull it back and get more than just this glimpse.

And I realized this moment would echo on in eternity forever.

The rest of church going was nothing like that. When you're raised Southern Baptist as a kid, it's to become a Sunday schooled, hymn turnin', Bible thumpin', dunked three times, back row sinnin', backward slidin', pass the collection plate, hallelujah-in', He saved me, goin twice on Sundays, once on Wednesdays, every night of the revival, prayin', singin', sittin', shoutin', jump down turn around can I get an amen Southern Baptist.

Nobody but nobody wants to hear of God actually showing up. Nobody is ready to deal with it.

But sometimes I wondered as that experience got further and further away every day if God had really showed himself. I hadn't seen him. Nobody has as God is spirit. Not even Moses who had to hide his face in the cleft of the rock when God passed by.

Only Jesus has seen the Father. Jesus was God in the flesh. And look what the religious leaders did to Him.

I've heard people whine if there was really a God then why doesn't He show Himself? Jesus showed up as God and whenever He would do some miracles, the critics would say, it He was drunk or demon possessed or challenge, Him on their finer points of law so when He got too popular and made them look bad, they conspired to Hill him.

People don't want God. They might say they do. But they say a lot of things. And do just the opposite.

Not if but when God decides to show up in His full glory, there will be no hiding from Him. There'll be no chance to hire a lawyer and file an appeal at the Supreme Court, or to vote on a U.N. resolution condemning God's anti-authoritarian action. God is the final supreme authority. Everyone answers to Him.

It's only when there's nothing left but God. When people have come to an end of themselves. When they admit everything they've ever done or known was just vanity and pride.

When they've hit rock bottom.

Then they'll call out to God. He'll never seem more real as when He can be someone's salvation.

We think there is this thing called free-will. To go where we want. Do what we want. Whenever we want.

O bring us our figgy pudding and bring it right here.

What does free-will have anything to do with God being able to save me? How much control do I have in the saving process? Who did the saving and why?

Not me. It was Jesus. When He climbed up on the cross. He came to die for all sinners to fulfill the law that requires a shedding of blood to cover sins. Also, it was love that kept Him on the cross for love covers a multitude of sins.

Jesus came to be born, not as a king in a palace but as a servant obedient unto death in a manger.

God's peace unto earth. God's grace unto man.

Sometimes I don't get it.

But I do know this. There are only two kinds of problems. Those we cause for ourselves and those that others cause for us.

So, it was a string of bad decisions that had gotten me here.

Who had made me get married to two women who I thought I could change thinking I would help them by changing them? Who made me get drunk time and time again? Who had made listen to sermon after sermon by a pastor or my dad? Who made me not want to read the Bible or not ask questions about it? Who made me choose not to listen to my parents or God? Nobody's fault but mine.

It was time to stop making bad decisions.

It was time to question my decisions before I made them.

It was time to ask just who I was listening to when I had a question.

I looked forward to coming back Thursday night. But what was I going to do about tomorrow night, Wednesday?

As Sandy L. signed our log sheets, she asked each that very question.

"I guess I'll go to that New Hearts meeting," I said.

Sandy L. smiled and nodded in approval.

Then I left and got in my Stratus that Blair had waiting by the front door.

I was shocked to see Blair sucking down an ash cherry on a cigarette.

"So, that's what you do at your Mom's? Smoke cigarettes? Whose bright idea was that?" I asked.

Blair gave a non-challant shrug and tried to tap ash out the driver's window with a cultured aplomb that was just affected clumsiness.

"It'll help keep weight off me since I'm not working," Blair said.

"'Not working' as in intending to work or not planning to work?" I asked.

"I'm not able to work. My mother wants me to try for disability. Since you're not going to take care of me," Blair said as she drove us home.

That was their big plan? I shouldn't feel guilty about that. It wasn't my fault she would have to try for disability. I couldn't take care of Blair, plus the house, plus the utilities, plus all the car payment, plus all the unsecured debt from impulsive needs.

That might sound callous. But that was the Floydian wall around my stony heart at work. Not that Blair respected boundaries and wasn't above trying to lob a Molotov cocktail over the wall to fire-bomb my heart.

"What else were you guys up to?" I dared to ask.

Blair pulled out some scratch-off cards. "We've been playing some scratch-off cards. My mom won a hundred and I won twenty."

"How much did you spend before you won?" I asked.

"Thirty," Blair said in ignominy.

"So, you're still ten in the hole," I said.

"You gotta spend a little to make a little. But you might win big," she said.

"So, you're gonna use your unemployment money to buy cigarettes to lose weight, and to play lotto to get rich," I said.

My first job at America's Bank had been in the mailroom where I signed in and signed out packages for different departments and companies. This was back in the days when people had their paper checks cleared and paid out. There had been a member of a family-owned messenger service who had won big at Casino Queen. By "big", I meant well over a hundred thousand dollars on a payout from a one-armed bandit quarter machine. His modus operandi was to pump in about a hundred quarters at a time on a given machine and then try a different one. Then he'd take a break and watch which machines people were pumping quarters into. He figured a machine would pay off when it was set for a certain dollar amount to be put in. And he guessed right. There was no telling how much money he spent to get the hundred thousand, but the casino took about twenty-five percent off the top for the IRS and there was still more taxes to give.

"Did you get to talk to your son?" I asked.

Blair looked down to the left. "Oh, yeah. It was nice to catch up. He told me all about his school. Only…only he doesn't want you over for Christmas."

Here all this time, Blair had been pushing me to get my parents to accept us being back together and now, her own son was throwing a red flag.

"Don't worry. I'll get my mother to ask you over. It'll happen," she said.

I shook my head.

"What?" she asked as she butted and threw the spent cigarette out the window.

"I can't believe I let you drive my car when you're not insured on it," I said. "It's not a good idea."

"So, call them up and add me," Blair smiled. "Or we can make it even more official and legal and I'll get an engagement ring in my stocking for Christmas."

She even tapped her left ring finger with her right index finger. It was like she thought all our troubles would go away if I consented to marry her again.

"Right now, the only thing I got to put in your stocking is a bill," I said. "I haven't bought anyone squat."

It was odd to be cast as the villain in her family's eyes. What had they lost? Money or appliances? "If your family doesn't want me over, I'll just stay home for Christmas."

"Nonsense. I'll get them to let you come over. They're not like your family," Blair said. "Your family'll have to get over being mad at me if they ever want to talk to you again. Besides, that's not being very Christian

No, my family would be having Christmas fudge on Christmas Eve.

"Can we make some fudge tonight? I'm really wanting some," I pleaded.

Blair put me off, "Honey, I don't know how to make fudge. Can't we just buy a refrigerated roll and bake some cookies quick? I'm tired from dealing with my mother."

"Ok," I said. I had let Blair buy me off cheap again.

We stopped by Best-Mart, and after bartering, decided on a roll of chocolate chip cookies. Then we got home, turned on the gas oven and broke apart the pre-portioned chunks onto a cooking sheet.

But it wasn't the same as home-made. They tasted like chocolate chip cookies but for only a half second. Then the taste went bland.

That's what I got for being talked out of what I wanted.

-9- Accepting Hardships As the Pathway To Peace.

Tuesday night was the same as every other night since I'd been back from Kelter Ward C: we watched Everybody Loves Raymond and laughed at the younger adult characters blaming all their problems on their dysfunctional parents. Then I drifted off to sleep on my pre-marital couch, which had become Blair's post-divorce property while she scurried back to sleep on her post-divorce bed.

The next day I repeated yesterday's arrival: Driving to park at the Metro station, riding the Metro to walk from Union Station to the bank building, standing in an elevator going up to sit down at a cubicle.

There was a numbing rhythm to it. Just not much inspiration. Not so much a comfort as a blanket that smothered you.

Work was better than Lexapro in that sense.

My job at America's Bank was a living. Just not much of an existence.

Then at four, I repeated the arrival process in reverse for the departure. I was getting into a new schedule by having to be somewhere every hour of the day and most of the night.

When Blair asked if I was staying home tonight since I didn't have a group session, I waved my log sheet.

"So, where are you headed tonight?" she asked.

"New Hearts Recovery at New Springs Church," I said. "What do you have planned?"

"Do you honestly want to know what will be the highlight of my evening?" Blair said. "Since, I don't have a car, I'll have to walk to Gas-mart to get a fresh pack of cigarettes and some scratch-off cards."

"Well, maybe you'll win enough to buy a new car. Then you can pay the game tax and the sales tax on the car," I said as we kissed. "Please smoke outside."

"Oh, I forget," she said. "It's *your* house."

"Yes, it is," I nodded.

New Springs Church was a pre-fab metal building with no cross or Christian symbols at all. The front atrium didn't like much different than the Hope Counselor's offices.

There was a sign on the door. A message printed inside an open heart that had a stake coming out ot the bottom ventricles with two crossbeams to take the weight of the heart. **"NEW HEART RECOVERY. WEDNESDAY MEETING. DINNER 6 PM. LARGE GROUP 7 PM. SMALL GROUP MEETINGS 8 PM. RECOVERY STARTS HERE. IN THE HEART."**

It was five-fifty-five.

A short man with a round belly opened the door for me. He was dressed in faded Levi blue jeans, gray Brooks running shoes with dark blue trim, a grey and blue Silver Dollar Hoodie. His beard was salt and pepper, his hair short and black, teased up and then smoothed down.

"Hello, I'm Jeff. A born-again believer who's overcome addiction to alcohol, depression, and suicide ideation. Welcome," the man called Jeff said. He even wore a name tag that said, *HELLO, I AM JEFF.*

The man called Jeff directed me to a welcoming table where other name tags and a magic marker lay alongside a brochure about the night's meeting and various other tracts in different colors: orange, white, green, red, blue, pink, yellow, black, purple, bronze, silver, and gold. Twelve in all. And each bore the same series label: *THE MASTER'S STEPS*. With each step being a different color.

I wrote *JUSTIN* after the *HELLO, I AM…* and put the name tag on my chest. There were about sixty other people present. Just what was the percentage of people who were in need of recovery? I answered myself with another question, *Just how many people did Jesus die for?*

From what I could see, this church building was one large open room. Food had been set out on two folding tables at this end. Beside them were ten circular tables. Beyond them were a hundred folding chairs set in ten rows of ten chairs broken in two sections with room to walk down the middle. Placed in front of the chairs was a podium with a smaller table beside it that held a box.

Most people, besides the man called Jeff, were seated at the tables or in the back rows.

Two ladies prepped and laid out the food. One table with cups, plates, and napkins, a bowl of ice, various liters of sodas and bottled water. The other with a large casserole dish of something with cheese and shredded chicken, bags of various potato chip flavors, and packages of sandwich cookies.

A man near the podium asked one of the preppers to bless the food and then everyone lined up.

As I partook of the spread the man approached me. He was six foot by six. A rather large lad. He had a long salt and pepper goatee and long thinning white hair. He wore black boots, black jeans, a black Pantera concert shirt, a black sleeveless leather vest. A silver chain linked his wallet to his black belt. The buckle was a championship style banner with gold printed lettering: **KING JESUS. REIGNS ETERNAL.**

As he came towards me, he stuck out a Popeye thick forearm that bore the inked face of Bela Lugosi as Frankenstein's monster. And on the other Popeye styled forearm was the face of Lon Chaney, Jr done up as the Wolfman. Two tragic hero counterparts who were also adversaries.

The only thing not black on his habiliments was the name tag. *HELLO, MY NAME IS LARRY.*

"Hello, my name is Larry. I am a grateful believer who has overcome abuse and suicide ideation and cutting," said the man called Larry.

"Hello, I am Justin. I am a believer, but in the Neil Diamond sense, and I am just overcome by being here," I said taking his hand and taking in the intricacy of his ink.

"Cool, man, that's so cool," Larry said and let go of my hand.

"Not many people prefer Bela Lugosi as Frankenstein," I said. "But there's only one Wolfman."

"'*Frankenstein Meets the Wolfman.*' A personal fave. One man cursed. One creature hated. Yet, they still can't or won't help each other. Plus, the script was written by Curt Siodmak. An out and out classic," Larry said. "Do you have a favorite old horror film?"

"Sure, '*Abbott and Costello Meet Frankenstein.*' It's got all of the classic Universal monsters and it succeeded in reviving one thing at least," I said.

"What's that?" Larry asked.

"Abbott and Costello's careers," I said.

Larry belly laughed. "It's got *three* of the classic Universal monsters. It's missing the Mummy."

I thought for a minute. "That was their penultimate film, '*Abbott and Costello Meet the Mummy.*'"

Larry laughed again. "True, true."

An older lady walked over. She had no make-up on besides her smile. And that was all she needed. She had iron-cropped hair clipped short and wore a name tag that read HELLO, MY NAME IS SHIRLEY.

"Hello, my name is Shirley. I am a blessed believer saved by faith and covered by the Savior's blood that's helped me overcome an abusive relationship and addiction to pain killers and suicide ideation," the woman called Shirley said.

"Surely, you must be," I said taking her hand and giving a slight bow.

As she took her hand away, I beheld a word tattooed in black ink across her wrist: **cont;ue**.

"Attention everyone!," Larry beckoned with Fezziwegian enthusiasm. "Welcome to New Heart Recovery. The best place for recovery. Because recovery starts in the heart. We offer you a safe place among friends. You can have a new healthy heart if you work the recovery steps. And you cannot work your recovery out alone.

"We're thankful for the ladies fixing chicken dorrito casserole, always a crowd favorite. We are ready for our large group meeting. We are having a testimony tonight. Which is better than covering all twelve steps in one night.   Then we encourage everyone to stick around for small groups. We will have both a women's and a men's meeting tonight."

I did not intend to stick around for the small groups just to earn an extra hour. I only needed two hours.

Everyone filtered over to the rows of chairs. Both Larry and Shirley went to the front podium. Larry sat down to play acoustic guitar to "Lord, I Need You" while Shirley got a microphone for them both to sing.

The song was about being humble and acknowledging needing the Lord every hour every day. Everyone seemed to know it and sang along. It was infectious.

Then he did the chips and coins. First, anyone whose first time it was to visit received an orange chip. I went forward to collect one along with another younger man about the size of Thad but without a hoodie over his head so it was Thad as I imagined him with more weight and less meth sores on his face.

The chip was about the size of a half dollar with the New Heart Recovery logo arced over the top. On a banner below was the inscription "Isaiah 36:26." On the back it read, "Welcome!" over the top and "Come Back Again!" on the bottom banner.

There were white chips given for being 30 days clean. A green one for 60 days. And a red one for 90 days. Then a blue one for six months.

Then they gave out gold coins for one year clean and two years clean. Larry gave Shirley a one year coin and Shirley gave Larry a two year coin. Larry said he had been at a national New Hearts Recovery meeting in Austin, Texas, where it had started, and saw a founding member get a twenty-five year clean coin.

Next, Shirley came up to do prayer requests. During the meal, she had made a circuit of the round tables getting people to write down their requests. Now she read them aloud.

"Our God is big enough for any problem. If He knows when a sparrow falls to the ground, He knows how to take care of us.   God's just waiting for us to call on Him. We work our recovery one step at time. One need at a time. One prayer at a time. One surrender a time. Heavenly Father, we lift up all these requests to you and know You will move in these people's lives so that they know it's Your healing hand at work and will give You the glory. Amen."

Larry came back up next to explain the program. "Here at New Heart Recovery we use Isaiah 36:26 as our anchor verse. *'I will give you a new heart and put a new spirit within you; I will take the heart of stone out of your flesh and give you a heart of flesh.'*

Larry had Shirley show the google slide for each step as he led everyone in a recitation over the twelve steps using "FLESHY HEARTS" as an anacronym.

1. For I am powerless to control my life and it has become unmanageable.
2. Leaning on God and believing that He exists and that only He has the power to help me recover.
3. Eagerly chose to submit all my will and life to the care and control of Christ.
4. Searched myself in order to make a list of all my wrongdoings and faults
5. Having done so, I have confessed all my wrong doings to God, myself, and another person
6. Yielded over my faults to God in submission
7. Humbly ask for God to remove all my shortcomings

8. Earnestly forgive those who have hurt me and offer amends to all those whom I have hurt
9. And make direct amends when possible unless when to do would cause harm
10. Repent of any wrongdoings after I promptly admit them
11. Take the time daily for meditation in the Word and with prayer to seek God's will and to choose to follow His Will.
12. Send me and use me to give my testimony to others."

Larry smiled and said, "Amen." Which was followed by others saying, "Amen."

"And now Shirley has consented to giving us her testimony. If any of you hadn't heard it before, it is so, so powerful," Larry said and having introduced her, stepped away from the podium.

Shirley came back to the podium in slow steps and took a piece of notebook paper from her back pocket that had been folded over several times. I could see that she had written very long paragraphs in cursive but before she could read it, she had smooth it out with the palms of her hands. She tittered like a school girl.

"Hello, my name is Shirley," she said and paused as Larry led everyone in a reply of "Hello, Shirley!" Then she continued, "I am a blessed believer saved by faith and covered by the Savior's blood that's helped me overcome an abusive relationship and addiction to pain killers and suicide ideation. I always thought that I was a good person and was good enough to get me into Heaven. And I also thought my being good meant that it covered whatever bad things my kids might do, can I get an amen?

"I'm a nester and I always wanted a family to take care of. But the man I married just liked to spend money on beer and to sit in a bar all night after working all day. He would come home and hit the kids and when I got between them he would hit me before he'd pass out for the night. He wasn't taking care of us. He was making us miserable.

"I made excuses for his drinking and blamed myself for his hitting the kids and even me. But when I started getting migraines so bad they would about make me blind, the doctor put me on hydrocodone. The more helpless I felt, the more hydrocodone I took, until I would be zoned out when my husband got home. I couldn't protect my kids which made me feel more guilty and I'd take even more hydrocodone which made me feel even more guilty.

"I was in a cycle of misery. And I thought the only way out was just to take a few extra hydrocodones so I could go to sleep in peace and never wake up. But then who would take of my babies? My husband sure wouldn't.

"Well, the kids got older and could drive themselves places by now and one night my husband came home drunk, but there was no one for him to beat on. So, he came into my bedroom--we weren't sleeping together anymore—and tried to shake me awake. He pulled me out of bed by my hair and threw me in the bathtub and ran the shower. He said it was my fault the kids didn't wanna stay home or be around him. And said everything was my fault because I was an addict.

"That's when I got mad. Real mad. So, I yelled the reason I had to take hydrocodone and why the kids didn't want to be home was because he drank all the time. Then he hit me. So, I hit him back. Then he took his belt off and whacked on me until I passed out.

"I woke up at Our Lady's, just down the street. I was all bruised up. My husband was in jail. And the kids were in temporary foster care. DHS tried to explain about the FINS they'd had to file.

"The hardest thing was that someone from DHS had to bring my kids in to see me in the hospital and they had to leave with that person. That hurt worse than any of the bruises. I felt so helpless and I asked God that my kids would never be taken from me again."

Here Shirley paused to turn her testimony over and began to read the back. She had read up to this point in a clear voice. Restating the pain and the guilt of a past that could no longer hurt her.

"I had to get a lawyer to file for divorce and DHS was the ad-litem for the kids. It was such a big mess. My now ex-husband refused to see the kids or pay any support and got arrested again. He still may be in jail but wherever he is, I pray he come to know the peace that only Jesus can give.

"One of the ladies from DHS took my kids to a Vacation Bible School. The kids hadn't been anywhere in years, so I thought, why not, as long as I didn't have to go, I still had bruises. But the VBS changed my kids. They came home singing and laughing and smiling. The teachers had given the youngest one a little music cd …" Shirley stopped to compose herself. She hadn't batted an eye when talking about her addiction or abuse. But it was at this moment of something small and beautiful on which her recovery hinged that she couldn't stop from being choked up.

"…so she could learn this one song that she liked a lot. It was a song for kids, but the words were Bible verses. Each day there was a verse for them to remember and a song to teach them the verse." The tears streamed out of her clear, shining eyes as Shirley wiped the corner of her mouth.

"It had a man and a woman singing to a guitar and banjo. Just so beautiful." She sang, as best she could, a little of the melody but was able to phrase every word. "'Come to me, all who labor and are heavy laden, and I will give you rest. Take My yoke upon you, and learn from Me; for I am gentle and lowly in heart, and you will find rest for your souls. For My yoke is easy, and My burden is light.'"

Shirley was overcome. Smiling. Crying. Amazed. Astounded. Happy. Euphoric. "And I thought, if a child could learn verses that way then so could I. So, those were the first Bible verses I ever learned: Matthew 11:28-30. How marvelous is that? Now it's my life verse.

"That was my first God moment. If God could make Himself so real to a child, why couldn't I believe in Him?

"On the last day of VBS, all the families came to see everything the kids had learned. It was so inspiring to see all these kids quoting scripture and singing to Jesus with their child-like faith. Then the preacher came up and gave a short sermon. It was about Hebrews 11:6 'without faith it is impossible to please God; because anyone who comes to Him must believe that He exists and that He rewards those who earnestly seek Him.' And isn't that our first two Master's Steps? Isn't that wonderful?

"God was dealing with me. He knew everything I had done and still He loved me. He had sent his son to die for me and for everyone. But when the preacher gave an invitation, it was my youngest who went forward! And when the preacher invited me to stand beside her, I told him that I wanted to be saved. He was just as shocked as I was. How marvelous is that?

"From that moment, I've known the peace that only Jesus gives. Not peace as the world understands it but the peace that surpasses all understanding. And though I was broken, God has been changing me into what he wants: first a single mother of three saved children, then a grandmother of a little baby girl, and now a mentor to other women who have it worse than I ever did.

"I am here to tell you there is hope. There is recovery. You can have a new heart! Amen? Amen!"

That elicited several amens and handclaps and a standing ovation.

Then Larry came back to share the podium with her and picked up his acoustic guitar so they could sing "Built For Glory" by the Lost Dogs, trading off each verse while singing the chorus together.

Another google slide came up with a prayer on it. Larry and Shirley stood shoulder to shoulder, arm over arm, and led everyone in this final recitation.

"God, grant me the Serenity
To accept the things I cannot change...
Courage to change the things I can,
And Wisdom to know the difference.
Living one day at a time,
Enjoying one moment at a time,
Accepting hardship as the pathway to peace.
Taking, as He did, this sinful world as it is,

Not as I would have it.
Trusting that He will make all things right
if I surrender to His will.
That I may be reasonably happy in this life,
And supremely happy with Him forever in the
next.
Amen."
With that we were dismissed from the large group.

I had heard part of that prayer before. Seen it in
home décor. And as bumper stickers and refrigerator
magnets.

I think it was called the Serenity Prayer.

But I had never heard it in full before.

I decided to stay for the small group session which
was divided into men and women only. It was very much
like a session at Hope Counselors, Inc. It lasted until 8:45
and then the New Hearts Recovery meeting was over.

Shirley signed my log sheet for me and encouraged
me to come back. I took a Master's Step pamphlet for
step one because that seemed the best place to start.
Driving back to 2112 Springhill Drive, I thought about
the music and the testimony and that last prayer.

Accepting hardship as the pathway to peace.

"Honey, the water heater broke," Blair announced
when I stepped out of that peace and through the door
into a world of stress.

I banged the back of the front door with the
against the side closet door that was open, and stepped
over several soaked towels placed over the front rug.
Blair was on her hands and knees inside the closet,
soaking up water with handtowels and sponges that she
rung out into a bucket with dirty brown water.

The water heater was located behind the small vented door and next to it was a bigger closer with a actual door to hold the heater and furnace. Next to that was the corner hallway going down to the bedrooms and bathroom.

Another utility on the blink. The water heater had "broke" as in we were going to be "broke" after having all these utilities fixed.

"I was taking a bath but the water never did get warm. It got ice cold," Blair said. "I got out and put my robe on and happen to come out here to find the front rug soaked and a gallons of water in the utility closet. The bottom of the water heater had rusted out and fallen off. And I've been cleaning this up ever since. How was your meeting?"

"Wonderful," I said bending down to pick up some soaked towels. I was quite sure where to put them, "You ever hear of the Serenity Prayer?"

"God, yes," Blair said as she blotted at puddles. "My grannie used to have it on picture frame in her kitchen. It goes something like *God give me the serenity to accept what I can't change and the strength to change what I can't accept and the wisdom to know the difference.* Is that it?"

"Sounds pretty close. Did you know there's more to it than that?" I asked.

Blair continued to press and blot. This was the most I've seen her at work at something. Evers. "No," she was slow to admit. "How does the rest go?"

"I can't remember. I think it's on this brochure I took," I said and took the two paged Step One pamphlet out of my back pocket. I found it on the back of the second page. So, I read it.

"That's nice," Blair said. "Either we're gonna need more towels or I'll have to ring these out."

"I'll ring these out in the tub. Then throw them in the dryer so we can use them again," I said.

"If we want fresh, dry towels for the morning, we'll be running the washer all night," Blair said.

10-The Twelve Days Of Christmas Trouble

That was now the rhythm of my life.

Trouble coming at me every day.
With no time to delay.
There was no time to think.
No time to hold my breath.
No time to pray.
I was in the middle of the fray.
Morning, noon, and night.
Everything around me was constant motion.
Thirteen days until Christmas.
The closer it got to Christmas, the crazier Christmas got.
Life had become a whirlwind.
Sucking away day thirteen and day twelve.
And then a whirlpool.
Either way, I was at the center.
I couldn't hold onto day eleven or ten.
They went down the drain.
Work no longer was the oasis of boredom it had been when coming back from Kelter Ward C.
In its own way, it was becoming more like Kelter Ward A.

With people stalking back and forth from meeting after meeting. Shufffling across the floor to annoy each other with busywork. Going behind closed doors for a job performance review and taking a beating.

Every year, my department would hire more staff before March but people would start to get laid off in October. We called it Black October. All Soul's Day became Survivor's Day.

This year, no one had gotten laid off in October. We thought we had turned a corner and weathered a storm. Broken a tradition.

Once we got past October, it looked as if everyone would have get a Christmas bonus and have the same job after the New Year's.

Or so we assumed.

Except the fifteenth of December check had pink notices enclosed in some people's envelopes on that final nine day stretch before our Christmas Break.

I was not among them.

But it dampened everyone's mood and the Christmas potluck was more a hugging and goodbying event than a Fezziweg festival. Everyone took their meager paper plates back to their cubicles while keeping their heads down, so as not to be noticed in this now Scrooge-like counting house. No one spoke a whisper.

This Christmas, my only Christmas bonus would be that I would keep my job.

The rocking motion of the Metro's coming and going was the only comfort to lull my disjointed nerves from my unsatisfaction about working at America's Bank.

I headed from the miserly counting house to a boiling crisis on the homefront.

We went from *"There's a gas leak!"*

To *"The water heater broke!"*

To finding out when the heat/air guy came to replace the water heater that "The heater coil is cracked! We'll have to replace it or the furnace will stop working!"

That would mean thousands of dollars for a new unit and the labor to install it. About two months salary. This Christmas, the family fire might be coming from having the stove on and its door open.

The heater was no longer up to code, even if I just put a new coil on it instead of getting a new unit. That meant that I had bought the house with a cracked heater which a house assessor had given thumbs up on.

Day eight my true love gave to me, instead of eight maids a milking--an eight inch hole in the roof of the new addition. As all of the snow and ice from the blizzard started to melt, it didn't run off the roof. It followed gravity to the lowest point by falling straight down the beams and through the ceiling plaster.

This time I came home to *"There's a hole in the roof!"*

I had about thirty minutes to think up a proper plan of action. It would mean even more money, perhaps even more than getting the heater fixed. At this point, I would need half a year's salary just to spend on repairs on a rehabbed house I had occupied for a little over a year.

I was hoping someday Blair and I would be together with my family at Christmas, but circumstances: fate, the Left Hand of God, God's will, were not going to allow it.

In fact, the troubles seemed intent on burying me. Pinning bills like tails on my donkey backside with such accuracy that if Lady Justice was blind then these troubles from the Left Hand of God could see in the twilight, in the evening, in the black and dark night.

I looked from the gallon bucket, half full of dirty water and plaster crumbs, up to the undeniable hole in our ceiling where I could see revealed wet beams. By now, I didn't know which problem was worse. I went and got another gallon bucket as Blair dumped the other out and we put both buckets side by side on top of two towels.

At least, we were working together, I thought.

For whatever that was worth.

We called the heat/air guy to recommend a roofing guy. The heat/air guy said he could help out but he couldn't come until tomorrow, Saturday. Until then, we would have to keep bailing out buckets.

And this was just from the snowmelt runoff. If it was to rain, it would be worse fast.

After that, I had just time to make a ham and cheese sandwich. Then on a split second decision I let Blair drive me to my Friday night group session at our Lady's.

As she smoked a cigarette with one hand to tap the ash out the cracked driver's window and kept the other on the wheel, she explained that her appearance at the court of her Queen Mother was to gain an audience to plead my case for coming to their Christmas family celebration. It all hinged on the whim of her son—he had the final say. He not only may not want me around—since I had no relationship with him whatsoever—he also may want to grind a guilty ax into his mother's back and not want Blair around.

Their family seemed to thrive on holding each other at arm's length, like a loathsome spider in their pinching fingers, making each other beg and plead for mercy, but never fully receiving it, just an extension on judgment so they could keep punishing one another.

She got me to the back side of Our Lady's with about five minutes to spare. I gulped down the last bite of my ham and cheese sandwich before I opened the passenger door. Blair delayed me by brushing crumbs off my turtle neck sweater.

As she leaned forward to kiss me, a young blonde girl walked by the Stratus and flashed the peace sign at me. Blair saw the hand movement and regarded her countenance. As she watched the group member open the glass corridor with narrowed eyes.

Blair took a forefinger off my chest to point it in the girl's wake. "Who's that girl? One of your group?"

She meant Hannah S.

I shrugged.

"I know her. She's gross. Her dad's a junkie. I bet she's hooked on it, too," Blair said.

"'Respect confidentiality: What you hear here, stays here,'" I quoted.

She looked at me. "She's probably whored herself out. She doesn't even wash up for your meetings. That's just gross. I'm glad you're not like that."

"I'm an addict. And all addicts play the same game," I said. "Get high and stay high until you die. And any reason's good enough."

"Oh, right. I forget. When you were in bands you were just rolling in drugs and groupies. Did you have to ply them with drugs to get them to sleep with you?" Blair asked.

"Everyone got tired of being who they were with and thought the grass was greener in someone else's pasture. So, everyone cheated on everyone else. Criss-crossing tracks behind each other's backs. All you had to do was bide your time and wait for your chance. I wanted friends with benefits. No strings attached. Strictly catch and release," I said.

"You were a man-whore. Well, not anymore. Now you're with me," she said and finished her kiss.

She was a good kisser. But I still was behind the pharmaceutical wall of ice. Any feeling outside the drug screen felt weird.

I got out.

"Don't talk to strangers," Blair cooed and drove off in my Stratus.

Tonight there were only four of us in group.

Thad G. was a no-show. Which was a no-no.

Sandy L. asked if anyone had been contact with him. Then Paul D. slipped into the back office to call Thad G.'s probation officer and accountability partner at the AA group Thad had been attending.

Jayne V. came in to take Paul D.'s place. She had on pin-striped slacks. Her auburn hair brushed to the shoulders of her light blue turtle neck.

She might have dressed professional but her blue eyes were moist. If the counselors were worried about one of their sheep, there might be something to be concerned about.

Sandy L. even let Jayne V. take the first part of the lecture.

"Most addicts relapse an average of seven times before they decide to finally stop or they die. Every day you have a choice to stop. But if you keep on using, you're just playing a game of Russian Roulette. Sooner or later, you run out of chances. You may lose that final chance at getting help and you may lose your life," Jayne V. said.

She continued, "But you won't even begin to get better until you've made the choice to stop using. And every day you'll have to remember to decide to quit using. Because each day is a new day with another chance which brings you a choice.

"Now let's go around the room and tell each other what's your drug of choice? Your home drug and why?"

"Man, only crack or meth would do it for me," Ja-Rod said. "It makes me feel like tha god invincible."

"A little weed and some whiskey," Everett said. "Anything to help make the world go away."

"Xanex," Hannah said. "They're called mind erasers because that's what they do."

"Alcohol," I said. "Being in bands I got paid in drinks, people bought me drinks, and there was always cheap beer at practice. Alcohol is the cheapest legal drug there is and it's just about everywhere. I got drunk on the cheap for years."

Whatever drug Thad G. called home, that's where he was at right now. In the cold solace of a chemical cocktail that was poisoning one or more of his major organs. Would he be home for Christmas?

Then Sandy L. passed around a new handout.

CYCLE OF ADDICTION:
IMMERSION PHASE:
Triggers: problems of abuse, stress, lack of self-worth, character faults

Experimentation: recreational use of drugs or using them to relieve the problems

Obsession: urgency of doing drugs to seek high or relief or escape, tolerance levels go up

Guilt: over losing control, loss of self-worth, feelings of dissatisfaction

Promises: to stop, triggers re-appear, and the brain remembers what it's like to be high. Cycle starts over.

Increase of tolerance levels

Withdrawal: more abuse and more guilt. Loss of interests, family and friends avoided, work and money troubles,

CRUCIAL PHASE:

Periods of heavy use, neglect of food, physical deterioration, tremors.

Decrease in tolerance levels, moral deterioration

CHRONIC PHASE:

Obsessive drinking and withdrawal, continued physical deterioration.

Rock bottom. Admits defeat, helplessness or **DIES.**

REHABILITATION:

Admits: addiction, Seeks help

Acceptance: addiction is an illness,

Adjustment: to therapy and physical needs, develops a support group

Personal inventory: honesty about faults, hurts, and guilt

RECOVERY:

Accountability: faces facts, strives towards emotional control, emotional growth, confidence in self, respect of self, winning confidence of others, has a **PARTNER**

Growth: New interests, able to be independent and form mature relationships

"All of you are at different levels in this cycle. None of you are at RECOVERY," Sandy L. said.

"Either you move forward to RECOVERY. Or you move back to RELAPSE. And the longer you stay there or more often you do, you'll reach the CRUCIAL or CHRONIC PHASES," Jayne V. said.

Then Hannah S. brought up a very good point. "If we aren't druggin' anymore how do we handle our depression?"

"How many of you have been diagnosed with depression?" Sandy L. asked.

Only Hannah and I raised our hands.

"There are many things you do for depression outside of taking medications," Jayne said. Then she went on name several as Sandy L. passed out another handout which listed them. "Use spiritual resources. Have an emotional support circle. Don't trust your feelings. Not everything is as good as it seems or as bad as it looks. Get regular exercise. Be outside as much as possible doing something. Eat healthy meals. Maintain a regular pattern of sleep. And develop healthy hobbies."

"Remember, everyone's got problems in life," Sandy L. said. "It's how you handle your problems that defines your character."

"I've heard it said that the situation defines us," Hannah S. suggested. "Isn't that true?"

"That's straight up bull," said Ja-Rod. "I am who I am every day. I carry mamma's love. I got belief in God above. I got dreams. And I got choices. I'm more than some situation."

"That's so true Ja-Rod. You're thinking the right way!" Sandy L. encouraged. "It is said that every day is like a thousand years and a thousand years are like a day. Every day is a just part of the same moment of eternity. With endless possibilities and choices."

That echoed inside me and brought embers of that God moment when I was about three in the old family church, with the music reverbing around me and the light streaming through me.

"We limit ourselves. Thinking there's just one choice. When there's dozens," I spoke up. "Every day can be a heaven. Or a hell."

"Depending on what we choose," Hannah S. finished.

Her big eyes lit up with hope. They stood out against her bleached out hair with dark roots and greasy skin that hung loose on her thin frame. She was only eating to live but this session had given her some food for thought.

"All change starts with a change in attitude," Janet V. said.

"In the heart, if you like," Sandy L. said. "We need a new heart."

Giving into the depression and drugging to mask it had just caused me more problems. And now that I had been sober for almost two weeks, my raw open feelings were squirming like worms. If being human meant to love and trust and be happy then I had forgotten what it meant to be human. Maybe I never had known.

"That's why we are all here," Sandy L. continued, "To learn how to make wise choices That means everyone here will have to develop new habits. One habit, one day at a time. It's a process."

"It only takes four weeks or twenty-eight days to make a new habit," Jayne said.

"And only two weeks to break it," Sandy L. warned. "It's harder to move forward. Because it's new and change can be scary. It's easier to go backwards. Because you've been there. And you know what to expect."

Everyone in the group had been down so long we'd forgotten what a few positive words could do.

Not only had I found I needed them, I wanted more.

There was sweet surcease to my sorrow.

I came outside to find Blair and my Dodge Stratus were not waiting for me.

Up to now, she had never been late and she knew better than to make me wait. She was on a short leash with just one more chance for something not to go wrong or else I would be quits, again.

I had been half-expected something like this to happen. The car wasn't her property. She wasn't an insured driver on the car.

I was just asking for trouble. Playing Russian Roulette against something happening to her while she was inside my car. Sooner or later, there would be trouble.

So, I texted and texted. I called and left messages.

There was no reply at all.

Looked like it would be sooner rather than later for trouble.

Everyone else had left the session, gotten into their cars, and exited the parking lot.

I was alone on a cold winter's night.

Stranded in a hospital parking lot.

The near freezing air cutting through my winter jacket and jeans. I had little cash on me. And even less on my debit card.

My options were few. I had no friends in this town. I only knew Blair and her family.

And I couldn't call them up and ask them for a ride home.

Or my parents. That would be a laugh. Especially when I had to explain how I had come to be stranded.

I didn't know if I had enough cash or enough on my debit card to call for a cab. But if I did, it couldn't be that bad. It was only a few miles to the house.

If it was just a few miles, then maybe I might be better off to walk home.

Getting home would be step one. Finding out what Blair had done with my car was step two. Getting my car back step three. And dealing with Blair?

Step four.

Did I need this aggravation anymore?

Wasn't I just proving my Dad right?

On a whim, I thumbed through my contacts to find Blair's mother's number—my ex-mother-in-law, the queen of the court. I tapped the call icon. She might answer. She just as easily might not bother.

"Hello, is this Justin?" asked a squeaky unsure voice.

"Yes. Do you know where Blair is?" I asked.

"She hasn't called you?" Blair's mother asked.

I gave a round "No." We were off to an auspicious start. Beating around the bush. Hiding things. Blair must have learned it somewhere. She sure didn't learn it from me within the year and some odd months we'd been together.

"She has my car. She was supposed to pick me up after my group meeting," I said.

Blair's mother gave a heavy "Oh, your car is here" and stopping there with any further information but weighed with indecision about how much more to give.

"Okay, Blair said she was taking my car to your house," I said giving into the logic of the earlier evening's events. That was step two taken care of. Now the last detail. "Where's Blair?"

"I'd imagine in jail," Blair's mother said.

"What? Oh, no," I said. My stomach drop-kicked, my fist clenched in a shaolin punch, and my heart raced to get away all at the same time. I wasn't too concerned about Blair's safety. Just at having been affected by her stupidity.

"What happened?" I asked.

"I'd rather not say. Only you'll probably be hearing from her in a bit," Blair's mother said.

"What? She hasn't called you to bail her out or come get her?" I asked.

"No! I'm not gonna bail her out!" her mother said with a histrionic hiss. "She just needs to call you. Don't call me again. Leave me out of this! What's done is done."

"What about my car?" I asked.

"No one's gonna mess with your car, Justin! Come and get your stupid car!" she shrieked and just like that the connection ended from her end.

And just like that, I was alone.

Stranded on a Friday night.

A silent night, but hardly a holy night or a night divine.

Just another freezing night in a desolate parking lot.

I wasn't homeless but I was wasn't home. 2112 Springhill Drive might be close. And my car not much farther away but home was gone.

Even if I called for a cab and took it to my ex-mother-in-law's house, I couldn't retrieve the Stratus. Blair had the only key.

And just like that, an angel appeared in the form of a medical technician of some sort. He drove up in a four door Nissan that had seen better days, smoking muffler and all. The passenger window slid down and the man had a dirty mac on over short clipped red hair and ruddy cheeks. I felt like I'd seen him before…an orderly on Kelter Ward C? He leaned forward in his dark blue Our Lady's jacket, with the medical technician name tag pinned to it to ask, "Need a ride? How far do you live from here?"

"2112 Springhill Drive," I said. "It's not far."

"Thought I've save you a cab ride. Get in," the med tech said and electronically unlocked the passenger door.

"You saved me more than that," I said and got in.

He dropped me off and we exchanged "Merry Christmases." Only he added a "God bless us, everyone." That was something Boz would have said. And though he looked like Randle McMurtry, what he had just said was more important than some fool going around "Merry Christmas" just waiting to get staked with mistletoe and boiled in figging pudding because he didn't mean a word of what he said.

When I went inside 2112 Springhill Drive, it was a quarter of nine.

At nine-thirty, Blair called me. From the city jail.

I demanded to know what had happened.

Blair wasn't much forthcoming. But I reminded her I could just ask the jailer when I got there and paid for the privilege of releasing her. It was all now a part of public information.

"I got into a fight with my mother," Blair said.

"You mean an argument?" I asked. I could see them yelling at each other and then cussing and then threatening.

"No, I mean a fight. We went at each other and my step-dad had to get between us," Blair said.

"Ok, well, that couldn't have been too bad. You just go to neutral corners. Cool out. Or you could have just left," I said.

"No. They took my winning lotto card from me. I wasn't leaving without it," Blair said. "I should have called the cops then."

"Wait, why did they take your lotto card and why did you have it other there?" I asked.

"Justin, that's what we do sometimes. We go get lotto cards from Gas-Mart. Well, this time, I won. Big. Over a thousand dollars!" Blair said like a child whose favorite toy had been taken from her.

"Why did they take it from you?" I asked.

"Because they say I owe them money from when we broke up, when they gave me money for groceries and utilities, until I got my WIC and unemployment cards. They said I'm a horrible daughter and unfit mother. They made me feel like scum," Blair said painting her family as treasonous, troll-like villains. Much like my family thought of me.

"I'm sure you said nothing but kind things to them," I said knowing Blair could use every cuss word in a Stephen King book within a single breath.

Blair paused to try and process my dry sarcasm. "What?" It was more important that someone believe her tale, no matter how absurd. She spun it to paint herself in the best light. She would get right in your face and watch your every response in your eye as she told her tale. But that didn't work over the phone.

"They said I owed them thousands going way back. I made it hard on them to give so much and I was so ungrateful and I've never paid them back a dime!" Blair blurted getting close to tears.

Did it hurt because it was true? Would it hurt so bad if it wasn't?

It didn't sound much different than what I had gone through when I'd come to genuflect and confess to my parents.

So many stones in so many hearts.

So much unforgiveness and hurt.

So many people were prepared to die with these stones in their hearts. Just to get the last word. Thinking they'd just go to sleep and that would be the end of it. At least, they'd leave the hurt and stones with the other person.

But did it really work that way?

What if people didn't go to sleep when they died? What if the stones were weighed and put on your back? You chose to carry it around in life so now you get to carry it…

I shook my head clear of such nonsensical nonsense. My God moment when I was three proved to me there was a God, but surely, He just let all those stones go. Surely, everyone was going to get a new heart?

"Look, I've got to get off. But I've got to know. Are you going to come get me?" she asked.

"What's the charge and what's the bail?" I asked. Basically, what was the bill? I was finding life with Blair always came with a price tag.

"The police are calling it domestic violence. My family is saying I slapped my mother. Twice. Yet my step-dad grabbed me by the throat and tried to choke me out. But the others are saying he didn't attack me. That he only got between me and my mom and tried to restrain me.

"So, I'm being booked with a Domestic assault charge. Class A misdemeanor. Like a slap on the wrist," Blair said justifying it to herself. Hey, if I believed her version then I was believing the truth.

"You mean you just get a slap on the wrist for slapping your mom? Isn't that just fair," I said with more dry sarcasm. "So, how much is this domestic assault misdemeanor A charge?"

"I'll get off cheap. Charge is just $2500. But I can get out on bail tonight with 20% tonight. I'll have to go to court where I'll fight it and get off.

"What is you're found guilty?" I asked playing devil's advocate in suggesting something that she would never

"I'll get off when I tell the judge my side about how they took my lotto ticket and my step-dad assaulted me—he's the one who should be arrested!" Blair said rewriting history to her solitary satisfaction.

"You say they took your lotto ticket. They've probably cashed it in and spent all the money. The judge won't make them give back the money. You'll have to have a receipt from the gas station and it'll be a civil law suit for that thousand dollars. There was a lotto ticket. No receipt? Then it'll be finders, keepers; grabbers, takers.

"The judge won't care about the lotto ticket. He'll just wanna know if you hit your mother and why you did it. It'll be your word against…how many of them? Two?" I asked.

"Three. My son was there and saw the whole thing," Blair sniffed.

I winced. Anytime violence was done in a house with a child, it could result in an immediate DHS investigation. And that was a whole other world of trouble no one wanted. Needed? Different story.

But it would not be my trouble.

From out of this whole ball of wax I just wanted my keys. So, I could get my Stratus back. And drive home.

"If I'm found guilty, I'll have to pay the whole amount. But I won't have to pay the whole thing at once. I could do it installments. I could stretch it out to five years if I have to," Blair said.

"How are you going to pay on it?" I asked.

"With money of course, duh, Sherlock," Blair said.

"Where are you going to get the money? You can't use your WIC. Can you use your unemployment?" I asked.

"I could have them garnish my unemployment. It'll all work out, trust me," said the spider to the fly, who had just let it back into the parlor.

"Or you could just pull another winning lotto ticket again to set you square and be done with it," I mocked.

"Ha, ha. Very funny. Now are you coming to get me?" she demanded.

"I suppose I have to if I want the key to my car back. Unless you think I could come up to the jail and ask for my key?" I asked.

"No, they logged in the key with my personal belongings. You'll have to bail me out so I can get my belongings back," Blair said like she had the routine done cold.

I wasn't stupid enough to ask out loud how much twenty percent of twenty-five hundred would be. I worked at a bank. I could figure out. But I already knew I wouldn't have the full twenty percent.

When I didn't say anything, Blair gave me more good advice. "It's cash or money order only. I'd do a money order if I were you. At this time of night, you'll have to go to Best-mart.

"Look, my five minutes are up. They're making me get off the phone now. Come and get--"

Once again, the call was ended from the other end.

Once again, I was alone. This time in a house that was not my home.

I would need five hundred dollars to bond her out.

I didn't have five hundred dollars.

I had about three hundred and fifty. Out of which I would also need cab fare. Thank God, I'd gotten a ride home.

So, I needed over a hundred and fifty. Closer to two hundred. Because I would need three cabfares. One to Best-Mart. One from Best-Mart to the police station. And one from the police station back to her mother's house where we could pick up the car and get back to 2112 Springhill Drive.

And go straight to bed.

What did I have that was worth two hundred dollars? Nothing left from the moving in and out after our divorce. If there were a handful of things I could pawn, I'd have to wait until tomorrow when the pawn stores opened.

No telling what you'd get on a pawn. Never enough of what you need. Pawnstores had a Scroogey reputation.

Without thinking, I took out my wallet as I walked into the front room where the Christmas tree waited to be plugged in. I opened my Star Wars trifold and dipped my fingers inside. Out came several folded receipts—I may not have listened to my dad about much but I had listened to about keeping receipts.

Most of them were before my admittance into Kelter Ward C. Gas. Drinks and chili tots from Sonic. Bank account balance. And a very recent Best-mart receipt.

For a tree.

One Christmas tree.

The item was one hundred and ninety-nine dollars and ninety-nine cents. Plus twenty-three dollars and ninety-nine cents for tax. Making a grand total of two hundred and twenty-three cents.

I called the number on the back of my debit card.

After choosing English and number one for several choices through the labyrinthine call menu, I got my on-line balance. Three hundred and fifty-seven dollars and forty-three dollars.

Giving me a grand total of five hundred and eighty-one dollars and forty-two dollars, according to my phone calculator. That would leave eighty-one dollars to use for the three cab trips.

It was now nine-forty-eight. Time to get started.

After Blair got home and realized how I had made bail she exploded, as I had anticipated. So, I reminded her of the choice: tree for bail or sit in jail. Which only made her madder, as I had also anticipated.

She stormed off to her post-divorce property queen sized bed to bawl herself to sleep.

And I in my clothes, settled down on the couch for a long winter's nap.

Thank God, tomorrow would be Saturday.

I'd have enough of the twelve days of Christmas. And there were still seven days left.

11-Six Shopping Days Until Christmas

Day seven was Saturday.

On the home stretch now.

Blair was plenty sore about the Christmas tree. She mad at her mother. She listed off everything that was wrong with her and somehow tied it to something her mother had done at some point in the past.

But I'd never spent a lot of time with her extended family: Blair's mother and step-dad and Blair's son. What little time we had, I'd heard quite a different take on Blair's life. Out of the good, bad, and the ugly it was mostly tales from the ugly and bad. Causing Blair to raise her middle finger to her parents and telling them to fornicate themselves.

I would have never thought of acting like that to my parents. But right now, they might feel as if I had.

Blair perked up when the heat/air guy dropped by. First, he looked at the hole from the inside by standing it to get a worm's eye vantage. Then he climbed the top of the addition to survey the damage from a bird's eye vantage. Then he came down to render his verdict.

It didn't matter what we did with the hole. We could patch it with drywall, but the hole would just appear again with the next rain. And that was because the hole was unfixable.

I asked him to explain this with the laws of physics.

He was only gracious enough to explain. Due to the slope of the roof on the addition, there was not enough grade for water to run off. Snow, ice, and worse, water, would only gather in the same spots—the back of the roof, and seek the lowest spot of gravity. And the lowest spot would be towards the middle of the roof.

That was physics.

But he told to wait because there was "more."

The reason that this would happen time and time again was because the grade of the roof was almost flat. And that the grade of the roof was not up to city code.

And then he poured more salt onto the wound.

The large air conditioning unit that been placed on a pile of sloppily laid patio bricks outside the kitchen was also not up to code. It was too large for the square footage of the house because that particular model was made to sit atop a four apartment building.

Whoever who had rehabbed the house had made some interesting cost-cutting decisions. What was worse was why had so many city-codes been flagrantly broken and yet passed by the property assessor who had been contracted by the realty company, who, in turn had contracted with the rehabber?

When they had put up the "For Sale" sign, it actually meant something else. In this case, "For Sale" meant "WANTED: SUCKER."

It was my house now.

I was that SUCKER. When I'd moved back in and had to clean the carpet from all of the backed up water, a neighbor dropped by. She'd heard about my divorce and asked if I wasn't going to sell the house. She could sell it for me. Only problem, I hadn't paid enough of the mortgage and I would have to pay at least three thousand difference after her suggested selling price plus her fee, naturally. In addition, I would have to be willing to make any necessary repairs.

Hmm. A cracked heater coil, a hole in a roof that was not up to code, and an uncoded air conditioner unit.

2112 Springhill Drive was becoming a bit of a black hole. And I was being stretched past the event horizon.

As it stood now, I might not have enough for January's house payment.

Blair's response was, "Just call them up and tell them you'll be late. They won't throw you out in one month."

There were consequences for not following covenant agreements. A sign of major trouble on credit reports was when someone couldn't pay their house payment. Usually, people would pay the house note over utilities. Over credit cards. Even a car. But they made sure the house got paid.

I knew this to be true because that was what I did all day—analyzed people's credit reports.

The bank had a policy for collection. They weren't just going to let you alone and forget that you existed. Oh, no. They had Scrooge-tactics to get their loan value back. Or they took back what was theirs—the car, the house, or whatever it was you had signed over.

Collateral, lien holder, covenant, compliance.

It was a Scroogework. An Iron Mary of penalties. Chains of criminal negligence.

Blair just couldn't skip down the Yellow Brick Road and run through the poppy fields of banking. Sooner or later, they would send the flying monkeys.

This house, 2112 Springhill Drive, was mine. My very first house. I hadn't quitclaimed it to Blair. I hadn't surrendered it in a bankruptcy as my divorce lawyer had suggested.

It was a property.

But it was a very flawed property.

It was a responsibility.

But that responsibility had seven heads and every time I chopped off one head, another three grew back in its place.

It was becoming a millstone.

And it was sinking me down into the Seas of Debt.

Under the waves of despair.

Day Six, Sunday, passed with all this dogging me like a black shuck.

Blair paid it all no mind. She stayed back in the bedroom and stayed on the phone. I figured she was talking to her mother and trying to get herself invited back over for Christmas. I was probably still *persona non gratis*.

I figured out a game plan. Monday and Tuesday, Days Five and Four, would be regular group sessions. Wednesday, Day Three, was pay-day. I would have to hold money back for the house payment, or be smart and pay it early.

I would also need at least two more hours that night at a twelve step; so, I planned to go back to New Hearts.

Thursday would be our last group session and our "graduation" and it would be Christmas Eve.

Friday would be Christmas. Which was unknown territory at this point. I didn't know where I would be and I might just be sitting on the post-divorced couch.

But on Thursday, Christmas Eve, the bank planned to close early. Probably about one. Which meant, we all had to come back from lunch and stand and be counted. Only then would we be released from our tanks to get the next day off, as well as the weekend—which may be inconvenient for the bank, but only if everyone was to get there all the more early the following Monday.

I had purchased few gifts. And next to none wrapped. But I had bought one thing apiece for my Mom and Dad. If they wouldn't let me over, I'd just swing by and put them in their mail box. Secret Santa didn't need stamps.

I suppose I should buy Blair a little something. A very little and something. And for her family as well. Even if I wouldn't get invited to their house on Christmas.

I was a guy. I was a power shopper.

On Christmas Eve, most shops and stores would be open until five or six. The most daring would risk being open until seven. And likewise, there was always one guy who showed up just minutes after the doors would be closed and locked, banging and pleading to be let in and promising to buying just one item and he even knew where it was on the shelf—I never wanted to be that guy.

My plan was a mad dash to the St. Louis downtown Famous Barr candy counter for last minute gifts—chocolate covered peanuts for my dad, chocolate covered cherries for my mom, an old fashioned assorted candy box with the schematic on the underside of the lid for Blair, whoppers for her son, a couple of turtles for her mom and step-dad, and a bag of white chocolate and chocolate covered pretzels for me.

That would cover from one to three—I would be pushing the timeline—I'd needed to be home before four and wrap gift like crazy until five. Then I would have to go to group therapy—our last session.

Only about five or six would be the time when my family would have a party style meal with cookies and Christmas Fudge.

All without me.

This would be my first Christmas without spending it with my parents or getting Christmas Fudge.

Or having Christmas Fudge.

But at least I had the comfort of spending Christmas Eve with the one I thought I loved.

Blair.

It looked like it would be just Blair and I at home for the holidays.

She no longer talked about getting a job. She was too wrapped up with cigarettes and lotto tickets.

But Blair was in no short supply of schemes. Some were crazy: she wanted me to get a financial license so I could advise people on money and invest their money to make us money, while Blair would be my secretary. The reason: Blair was convinced that looking at people's FICOs every day made me some kind of financial expert. The cost: three thousand for the three week course to get a financial license, which would be cash advanced off a credit card that she wanted me to open up. The promise: she wouldn't call in sick on me and I'd make bank.

Some were logical: I could take out a loan against the amount of my pension I was already vested in. The payment would come out of my check and I wouldn't lose my pension. The problem: it would barely float us through two months and wouldn't make a dent in the unsecured debt I still had weighing on my back.

Some were a long shot: Blair could apply for disability for having bipolar manic depression disorder. It would only need Dr. Frost's referral and her entire medical history to be sent off to the Supplemental Social

Security office. The machinery of her mind moved fast with computing the end result. She was positive she would receive at least two thousand a month—more than what I made, she was quick to point out—and that she could apply for a back payment for all the time she had been out of work—about the whole year and a half since I'd met her—and that would come out to forty thousand dollars.

More than enough to pay off the unsecured debt and pay for repairs to the house. With enough left over for a trip to Disney. And even a Caribbean Cruise.

She'd spun a glamour. Her words were crystalline chimes. Sugar coating the bitter medicine.

Because the bitter was coming: the ball under the moving shell.

Blair used a slight of hand. Keeping my eyes on her hand that made the magic wishes while the other hand was kept behind her back. The hand full of crap.

Then she presented her hand full of crap and she laid bare what she wanted. "If we got married again, half of it would be yours. There might even be enough to pay back your parents."

If we didn't go to Disney or take a couple of cruises, that is. But why keep your word in paying off debts and fulfilling responsibilities when you could celebrate and throw money to the wind and make some memories? You can't take it with you: the money or the debt.

But what exactly did you take with you?

Your words. Your deeds. Your guilt. Your legacy. Your true worth.

The glamour had been powerful. The sugar sweet. Poured into the acid-test kool-aid variety and not the

Jonestown flavor. A promise made great. And better than an American Traveller's check since it was coming from Blair's mouth.

She grinned to seal the deal. Her eyes bigger than the wheels spinning in her mind. All I had to do was just believe. Have a little faith.

"Maybe there will be a brand new engagement ring under the tree for Christmas," Blair said. "We could go back to that bed and breakfast. Get married on the way. Then we could call your mom and dad and tell them the news."

Wouldn't that be tidings of comfort and joy?

If my Miami-Dolphin-pajamed-six-year-old self would have found a ringbox with Blair's name on it under the tree, he would have thrown it in the trash can outside on a cold winter's night. McMurtry would have stolen it and pawned it to feed the poor. Grandpa would have given the ring to Blair on a string and then jerked back on the string to clutch the ring in his fist. Grandma would have been a little more subtle. She would have given Blair a piece of her choice fudge. And instead of a biting down on a walnut, Blair would be biting down on the diamond engagement ring.

Boz would have approved any of these measures.

My head still dizzy from her glamour, I changed out of my business casual polo shirt and khakis to jeans and a turtle neck. Anything with long sleeves to hide the still healing cuts on my wrists.

It was Monday.

Five days left now.

I grabbed the keys to the car.

"Now, are you going to be alright here alone?" I asked.

"If it really bothered you, I guess there's no chance in letting me have the car tonight?" she asked with an eye roll.

"Not a chance," I said and grabbed my coat out of the water heater closet and made to leave. "You could do something else rather than smoke or play lotto tickets."

"Ha, ha," Blair said and rubbed her eye with her middle finger.

"You got a license to fly that bird?" I asked.

"What?" Blair asked retracting her cat claw with a feline "who me?"

I wonder what she did when she at the house alone while I was at group. I already knew what she did when she was over at her mother's.

"I feel like I'm being punished. Like I've been a bad kid and I've been grounded," Blair said.

I shrugged. "I guess if you don't like the arrangements you could do something about it."

"Like what?" she asked.

"Get a car on your own. 'Cuz I'm not signing anything for you again," I said.

Blair looked at me askew. "I can't get one on my own right now. Unless I get on disability I'll just end getting another broken-down piece of crap.

"It's like you don't even trust me!"

"Bingo," I said as I opened the door.

"Are you ever going to trust me again?" Blair asked.

With my hand on the door, I stopped and looked over my shoulder. "I don't know. It depends. Are you ever gonna be sorry for anything you did and ask forgiveness?"

"But I didn't do anything wrong!" Blair said.

"Sure, it's *never* your fault. You never do anything *wrong*," I said.

"If you're not gonna believe me then why did you even take me back?" Blair began to cry. She did that a lot lately after she'd been arrested.

I remembered the sound of another woman whose broken-down-beside-herself-crying jag had caused such a clatter than I jumped up of my deep sleep to see what was matter.

The truth was I was afraid of being alone. Or what was waiting for me. I was scared.

I thought having Blair around was better than being alone.

I thought if we weren't married this time I could control the situation.

And what a bang-up job I had done. Peeling back all the problems of this house was like peeling back an onion—it sure made me cry.

12-Silent Night

This time I gobbled down a bologna and cheese with mustard sandwich before I got out of my Stratus and entered the ancillary entrance to Hope Counselors, Inc. Most of the others were there before me. True to form, Hannah S.talked to everyone—even me. And true to form, Ja-Rod laughed the most with supreme confidence. And true to form, Everett P. was about the last to get there and just a little sour and put out at having to be there at all.

And, maybe, just true to form, I was still trying to be Mr. Too-Cool-For-School.

All three counselors were there tonight: S Sandy L., Paul D., and Jayne V. , and Paul D.

Again, there were only four of us. One chair was still empty.

And true to form, it was Ja-Rod who first expressed concern, "Where Thad?"

He'd missed so many days, he must certainly be in danger of being expelled from the program. Which meant in this case, breaking conditions of parole. And probably a drug test. And since we assumed he'd been using, probably meant jail time.

"His family finally notified the police he was missing," Paul D. began. "Last night I got a call from the police. The kind of call I don't want to get."

"He's dead, isn't he?" asked Hannah L.

Sandy L. and Jayne nodded but let Paul D. finish. "They found him in the basement of an old building downtown. At this point they don't know if he died from an overdose or from exposure."

"Do they know how long he had been there?" Everett P. asked.

Paul D. frowned. "Probably a few days at least."

Hannah S.blurted out with tears and sobs. Ja-Rod shook his head with a "Dear Lord, no." Even Everett P. wiped at the corners of his eyes.

Only I refrained from saying anything. Only I kept myself behind a wall of ice where I was safe from being touched. Mr. Ice, that was me.

"Justin R.?" Paul D. prompted as the three counselors took in my non-reaction.

"He made his choice. He made up his bed and now he's asleep in it," I said. Though, I was doubtful he was resting in peace. Having sought escape in this life from the hell-hounds that had dogged him, he might have put himself in a place where he was their play-thing.

"Man, that just a stone-cold thing to say 'bout someone," Ja-Rod said.

"I ain't speakin' ill of the dead," I snapped. "I'm saying that he *is* stone-cold dead. He gave up and thought he'd get what he wanted. He's beat my record at least."

"You was dead long 'nuff to know what he's goin' through now!" Ja-Rod accused. "You was dead and come back. Yet you come back with a heart a stone. Man, you still dead. You just a dead man walkin'."

I can't deny that I experienced something while I flatlined. I can't deny that I've experienced seeing things after I was revived. But what did it all mean?

I was still here by God's grace.

Every day was a second chance.

And I was blowing it.

Ja-Rod had put his finger on the truth.

I wasn't being grateful.

"We are not here to judge one another. Or give advice. Or help counsel one another. The way I look at it, the time I spend serving my clients and getting' their trust by listening earns me the right to chew them out. But that's a card I don't to play much," Paul D. interceded.

"We are better off listening in this group for the time being. I wanted to tell you this. You all needed to hear it. Thad G. is dead. Deader than a mackerel. Deader than roadkill. Deader than Disco. Deader than a sabre-tooth tiger. Deader than a doorknob. Deader than a graveyard. Deader than dead.

"And you know what? You all are still alive," Sandy L. put in.

"Be ye therefore grateful," Jayne V. added.

"Show a little respect. For everything," Paul D. said. "I can't state enough how important a group like this is to your future. We are almost done with our intensive outpatient group therapy. But none of you are fully recovered yet. You're barely on the mend. You've just started. You're still taking baby steps.

"And it wouldn't take too much stress for you to go running back to your dirty-dog-drug-who-you-call-mama-but-who's-a-goddess-of-death. That's all drugs got to offer: death, death, and more death. Let what happened to Thad be your best illustration. Every day we have a choice. It's either you live or die. You can build your life. Or you can destroy your life.

"It's your choice."

No one had said a word. Even Boz and McMutrty would have been church-mice quiet.

"If you want to work your recovery, you've got to remember this: it won't start until you've hit rock bottom. Until you've had enough and you're ready to let go and quit.

"You'll know when you've hit rock bottom. Because you can't go any lower. I know I've said it before, but in the light of Thad G., I might as well say it again: you might hit rock bottom one time too many and the next time you might not get back up," Paul D. said.

"Remember, you can't grow until you let go," Sandy L. said.

"You each have been given a unique irreplaceable gift. Your individual life. Each of you are a walking miracle," Jayne V. said.

"So, quit playin' Russian Roulette with your life," Paul D. said. "And start workin' your recovery."

Jayne V. passed out tonight's work sheet.

Recovery vs. Relapse	
Recovery Bound	**Relapse Bound**

Honest about self and your problems	Minimizes, distorts problems
Socializes with others	Withdraws from others
isolates	
Asks for help	Will not ask for help
Trusting, sharing with others	Suspicious, distrustful
takes full responsibility for behavior	Blaming, resentful, "victimized"
Acts mature, has attitude of gratitude	Acts immature, pities self
Understands need for abstinence	Hides use/denies need for abstinence

"We strongly suggest you all be a part of a twelve-step program after our group is over," Jayne V. said.

"So, we have tomorrow night. You all will need to attend a twelve-step group on Wednesday. Then we have one final meeting on Thursday," Paul D. said.

"Christmas Eve," Jayne V. said.

"Remember to turn in your log sheets after we sign them on Thursday. Thursday night will be special," Sandy L. said.

I wondered how Thursday night would be special.
I wondered what was so special about me.
About anything.

13-Hark, the Herald Angels Sing

"I almost died," Blair said big as
life the moment I walked the front
door 2112 Springhill Drive.

To paraphrase John Lennon, I knew what it was like to be dead. Blair wouldn't be able to handle it.

But like a good partner, I played along. "Oh, what happened?"

I hung up my coat in the water heater closet and she followed me to the kitchen as I got a glass of ice and poured some water. Then I followed her into the back room addition. The tv was on and *Everybody Loves Raymond* was showing, but it was muted.

"Like I said, when I tell you what happened, I almost died," Blair said.

"Almost doesn't cut it," I replied.

"What a cruel thing to say to someone," she pointed out.

I thought it appropriate. Since we were newly divorced. I shrugged and made the mistake of asking. "So, tell me already."

And so Blair told me what had happened. She'd walked to the Get Gas Mart on Main Street to get some more lotto tickets. She had enough left on her IDES card to buy maybe two if she had to stretch her luck. Well, she hit paydirt on the first card! Fifty dollars! So, she bought a red hot hot dog, a twenty-four ounce Mountain Dew. And played a string of losing cards.

When I asked her how much of it she had brought home, she pulled the sum out of the pocket of her sweat pants: twenty-three dollars and eleven cents, thank you, very much, then she shushed me.

During all that time, she was up at the counter talking to Tim. Tim was great. He was the assistant manager and loved his job because he knew how to deal with the crap that came with it. Not just the crappy customers but his crappy regional boss. Tim worked hard. He worked very hard and kept a smile on while he did it. Soon, Tim would be the station manager. Then he'd work even harder and become the regional manager. Then he'd be smiling big. Tim had a goal. Tim was going places.

So, instead of buying just one more card—did I know that each station gets a bonus for selling winning lotto cards—and yes, I did—they were called incentives—and then Blair got back to the meat of her story because up to now we had just been chewing on the fat—Blair got ready to leave and they exchanged numbers, she hoped I didn't mind. (Definite Red Flag and yes, my heart kicked a beat and I felt blood rise in my cheeks but I tried to stay behind my Floydian wall of ice). A guy came in to pay for his gas so, Blair left and hadn't gotten but ten steps from the front doors when a bigfoot truck just rolled right through.

It took out the doors and smashed up the front counter. It threw Tim against the hot dog rollers and he got burned and broke some ribs. But it pinned the man buying gas against the bumper and the lotto machine, which is pretty much built like a safe.

What happened was, the wife of the guy who came in to pay for the gas thought she'd do him a solid and put the truck in gear—since he'd left it running while he gassed it up—and just have it rollup to the front door to be there for him when he came out. Except she did this while she was in the passenger seat and hadn't thought about riding the brake.

Blair decided to stay as a witness. She had stayed out of the store but Tim told her he had been able to call the cops and an ambulance. The cops had gotten there first. Then the Fire Department. Then one ambulance. Then a second ambulance.

Nothing had happened to the wife during the accident. Blair watched the cops have her use a breathalyzer. She blew a 1.04. Her blood had enough alcohol for a Sangria and a Bloody Mary.

So, they took her away in the back of a cop car. Tim and the husband each got to ride in an ambulance.

"Well, I'm sorry that happened. That would have been weird to watch. And I hope they all get well quick," I said.

"Except for the wife. I hope she goes to jail," Blair said having just gotten out of the pokey herself.

"Hard to tell. She might get a DUI or just a drunk and disorderly. The husband's car insurance will have to pay for everything. They might suspend her license or put her on probation. It could have been worse," I said.

"She could have ran me over turned me into road kill," Blair said.

"You must have a guardian angel," I conceded.

"I could be your guardian angel. I could take care of you, if you'd let me," she cooed like a babysitter on acid. Blair reached up to put her arms around my neck and kiss me full on the lips.

No dice.

I was still on ice.

14-I Wish It Was Christmas Today

Tuesday was a new normal day.

Rise, shine, arrival routine, looking busy in the cubicle, making a very short Christmas list during lunch, and figuring out how much money I could use by writing down bill due dates and amounts.

Blair called me up in the afternoon.

"Honey, I've got great news!" she about screamed through the phone.

"You got your disability," I said.

"No, I'll have to pay a lawyer to file that. Unless you want to pay for the lawyer and filing fee," she offered.

"No, thank you," I said. "The last lawyer I paid for was my divorce lawyer."

"Ha, ha," Blair said. "Anyway, I've been talking to my mom--"

"I thought you'd've called Tim by now," I said.

"I did, I called to check on Tim today. He's doing well. Should get released today," Blair said. "Anyway, I called my mother today and she's want to talk!"

"That's a good first step," I said. "When are you going to talk to her?"

"I can't unless I go over there," Blair explained. "So," here she paused. "So, I was thinking that maybe you could let me drive you to your group meeting and I could go talk to my mom."

"Nuh, uh," I said. "No way. Nothing doing."

"Because last time, it cost me five hundred dollars. Plus cab fare," I said.

"She might be willing to drop the charges. That would save us another two thousand dollars," Blair argued.

"Can you guys even be in the same room without fighting?" I asked.

"Well, sure. We were fighting about money then. They got some. They'll play nice," Blair said.

It would be a favor. It would be on her word, Lord help me. I was about at the end of doing her favors.

I shut my eyes and felt my heart pound against the back of my eyes. Why, oh, why had I—

"Why can't she come over to--"I almost said "our" but instead I substituted—"the house?" I asked. Maybe she thought I had tried to stifle a burp.

"Because she's still mad at you. She blames you for hurting me," Blair said.

I tried to count all the times my mother-in-law had come to my house when it was our house when we were married. I couldn't even count them on a one hand. Because she had never come over. Not once.

And then I counted the number of times she had invited me over. Once for Thanksgiving (and only after Blair's son had eaten and left because they were speaking that week). Once during our first Christmas. And once for Easter. On those last two occasions, I had been given the opportunity to sit and eat at the same table with Blair's son but with the strict instructions not to talk to his majesty unless spoken to first which never happened. No matter, he had ignored every question posed to him by his mother.

Maybe I should be taking Blair and her whole family with me to New Hearts Recovery tomorrow night. Wasn't one of the steps to make a list of everyone I had wronged and be willing to make amends?

I exhaled a long sigh. "Okay."

"Great!" Blair squealed. "I love you!"

"Mm, mmm," I said.

"What can't you say it anymore? You haven't told me it much lately anyway," Blair said.

"I. Love. You. Now, see you tonight," I said.

Blair squealed again like a babysitter getting to put her favorite nail polish on her ward.

I wasn't sure who was babysitting who anymore.

The rest of the afternoon, I regretted my decision. On the departure routine, I thought about rescinding my ruling with a stay. But I didn't.

All through the group meeting, I thought of another round of Family Feud Upclose And Personal. Only this time, it would make the paper. Blair still had my last name. And if there was another police report filed, the newspaper had no qualms with publishing the subject's (the one who got arrested and charged) home address.

Oh, tidings of comfort and joy.

I walked out of the hospital to my Stratus in a good mood.

"Did you have a good group session?" Blair asked when I got into the passenger seat.

"I did," I said.

"Good," Blair said.

"Did you have a good visit with your mother and son?" I asked.

"I did," Blair said.

She was in a good mood, too.

"What was the verdict?" I asked.

"Oh, my mother's agreed to drop the charges," Blair beamed.

"Great! Will I get my five hundred back?" I asked.

"Uh, no. County fees. The arrest still stands on the books. But the charge will be wiped out," Blair said.

"Well, that should be a comfort to you at least," I said kissing my five hundred goodbye forever.

"And guess what else?" She prodded as she came out of the parking lot and to the boulevard,

"I don't know. What?" I asked.

"We are invited over on Christmas Eve! They're going to get together on Christmas Eve instead of Christmas! My step-dad has to work on Christmas! Isn't that freakin' fantastic!" Blair squealed. And then tried to goose me in order to get me to squeal.

Though, I let her touch me, which I didn't really like, I didn't squeal.

"'We?'" I asked.

"Yes, we. Or *oui*, in French. We two," Blair said.

I was impressed. "The both of us? Wow."

"But there's a catch," Blair said.

I was still way open-minded. "What's that?"

"We can only come over after they've eaten and when they're passing out candy and the presents. Then we are to take our presents and leave," Blair said.

"Wow," I said again. I wasn't so impressed now. Instead, I was insulted.

That was some major restrictions.

"I wish it was Christmas today. Right now. And tomorrow. Everyday, too," Blair squealed.

I wondered how Blair's mother treated Christmas Carolers if she knew they were juvenile delinquents.

15-Way Of Lights Another Way

Down the boulevard, green wreaths and red holly ribbons decorated city lamps and streets. Christmas lights had thawed out along people's gutters and bushes. Christmas inflatables waved and beckoned and bent. And in many front living rooms, plastic Christmas trees stood tall and proud and bright.

"Why are you smiling so much?" Blair asked.

"I just hope no matter where I am come Christmas morning, there will be peace on earth and goodwill to men, at least for a little while," I said.

"You're gonna be with me Christmas morning and we're gonna have a holly jolly time," Blair said.

Another promise. We would wait and see if this one would be fulfilled, too. I was still waiting for my Christmas fudge. I wished she would stop making promises she didn't intend on keeping. It turned the future into a black shadowy figure in graveyard habiliments over a skeletal frame.

The streets were cold but dry. Snow still clung stubbornly to hermitish bushes and cold curbs

I kept my eyes on the lights. With the future bleak, I reversed course to the past. It was better than a painkiller. "When I was little, my mom would drive us through different neighborhoods that had put up tons of Christmas lights. Sometimes, we'd even go to Our Lady's Shrine and see 'The Way of Lights.'"

"You used to do that, too? We got such a kick out of it," Blair said. At the next intersection, instead of turning left, Blair turned on the right blinker and cut across two lanes of traffic to pull down a frontage road. "It's right next door. Let's have a look."

Blair was fearless. It was part of what had attracted her to me. Because I was just the opposite.

Just as a strength can also be a weakness, Blair's recklessness often got her into trouble. But every once in a while, she would come up with a wondrous gem of an idea that wasn't all about her.

Two volunteers in orange caution vests were on either of the frontage road to face traffic coming and going. On the entrance side, Blair slowed so I could put the window down and take a tract hand-out. On the exit side, a person stood with a bucket for donations.

According to the tract, Our Lady's Shrine had been established in 1970, by a Catholic order of nuns, the Society of the Holy Mother of the Flaming Heart. After one of their members had come to the bluffs along the Mississippi for quiet meditation and had seen a vision of the Virgin Mary.

The grounds had been bought.

The shrine built.

A grotto with an statue icon of the Virgin Mother Mary.

A convent established.

And then Our Lady's Hospital had been founded.

Since it was owned by the order and it had been zoned in a commercial property but designated as a non-for-profit, they ran it according to the edicts of the Holy Father on the throne of St. Peter in Rome.

Now we were on a pretend pilgrimage. With a few other fellow car travelers. It was a journey along a winding one lane road that told the birth of Jesus through signs and two-dimensional wooden figures, quoting and acting out the first chapters of Matthew.

"I don't know why more people don't come here now," Blair said. "I remember it used to be bumper to bumper."

"People want the season but not the reason," I said.

"They want the gifts. The stuff," she said.

"And dump the baby back in the manger," I said.

When was the last time either of us had been to church?

I continued, "I guess people just don't want to be reminded. Christmas was supposed to be about the first gift. Peace on earth and goodwill to men. We were to be given those things because of the prophecy of a Messiah. The Annoited One. That was the reason for the peace and goodwill. The gift was Jesus.

"'And they shall call His name Immanuel' which translated means 'God with us,' 'For unto us a Child is born, Unto us a Son is given; And the government will be upon His shoulder. And His name will be called Wonderful, Counselor, Mighty God, Everlasting Father, Prince of Peace.'

"But people don't want God. They say they do. But having God show up means they'll have to change their ways and people won't do it. They say, 'No thanks. Changed my mind. We likes our ways.'"

"Do you think most believe in God and Jesus?" Blair asked.

"Most people believe in God or some kind of god they can make deals with and who won't demand too much of them. Many people have heard of Jesus, less believe in Him. More and more people hear nothing but negative stuff about Jesus and church and the Bible. So, it's easier to say it's just a fairy tale.
Up there with Santa Claus and the Easter Bunny and Bigfoot. To them, Jesus rides unicorns down the Bi-Frost Rainbow bridge to give out candy wafers and shots of Jesus Juice," I said.

"There is no fear of God anymore," Blair said.

"My dad says, 'When you take away God, all that's left is fear.' There is only fear. And plenty of it," I said.

And for twenty minutes, we tooled down the one-lane asphalt on a pilgrimage to the grotto shrine. The signs and figures told the story: Behold, a Virgin shall conceive—Fear not, Mary: for thou hast found favor with God—And it came to pass in those days that there went out a decree from Caesar Augustus—And Joseph also went up from Galilee…unto the city of David—And she brought forth her first born Son—And there were in the same country shepherds—And, lo, the angel of the Lord came upon them…and they were sore afraid—I bring you good tidings of great joy—And they came with haste, and found Mary, and Joseph, and the babe lying in a manger—behold, there came wise men…saying…we have seen His star in the east—and when they had come into the house..and worshipped Him…presented unto him gifts; gold, and frankincense, and myrrh—the characters and the names of the three wisemen struck me. Caspar, the young one in blonde hair in a green cloak; Melchoir, the oldest with white hair and a gold cloak; and Balthasar, a middle aged African in a purple cloak.

There were to represent not only the three gifts but the known continents: one young European, one older Asian, and one middle aged African. They represented global humanity.

The end of the pilgrimage brought us to the manger scene set up in the grotto. Real animals were kept nearby in a sheltered petting zoo. On impulse, Blair parked at the zoological station and we got to wander among the goats and sheep and burrows. I even fished out a few quarters to get hands-full of pellets to feed the creatures.

Then we were back in my Stratus and I was fishing the rest of my change out of my pocket to give a drop into the bucket of the person at the exit.

We drove back to the Dutch Hollow neighborhood where more secular decorations were in vogue.

These celebrated the season.

Not the reason.

Secular displays. In place of angels and shepherds and animals feeding at a manger that held a little baby were fiber optic reindeer with rotating heads, penguins with open umbrellas rode on a merry-go-round, inflatable headless snowmen surrounded by yard elves with snowmen's heads glued to their mitts ready to pitch them at a bullseye target on the neighbor's privacy fence.

Instead of a manger in a grotto, our neighborhood scenes climaxed in a roof top display of a wooden sleigh, with reindeer who had paused. Next to them was a bent over Santa Claus. He had dropped his red trousers to show the backside of his goodwill to men. Across the crack of Santa's moon a sticker had been plastered that read CENSORED!

"Now that is just ugly," Blair said.

"A dog-butt nasty Santa," I said.

"People are just so dirty anymore," Blair said.

Another left. Then a couple of rights. And we came to the end of the culvert. Right where it slipped under the curb. At the front yard of 2112 Springhill Drive.

16- For I Am Powerless To Control My Life and It Has Become Unmanageable.

Wednesday, I went back to New Hearts Recovery.

This time Larry had on a different concert t-shirt. A more gun metal gray with the cover of Rush's Caress of Steel. I gave him a thumb's up.

"That's my favorite band," I grinned.

"Well, I like a lot of the early stuff up to 'Hemispheres' for sure. I dropped out after 'Signals.' They're good. Just got into too many keyboards for me. Must have been tough on their guitar player. He is so first class," Larry said.

"Rush is one of those bands that went through so many phases, it's hard to find a fan that stayed with them through it all," I said. "Are you a pastor?"

"Not ordained," Larry said, "I did the steps and program of New Hearts to be the Group Leader here. When I was younger, I did some seminary classes but I dropped out. That's a long story. But I was a youth leader for a long time. I got into all those 90's metal bands. I would do youth rallies for a lot of young metal-fans. They called me the 'Rock N Roll Preacher' or Pastor Larry. Pantera was my fave if you hadn't guessed. But when Dimebag got murdered, a lot of people starting asking why God would let that happen. God opened a door for me to minister to a lot of hurting people.

"But then an old childhood experience hit me like PTSD. I lost my job and we lost our house. We were living in a car. So, I had to move in my with mother-in-law, God love her. While there, I got addicted to her pain killers. Then I found New Hearts. And God got me back on the Right Path.

"Now I have a dual diagnosis. Jesus is my Rock and my name is on His Roll. And God has given me a new circumcised fleshy heart."

Then he asked, "What's your story?"

I shrugged and pulled out my log sheet. "I got admitted to Kelter Ward C. I was on lock-down for three days. Then I got released but I've been having to do

358

intensive outpatient group therapy. This is my last week," I said.

"Do you mind asking why you were in Kelter Ward C?" Larry asked.

"I took some of my ex-wife's darvacet and did this," I pulled up the sleeve of my left wrist with my right hand to show the pink scar that was turning into a frown. "Got one on the other wrist, too. I was dead for at least five minutes before they brought me back."

"Dear Lord, you've been through hell," Larry said. "I know about the lock down. Kelter-Skelter is what I called it."

I grinned and nodded. "The whole thing was like *One Flew Over the Cukoo's Nest*.

"I would encourage you to continue going to a support group. Especially, a Christian twelve-step program. Ours is a safe place that would welcome you. I encourage you to continue working your recovery," Larry said.

Tonight's meal was more a potluck of party-style food and various deserts since this would be their last meeting before Christmas. Finger foods: there were smokies, hot wings, cheese dip, salsa dip, chili cheese dip, salsa and cheese dip, dip dip, sausage and cheddar cheese slices with Ritz crackers, assorted cheese slices, grapes. Deserts: sugar cookies, ginger bread cookies, fruit cake, pound cake, chocolate chip cookies, M and M chocolate chip cookies, and…Oh. My. God.

Ffffuuudddgggeee.

"*Fudge* me," I must have breathed out.

Except I didn't say *fudge*. I said the f-bomb. Fornication under consent of the king (both heavenly and earthly).

And I had said it in a church. Amongst God-fearing people. At a recovery meeting.

The serving ladies did not pretend not to hear me. They had heard what I said plain as day. One of them was Shirley.

"You know, God has heard it all," she smiled. "Only he knows what's in our hearts. And our hearts are deceitful and wicked. Yet, God still loves us."

I sighed and relaxed.

I was in a safe place.

I ate two plates. One for the finger foods and dips and one for the deserts. I ferreted two more pieces of fudge from the remaining three pieces and wrapped them in a napkin I secreted into the pocket of my coat.

It was good fudge. But not as good as my grandma's. Or my mom's. Both of them put half a piece of walnut on top of each piece.

Next was the large group meeting.

It followed the same form as last time, but seemed all new to me. They opened with a welcome and a song, "Lord, I Lift Your Name on High." Then the chips. At this point, I looked around for the man who looked like Thad G. I did not see him.

Next, was reciting the twelve steps. When Shirley came up with the prayer requests, she began with, "I know we have some visitors here tonight and some first timers. That really warms my heart. One of the most important things we can do other than have faith, is to pray and it is important to pray for others.   Some of you may remember Todd J. The little guy? Well, he lost his struggle with drugs." Her entire countenance changed: Her checks flushed red, her nose ran, and tears poured. She had to sniff them back and wipe off her chin with the back of her hand. "He OD'd. They tried to shock him but his heart just gave out. I hate it for his wife and his kids." There was a fresh round of tears out through her nose, which she had to wipe away. "And I hate it for him, too."

Larry came up. He and Shirley exchanged hugs and then they exchanged places. Larry began a lesson over Step Number One: For I am powerless to control my life and it has become unmanageable.

"What can we control? Not much. In the grand scheme of the universe, we have our breath and a free will choice. We can't stop the earth from spinning. We can't stop the rain. We can't stop the bills from coming or the taxes we have to pay. Can I get an amen?

"So, we want power. Position. Titles. And authority. Usually, to get power you need money. Everyone's respects money. Everyone respect you when you're rich. What's the saying? Wanna get rich? Get into politics. People are chasing after power and money. Rich or poor, they always want more.

"You see, when it comes to power, there's never enough of it. Because someone's always got more than you and you want more of theirs. Or someone doesn't have enough and envies what you got and wants more of yours.

"We think if we got money, then we got power and respect. And if we got those things then we got control.

"But what do we have control over? Like I said, not much.

"So, who does have power? The ultimate power? Who does have control? Over everything?"

Many people at the meeting said it out loud in chorus, "God!"

"That's right, fellow struggle buddies. When we try to control things, we tend to make it worse. Or royally screw it up. But we don't want to admit that we are helpless. Weak. So weak that one day we are going to die. There's no one here who is strong enough to escape death.

"I always hate it when someone says, 'Yeah, my ninety year-old grandpa fought for his last breath. He went out fighting. He was one tough old mule and there was no one tougher than him.'

"Well, yeah, there was. Death. And one day, everyone here is going to meet Death up close and personal.

"But there is someone who beat death. Someone who said no man takes my life from me but that I freely lay it down and if I lay it down then I will take it up myself. There is someone who died for all our weakness, all our sin. Someone who became weak and suffered and became our sin. Someone who died and then defeated death when he arose again."

Many in the crowd shouted, "Jesus!"

"Yes!" Larry encouraged. "Jesus!

"Things can get out of control fast! And we still try to lie to ourselves to keep playing the game. Even as we know we are losing!"

Larry had Shirley throw up another slide.

He read it out loud:

I've lied.

I've been vicious.

I've slandered and condemned.

I've been unforgiving and cruel.

I've been boastful.

I've had dirty and nasty thoughts.

I've used curse words.

I've chased after money and loved it more than anything.

I've struggled with my addictions to substances or things that make feel good.

I've refused to help someone in need because I had something against them.

I've hurt others on purpose and I've hurt myself by cutting.

I can no longer control my will. Time and time again I have done what I shouldn't do knowing that I shouldn't do it but I've kept right on doing it.

But thank God that I wasn't too lost to be saved. Or too broken to be made whole. Or my heart too stony to be melted like wax into a fleshy heart. It's not because I'm a good person, but because I am not that I must have faith in Jesus to save me because only God is good.

Despite my faults that I do not have control over, through my faith in Jesus Christ:

I am **LOVED** (John 3:16)

I am **APPROVED** (Romans 15:7)

I am **REDEEMED** (Psalm 111:9)

I am a **CHILD OF GOD** (John 1:12)

I have **PURPOSE** (Proverbs 16:4)

I am **FREE** (John 8:36)

I am **FORGIVEN** (1 John 1:9)

I am **SAVED** (John 3:16)

I will not let myself or anyone define me by what I do or let circumstances define me. I am not my past. I am no longer trapped by my sin nature.

Then Larry said, "Ephesians 2: 8-9 says, 'For it is by grace you have been saved, through faith—and this is not from yourselves, it is the gift of God—not by works, so that no one can boast.'

"Guys and gals and everyone in between, it all starts with Genesis 1:1 'In the beginning, God created the Heavens and the Earth.' If you don't believe that then you won't believe the rest of the Bible. It takes faith to be saved.

"Hebrews 1:1 says 'Now faith is the substance of things hoped for, the evidence of things not seen.' And verse 3 says 'By faith we understand that the worlds were framed by the word of God…' which takes us back to Genesis 1:1.

"You gotta believe that God exists. You gotta have faith. A lot of people stumble right there. But that's how it is.

"Even Hebrews 11:6 says 'But without faith it is impossible to please Him, for he who comes to God must believe that He is, and that He is a rewarder of those who diligently seek Him.'

"So, we'll wrap it up there for tonight. Because now we're getting into Step Two."

At that point, Larry picked up his acoustic guitar and led the group through the Newsboys "We Believe." Most of the group raised hands in praise and quite a few shed tears.

I was beyond moved.

Something was tugging at my sleeves.

Pulling at the stones in my heart.

I so wanted to go forward and have all my stones removed.

I longed for a fleshy heart.

But I chickened out.

Then Larry ended the large group meeting with the Serenity prayer.

Serenity. Accept. Change. Courage. Change. Can. Accepting. Taking. Trusting. Surrender.

There was a lot of surrender in order to get that *serenity*. And what did *serenity* mean? Peace.

Peace on earth, baby.

Peace on earth because of a baby, baby.

A King.

A Savior.

For eternity.

I didn't go forward.

And I didn't go to small group. I was troubled. And I didn't feel like sharing.

So I went back to 2112 Springhill Drive to ponder these things in my heart of stone.

17-From Burning Fudge To Hot Chocolate

2112 Springhill Drive had been my first home. Now it was twenty-three hundred feet full of mildewed rugs and closets. A brand new water heater. New coils for the furnace. An oversized air conditioning unit. And a hole in the back room addition.

Why was I so attached to it? Why had I not want to let go of it? Because I didn't want Blair to have it?

I sure hadn't been able to control much about what was happening to the residence now.

If I wanted to put a band-aid on the roof then I should have climbed up there and shoveled off the rest of the snow. Since what was left wasn't going to run-off on its own. Maybe I could nail a tarp down over the wet spot. But the heat and air guy said the water would just find another way in through the ceiling. Didn't matter what I did since the slope was too flat.

"Justin, what are you doing?" Blair asked.

"Looking at the hole in the roof," I said surveying the foot long wet gash in the ceiling noting that even the exposed beams looked wet. The water buckets had been replaced by a slender trash can that could hold more and take longer to accumulate. There was already a good amount of cold dirty water sloshing around in it now. "What are you doing?"

"Getting ready to fix you some Christmas fudge," she said.

"Really?" I asked. I wasn't going to hold my breath. And I had forgotten about the two pieces I had copped from the New Hearts meeting. Best I keep them hidden a while longer. "You ever made it before?"

"No. But I will for you. I just found a recipe in the paper. We got all we need," Blair said. She was going through the cabinets and drawers getting out every pot and pan. "You could help."

"I'll help clean," I offered.

"You turd," she said. The pots and pans banged together in cacophonous tones. She cussed as she made a ruckus.

I sniffed the air.

Whatever she was cooking was now burning.

Blair cussed some more. She could cuss more than a Stephen King book.

Then the pots began to fly. Making a landing in the sink.

"Screw your fudge! I'm going to bed!" Blair said, surrendering on her promise to do something outside her comfort zone. The task was too daunting. The patience required beyond her.

After she slammed the bedroom door, the house quieted.

But there was no peace.

I could feel something. Coming down like a smothering blanket. Something dark.

Fear? Hopelessness? Despair?

It descended from the ceiling like a spider to hide and skulk in the corner.

The pink scars on my wrists itched. Fearful of those things getting a hold of me again. And of me getting a hold of a knife again.

My head throbbed. From what might happen next.

First, the gas line.

Then the water heater.

Then the furnace.

And now the roof.

Each problem had grown in expense but the roof seemed the biggest obstacle. Would it need to be torn out and replaced? Or somehow detached and propped up to the correct slope?

Was I just throwing good money after bad? I didn't have any money to throw. I needed about fifty thousand dollars wrapped in hundred dollar bundles stuffed in my Christmas morning stocking.

Where was I going to get fifty thousand dollars by Christmas? By New Year's? Was my New Year's going to be like my old year?

Sucky.

I pushed myself out of Grandpa's old tweed recliner and went to survey the wreckage in the kitchen. She had left a gas burner on. A trail of coca clumps across the stove top from where some of it was smoking on the burner.

I turned the burner off and used a wet rag to rub off the burner and then clean up the clumps.

Blair had left the cocoa container and the flour bag out. As well as a can of condensed milk. So, I put those items up.

The abandoned sauce pan of watery chocolate concoction sat tilted in the sink with chocolate splashes around. I lifted the sauce pan out and clean off the bottom and set it back on the burner. The sink was easy to clean out with the sprayer.

The concoction was very thin and watery. But, I could smell the chocolate. So, on a whim I turned the burner back on and poured in some regular milk until it began to smoke and bubble.

I turned off the burner, lifted the sauce pan from the stove, and poured the contents into my biggest Star Wars mug I could find: an open head of Darth Vadar.

Taking the warm mug of smoking hot chocolate, I eased back into my Grandpa's recliner to quaff some nepenthe and try to absorb some peace and quiet.

That was the last respite I got for the rest of week.

18- Sugar Plum Fairies Wear Boots

America's Bank was true to their Scrooge-ish promise. They did it all and infinitely more: they let us out at twelve-thirty—a whopping thirty minutes earlier than promised--without docking us for half a day. The exchange was that no one could get a lunch break.

It was Thursday and the day of the night before Christmas!

Christmas Eve!

I was plenty excited. For why I didn't know! I took the elevator to the first floor. Then I hit the street and got on the Metro at Union Station. I got off of at the Locust Street station.

I came up at the corner of St. Louis Center and already stores were beginning to pull their front gates down. There were lunch-breakers and merry-makers and shoppers still out on the street.

I entered one end of the Center, hit the ATM at the street level and got a paltry sum, took the elevators going up, and walked through the second floor wing into the side entrance to the old Famous Barr building. The classic style department store. Departments for each category and item. Housed on old wood floors with commission based sales clerk. It all had some kind of style and panache.

Once there, I powered shopped. Something for my dad—a Dr. Pepper Christmas tie. Something for my mom-- a Mary Engelbrite ornament with a freckled face girl holding a bowl of chocolate covered cherries that read: *Chocolate Makes Everything Better.* . Something for myself—something Star Wars (I typically put *To: Justin, From: Santa* on self-bought gifts like this; this way at least I know I had at least one gift and it would be something I'd want).

Then I stopped by the jewelry stand, which wasn't too far from my goal: the Famous Barr candy stand. I picked out a heart necklace for Blair. And some earrings for my mom. It was always easier to buy for my dad than my mom—my dad never asked for anything and I really had to use my brain to come up with a gift that would surprise him.

Stepping over to the candy stand, I saw such wondrous things on display: Bins of ju-ju-bees and goobers. Tiers of chocolate covered cherries and raspberries. Trays of fudge in all different varieties: walnut, vanilla, and pecan.

All kinds of sugary concoctions. All manner of dainties stuffed with either fruit or nuts. All sorts of shapes and colors.

And large items like chocolate covered oreos, large pretzel sticks dipped in chocolate and dusted with sprinkles. Different sizes of gingerbread men with colored clothes made up different icings. And the richest of all creations: large turtles with pecan dotted shells over caramel stuffed insides.

I got a package of both white chocolate and chocolate pretzels for me, goobers for my dad, chocolate covered cherries for mom, peanut brittle for Blair, and a turtle apiece for my ex-mother-in-law and ex-step-father-in-law.

That was it.

I was done with my list.

I was about through all the cash I taken out of the ATM.

America's Bank had deigned to pay us our pittance today, but I had to save the rest of my check for the house payment and utilities and God knew what house emergency next.

Then it was out the door. Back down to the corner to Locust Street. And then across the street to the opposite side to catch the Metro going EastBound as I lived on the East Side.

I took a seat on the concrete bench that had been set into a wall recess and cooled my heels until we could hear the whine of the Metro's trams, as the pantograph moved down the electrical line.

As I stood up with the tram cars coming into the station, I heard, "Justin!"

I looked around and moving through the crowd of riders was my Dad.

We moved towards each other and gave each other a hug. No words. No regrets. No recriminations.

The tram cars were slowly down.

"Dad, I got you and mom something for Christmas!" I said and held up my Famous Barr bags. "I don't have them wrapped. Do you want them now?"

Dad smiled. "Wrap them first. Give them to us later." His word was better than 'change. He'd never welshed on a promise to me yet.

It was a seed of hope.

The tram doors opened and the riders passed between us.

"Goodbye for now, Justin," my Dad said. "Love you." Which I'd heard him say as many times in my life as my ex-mother-in-law had invited me over.

"Love you," I said. The last of the riders were boarding now. There was a buzz. The doors began to close.

I moved forward to the next tram and got on just as the door closed behind me.

And just like that, on the tram went eastbound.

19-Coining

I got home before four. And I took my gifts and found the wrapping paper and name tags and scissors and tape and went into the back room addition. I wrapped like crazy and got it all done by five-thirty.

I had a good thirty minutes before I had to report to my last—*last*—intensive outpatient group therapy.

Blair was just waking up. The meds Dr. Frost had her on made her so doggone tired if she took them all and on time everyday. I told her she'd better kick it into high gear if she wanted to ride with me to my last group meeting so we could go straight from Our Lady's to her parents.

I have to admit she looked cute when she'd woke up from a long winter's nap. Even if her brain hadn't reset yet, her checks burned with ruddy marks and her lips were full.

She mumbled something about gifts to wrap, dip to make, and muffins to bake.

I asked if that meant she didn't want to ride with me. That meant I'd have to come back here and get her. And might put us at her mother's by eight-fifteen.

In the end, she mumbled something and closed herself off in the bathroom. Trying to get a proper response, I repeated my question. Finally, she yelled a healthy, "NO! Go ahead to your stupid meeting. Lot of good it's doing us!"

So, I left and arrived at the back parking lot to the ancillary entrance into Our Lady's. Only it was locked. And the lights were off in the utility corridor and no lamp was on in the Hope Counselor's office.

I hadn't missed it, had I? I was about ten minutes early. It was Thursday, December Twenty-fourth, wasn't it?

I checked the back screen on my phone.

Correct time, correct place.

I thought about going back to my car where I would wait until six-thirty before leaving. I saw other cars pulling into the parking lot. Maybe I had arrived too early.

Then three cars pulled into the front of the parking lot, one after another, and parked near the top of the row. One by one, the three counselors: Sandy L., Paul D., and Jayne V. All three were carrying gift boxes.

Sandy L. unlocked the door and I took it to go inside first so I could hold the door open for the counselors. After the counselors had gone in, Hannah S. walked past me—I must have been standing downwind from her before then because my nose let me know she hadn't bothered with a bath in quite a few days. Next, came Ja-Rod who wanted a fist bump. Sure, why not? It was Christmas Eve!

At about three after six, Everett P. made his last appearance for the group therapy.

"Last one," I said with a smile.

Everett gave me a 'What? Me worry?' look and went in with a scowl.

"Well, here goes nothing," I said and went inside.

The meeting was brief. There were no reprimands. No hand-outs. No warnings.

Instead, we went around the small circle and had three minutes to talk about what we've learned the past two weeks about ourselves.

"I learned I'm not in control of much. But that I should take anything that comes at me, good, bad, or ugly moment to moment, breath by breath, and to accept hardships as the pathway to peace. That's what I think I want for Christmas. 'Peace on earth and toward men goodwill.' Up to today, I would have told you 'fudge,'" I said.

"I learned about how close I am to addiction rebounding. I've been off xanex for a week. And it's been a different experience. I've got to get better at just breathing and not panicking. Like Justin said, it's one day at a time," Hannah S.said.

Ja-Rod said, "Recovery is an attitude. Sobriety is a choice. I'm gonna take it one day at time. Each day is a celebration. I used to make excuses to get high. Now I make excuses to stay sober."

Everyone looked at Everett P. who looked like he was chewing on something to say, but trying to swallow it at the same time.

"When I first came here, I didn't think I should be here. I didn't think it was fair. Lots of people drink and it don't bother 'em. Lots of people blow weed which I think should be legal. It's them pills. It's so tempting. I could name half a dozen people I work with who pop 'em like candy. Yet, they never get popped.

"Well, I did. And I hate to admit it, but maybe what y'all been saying is right. Maybe I got a problem. Maybe I needed this. I'll still need help. I don't want to lose my job. Or my wife." Here, Everett began to choke up and flow with tears. "Or my kids."

He stopped talking so he put his head in his hands and squeezed his tears back. Everett gave a good sniff to suck back the tears.

"You can do it, man," Ja-Rod encouraged. "Just don't give in or give up. One step at a time. One day at a time. Hour by hour. Moment to moment. Breath by breath."

"Congratulations," Paul D. said. "You all have been clean. You've come to every meeting. You went to your twelve steps. You are ready to graduate."

"But you all need to continue to work your recovery," Jayne V. said. "You all need a good clean and responsible support group around you. Someone you can ask to be an accountability partner with. You can't do it alone."

"Okay," Sandy L. said as she stood up and Jayne V. and Paul D. stood behind her and gathered up the small gift boxes. There were two. Each counselor opened the lid on their boxes as they held them out.

"We will begin our graduation commencement," Sandy L. said.

"Hannah L.," Sandy L. began. "You are stronger than you know. Don't doubt yourself. Your biggest fear is that you might turn into your dad. Don't carry his guilt. You are your own person. You're your own choice. Choice to say sober. Choice to work your recovery. It won't be easy. But remember, it's easier not to try and give up. So, don't give up."

Hannah S. stood up and went forward to be handed a coin. And we all clapped.

Paul D. stood up to facilitate for Ja-Rod. "Ja-Rod, you are strong and determined. It takes courage to want to be sober. But you need a good accountability partner or will you get tired and weak and want to quit. Because no matter how strong you think you are or indomitable your think your will is, you will get tired and worn out. And that's when your stress triggers come at you to go back to the old ways. You are enthusiastic about being sober. You won't go far on enthusiasm, you won't go far without it. Have a plan for the bad days and when you come up against a trigger," Sandy L. said.

"I will," Ja-Rod said as he came up to get his coin. We all clapped.

From what I could tell, the coin was gold with icons and printing. Fairly large printing. A banner arced over the top and bottom.

Jayne V. stepped forward to matriculate Everett P.: "Everett P., you don't have to be a follower. Strike out on your own. Not everyone around is doing the same thing. That's just an excuse. As you know now: find excuses not to drug. And when everyone else is letting you down realize that doing the right thing never lets what's right down. It's not easy. It never will be easy. But you won't be letting yourself down. I challenge you to find the reasons and the strength to be sober one day at a time."

Everett P. gave an "aw, shucks" gaze at his feet and stepped up to get his coin. All we all clapped.

It was Sandy L.'s turn again. This time it was to commend me. "Justin R.," she said and paused on a smile. "You worry too much about what others think. You can't please everyone and if when you try you'll find out that you are making yourself miserable. Be your own person. Stay true to what you know is right. Find your boundaries. Make your boundaries. And stick to your boundaries. Work your recovery. You won't be alone even when you think you might be."

Every word she spoke struck home. Every word was like gold to mine ears. Every word was true.

I stepped up and she handed me my coin. All they clapped.

And I sat back down to savor my coin. I looked it over. Turned it flipside time and time again.

The front had a dove in the middle. The dove stood for peace. The dove stood for the messenger that the floods had receded. And the dove stood for the Holy Spirit. God's favor upon a person.

The top banner arced with the words: ONE DAY AT A TIME.

I now knew where this famous line came from.

That prayer.

The prayer that was becoming a lifeline for me.

I turned the coin over.

On the top banner the words were arced: THE FREEDOM TO BE ME.

And below was another banner that read: TO THINE OWN SELF BE TRUE.

And below it was a streaming ribbon, the kind used for decoration for celebrations.

Because recovery was a celebration.

Life was a gift.

Meant to be lived with the good, the bad, and the ugly.

And sometimes, the ugly can be where the pearl is hiding.

The pearl that is like the kingdom of heaven. The pearl that the farmer found and went and sold all he had to possess it. The pearl that is not to be thrown before swine because it would be trampled underfoot.

We lined up for final handshakes and for our counselors to sign our log sheets and sign them. Then they gave us certificates of completion.

We had graduated.

Now we would go forth into the cruel world. And cruel it was indeed. Full of darkness and wailing of gnashing of teeth.

We all hugged and said our goodbyes.

I got behind the wheel of my Dodge Stratus and hummed a simple little Christmas song.

20-Mixed Nuts

When I got back to 2112 Springhill Drive there had been an attempt at cleaning. Most of the tubs and boxes were still out. But they had been restacked. Even the vacuum cleaner, often forlorn and bored in this house, waited at attention. I couldn't tell if it had been used or not.

Above our open kitchen area, two tube socks hung there. Long and white with red stripes and emblazoned with the St. Louis Cardinals logo. At the top of each Blair had put two names in black magic marker: Blair. Justin.

"You're back early," Blair said.

It was just before seven. Usually, I got back after eight.

"We had our last meeting. We had a 'coining," I said.

"What's that?" Blair asked.

"Kinda like a graduation," I said.

"I wouldn't know. I've never really finished any group sessions," Blair said. "So, if you're done are you not an addict anymore? Did they fix you?"

I laughed at her naivete. "Once an addict. Always addict. Being sober is a choice. Working recovery means working it every day."

She was in the kitchen fixing up something on the quick. From the smell of it, it was French onion dip. For ingredients, she had used a sixteen ounce container of fresh sour cream and a dry packet of French onion soup—that would make it strong enough for the hair on your arm to stand up.

"Speaking of work, did you get a Christmas bonus?" Blair asked.

"No," I said.

"You work at a bank and you didn't get a Christmas bonus?" Blair asked incredulously.

"After all the days I've missed, my Christmas bonus is that I get to keep my job," I said.

"We could have used that money. To fix the roof," she said.

I nodded. She was showing wisdom and giving priority to what needed to be taken care of. Usually, she was thinking of six ways to Sunday on how to spend money she hadn't even gotten into her hand yet.

"Your mother ask you to bring something over?" I asked. It was my turn to be incredulous.

"No, Sherlock, she didn't," Blair said with a tinge of venom. "I don't care what she thinks. You're supposed to bring something to someone's house when you get invited. Especially, for a party."

"But we're not going to be there for dinner. Your son wants us to come after dinner," I said. "Why?"

"He thinks I'm ruining the family. Again!" Blair snapped.

I hadn't thought about what effect our reunion would have on her family. Nobody but nobody was in favor in our getting back together. Or, was there more to the story?

"I like how my son gets to call the shots. They let him dictate who comes and goes at his whim. They're getting together tonight just to have us over. But tomorrow, they'll have their real Christmas party!" Blair wailed.

"Why do they let him tell them what to do?" I was stupid enough to ask.

"Because, somehow every holiday, somebody in my family always manages to ruin it. Someone says something about me and I tell them off. Then I don't get invited to dinner for a couple of months. Then they decide at the last minute to let me come. Only they won't let me cook or bring anything! That's such an insult!

"And I am a good cook. Better than my mom. And my grandma's—sorry, step-grandma's—cookies are crap! Then, whenever someone says something about me or my son do they really expect me to sit there and take it? I don't care whose house it is! I'm gonna defend my little boy! I hate my family.

"Something will happen. Mark my words. Something always happens. How much you wanna bet everything will be fine for a while? Then someone will open their big freakin' mouth. Maybe about you this time. So just be ready. That's all I'm telling you," Blair prophesized.

I thought that was the final word on the matter but Blair had more to add. "I'm gonna freakin' bring something this time! You know what? I don't care if anyone brought a different dip, I'm bringing something. This will be the greatest dip ever. It's your dad's recipe, Justin. And I'm gonna set it out there along with all their food and not say a word. And then someone asks who made this awesome French and onion sour cream dip, I'm sing out, 'That was me!' And they'll all say it was the best freakin' dip they've ever tasted and let's see how grandma likes that!"

"Step-grandma," I corrected.

"Step-grandma," Blair echoed. Then she finished getting ready and put her wrapped gifts and the dip concoction and a bag of Ruffles for dipping into one of my paper Famous Barr shopping bags. And I had a plastic Best-Mart sack to carry my gifts for her parents.

We left the house and got to her parents by seven-fifteen. Blair had been on the phone with her mom right up the moment I parked along the curbed and turned the fob off. We both breathed in.

"Well, here goes nothing," Blair said with an exhale.

I held my breath.

We took our meager gifts inside.

The extended family was there. Grandpa Clark, who said when he met me: "You're the one what married her last year, then divorced her this year and now you wanna get back together by the end of the year? Trying for that tax break?" His new wife Miss Lois, who smiled and said, "Nice to meet you, I'm sure" and gave me a limp cold hand to squeeze. Uncle Ralph and Aunt Alice, who didn't bother to shake my hand and just gave me a nod. Cousin Ted and his wife Carol and their three children, Tex, Susan, and Patty. The husband and wife gave me a hardy hello but one of the kids—probably Susan--stuck their tongue out at me. Then was my ex-step-father-in-law, Trent, was a security guard and worked off nights. Finally, there was my ex-mother-law who was ten years older than me while Trent was a few years younger than me. She was done head to toe with lipstick, nail polish, gloss, and glitter. The queen reigning in her court sitting in the best chair.

I noticed two things straight away.

One, not only had they finished their Christmas meal, but they were passing out the candies and other goodies. It looked like Best-Mart brand store bought items taken out of a bag or box and put onto cheap glass and plastic trays. I hadn't missed much (but what was I truly missing—my own family's Christmas Eve party foods). The spread at New Hearts had been delightful next to this tacky, boring fare.

Two, Blair's son was not in attendance.

Blair with her super-tuned perceptive powers noticed both things, too. Only it was her place to say something. Not mine.

So she said, "Where's my son?"

"After he ate, he asked if he could open all his gifts. Then he went back into his bedroom with his new toys," Blair's mother said.

Blair was crestfallen. She lifted up a paper sack full of gifts. "But I brought him these. I'd like to see him open them."

"We'll give them tomorrow. It'll be Christmas, dear," Blair's mother said.

"But I won't see him. I won't be here," Blair complained.

"I'll call you on the phone and you can talk to him then, dear," Blair's mother said.

"No, I want to see him open the gifts I bought for him," Blair said. She left the living room calling out the name of her son and walked to the hallway leading to the bedrooms.

"Now, don't bother him, Blair," Trent said. "He may change his mind and you can get to come over tomorrow and he can thank you."

Blair made circles like a lost mother hen. Then she came back to the family circle. She looked at the trays and the individual plates that the family were nibbling from.

She still had the Famous Barr paper bag in her hands. She came into the kitchen and tried to reach into the bag to pull out the container of French Onion dip and the bag of Ruffles without anyone hearing or noticing. But she made too much noise for them not to.

"What's that, dear?" Blair's mother asked.

"It's French and Onion dip," Blair said.

"You didn't have to bring anything," Blair's mother chided.

"She doesn't have room for that," Trent harped. And then added, "No one's going to want to eat it anyway."

Blair was resolute. Her smiled unchanged. Her course of action unfazed. "Well, you don't have to be so mean about it. It's Justin's dad recipe. You might like it if you try it."

"I'm sure it's great for Justin's dad. But it'll give Trent heart burn," Blair's mother said.

"Mom, you should have made some fudge. Justin won't get to have any of his mom's this year," Blair announced. That was the last thing I wanted any of them to know.

"You're not going to get to see your parents for Christmas?" Blair's mother asked. "And I did make some. It's in the kitchen with the sandwich fixings."

"I haven't got that quite coordinated yet," I said. I guess I was still hopeful.

"They're not talking to him on account of we're back together," Blair said.

"They'll get over it," Trent said.

"Or maybe not," Blair's mother said.

"You already got into the Christmas cookies and candy?" Blair asked with an air of disappointment.

"We said you could come over at seven for dessert. You showed up late," Trent said.

Some of the family laughed.

"Now Blair," her mother chided. "You and Justin go get yourself some food and cookies. Then we'll exchange gifts. We'll even wait for you."

Blair led me into the kitchen and dinette room. The spread was laid out across the kitchen counter and breakfast style table. Various cold cuts. Cheap individually wrapped cheese slices. Loafs of store bought bread. Bottle of mustard. Bottle of mayonnaise. Pickle tray and celery tray—both snug in the black plastic Best-Mart trays. And to wash it all down was your choice of Best-mart's Best Choice soda flavors in two-liter bottles.

A veritable holiday feast.

Only the best for your family.

Under it all, I sensed the barest fulfillment of obligation. I'm not sure I sensed any filial love.

I was not impressed. My work potluck had more interesting fare given with tender loving care.

We fixed ourselves a quick sandwich on plastic plates and came back into the living room. I sat on the floor away from everyone and Blair sat at her mother's feet. She was in her majesty's court, I had to remember.

"Honey," Blair addressed me. "Want some of my mother's fudge?"

Since she asked me in front of everyone, I had to try it. And not one, but two pieces. It was dry. And the walnuts bitter.

"Honey," Blair addressed me again. "Care for some French and Onion dip?"

I knew better than to pass on something she had brought over. So, I tried a couple of chips full of dip. It was a bizarre combination to hit my stomach: fudge and French Onion dip. "Good," I lied.

"Well, maybe my son would like some. If he would come out of his room, that is," Blair said.

"Just let it be, Blair," Blair's mother said.

The family members passed the plates of desserts our way. I took a couple of mixed sandwich cookies and a double stuffed hydrox.

After we'd caught up with the calories, Blair handed out her gifts for each of the family members present. They were kind enough to accept them. She got a few in return: one from Grandpa Clark and Lois, one from Uncle Ralph and Aunt Alice and one from Ted and Carol.

I got nothing. And that was ok. So, I sat in silence and watched as they opened theirs and showed minimal gratitude even though Blair tried to connect each gift with a need to show how doting she was and then Blair opening each gift with the zeal of an excited child discovering something precious.

After the rustles of tissue paper and wrapping paper had subsided, I asked Blair to hand out my meager gifts to her parents.

"How nice, Justin. It looks so rich. Thank you," my ex-mother-in-law purred.

"Cool. Thanks. I do like turtles," Trent said. And then he got out of his recliner and came over to me. "This is from all of us." He sat their joint gift down at my feet. "Merry Christmas."

It was a can of Best-Mart Mixed Nuts. The lid black and sides wrapped with a picture of the nuts inside. Complete with a red bow.

It was the most insulting gift I had ever received in my life.

I took it with gratitude and I smiled at their little joke.

"Thank you, so much," I said.

"I'd really like to see my son open the gifts I got for him," Blair said as if she were putting her foot down. Or putting it into her mouth.

"He's not coming back out until after you leave, Blair," her mother said.

"That's so stupid. Why does he want to ruin Christmas? What's his problem?" Blair pouted.

"He's not the one ruining Christmas," Trent said. "And I think you know what his problem is."

"Are you saying his problem is me?" Blair taunted. "Is that what you're saying?"

"Blair, I think it's time for you to leave," her mother said.

"Why? It's only seven-forty-five. I've only been here a half hour," she said.

"A little of you goes a long way," Grandpa Clark said.

"I don't need your advice. Not on anything. You didn't do so great a job on raising my mother anyway," Blair snapped.

Aunt Alice was the next to chime in, "Blair, you're a miserable person and you make everyone around you miserable."

"How many times have you've been married before Uncle Ralph? How many times did you sleep around?" Blair accused.

"Time's up. That's enough of that. Out you go. Ex-husband. French and Onion dip and all," Trent said standing up to get his swagger on and back up his bluff.

Blair stood up next. "If I leave now, I'm never coming back here again."

It was Trent's move next. "Fine by me. I never wanted you or your ex-husband here anyway."

Blair huffed, "Fine. We're going but I'm never coming back."

I got into behind the wheel and Blair kept quiet.

We came. We saw. We had been asked to leave.

A holiday first for me.

On the way home, Blair didn't apologize for her family. She continued to sulk.

I remember times hating my dad because he'd get mad at my not talking to him. I hadn't wanted to bother when all he did was find fault. But sooner or later, you have to talk to each other, at least out of some desperation.

And I could remember my paternal grandmother and my dad getting into arguments over religion and my dad standing his ground and not giving in under my grandmother's childish insults, to the point that he threw her out of our house on more than one occasion. She would be crying at the door, her hand on the knob, and turn and say, "Son, I love you, but you're wrong. And I'm never coming back."

He reminded her that her only job was to leave the house.

So she did.

But they didn't stay mad that long. She'd be back soon enough. Whistling as she did our laundry. She always helped with the laundry or clean the windows. My dad would even say she was a big help. Not a big mouth, which she was that, too, but he'd never say. Except I never saw them apologize or hug or say that they loved each other in front of we kids.

Then again, despite her family's poor execution of the type of food laid out and its presentation and their snubbing and belittling of me, and her son's ignoring of Blair, and then the picking of the fight between Blair and, well, everybody else, I still hadn't heard a word from my own family.

Surprisingly, in reverse irony, it was me who said, "Sorry."

"Yeah, well, Christmas has sure been sucky," Blair said.

There was no denying that.

21-Merry Christmas (I Don't Want To Fight Tonight)

It was the night before Christmas.

And all was quiet throughout the house.
But there was no peace.
No cheese even for a mouse
Tubs and boxes stood in monolithic columns.
Holding stuff and junk to be hoarded and lorded over.
Dust danced on top of the lids.
There wasn't even a Christmas tree to plug in.
Tube socks hung on the wall in despair.
Would Santa Claus even show up?
Would he even care?
And Blair in her nightgown, and I in my clothes
Couldn't settle our brains, let alone our souls
Down for a quiet winter's nap.
I had heard Blair sobbing again. Probably laying under the quilts of her queen sized bed.

I sat in my Grandpa's recliner in the back room addition to numb myself with *Everybody Loves Raymond*. Only that wasn't what was being streamed.

A third of the channels showed *It's A Wonderful Life*, a third *A Christmas Story*, and then there was a mix of cartoon classics: Rankin and Bass' unforgettable story of misfits *Rudolph the Red Nosed Reindeer*, *A Charlie Brown Christmas* which dared to trigger haters with its presentation of the nativity story told in Luke, and the classic neo-gothic *How the Grinch Stole Christmas* with Boris Karloff's narration and a "You're a Mean One Mr. Grinch" sung by gothic bass Thurl Ravenscroft with Chuck Jones jazzy-gothic animation. There was nostalgia fashioned old with *The Homecoming: A Christmas Story*: the first show about the Waltons. Even *A Christmas They Never Forgot*: about the Ingalls family's Christmas settler style (before they got cancelled from the air and culture). And then there was the Hallmark Channel that gave itself over to non-stop 24 hour Christmas story saturation of do-they-love-each-other-they-don't-love-each-other-they-do storyline told through a female perspective, then a male perspective, and then a canine perspective.

And there was the granddaddy of all Christmas stories: about a hundred versions of *A Christmas Carol*. The second-best known Christmas story next to the original.

Every generation had a Christmas movie they claimed for their own. It was always built around nostalgia of celebrating Christmas with family. And this current generation's choice of Christmas no doubt was *Elf*.

I had a plethora of choices to watch Christmas unfold itself through pixilated digital perfection.

Preparing my heart for the inevitable.

Tomorrow would be Christmas morning.

The promise of peace on earth and goodwill towards men. Would it be fulfilled?

Or would it turn out like Blair's promise of fudge?

And then a thought, with free-floating wings, popped into my head. *Why don't you make the fudge?*

Why hadn't I thought of it before?

Why hadn't I done it by now?

I could do it, couldn't I?

What was stopping me?

I had a body, two capable hands, and a mind with a freewill.

Why not?

I started to get out of my Grandpa's recliner, but another thought came to me: why had I taken Blair back?

I did not have to. At point, I had chosen to.

Yes, she had pestered me with pleas to reconcile before the thirty days were up and we could annul the divorce. I'd heard of annulling a marriage but never a divorce.

Yes, she had come over one day to 2112 Springhill Drive, unbidden and uninvited to make a pass.

Yes, she had called me over to her apartment where I had seen her messy hoarding in all her spider web glory.

But the final chink in the chain had been when she had called me on a Saturday with the plea: "You've got to help me. I've got nowhere to turn," Blair spat out.

"Why?" I had asked.

"Because I'm in jail," she had said.

"Why?" I asked again.

It had been her day to see her son. Only her son had not wanted to spend any time with her and had gone to his dad's. With his new pregnant girlfriend. That had sent Blair into orbit. She convinced her new boyfriend to drive her over to her ex-husband's.

She had stood on the front porch and huffed and puffed to be let in so she could see her son as per their court agreement.

The son refused. The ex-husband refused. And then his girlfriend had stepped outside.

Blair's hands had flashed out. There had been a struggle. Her ex-husband had come out just as Blair had picked up a garden trowel from the porch and was going to attack the pregnant girlfriend Manson style.

The ex-girlfriend had defended herself and pushed back.

Blair had fallen off the porch and broken her knee, so she claimed.

They had called the police. And Blair had called for an ambulance.

The ambulance had arrived first and three paramedics had taken her to the emergency room. The sheriff's deputy had shown up at the hospital after assault charges had been filed. He couldn't arrest her because her knee had been broken and needed to be treated. So, the deputy had cut her a deal. He let her go on her own recognizance on the condition that she would turn herself in to be booked on the charge.

Blair hadn't and a bench warrant had been issued.

Her ex's pregnant girlfriend kept calling the police on Blair everytime she'd called to talk to her son, to let the police know where Blair was calling from.

Blair had wisely turned herself in. And now needed two hundred dollars to be bailed out. Or she'd stay in the county lock up until she went before the judge.

The new boyfriend had decided to back out at this point. He'd seen enough to know it would never change.

Blair's mother didn't have the money. And wouldn't have given it to her is she'd had it.

So left that me.

I was her only hope.

"You're my only hope," she pleaded without the Obi-wan tagged on.

I swallowed bitter pride and had hocked one of my bass guitars for the two hundred dollars. It was a 1986 Precision Bass Special. A one of kind. How I would miss that bass guitar.

Then I had gone down to the county jail and bailed her out.

I drove her back to her ratty apartment in my Stratus. A hug had turned into a kiss and then she was pulling me through the rooms of hoarded treasure to her bedroom.

I saw all my old stuff. My parents stuff. Stuff I'd grown up with. Stuff she had taken. Stuff she had been selling on ebay to help make her rent.

I had come to a shrine of spite.

It was sick.

I had torn myself away and went back to 2112 Springhill Drive.

The next day she was knocking at my door.

And one thing had led to another and now she was back with all her own stuff and what she hadn't sold off that used to belong to me.

And now I was getting what I paid for.

People don't change, I was learning the hard way.

I should have learned it the first time. After eight years of frustration and misery. Instead, I had wasted a year and a half feeling sorry for myself. I had partied all night and I didn't care if didn't make it home by morning. I was perfectly unhappy in trying to throw my life away.

Through all that, I had learned just how empty the bottom of an empty bottle was. And how sharp the broken glass of an empty bottle could cut.

I had learned the truth of the lyrics from the Animals' song "Good Times": I'd traded the chance of making good memories by partying it up and getting nothing in return but a hangover and alcohol poisoning and guilt and shame and empty friends with empty words spending empty nights wasting our lives.

Oh, what fun it is to sing a drinking song tonight!

Yeah, right.

What crap.

I got up from Grandpa's recliner and went into the kitchen. Determined to make some fudge and have something to show from this whole mess.

As I began to search for the recipe Blair had used and the necessary pans and ingredients, I heard something. Low and steady. At first, I thought it was the gasoline gone bad.

It was the hissing of gas.

It was the whispering of words.

Coming from the bedroom.

Blair was on her phone. Talking to someone. In low conspiratorial tones.

Another thought took me. Not quite as free floating with freedom ringing as making the fudge myself. It was more like the buzzing of a fly in mine ear.

Get on her laptop. Email your parents. Let them know you're okay. And maybe…maybe you should check her IM history.

What a wild hair of a thought. I hadn't thought about that. In weeks.

That was like spying.

That was mischevious.

That was devious

That was delicious.

But that's what I did.

I went into the living room where Blair kept her laptop tucked away on the half buried living room couch. It was a pink floral print and very stiff. And barely open because of the columns of tubs surrounding it.

I opened the laptop, put in her password, which was the name of her son. And opened a web-browser. Then I opened my yahoo email account and started to draft them an email.

TO: Mom and Dad

FROM: Justin

Re: Merry Christmas!

Merry Christmas Mom and Dad!

I hope you have a great Christmas. Hope your fudge turned out well. We went over to Blair's family's for Christmas Eve. Didn't stay too long. Had a nice time. They even got me a gift!

Hope Santa brings you everything you want!

Love,

Justin

Before I hit SEND an IM window popped open.

MERRYPRANKSTER101: Want sum fun?

BLAIR1975: (idle)

Merry Prankster rang a bell. But I thought that had just been weird dream. Or flashback.

Or it could be one of Blair's friends sending a Christmas message.

Only Blair didn't have too many friends.

Acquaintances? Tons. But they were kept at a safe distance.

How about on-line friends? That was the best way to keep an acquaintance at a safe distance.

So, I typed back. BLAIR1975: Merry Christmas to the Merry Prankster

MERRYPRANKSTER101: Screw Christmas Let's play Like before

BLAIR1975: Sorry. Tired Better get to bed so Santa can come

MERRYPRANKSTER101: I can be ur Santa When u want me over again

BLAIR1975: Im back with my x

MERRYPRANKSTER101: Didnt u kick him out Did u get the house

BLAIR1975: Got something better Got my husband back Merry Christmas

MERRYPRANKSTER101: K If it dont work out let me no Im ready when u r

I didn't click off the message box. Instead, I went to USER ACCOUNT. Then MESSAGE. Then HISTORY. There were a half dozen usernames in the history. All of them dating back to last summer about two weeks after I'd left.

While I'd contacted all my creditors and had consulted with bankruptcy lawyers Blair had been busy, too. I opened up a few of the dated chats of each user. But the most dated messages had been with the MERRYPRANKSTER101. The chatting had turned quickly to flirting. And a few sextings. Then the browser history showed that pictures had been shared. And then a webcam had been shared. Then the texts had gotten quite graphic.

"What are you doing on my computer?" Blair's voice was caked with sleep as she leaned against the hallway. Her beauty had been stripped away. And her pride. I was talking with the ghost of her old wounds now.

"Just was going to ask you the same thing," I said.

"What do you mean?" she asked.

I turned the screen around so she could see the browser history.

"Why are you looking at my browser history?" she demanded. Her cheeks were growing livid again.

"Why were you sexting this guy?" I asked.

"I told you I was flirting a little after you left. Just to make you jealous," Blair said.

I opened the most torrid email and began to quote it.

"'MERRYPRANKSTER: 'SHOW ME WHAT U GOT!

MERRYPRANKSTER: YEAH BABY!

MERRYPRANKSTER: SHAKE IT DON'T BREAK IT!

MERRYPRANKSTER: U WENCH!

BLAIR1975: NOW IT'S MY TURN! WHAT U GOT FOR MAMMA?

BLAIR1975: HOT STUFF!

BLAIR1975: IS THAT ALL U CAN DO?'"

"I told you about it already. Nothing happened," she said.

I opened another dated chat. And quoted from that:

"'MERRYPRANKSTER: WHAT'S UR ADDRESS AGAIN?

BLAIR1975: 2112 SPRINGHILL DRIVE

MERRYPRANSKTER: R U HOME RIGHT NOW?"'"

"You keep saying 'nothing happened.' Why don't I believe you? Was the Merry Prankster over here? Did you ever have a guy spend the night?" I asked.

Blair said nothing. "I didn't think you weren't coming back. You just left me. With all the bills."

"I wasn't coming back as long as you were in the house. And you couldn't pay the bills. And you wouldn't've even if you had the money. Not until I gave you the house. That's how you operate," I said.

"Why are you being so mean? It's Christmas Eve. And it's been a really crappy one," she moaned.

"It's about to get worse," I said.

She flinched. "Why do you want to bring this up?"

"I'm not the one who's bringing this up. The Merry Prankster just did. I got on and he eye-emmed. Looking for you. Looking for some fun. Have you been chatting with him again? Or flirting? Or sexting? Or getting it on behind my back?"

Blair pursed her lips. Being careful about what she wanted to say next. "You got the browser history right in front of you. Why don't you tell me?"

I saw the second most recent date from the MERRYPRANKSTER101 and clicked on it.

"'MERRYPRANKSTER101: IT'S BEEN AWHILE FORGET ABOUT ME

BLAIR1975: NO I COULDN'T FORGET U

MERRYPRANKSTER101: SO WOT'S THE DEAL R U DONE WITH YOUR X WHEN WOULD BE A GOOD TIME TO COME OVER NOT SURE ABOUT ROOMMATES I LIKE HOW IT'S BEEN SO FAR"'"

"I wasn't talking about moving in with him," Blair spat acid.

"Then it was just friends with benefits," I said.

"Look," Blair said. "I won't talk to him anymore, okay? Can we just forget about this?"

I shrugged. "Why give up on him now? You got him hooked. Who were you talking to just now?"

Blair looked down to the left. "To my mom."

"I can always check the phone call records on-line. Get the number and find out who is it by an on-line search," I said.

"You don't want me anymore. We haven't had sex since you got out of the hospital. I can't take the chance that you'll kick me out. We're not married. I don't have any ties to the house anymore. So, I've got to keep my options open," Blair said.

"Then leave. If you think this Merry Prankster will ring your bell long enough to take your tubs over there, then more power to you. Have fun. Best of luck. Have a blessed union. Later, gator," I said.

"I've changed, Justin! I'm better," she lied. "You're the one who left me."

"And now I remember why!" I yelled. Not unlike with the same moral force that my dad had done with throwing out my paternal grandma. "I was a fool to take you back! Actions speak louder than words! You say anything to make yourself look good, but you don't follow through. You're a big fat zero when it comes to keeping a promise. It's like if you were the star of a movie that went straight to the five dollar Wal-Mart bin, I'd believe it."

"You think you're too good for me! You're no better than me. You've done drugs and slept with how many girls? And how did your first wife, your precious Lauren, handle all that? What happened to her? Isn't that your fault? Think she'd ever forgive you if she were still here? You're nothing. Always feeling sorry for yourself. You're weak!"

I was up off the couch before I knew it. The laptop bouncing to the floor.

"Don't hit me!" she cowered in a defensive position.

I stopped. I'd never hit a woman before. And I still had the presence of mind not to start now. But I had come close. I was shaking. We were toe to toe. Ready to duke it out. Get as nasty as we wanted to be. No holds barred. Kid gloves off. The words were gonna pile up until someone lost their temper. And took a swing.

Then it all would be over for the loser.

"You're not worth it," I said. "Get out."

"You can't touch me. And you can't make me leave," Blair said setting her feet apart and folding her arms over her stomach.

I knew the next move. Always call the bluff. Always up the ante. Until they lost their nerve.

Time to up the ante. "You'll be going. I'll get you out tonight. And I won't even lay a hand on you."

I got out my phone.

"What are you going to do? Call your parents? They won't come over! They're never going to talk to you again! Cuz you're with me now! And you're never gonna get rid of me again! You might have divorced me, but you're still stuck with me! You're gonna be stuck with me until the day you die!" Blair taunted.

Time to prove her wrong.

I pressed in just three numbers.

Nine-one-one.

Blair's eyes grew wide. Her fists became claws. "What are you doing?!"

"You should think twice about making threats. Especially, when you've been bonded out twice for domestic abuse. This will be strike three," I said.

"They'll put me in jail! Without bail this time!" Brandy screamed. She had become unhinged and it was not pretty.

"Hello, Nine-one-one, what's the nature of your emergency?" the dispatcher asked.

"There's a person who won't leave my property peacefully," I said.

Blair spat loud thunder. She cursed blue lightening. She threw up vile hateful words.

I gave the address. "2112 Springhill Drive."

Blair ran out of breath or steam. At a loss for words, her mouth hung open, empty of rage. For a few moments she stumbled towards the sofa. Her advantage lost. Outflanked. The game about to be called.

She fells backward in shock into a seat on the stiff cushion. All she could do was breathe. Then she found the words to voice her outrage.

"You're gonna have me arrested? On Christmas Eve? They won't keep me in jail. The first time it was the county sheriff who arrested me. The second time it was here in town. This won't be domestic abuse. The worse I could get is a disorderly," Blair said. But then she turned to the dark side. "All I have to do is tell them that you hit me and you'll be arrested. Then you'll have to call your precious mom and dad and tell them you're in jail for domestic abuse. But they'll tell you that's what you deserve for me taking me back and they'll let you rot in jail."

I had been around Blair long enough to know not to be afraid of her threats. It was just talk. Nothing but smack talk. She didn't know how things would turn out. And she had little influence other than the hate and venom that she chose to spew out of her pretty mouth.

She could say anything: like she was going to go to Mars tomorrow on a rocket. What was the chances of that actually happening? None. So, what were the chances of anything happening that she promised or threatened. Slim to none. It was like a spell: it only worked if I believed.

The spell was broken.

So, I went back to square one. "Go ahead. Tell them a lie. Sooner or later, it'll be your word against mine. After all, there's the IM history for everyone to see," I said.

Blair screamed and her face turned colors as her hands twisted into talons.

All at once there was a clatter. The neighbors would soon know what was the matter. Blair flew to window and saw the flash. Of strobe lights from the police car coming for a clash.

From out of the car and at the door appeared two police officers in uniform. They came knocking, expecting the worst. Hating family fights, they wanted to solve crimes. Not be marriage counselors.

Blair opened the door and let them in. Two men in blue with cuffs on their belts and guns snug on their hips. They weren't jolly old elves. They didn't shake like bowls of jelly. They were ready to snatch up the person who was yelling.

"What's going on?" demanded the first, the shorter of the two.

"Nothing," Blair said.

"We had an argument. And she won't leave. But she has to. This is my house. I'm on the title. She's not," I explained with care.

They listened but then the first turned to Blair. "Did he touch you at all?"

Here, to her credit, Blair finally told the truth. She shook her head. "No."

"Who called us, then?" demanded the second.

"I did!"

The first cop backed me towards the kitchen. "You need to cool down. Be smart. Don't yell. Don't argue. Or we'll haul you in."

"But I'm the one who called you!" I protested.

"We got better things to do than sort out fights at home," the second one said.

"Then make her go," I said.

The second turned back to Blair. "Are you on the house?"

"No."

"Do you get mail here? Bills. Correspondence?"

"Yes."

"How long have you been living here?"

"About a month and a half."

The second turned to me. "We can't make her leave. She's been here too long. There's an occupancy law here in Belle-Valley."

"How do I get her out of the house?" I asked.

"You'll have to file an eviction notice with the sheriff. And post it on the door. She'll have thirty days to vacate the house. If she hasn't vacated the house by then you can go to court and get the sheriff to enforce the notice. Not you. Do you understand?" the second said.

"In the meantime, I would try to have a silent night," the first added. "This is a big house. Stay in the back if you have to. And keep away from each other."

Having written their report and taken our names, both officers moved to the door.

"And try to have a happy Christmas," said the first cop as they both left to get back to their cruiser.

Blair began to blubber with tears. "I can't believe you called the cops on me! I can't believe you wanted me to get arrested! It's another awful, horrible Christmas thanks to you! You're never gonna get rid of me! You can't! I'm gonna be with you until you die and then I'm gonna haunt you in the afterlife!!"

O, tidings of comfort and joy!

The she fled to the bed.

Slammed the door.

And wailed and gnashed her teeth.

There was nothing to do but retreat back to Grandpa's old tweed recliner and choose a Christmas movie to watch that would end in a safe Hollywood fairy-tale ending that demanded a sequel or at least six more. Why? We Americans like repetition. We didn't like stories to resolve. And the producers wanted to make money. Not art. Not crap. Art might be crap. Crap might be crap. Except money. Money was always money, honey.

Except what was there in this world to buy with your money but crap?

Hollywood didn't care. The investors didn't care. The marketers didn't care.

Right now, Christmas spelled money in the bank. Black Friday. A whole year's profits in one quarter.

It was always Christmas on the Hallmark Channel.

Chuh-ching!

22-A World Gone Humbug

I was angry.

And sad.
And helpless.
Where was my peace on earth?
Where was my joy?
Every mistake and failure I'd ever made paraded by flipping me off.

I thought everything that had happened was my fault. After my first marriage, the counselor had taught me this invaluable truth: "You chose to get married." Well, I had chosen wrong. Twice, now.

I was a two-time loser. And my live-in girlfriend was my ex-wife. Who may be two-timing on me.

So, divorcing Blair and forcing her into that rat hole apartment with all our collected junk, her son finding fault again and not talking to her, getting thrown out of her parents' home on Christmas Eve, my parents turning their back on me when I took Blair back, every wild hair money making scheme of Blair's, everything that was going wrong with this property, Blair's getting arrested—twice—and now calling the cops to threaten her with a third arrest, this crappy Christmas—

My fault.
All of it.
Every last bit of it.

Whenever someone got angry, I always thought it was my fault. I would slump my shoulders and shrink down inside myself. I wanted to shut down. Go someplace and hide.

Often it was my dad's anger. He was always mad. He found fault just to get mad. He would yell and rage. Bluster and thunder. He would annunciate every word with just enough venom to shake the sky. All that he had to do next was reach for the lightning and hurl it down on us mere mortals, to scourge us into little ash heaps.

I would go and hide from his anger. I don't remember much of his love. Often TV, not God or His Word, was my refuge. Old tv movies and shows: adventure, sci/fi, and horror—lots of horror. I got so lost in the stories, I thought they were real and I was in them. I was every hero who faced a monster to save a heroine or the world.

And the greatest of these stories was the first *Star Wars* from 1977. No other movie had ever affected me. It changed my life. Next to knowing God and going to church and learning about His word, it has had the biggest influence on my life.

I lived, breathed, and ate Star Wars. The comic books, the storybook soundtrack, the toys—oh, the toys. I was Luke Skywalker, I was Luke Skywalker's younger brother getting totted along and left with the droids in their misadventures. My older brother was Han Solo. Princess Leia—uncast, until maybe I met my first wife, Lauren. And Darth Vadar? Grand Moff Tarkin? Evil Emperor Palpatine? I think I knew who to cast.

There was no peace.

There was no joy.

Because Despair was strong. The Dark Side, if you like.

And Hate mocked everything good. And seemed to be winning. Big time.

According to Yoda, hate led to the Dark Side. And so did fear and pain. Because fear led to pain and pain led to suffering and that was the path to the Dark Side.

I wasn't filled with Hate, though, necessarily.

I was filled with Guilt. Shame. More than that, failure. Which was evident. Manifest. It was my destiny. A legacy of everlasting shame.

That was all there was.

That was all I would ever be.

Every decision led to a fresh trainwreck. Every move I made. All for the everlovin' sake. Of Guilt. And Failure, buddy boy.

I was a failure. With a lower case f. justin r. is a big fat failure.

For I am powerless to control my life and it has become unmanageable.

A lot of fat good it did to know that. I could admit that much at least. But I had forgotten step number two.

There was no hope. Not for this Obi-Wan.

There was no peace.

No joy.

There was no escape.

Well, there was one way out for sure.

One dark door to whatever waited for me beyond. It was time to square up with the Dark Side. But how could I ever face it when what I called goodness was nothing more than filthy rags.

I had nothing good to pay the price.

But at least I would be free of here. The guilt and failure here. They would stop.

I turned off the tv and sat before a blank screen.

In the corner of my ear, I thought I could hear Blair snoring. Then muttering. Then yelling and cussing.

She was arguing with someone in her sleep.

Keeping in practice? Reliving her favorite fight? Or fighting her inner demons? Who was winning?

Then she fell into snoring.

Having let chaos out of its bag, Blair had fled to her lair. A mother bear hunkering down for a long hibernation in cold winter. Burrowing under sheets and blankets.

I just let her sleep.

And listened to her breathing.

Sinking.

Deeper.

And deeper.

Snoring.

I walked into the kitchen and stopped at the sink. My hands reached out and found the tab sheets of trazadone. My fingers punched out four. Then two more--three times my prescribed dosage.

I put them in my mouth and dry swallowed.

Down the hatch. Straight. No chaser.

Then my hand went into the open knife drawer and pulled out the butcher's knife.

It was going to be a replay of fifteen days ago.

If first you don't succeed, etc, eg, ergo, ad adstra, asterisk, vice versa, and versa vice.

It flashed silver. Tempered stainless steel. Made to cut and sever.

I put it to wrist. Just above my two week old scar.

I could make a new one.

I could make a better one.

All I had to was cut down, then slice across. And the Guilt and Failure would stop.

But would it? What if the guilt and failure wouldn't stop? Even when I crossed through Death's door.

I had been a chump.

I had chosen poorly again.

I was going to fail at escaping Guilt and Failure through Suicide.

The trazadone was working already. Water boarding my brain.

I grew dizzy.

My head became too heavy to hold up.

My hands couldn't feel to grip.

The knife clattered to the floor.

I limped to the back addition. Stumbled back to Grandpa's tweed recliner. And tripped over my own steps to fall in.

My eyelids were collapsing.

A deep weight pulling down in my chest.

Pressing down on my heart.

I was falling inside myself.

Into a basement.

My body was shutting down.

One sense at a time. I couldn't feel my hands or legs. I couldn't touch anything. My eyes were closing. I couldn't taste the bitter pills I had swallowed.

The last one, the only one, working was sound.

I heard breathing.

Respiration.

Louder and louder.

All around me.

It was a wind outside the house.

It was the heater blowing inside the house.

It became a wail.

Something was coming.

I struggled to take back my sight. To keep my eyes open. And see whatever was coming for me.

I looked up to the hole in the roof. Fog slipped through. In serpentine coils. Billowing tendrils.

It poured onto the floor and spread across the family room. Illuminated by a sickly green.

The breathing and wailing had become a cry.

A moaning. A deep mourning.

For something precious lost.

A heart broken.

Dreams emptied.

Peace forsaken

Joy taken.

Riding over an ocean of hurt. A river of sorrow. A lake of fire.

My ears were full of the sound.

The fog engulfed the room and the hole in the roof grew bigger. Big enough for clouds to descend. An aperture for a herald angel. Or one of its long lost brothers.

The moaning was a voice.

A woman's.

Down came a feminine shape. Clad in a lace bridal dress with lace sleeves. Once the gown had been snow white but now it was spotted and dirty with the lace frayed and smeared with the dust of ages and dotted with moth holes.

She descended down through the hole. Her train spread out behind in wings of torn fabric. A bridal veil covered her face. The veil held blue crystals like tears caught in a spider web and frozen. Above the veil, I could make out eyes of polar ice. Beneath it, there was a mouth, a deep orifice. And tombstone teeth.

When her bare feet rested on the floor and she stood tall in her frame, the dark lady faced me.

"Hello, Justin R.," she said under the veil. Her words were a cold front. The frost slapping my face.

It was a voice I should have known. No-nonsense. Stubborn. Unforgiving.

"What do you want with me?" I asked.

"I've come to show you what might be if you let it," the veiled woman said.

"I think I've seen enough," I said.

She clapped her hands. A sheet of light pulsed around me. A static charge passed over my skin. There was a pause and thunder rattled 2112 Springhill Drive right down to its slab foundation. The type of sturm and dang my dad had sought all his life without having to stomp his foot.

"Then you aren't paying attention. That's why I've come here," she said.

"Leave me alone. Go away," I said.

"I will do neither," the dark lady declared. "Not until you see. And admit what you did."

Did I know this woman? I think I did. Did I know what she wanted? I hoped to God I didn't. If there was one time the cup could pass from me and my own will be done let it be now.

She held out a laced arm. "Come with me."

"Where are we going?" I asked. I hoped not to a chapel. Not to a ceremony.

"Abroad," she said.

"I'd rather not," I said.

"I don't care what you'd rather. Your time is short. Mine is shorter," the veiled woman said.

I held her by the wrist. It was a wintry glacial surface.

The fog enveloped us. We began to walk. The veiled woman in her lace gown with me at her side. Barefoot the both of us.

We proceeded out into the world. But not the world as it was on Decemeber 24, 2004 as I experienced this. An altogether different world where it felt strange and the air smelled weird and tasted bitter.

It was a bitter future we traversed into.

I could no longer see the four walls of the family room. Underneath was soft asphalt.

We weren't in 2112 Springhill Drive anymore.

The air was wet. Humid, not as cold. More like early fall or late spring.

By touching the dark lady's laced wrist, my hand was going numb. The longer the numbness stayed, the more it would grow and overtake me until the cold could touch me no more. And she had been cold so long she would never bother being warm again.

The fog receded to its four corners.

We were outside. It was December the twenty-forth, whenever it was where we were at. It should have just turned winter, but it was warm for winter and there was no snow.

It was still night.

But it was not a silent night.

It was full of noisy voices. Strains of cacophonic music. With little rhythm or melody.

We crossed the street and came to a gated neighborhood. Guarded by two iron portals meant to turn us away. But the veiled woman passed a hand through the air and the gates swung back on their wheels.

Two men with dark Kevlar vests and walkie-talkies came running with guns drawn. They looked outside the open gates. They looked inside. Behind them. Then they pressed a remote and the gates swung shut again. Then they went to check the security cameras and reported to HQ on their walkie-talkies.

"They didn't see us," I said.

"We are not natives to this time. We are but strangers passing through a shadow land of what is to be. We are shades of the past," the dark lady said.

"Are we dead?" I asked.

"We are shades. Thinking and aware. With a core of energy. But no substantive mass," she answered with little meaning to me.

We walked into it on well paved roads and manicured lawns with trimmed bushes and adequately spaced trees.

It was the old Signal Hill neighborhood. We were still in Belle-Valley then. But it was different somehow.

The curb appeal was even more immaculate. Even in this warm winter. The layout of each home custom built and tailored to individual taste however aesthetically gauche or eccentric.

"If this is winter," I said. "Something's missing."

I did a three hundred and sixty degree look around for the absence of something.

"There's no Christmas here," I said.

There was not a trace of it outside. No Santa Claus or reindeer or snowmen or angel or shepherd or wise men or nativity. Nothing at all. Secular or religious.

"Strip away Santa Claus and you have a white male forest demi-god. Dig a little deeper and Santa Claus becomes Father Christmas and Father Christmas becomes Sinter Klassen and Sinter Klassen becomes St. Nicholas and St Nicholas becomes Bishop Nicholas of Smyrna. And the bish was just some kind old man who orphans brought gifts every Christmas Day. There isn't some old white guy who lives with elves up at the North Pole. Nothing could live up there. It has an average of minus thirty-four degrees. The life of a kind hearted man was turned into a myth," the veiled woman said.

"And the Christmas story?" I ventured.

"Here a virgin might conceive. Through artificial insemination. Under scientific controlled conditions. Not out of some divine plan of redemption," she said.

"What about the birth of Jesus?" I asked.

"In this neighborhood, a child being born in a manger would be a sign of child abuse and parental neglect. The state would take the child away and the parents would be arrested, their mug shot spread virally on-line, and they would be rehabilitated.

"The state would ensure that the child would be placed with two mutually consenting adults who had signed a contract to raise the child together in order to receive state aid," the dark lady said.

"Here there is no nativity. No mother and father. No birth parents on a birth certificate. No sex assigned. The State determines the role of the offspring. There are no wise men. And there are no angels. No heavenly multitude. No glad tidings. No shepherds. But there are sheep. And there are census laws. All manner of laws. New laws are being added every day. Which only makes new criminals," she added.

"Doesn't anyone celebrate Christmas here at all?" I asked.

The dark lady shook her head. "It is forbidden to observe it. First, there was Separation of Church and State. Then, there was Freedom from Religion. And then there was no Church. The word faith is not allowed to be spoken here. All belief rests in the State. The State supplies all wants after it weighs the need."

"What's there to even celebrate then?" I asked.

"Let us look," she said and waved us on our way.

The veiled woman led me up the path to the nearest house. The front door opened for us but no one was at the door to open it. We walked inside to a house party. Everyone turned their heads to us gatecrashers. Then they looked away and got back to business—talking about themselves.

Neither of us was dressed for this party. Or for any party. We had come as we were. Me in my ragged blue jeans and blue turtle neck. And she in a tattered bridal gown with a long dirty train and a veil covering.

We were the uninvited. Unwelcome. We went among them but we weren't of them.

Whereever we walked, the partiers cleared out a path. They kept chained to the sides of their friends. They were safe. Accepted.

We were not.

No one talked to us.

No one wanted to know who we were.

They let us be.

We were invisible.

"They cannot see us?" I asked.

The dark lady shook her head. "We are like vapor or shadows to them. Even if we were in the flesh, they would ignore us and have us removed."

"Why?" I asked. "Do they not entertain strangers?"

"They will not entertain the strange. It does not fit in their narrative. We are not of their tribe. We do not share their values; therefore, we do not have any value to them. It is easier to ignore that which they'd rather not believe."

Everyone had come to the party to gorge their senses.

They wore clothes swabbed with neon paint or threaded with LED lights that flashed the same color as their hair and makeup. Some even had teased the ends of their locks and beehive hairdos with LED threads that ebbed with changing color spectrums.

Anything to be noticed.

At least for a second. Because the shock value didn't last. Especially, when it was always expected to out Herrod'ed Herrod.

The music throbbed and belched and rumbled and burped high pitched squeals and low end mumblings having no set repeating pattern of melody or rhythm. It flowed, or rather gushed, like broken machinery that formed a drone of dying automation.

The party-goers filled up their eyes and ears and noses and fingers with lavish things. And they were filled with pride.

Here in this antechamber, there were several tables arrayed with various kinds of foods. Bowls of tangy bean dips surrounded with all sorts of baked veggie straws. Trays of cut fresh red and yellow and green vegetables. Platters of veggie tots. Veggie noodles. Veggie pizza pieces topped not with cheese, but with strange pieces that wasn't pressed or cut meat, but had definite shape and form.

I came closer to these platters and picked up a piece to investigate it. The veggie dough was waxy and flaky, like poorly executed bread dough. But the toppings were bizarre to me—they had abdomens and thoraxes; feelers and segmented legs.

Insects. Instead of layered meat, this strange pizza was sprinkled with baked insects.

Worse, the next table had cooking pans full of more roasted insects. A pan full of grass hoppers. Another of mealworm larve. Both of which the party-goers grabbed, ripped, bit, and sucked. The effect was that it turned their teeth green and blue from the insects' viscera.

Next to this table stood two vertical bread oven and warmers. Only the smell was not warm soothing yeast and sugar and flour. The one on the left radiated with a pungent and sulfuric aroma of barbequed stink bugs. The one on the right radiated with the nutty or fishy scent of baked crickets.

Around the food source tables, on the tables as settings, were large ice sculptures of the kind of food sources humankind used to eat: flying fish, large shrimp, alligators, turtles, deer, and various ruminoids.

For desserts, there were bowls of colorful fruits, where each piece of fruit had been diced and pressed back into its original shape. And bowls of larks' tongues in vegetable fat based aspic. And candy bowls of various nuts—cashews, almonds, pecan, walnuts, and pistachio.

I took a few nuts of each kind to fill up my hand. But my stomach was full of trazadone. And began to burble.

There were carafes of various teas: teakwood, green, and ginger. And bottles of wine. Corked bottles in racks against the walls. Rich vintages from favored years. From savored terrior vineyards from around the world. Each possessing a unique boquet and robust body.

These people knew each other. They approved each other. They were all members of an small elite group.

They praised each other on knowing they were in the presence of fine quality things. The finer things they had worked for themselves. Affluence that they deserved. Things of power that they meant to keep.

They commented on the one thing they wanted for this Winter Solstice. They pestered each other over what they got for each other. Then they bragged about the unique item they had acquired for a tax write-off. Taxes were for the poor.

It was not quite a gift exchange as a swap meet.

Unique one of a kind items. Paintings and sculptures and pottery. Artifacts empty and void of any discernible known shape.   Out of any geometric sequence. Non-fibonacci. Un-prime numbers. Sickle celled blobs.

The paintings looked as if they had been smeared with larva viscera, or mud, or snot, or vomited veggie noodles.

The party was held in a suite of rooms. Seven in all. The rooms were wide, but each side had a sheer netting draped from ceiling to floor. Like a see-through screen. From behind these screens light swirled through fog. And projected in the fog were shadows of anamorphic shapes. Lost souls running to and fro without hope. For these elites loved to lord over the pain of others, while being detached from it themselves so they could condemn the actions of others, while they remained aloof and had a pathway that kept them separate from the suffering.

The screens made a narrow corridor. A hallway. Down each room with a different room. The first was blue; the second purple; the third green; the fourth orange, the fifth white, the sixth violet, and the last a deep velvet red. And in this room stood an ebony grandfather clock with the brand name CHRONUS.

The time was two minutes to midnight.

Slowly, every gay party-goer drifted through all the rooms into this last one: the red velvet one. I stood holding the Dark Lady's cold hand as the minute hand crept to meet the hour hand until both were straight up twelve midnight.

And the clock began to strike the hour.

One stroke at a time.

One peal of the bell after another.

As the hour was counted, the party-goers passed around a tray. Upon it were pieces of flesh. Raw and uncooked. Colorless and dull and having algor mortis. The skin of some hairless and pink animal. So fresh that it had hair as fine as a frog.

"No, it couldn't be," I breathed. "They wouldn't dare."

"There is nothing left to shock anyone about. Everything is accepted. Every behavior normalized,"the dark lady said.

"Eat of the body. Partake," they said.

And they ate.

Then they passed about trays with shot glasses full of what I took to be Merlot styled wine.

"Drink of the blood," they said.

And they did.

I did not care to know if they were drinking wine or not.

"Merry Winter Solstice!" someone said.

And they all drank.

The partiers were keeping Christmas in their own way, by not keeping it at all.

They were celebrating themselves.

I retreated down the colored hallways to the front door.

"I've seen enough. The rich always survive. They're eating the poor!" I complained to the dark lady.

"All tomorrow's parties are in vain. When all is vanity, it soon will eat itself," she said. "Let us walk on."

We left tomorrow's party early. The same as we'd entered. Unnoticed.

We walked from Signal Hill back to Main Street. And followed it down. I recognized a corner where an old tool and dye shop had once stood.

It was now a quick payday loan and pawn shop. The old fashioned inviting windows with warm logos now barred with iron and the lettering scraped off.

We were six blocks away from Dutch Hollow. In the west end of Belle-Valley.

There were no longer public Christmas lights on the light poles. Most of them were broken and turned off. The dark lady had warned me that there were no carolers. No angelic choir. No heavenly multitudes.

But there were multitudes. Shiftless and homeless. Strangers to themselves and each other. Banded into tribes and stratified by hierarchies.

They saw us. And eyed us with envy and hunger and wariness. Which group did we identify with? Did we have anything worth trading for? Did we have food portions? We were told we couldn't stay here. That there was no room. No beds to let. Every building was overcrowded. And we couldn't sleep on the sidewalk. It already belonged to someone else. We couldn't stay here. We weren't welcome here. We had to move on.

We walked on through the night. The homeless thinned out and became more of a shuffling herd with an undead glaze. Not much alive other than breathing or walking. It was like they had opened the doors of Kelter Ward A and let all the catatonic patients loose.

The storefronts receded back into empty spaces as the buildings housing them disappeared into open holes in the ground where the foundations had been filled in with rubble to create a colony for a mischief of rats and trash and a murder of noisy crows. Rats were omnivores, eating fruits and nuts and insects and birds and reptiles. And flesh. And so were the crows. They made a symbiotic and competitive pair. The mischief rats and the murder crows.

There was a single light from a single store at the end of this miles long Main Street.

It was set apart from the old derelict business district. Here the city lights still worked and the sidewalk was paved with fresh cement and without a single crack and there were bike racks aplenty.

A large sign with harmless light frequencies sat atop the store. Its light a beacon to the community. A proclamation of glad tidings of comfort and joy through the stuff in stock. A promise of surcease of sorrow, though temporary. A chance to purchase peace on earth and good vibes for humankind.

Though the store was new and neat, the first letter of the sign had gone dark.

HARMACY it read. With UNITED STATES DISPENSARY below that.

"America is not allowed. No longer spoken. No longer written. No longer accepted," the dark lady said.

"Then what is it the United States of? Depression? Misery? Feudalism?" I asked. "And just what are they citizens of?"

"There are no citizens. Residents and Denizens. Herders and Hordes. The Shoulds and the Shouldn'ts," she said.

The store was well lit and clean. The front doors slid open for us. We stepped over the threshold into an environmentally controlled atmosphere. Out of the muggy unseasonal winter night and into a business full of a cornucopia of smells. Pungent. Acrid. Sweet. Bitter. Salty. Minty. And Tangy.

Aisles of assorted pharmaceutical blends. Shelves of homeopathic strains. Endcaps of special buys on synthetic concoctions.

All these were pharmakeia. Plant derived potions that could heal or poison. Or both.

Nothing was illicit.

Everything was permitted.

The choices were endless. The variety limitless.

A pill.

A tablet.

A capsule.

A dose.

Too many to count.

Too many to name.

They had a pill for everything.

And for anything.

There was a pill to pick you up in the morning.

And one to put you down at night.

One to make you feel like a million dollars.

Another made you feel like the loser your dad always said you were.

There was a pill that made you see acid trails.

There was a pill that made your childhood companion who never aged finally disappear.

There was a pill to make you feel loved.

And there was a pill that made you feel nothing at all.

Some had more side effects than the symptom you were showing.

Some had patents.

Some did not.

Some were government approved.

And some were experimental trials.

Medication.

For the whole nation.

Just to function.

From generation to generation.

I picked up a bottle of Tumeric Curcumin with Ginger. There was a National Zone Tax, a regional infrastructure tax, and a local social safety net tax. Which almost doubled the price of the product.

And everything was taxed beyond reason. Value added and carrier taxes. For each level of government to get their crumb from every transaction.

An anamorphic figure appeared from out of the bank corner. A hybrid figure. The top part being in the likeness of an audioanimatronic person of bland and non-threatening features with thinning hair, possessing a head and thorax and waxy arms striding atop a large box containing servos and wires fitted to wheels with shocks.

"May I be of service? Which brand or blend are you needing? Do you have your Department of Human Health and Services Card?" it asked in a baritone voice through a speaker in its throat. Its head moved to one

side and its eyes snapped in order to show the human
affinity of blinking.

I turned to my dark lady companion. "Is it AI? Is
it sapien?"

"To be a being, your mind must be able to think, to
have a will, and to have emotions," she said.

So, I tested the machine. "Me and my dark lady
companion were just walking Main Street and we just saw
a polar bear. So, I said to the polar bear, 'Hey, polar bear,
what are you doing this far south?' And the polar bear
said, 'I seem to have lost my bearings.'"

The audioanimatronic figure on wheels clapped its
eyes shut. Open. Shut. While its servos whined in its
lower abdomen box. "There are no polar bears. Now,
you must have a Department of Human Health and
Services Card in order to purchase your choice of brand
or blend. And you must purchase something to remain in
this store premises. You may not loiter or 'squat' as if
your class' mode of behavior. If you need shelter or
assistance, you may go to the former St. Michael's
Catholic Church, which is now a refuge and sanctuary for
the non-homed or non-essential worker class.

"Do you have a Department of Human Health and
Services Card? If not, you must leave the store premises
within thirty seconds. If not, I will be forced to notify the
constable who will counsel you and determine your need
or threat level. You may not damage me as I am a
representative of this township and have legal rights and
am identified as a person."

"But you have no emotions. You're a machine.
Not a person," I argued.

"It has been determined that you do not have a
Department of Human Health and Services Card. I
cannot identify you by my facial recognition system, and

therefore, it is impossible to determine your social credit score or possible deficits or possible warrants, and therefore, I must prescribe you as a threat level of three—possible intent to do harm to yourself or others. With a threat level of three, the constable has been notified and will be dispatched to this store premises' location shortly. It is well-advised that you and your 'dark lady companion', leave forthwith and with all immediate dispatch," the audio-animatronic person with legal rights said.

"We must be on our way," my dark lady companion said.

Still, holding her wrist, she whisked out of the Harmacy.

The doors slid shut and only then did I notice the signage on door depicting the store hours: **365-24/7**. And a lengthier notification on the other: We exist to serve the needs of the many from cradle to grave. **This store operates under the "Freedom from Religion and Hate" and "Commerce Clause" as expressed in our global Constitution. We believe in a free and open society. The security cameras are here for your protection.**

"Looks like they give you a whole lot of cradle. Then they shove you into a grave," I said.

"These are the shadows of what might be. Such things hinge on the heart and will and humankind. From out of the heart comes the abundance of its treasure. And that treasure is what people have stored in their heart: all what they think is important," said my dark lady companion.

"Nothing but stones then. No hope," I said. "Looks like they nailed Pandora's Box shut. And left hope inside."

"I know what it is like to have your hopes buried," she said.

"You live only to relive your hurt, don't you?" I asked.

She gave me an icy stare. It made the stones in my heart turn cold and shake. "Look upon this fearful rundown world."

The few working streetlamps were bare of any signage. The storefronts were all labeled with perfunctory titles. There were no decorations: not a single wreath or red bow or strand of light or lock of holly.

Not a silhouette of a reindeer. Not a trace of Santa. No evidence of a nativity.

There was no Christmas music being played. Christmas wasn't white or blue or gold or silver. There weren't any days of Christmas. No one was coming home for Christmas. No one was wishing their baby a merry Christmas. Rudolph wasn't running. Because Santa didn't need his red nose. Because he wasn't coming to town and he certainly wasn't going to come down any lane. Mommy wasn't even going to kiss him. Because he didn't exist and no one was allowed to dress up to symbolize a stupid myth. No one wanted a hippopotamus or their two front teeth. Kids didn't have visions of sugar plums in their heads.

They weren't even allowed any processed sugar of any kind. And instead of plums, they were given prunes.

The streets were graveyard quiet.

Quiet as a crypt.

Deader than a sensory deprivation tank.

For a moment I couldn't hear my feet move. Couldn't even hear my own heartbeat.

"We must get off the street," my dark lady companion warned.

Sirens were coming. Not the blaring , wailing sirens that might cause a resident distress. But a blipping noise not unlike the video game *Space Invaders.*

We turned down an alleyway a few blocks away from the Harmacy. It was full of the tired poor, the huddled masses who couldn't breathe freedom, and the wretched refuse of the world.

Dear Lord, why were there so many?

They stood or sat or lay in greasy unwashed clothing sharing warmth and tics and lice. The alley had become an open sewer full of urine and defecation and flies and rats and crows. The animals sorted and sifted through discarded plastic containers of empty assorted caloric servings.

We passed people seeking surcease from sorrow vainly trying to borrow hope from state branded synthetic alcohol and medicinal low yield cannabis.

Some had given up the ghost and lay decomposing where they had fallen. Others lay face down in their vomit. Others marked the passing of time by urinating on the walls. The trace chemicals running down the drain to filter through the sewer and merge with the water supply.

Once past the sick and dying, we came upon children and youth half undressed and gathered in dyads and triads of different gender combinations, bent over one another or kneeling at each other's feet performing favors and supplying biological gratification.

Then we came to a large crowd. Men and women pressed together. But none were mother or father or husband or wife or brother or sister. They were simply a herd living and dying together.

They were gathered around an old storage rental facility. A single row of units with locked roll up doors.

One by one the doors were unlocked and rolled up, the items brought out and auctioned off.

There was no money exchanged. And no promise of credit. Wanted items from the storage unit were bartered off for unwanted items from the gathered crowd.

The auctioneer was a woman. She held sway in a coarse voice. "It's just stuff! But it's great stuff! And it's stuff you need. Stuff you want! But the question is, what you are willing to give to get it! Look here! A quease in nart! A best of twentieth century appliances!"

"What good is it if you can't plug it in?" yelled a man in the back.

"Yeah! We only get five electrical volts a day! Can't even run that on a battery!" shouted out a woman.

The female auctioneer held up a half gloved hand. The ends of her fingernails were long and polished from living below the poverty line and caked with the gloss of city sewer. She held up the squat glass appliance high overhead. Then she took off the top and unscrewed the glass container from the bass and blades.

"It's got blades. Metal blades. Past the legal safety length. Very sharp. And nasty," she said. Then she twisted the base away from the glass container. "Use the container for whatever you want. Only you gotta offer something for it."

Then someone started off the bid with a bag of plastic cutlery. It was met by an offer of three metal spatulas. That was met by an offer of a book of half used matches.

The woman auctioneer cheered each new offer and championed the next matching offer. Up and onwards she drove the price in value and item. The winning barterer gave up a sealed bottle of deli pickle spears— which was illegal due to the calorie law for its high salt and preservative ratio. Everyone deemed it a fair trade: a delicacy for a rarity.

At first I had been repulsed. Why would anyone be desperate enough to barter for stuff that wouldn't work? But here junk was treasure. The only currency that mattered. And the more odd and rare it was, the greater the value.

The woman auctioneer proved that with the next item.

"Look everybody!" she cried. "It's a Luke Skywalker toy! From the original Kenner's 1977 line!"

She held it up. The action figure as four inches tall and poseable at five points. The white tunic as dirty as Tatooine, the lightsaber that extended out its right hand missing the tip, and its blonde hair rubbed white to its base in places.

The last one I'd seen was the one my mom had bought for me after I'd seen the figures were for sale from an ad on the back of my Kellog's Frosted Flakes box.

Then the crowd bartered and haggled over the worth of the item. Each trying to find something of comparable worth. A sleeve of electric light bulbs. A saucer and gravy dish. A jar of beef jerky. Two packages of sugar.

And as the worth increased, so did the mania to possess it. The mob became excited and rude. Jostling each other.

But the female auctioneer held them at bay. She choked back their greed and reminded them to play fair. Promising items even more mysterious in the next storage unit.

The deal was bartered. The exchange was for a box of lego blocks. The box and Luke exchanged hands.

The mob subsided. Disappointment rolled off their backs. Then their heads were back in the game for the next round.

The auctioneer smiled. Showing missing back teeth on her lower left jaw.

I knew that grin of missing teeth.

Grown older. More stooped. Hair now thinning at the scalp.

It was Blair.

She stood in front of me and did not recognize me. I hadn't changed since she'd fallen asleep tonight. Whereas, she had become an old crone. Full of piss and vinegar. Or just more of it.

This time a few shabby helpers pulled out the next item. It was an old table with dark wood. Stolid and heavy enough to take her weight as she was lifted to sit atop it.

Blair was the auctioneer. Queen of the storage units. Mistress of the barter.

Her clothes were threadbare. Even if she ran the auction she didn't want to dress too far above her audience.

"It's just a table!" someone cried out.

"It's too big for my tent!" yelled a woman.

"Nothing is too good if you want it!" Blair shouted from her perch. "You come into this world head first and they take you out feet first! You are born with nothing and you leave it with nothing! Cradle to the grave they say! That's nothing but a lot of cradle then you dump you into a grave! Might as well get as much as you can while you can! Who doesn't need a table? This is a table from the twentieth century! An Ethan Allan colonial style table!"

"How did ya talk 'em out of it Breezy?" laughed one of the mob.

Blair held out her dirty long nails and flexed them into a claw. "I knew the previous owners! They had a true sentiment for it! I gave them an offer they didn't dare refuse! Now who will make me an offer?"

The mob laughed and began to deal.

Just as the cuisinart had struck me odd and the Luke Skywalker action figure had jangled a chord of memory, the dark colonial table made me cold and then my blood grew hot.

It had been my mom's. The one that Blair had taken out of the house after the divorce. And had brought back with her when she'd came begging, with her tail between her legs.

The table was one and the same.

It was easy to push to the front of the mob. More like I squeezed past them all. I was able to get a good look at what was in the rest of the storage shed that Breezy sold out of. There was my Grandpa's tweed recliner. There was a lamp plugged into an extension cord ran to an old commercial grade socket. There was a cot with ruffled bed sheets.

This is where Blair/Breezy lived now.

The rest of the storage space held storage tubs. Ones that I had come to recognize. Mine and hers. With our names written on them. One tub was full of my favorite books that I had saved from my childhood: hardback copies of *Treasure Island* and *20,000 Leagues Under the Sea*. They were older than me. They had been my brother's and I had inherited them from him. On top of those books, was a Double E ticket ride item. My board game version of *20,000 Leagues Under the Sea* made for and licensed by the Walt Disney Company. Based on their ground breaking movie.

"Three Atari video games?" cried Blair. "That's all you give me? Why this is solid wood! It'd take an ax, which you ain't got, to tear this table apart. You could live under it!"

"Just what I'm gonna do!" said the barterer as he sat down at the table.

The crowd laughed.

"What you got next, Breezy?" the mob asked in anticipation.

She held up two items. A grayish ribbed turtle neck shirt and worn blue jeans with a holes in the knees. "These should probably still be warm, as they've just been pulled off the deceased!"

"Ooo," went the crowd.

I went cold in my belly down to my thighs. Yet, something else snapped and I rushed forward.

"Give me those back! Those are mine!" I yelled. Yanking back on the man's dirty jacket, he was flung to the ground. And just like that, I could move among them and touch them. And they could see me.

Blair looked down her wrinkled nose at me. "What's your beef?"

"These are mine! All this is my family's! You've no right to sell them!" I yelled.

She paused as if to consider my statement. And just what it meant to her, if anything. And though the years had not been kind to Blair, she still could not recognize me.

"So what?" she shrugged. "If you want it back then offer us something. That's what we do here."

Many in the mob voiced their agreement.

"What have you done with my mom and dad? How come you have all their stuff and mine, too? You got my furniture and my toys and my books!" I yelled.

But Blair didn't have to deal with me. The mob did. They laid hands on me.

"Where are my mom and dad?" I cried out.

I was spun around by filthy hands and faced faces, dirty and angry. I asked them the same question and more besides. "Where are my mom and dad? What is going on here? Why don't you take a bath?"

Hands shook me. Hands slapped me down. Hands pushed me back.

I was pushed back to the crowd and out of the barter.

I fell to my hands and knees before a torn lace dress with a dirty train.

I looked up at my dark lady companion. "Where are my parents? What has happened to them?"

From behind her veil she was unmoved. "Did you not tell them that you were never going back there? Were those not your last words to them?"

I had meant it then. I had meant to hurt them. But I hadn't thought it through.

What had happened to them after I had abandoned them?

"How did she get all their stuff? Now where are my parents?" I yelled and pointed back towards the open storage unit where Blair's next item was Grandpa's tweed recliner. "Take me to them! Take me to them now!!"

The veiled woman said nothing. She pondered my heart with ice blue eyes. Then she waved her laced arm, palm up, her fingers bent and only her right index and middle finger sticking up.

We became insubstantial again. Like shadows. Or vapor.

We floated past the square downtown.

Facing each other on opposite cardinal points were two buildings. The one farthest away used to be a branch of America's Bank. Now it held a new sign MUSEUM OF CAPITALISM. The building closest to us was the old county courthouse complex. It, too, had been renamed: EQUITYAND EQUALITY CENTER.

We entered and found the lobby full of people in crisscrossing lines. The building smelled no better than a barn. The air was rank choking me with the stink of miscarried justice.

In each court room, people stood as their own advocates; giving depositions and reading charges. Every case came from a family member or neighbor suing someone for uncivil or insensitive behavior: saying hateful things about their values, not agreeing with the science posted in the government emergency bulletins, accusing others of threatening and making them feel unsafe. All this was done by citizen's arrest and was binding.

The judges had to hear these trivial suits because long ago it had been discovered that the rule of law was not an unbendable stone. It had proven beyond a shadow of a doubt that law was porous and could absorb everyone's complaints and squeeze out equity and equality to all in some measure. The judges now wrung out decisions in diffused justice.

Below in the basement were the holding cells. There were no police. Each cell was warded by trustees. Each person a criminal by accusation and placed for booking by the apprehending resident who was making the charge. Each one a heinous outrage that blacked the eye of blind lady justice.

The worst of the lot were those who flouted the Christmas Laws. These criminals were sure to be prosecuted to the full extent of the law: they would be boiled in their own Christmas pudding and staked through the heart with mistletoe.

"The whole world's gone humbug," I said.

"There is no Christmas. They have turned their back on Christ. There is no mercy here. Only condemnation. Here, they don't give gifts; they give payback," my dark lady companion said.

"Well, I don't see my parents here. Where are they? How did Blair get my clothes?" I asked.

She waved her hand again.

Mists swirled.

Then we were at the Our Lady's hospital.

It was dark and shut up. Derelict and abandoned. Condemned.

Again, she waved her hand.

We stood at the grotto of the Our Lady' Shrine. Here the night was no longer holy. Only nocturnal.

Here people gathered, not wanting to explain phenomena mistaken for myths. Seeking meaning. And belonging.

They observed Winter Solstice.

For something to believe in.

Though the stars that marked the turning of the seasons could not hear the shaking of their tambourines, nor see the whir of iron needles carving new tattoos with the old astrological signs. Nor could they speak to those who wanted to have faith in something they could see; the people were seekers looking for answers in their chaos and reason in the face of a cold and deaf machine.

They believed in a Cosmic Joke over a Grand Design.

"The State wants faith and belief to go extinct. They don't want people to think. Just to accept. People still gather here out of a shared need. Perhaps a psychological compulsion. Or a wired biological impulse. It may be creating a neurological pathway in the brain to the memory center. Not a religious or spiritual experience.

"That is their new hope. Or it may be that their hearts have been hardened to the most obdurate stone. And they have turned their backs on the God shaped hole at the core of their very being," my dark lady companion said.

"Humans are special. We don't follow magnetic streams or build hives. Life is not some random pattern until we fall back into dust. We don't just breathe and defecate. Something's happened to these people. They're no better than sheep or ants or bacteria living on a dead log," I argued.

But she said nothing to refute me. She had already shown me the evidence.

I hung my head and said, "Now for the last time, where are my parents?"

Again, she waved her hand and we walked through the ruined gates of an old forgotten cemetery. Most of the tombstones were cracked and the monuments bent sideways, slowly being pulled down into the bed of earth. The names had been wiped clean. The slates blank.

Seeds planted in the soil. Sleeping. Waiting to slough off their coils. And rise up like the morning dew.

Here the memory of the dead was *Lethe*-al.

We came to a large family crypt with angels on all four corners: one blew a trumpet, one held a sword, one held a harp, and one held a baby. Next to the locked door were four tablets. Three of them had a name with a birth to death date. There was one for my father, one for my mother, and even one for my brother. But the last one was blank.

Stunned, I fell to my knees. "I didn't even get to say goodbye."

"Yes, you did. When you went out the back door," my dark lady companion said.

"Blair had my clothes? Have I died in this godforsaken world? Why isn't my tombstone filled out? Where am I buried? Why haven't I been gathered up with my family?" I sobbed.

She had me take her by the wrist and led me on to a grove of oak trees with dogwoods growing beneath them. They had spaced out to give each set of trees room to grow and spread. A sign had been placed in front: MEMORIAL GROVE OF THE UNCLAIMED.

"In this world, you are born at the leisure of the State. You are awarded station and class at their pleasure. You have to maintain your social credit score or else the State deems who gets what resources or if those resources are turned off. Here, once a life has served its purpose, death is a biological function. Since there is no belief in an afterlife and not much use to life, there are no funerals or burials. The dead are salvaged for parts or food, the leftovers are frozen, then diced up by lasers and turned into mulch.

"That's it? That's no reason for living. That's not even living. Just because people don't believe anymore doesn't mean there isn't a God. God is God. He doesn't change. He's still on his throne. There's eternal life. Heaven and Hell," I argued.

"Yet, you are trying to throw away your life again. For the second time. You are giving up. You don't believe in that hope anymore, do you? Haven't you renounced it?" my dark lady companion asked.

"So, there's no more peace on earth? No more goodwill to humans anymore? Aren't there any believers anywhere?" I asked. "There must be! Show them to me! Take me to them at once or I'll be haunted with these horrible scenes forever and a day!"

I could see my dark lady companion under her ruined veil. Then with a weak pass, she waved her hand.

And we were in a ramshackle church. With boarded over stain glass windows. And candles lit instead of the dusty spiderwebbed chandeliers.

The decrepit pews could have easily held three hundred people but fifty might have been spread across the benches that still stood.

A man stood behind the half ruined pulpit. Six foot by six foot. With a long stark white goatee and whispy hair pulled back over a bald pate into a long white ponytail. He wore a Black Sabbath t-shirt under a black vest. His legs clad in black pants with a silver buckle that held a diamond cross.

"Hello, my name is Larry."

"Brothers and sisters, whatever we suffer, down here is the only hell we will ever know. We are promised a heavenly estate, goodness, mercy, and everlasting righteousness by the Ancient of Days. For we are His children. And whatever riches or fun the wicked know is a but a short season. This will be their only heaven they will get.

"What do we do while we await our Savior's glorious return? We abide in His will. We remain in His love. We endure in His hope.

"I am reminded of this prayer by St. Francis of Assisi:

'Lord, make Me an instrument of Your peace,
Where there is hatred, let me sow love.
Where there is injury, pardon.
Where this doubt, faith.
Where there is despair, hope.
Where there is darkness, light.
Where there is sadness, joy…'

"In this holiday season, we still celebrate the birth of Jesus Christ," Larry said and got fifty amens and everyone on their feet.

He picked up his guitar and led them in a song, "Hark the Herald Angel Sings" as their benediction. Then everyone left the shattered sanctuary of the underground church. Leaving us two alone.

"Why show me these things if there's no hope for me. No hope for Christmas. No hope for humans?" I demanded. "What do you want from me?"

The spectre in a dirty lace gown turned her head to me. As if waiting for me to be peeled back to my core. I already feeling nauseous. I was broken.

"Do you know what I want? That one special gift I wish for more than any other for Christmas? The only thing that would satisfy my heart?"

"What is that?" I asked.

Then she pulled back her veil. "I want to see you dead."

The veiled woman was an ex-wife.

The dark lady was my first wife.

"Hello, Lauren," I said.

She did not return my greeting. Instead she lifted the lace back from her arm and to reveal a silver icy wrist.

"Remember when I said that you'd better be careful what you say because it echoes into eternity?"

Before I could even try to remember, she grabbed my arm and yanked my sleeve back. And then put her cold wrist next to mine. Parallel. Side by side. The two antipol scars made a parenthesis. (Both our lives were encapsulated within it, but with different results and destinies).

I had becoming cold from head to toe. Numb to the bone. Only my stomach churned and burned like a smoking volcano.

"I'm sorry," I managed.

Lauren said nothing. She waited for her wish to come true.

"God knows you had your problems. You tried to block them out of your mind. I don't even think you know what happened. I tried to help. I thought I could be your friend. Provide a home. And I thought you'd come out of your shell. That we would both finish school and get decent jobs, enough to start a life together. I thought we would grow together. Well, you taught me you can't make people do what they don't want to do. We resented each other. Until we hated each other. I married for expectations and they didn't come true, God knows," I said.

"'God knows?'" she echoed. "Know what God knows? 'Vengeance is mine. I shall repay.'"

She said nothing more.

She merely waited.

"Yeah, but you're not God," I said. "The worst thing I did to you was to marry you. It was a mistake. That we both made."

Lauren startled.

"You might be dead. And you might be angry. And you might be trapped here still looking for justice. And I'll admit that I'm partially responsible for what happened to you. But it wasn't all my fault. Unforgiveness just hurts you, that's all. And revenge may get you even but it won't get you ahead. It won't set you free. Only when you forgive will it set yourself free. Unforgiveness is not God. God is love. God is mercy. God is forgiveness. Here and now I forgive you for all that I put you through and all that I let you put me through. Now can't you even try to forgive me?"

Lauren cast her crystal blue eyes down. "'The blueness of a wound cleanseth away evil; so do stripes the inwards parts of the belly.'

"You forgave that other one. Even if isn't working out and you two shouldn't be together, you forgave her. Even if your parents won't forget enough to forgive her. I just wanted to hear you say it to me," Lauren said.

Say it to me.

The mists of this future swirled around her and her features were lost.

The coldness left me.

And with it the fear and the hopelessness.

And in their place, a surefire heat. Internal combustion. Rising up. In me. In my stomach.

FIFTH VERSE: One Special Gift

1—Christmas Everyday

***I woke myself up by throwing up
all over my grayish ribbed turtle neck
sweater and my worn blue jeans.***

By looking at the chunks, I could see what had not
been digested. Chunks of my coldcut sandwich with
cheese from my ex-mother-in-law's. Frothy strips of one
of her family member's awful fudge with nuts. And
several parts of undigested tabs of my trazodone!

Something I ate, probably the fudge and/or the nuts
had kept me from fully digesting the trazodone!

I wore the vomit as I walked into the kitchen, where
the washer and dryer were. I stripped to my skivvies and
put the soiled clothes into the washer. Then I thanked
God that Blair had done a little laundry and I had clean
jeans and a Silver Dollar City pullover and fresh skivvies.

Taking the clean clothes, I crept into the only
bathroom down from the master bedroom with its closed
door and slumbering occupant.

The hot shower did me wonders.

And it put my mind at work.

It was Friday, Christmas morning.

I had been given a third chance.

I had faced some of my guilt and fears.

I had been weighed and found wanting. And the only
thing I could do was ask forgiveness.

Here and now in this life.

Because I doubt I would get it in the next. There, I would only get what I deserved.

When I got out and toweled off, I bent my knee beside the toilet.

"Heavenly Father, I am so weak and undeserving. I have made a mess of life. Yet, twice you have helped me escape death, but I still don't know how to live. I want to be reborn. I want to be saved. I believe that Jesus Christ is your Son who died in my place for my sins. And He rose again to the glory of You, the Father. Please save me now and give me a fleshy heart. Melt my heart of stone like wax," I said.

And like that, I was saved and received Jesus Christ as my Savior.

I was jittery and excited as I tried to hold my razor to my face and use the mirror to shave.

"Razor, you are for cutting the whiskers on my face, not my wrist. Never again," I said as I shaved.

And this time when I cut myself in a couple of places, I stuck pieces of toilet paper on my cuts and laughed when I saw myself in the mirror.

"There is another mirror. The Living Word of God that shows us what we truly are and who God truly is," I told myself. "And I want to know more about the Word. About New Hearts Recovery. About the Lord's Prayer. About Psalm Twenty-three. About the Serenity Prayer. About the prayer of St. Francis Assisi—wasn't that just a dream? Maybe I heard Larry say that at the last meeting? I so wish they were meeting today!!" I said and meant it all.

I finished dressing and went back into the back room addition, said hello the trash can and the hole in the roof, and got my wallet and keys.

Then I knew what I must do.

And what I wanted to do, with God's help.

Only then did I grab my cell and check the time. It was six-thirty.

What would be open on Christmas morning?

Gas stations.

Without a doubt.

And so I left 2112 Springhill Drive on a Christmas Morning. With its sole occupant still asleep.

I stopped at the biggest Gar-Mart I could find. I startled the sole cashier with a "Merry Christmas!" and then shocked her with buying up little novelty gifts and some accessories. I almost bought a hundred dollars worth. Including something better than gift cards, and many of the gift bags and tissue paper she had just set out.

"My, my, going to load up some Christmas stockings?" she asked.

"Something like that," I chuckled and was sure to give her, "A very merry Christmas!" as I left.

On my way to my first destination, as I played some classic Christmas songs, I had time to see God's hand in things. It was a little clearer than mud. The mud being the junk in my mind.

I had become an addict by choice. No one had made me get drunk or try those other recreational drugs or have empty and quick unattached relationships. But I'd slowly made those things a habit and handed my life over to addiction and caused myself far more suffering than I had deserved or what my friend and family would have ever wanted for me.

It had gotten to the point that when I would get triggered or stress, I used those to solve my problems in order to try to cope. Which wasn't coping at all. More like crawling through cut glass while pouring salt on my wounds.

For years, I thought that I was the only one in the world with problems and failures and guilt and later, after acknowledging my addiction and depression, the only one sitting in Ketler Ward C with that many problems. Now I knew why suicide had seemed so attractive. But, in the end, it was another form of Russian Roulette.

I thought it was a weakness to talk about it, because that meant I was admitting my failures.

But I knew there were far too many people going through the same thing.

We were all suffering.

The whole world over.

For an addict, when you had problems, it was easy to go run and hide and get high. Now I knew it was harder to stay sober day after day; to get up and work your tail off and get behind on a bill because of some emergency, and get up the next day to stay sober again, just to work harder.

I had been down so long, I'd forgotten what is like to be human. My heart had filled up with stone after stone.

To work the recovery steps, one would have to turn to God and trust in Him to solve their problems as soon as their problems appeared.

But was there surety that your problem would get solved? No. Only that you would have peace.

Wasn't peace a promise? Part of the gift? In spite of all our problems.

Tidings of comfort and joy.

For unto us a Savior is born

Unto us a Son is given.

This was Christmas.

This was hope.

I pulled into the back parking lot and prepared some things and put them into two bags. Then I went into the ancillary entrance and made two stops at two different windows. Both secretaries were happy to see me and very glad to be messengers for me.

Next, I was going to make the hardest stop of my life.

2—My Christmas Card To You

The dawn rose. It heralded Christmas morning with warmth and hope. And good tidings of great joy.

The patients on Kelter Ward C woke up on Christmas morning. There was a huge tree in the patients' lounge. And half a dozen packaged string guns. Nurse Rochelle and Nurse Michelle passed them out to each of the patients. They ripped open the packages, took the guns in hand, and ran down the hall squirting string on everyone and everything. The walls were decked with string. The beds covered with spread string. And the stoic orderlies stood guard with string hanging from them head to toe.

The nurses even got Kathy D. out of her room and gave her a string gun. She didn't do anything with it until Lizzy B. shot her with string in the face.

Kathy D. shrieked. And then she got mad. And shot Lizzy B. in the face with string.

Lizzy B. laughed even as Kathy D. was too shocked to change the look on her face.

The hermetically sealed door buzzed open.

Visitors on to the Ward.

Well, just one.

A man, a little older than Justin R. came walking in with a fleece lined hoodie parka and gloves buttoned to the sleeves.

This time it was Lizzy B.'s mouth that went wide, showing her gumline and tongue.

"Mom," said her son. "I want you to come home with me for Christmas."

Lizzy B.'s face soured. "You'll just kick me out again."

"Have long have you been here? Have long have you been sober?" her son asked.

"This is day sixteen," Lizzy B. said.

"Let me help you work it. I'll take you to the meetings. Go when I can, if needed," he said.

They hugged. Cried. And hugged again.

Nurses Rochelle and Michelle smiled at each other and wiped a tear. Nurse Michelle saw Kathy D. trying to get their attention.

"Yes, Kathy?"

"I want—I want—I want to call...my fuh-family," Kathy D. said. "I want to go home."

It was Nurse Michelle's mouth that dropped this time. While Nurse Rochelle gave a "Hallelujah!"

Up on Ward A, two orderlies entered a solitary room. Bud C. sat barefoot in a straitjacket, black circles under his eyes. The first orderly stood behind him and produced a thin rod ending in a wooden claw. The second orderly got on his knees before Bud C. and produced a second clawed rod.

Bud C. sat with unblinking hollow eyes.

The first orderly stuck the rod under the back of Bud C.'s jacket and began to scratch between his blades.

The second began to scratch his toes. Then tickled the bottom of his feet.

First, Bud C. sighed.

Then he began to giggle. And a flicker began to glow in his iris.

"Merry Christmas, Bud C," they said and hummed a Christmas song.

The secretary for Hope Counselors, Inc. brought in the morning mail. All three counselors had agreed to come in this morning, Christmas morning, for just a brief meeting and take the rest of the day and the weekend off, other than being on perpetual call for their many, too many client list. It was Paul D. who sorted through the mail, piling up bills and service notices by vendor and patient.

Then he came across three cards. One addressed to each counselor. He set them on his desk and called for Jayne V. and Sandy L.

"How nice," Jayne V. said.

Sandy L. gave her an incredulous look.

Paul D. shrugged.

They each opened theirs. The outside had three wisemen on camels on a pilgrimage at night in the desert heading to a walled city with palm trees under a bright solitary star. The inside read, "Peace on Earth and Goodwill toward men." And then it was followed by a personal note. And signed.

"You know, we don't get a lot of thank you's from any of our group attendees," Paul D. said.

"How nice," Jayne V. said. "I'll stick it on my board."

"Of all the ones out of that group, I thought that one thought he was too cool for school," Sandy L. said. "I hope he's had a change of heart."

The doorbell rang on a dingy apartment door.

It rang twice.

The husband expected his wife to get it, as usual. He was still busy eating his Christmas chocolate chip waffles she had prepared for him.

The wife shuffled to the front door in her robe and opened the door.

To find their estranged daughter, Jacque A., standing at the door. She had a black eye.

"Mom, Dad, I've left her. She was abusive. And I've been sober for sixteen days today and she didn't care. She said I've got the problem," Jacque A. blubbered.

She fell into her mother's arms.

"Delores, close the door, you'll letting all the cold in. Well, you'd better come here and help me finish this waffles. They're your favorite," the husband said.

The lounge room at the emergency station had a party-sub laid out. A case of snack bags. A pecan pie. A swiss roll log. And a bowl of egg nog.

For the three paramedics, it was a quiet respite and a small space in time for a meager feast.

Young red haired Mel filled all their glasses with a ladle of eggnog.

Bart took up his drink and smiled. He'd been smiling all night as their shift had proved quiet.

Gaspar was looking over his toy package again. It was a remote helicopter. He couldn't wait to get outside with it. And fly it. See how high it could go. How safe it would land.

A new song started on the streaming service.

The winsome tones of an electric piano. Soft snare and brushed hi-hat. Floating triple harmony over plucked strings.

Gaspar started to laugh. "No, you didn't!"

"But of course!" Mel said and held up his glass of eggnog.

"Here's to peace on earth. If at least for one more morning!" Bart said and clinked his glass in mid-air.

"Merry Christmas," Gaspar added his glass to the toast.

Then Mel began to sing the lyrics to the flowing ballad. Bart coming in at the end of the verse. And Gaspar taking the low register of the chorus, while Mel doubled it an octave above.

"'How deep is your love?,'" they crooned. Out of pitch. Out of time. But smiling.

Somewhere in time, my six year old pajamed self had his fire helmet. And his *20,000 Leagues Under the Sea* game. And his grandpa had his plate of homemade fudge.

And they both still had their family and their gifts in that basement for that one night forever.

Boz sat in his chair reading a story to his audience with his legs crossed.

"'May that be truly said of us, and all of us! And so, as Tiny Tim observed—'"

McMurtry handed him a cup of grape juice. "This'll straighten your curls out, Boz." He himself already had a juice stache.

"Not cider?" Boz asked.

"Not cider."

"Not punch?"

"Not punch."

"Not wine?"

"Not wine."

"Then what is it?" Boz asked.

"Grape kool-aid," McMurtry said.

"Without those doors of perception?" Boz asked.

"Even better, my man!"

"How so!"

"It's sugar free!" McMurtry said.

Boz held up his cup of grape kool-aid. "A toast!"

Everyone on stage and in the audience held theirs up likewise.

"Merry Christmas! God bless Us, Every One!" Boz toasted.

Everyone toasted and threw back their heads to toss the kool-aid down the hatch.

Boz licked his lips while McMurtry smacked his and slapped his belly.

"Hair of the dog, Boz. You gotta bite it right back," McMurtry laughed.

"Mr. McMurtry, I'm reminded of that old saying. 'Beyond me and thee, the whole world is quite mad, except that I'm no longer sure about thee,'" said Boz as tried to swallow the after taste.

McMurtry belly laughed and clapped the gentleman on the shoulder. "We're just two peas in a pod, Boz."

Somewhere in a church, it was dark and quiet. The light always grey. Either dusk or dawn. Or both.

The veiled woman sat in the pew listening to the peal of the bells.

There was a light on the empty altar.

Through her veil she could see it wasn't empty.

There was a something black on the Lord's Table.

She got up. Folded her lace arms across her dirty gown and came forward. The dirty train sweeping behind her.

It was a box. A small box bordered in black velvet. She took it up in her pale hands.

And opened it.

What was inside it was luminous. Golden hued. Glorious.

The light pierced her veil and smote her face with color.

She lifted her veil to get a better look. To make sure what she was seeing was real.

It was.

Her crystal blue eyes twinkled.

Her icy cheeks warmed.

Hot tears began to fall from her chin and onto her hands.

She lifted the precious thing out of the box.

It was a necklace.

With a gold heart.

She put it on as she began to fade within Justin's mind.

3—What'd Ya Get Me

Blair woke up sometime that moring.

On Christmas morning, she reminded herself.

"Justin!" she yelled as she came out of the master bedroom and past the mess in the living room and past the two tube socks on the kitchen spindles. "Merry Christmas!"

"I'm sorry about last night! I don't want to lost you!" she called as she came into the kitchen. "I'll cook you a very Merry Christmas breakfast! Do you want chocolate chip waffles?

"What'd ya get me? No use in hiding it! I'll just find it!"

Then she saw the punched out tabs of his trazaodone. Too many for how long he'd had them. And the butcher knife was upside down in the sink.

Blair screamed. "Oh, Lord! Not again!"

She screamed his name and ran into the back addition. But he wasn't in his Grandpa's recliner. And he wasn't in the extra bedroom being used for storage again.

Blair backtracked and came back into the kitchen and saw that the clothes he had on last night had been thrown into the washer.

The little creep left me to go out, Blair thought. "He ditched me on Christmas morning. Wait until my mother finds out! He probably has gone over to his parents. Without me!"

Blair was burning mad. She picked up her cell phone to call Justin. But her phone was dead. She hadn't paid on it since they'd gotten divorced. She would have to use some of what she had left on her unemployment card and that wouldn't still be enough. She'd have to set up a payment plan and hope they would take at least fifty dollars. Or less. It was Christmas after all.

She noticed there was a lump in her tube sock stocking. Next to Justin's empty stocking. She should have filled it earlier. But there had been too much drama.

Blair reached down inside it and grabbed what was inside. She pulled out two items.

A letter wrapped around a jewelry box.

She opened that first.

Bewildered again, she remembered to read the letter.

Blair,

It is best if we go our separate ways. We are not in a healthy relationship. I'm not sure I know how to be in one right now. I broke my sobriety and self-harm agreement last night. But somehow I threw up and God used that to save my life. I'm not blowing it again, with His help.

There is no ring. I am not going to marry you again. That would not be wise for either of us.

I did buy you a heart necklace but I think it best if I return it. I'll need the money to file an eviction notice. You will need to leave the premises within thirty days after I serve it come Monday.

This is all for the best.

J.R.

The front doorbell rang at 2112 Springhill Drive.

Blair answered it, and given who was standing in her doorway, wished she had taken a shower. Or at least brushed her teeth. Or combed her hair.

It was Tim. The assistant manager at Gas-Mart. The Merryprankster101 himself.

"Hi, Blair. Merry Christmas!" he said. "I hope I'm not imposing but you seemed pretty upset last night. Did he really call the cops on you?"

"Yes, he did. They told him how to get me evicted. And that's what he's doing come Monday," Blair said.

"He can't do that," Tim said feigning support. And coughed, due to his punctured lungs.

What did he know? Blair knew more about civil law than she cared to, what with two arrests in the past three months.

"Oh, yes, he can. The house is his. He can do what he likes with it. We are officially broke up on Christmas Day," Blair said and managed a tear for some sympathy.

"Well, then move in with me," Tim said. "I'll be manager soon enough."

"I'm not going to be able to contact the Social Security office until after New Year's," Blair said. "But when I do, I'll start my disability process. If I get denied the first time, there's a lawyer's office where all they do are disability claims. We're talking big money here. They'll be a back pay check."

"With the way you win at my lotto tickets, you'll get the whole hog!" Tim said and coughed.

"Poor Tim. You shouldn't be outside with your bad lung. You'll get pneumonia. Come on in," Blair and ushered in her personal Christmas Caroler.

I had never missed a Christmas with my parents. Even when I'd been married to Lauren, we had all spent Christmas Eve together. I liked Christmas Eve better – especially when growing up—my grandparents had been there and there had been fresh fudge.

What were they going to do for Christmas this year? Where might they go? It could be just the two of them. Unless, they had decided to leave town to visit my brother.

I knocked on the door.

Twice.

Then the door opened.

"Justin!" my mother cried. She was still in her pajamas. "We were just praying for you."

Behind her I could smell the fresh sticky buns. Two packages of Rolls put in a bundt pan. Left in the refrigerator to rise. Then caramel and butterscotch pudding and pecans added. Then cooked in the oven. Taken out and turned upside down onto a cake server. Hot and ready and delicious and sweet. Love. Family.

"And cooking, too," I said.

"It is Christmas," she smiled. Then she hugged me.

My dad came into the living room from the bedroom. He took one look at me and a smile light up his face. Brighter than any pre-lit tree. Louder than a carol.

I held up my bag of presents. "You said to bring these over later. I even got you all some stocking stuffers. Now a good time?"

"Son," he said. And threw his arms open.

Mom joined in on the group hug.

"We really didn't get you anything. And you didn't even give us a list this year," Mom said. "We've opened all our gifts last night. But we did stuff your stocking."

Three stockings were above the electric fireplace. One for each of us. They would be full of candy, a new toothbrush, pens, and batteries for electronics.

"We already mailed your brother's off last week. I thought we might have to do the same with yours," Mom said.

"I'll just put these in with the others," I said. There was barely room for my gifts in their stockings. Their's were pretty full at it was.

"All that matters is that you're here safe with us today," Dad said. "That's the best gift we could have from you."

"You look good. Healthy. Happy," Mom said.

"I feel good. And I am very happy," I said.

"You're just in time to help us eat the sticky buns," Mom said and dragged me into the kitchen.

"You did remember to make fudge this year? Didn't you?" I asked.

--cont;nue--

AFTERWORD

02/01/23
Dear Readers,
I revise as I go, so a finished draft is a well-worked draft for me. And once the work is done, I give it to a reader (usually, it's my dear mother). And then wait for the feedback.

This project made it to the reading stage and after that it went back to the shelf (*shelf* is a writer's word for cryogenic freezing or order of stay or skeleton closet) for another ten years while I moved on to other projects. I had (and still have) confidence that it was good enough to be published but I worried about its reception.

Because of the subject matter.

Even though it is a work of fiction, I thought it was very personal. Maybe too personal and not just personal for me, but personal enough to make people squirm.

But after the Covid shut down, I ran into more and more people with stories of struggles with mental health, and the worst case scenario where some lost their struggle. And I thought, maybe this story might be helpful. Though it is a fictionalized memoir, it does contain several different stories of recovery from suicide ideation, depression, toxic relationships, addiction, mental and physical abuse, dysfunctional families, as well as sobriety, safety, therapy, recovery, Christmas, hope, peace, joy, cookies, fudge, movies, and forgiveness

We should never give up.

Cont;nue.

Why bother, why cont;ue, you ask? Because in life, there is the good, the bad, and the ugly.

The good and the bad are public faces for people to brag or gossip about. Nobody, but nobody, likes to talk about the ugly. Or admit that it exists.

The truth is often ugly. Because it is a mirror. And the first step in recovery or achieving real growth or healing is in admitting the ugly.

So, that the truth may live in a fleshy heart instead of a stony heart.

There are many hurts and many recovery needs. So, there are many programs for those recovery needs. Some have twelve steps. Some have eight steps.

The basics of the steps are admitting we are not in control of much at all and especially not of our weaknesses/flesh/sin. Next, believing in a higher power (God/Jesus) and that only He has the power to save me, heal me, and recover me. Next, admitting my need of help and faults (sin) and choosing to live a life for Christ (This step is where many people drop out of recovery). Next, submitting to God so that He can change my faults one surrender at a time. Next, offering forgiveness to myself and others that I may hurt or have been hurt by (this is another stumbling step for many) and to make amends, except when it might do harm to them or others. Next, making time for God to work on my stony heart and melt it into a fleshy heart by reading His Word and praying to know His will and choosing to follow it daily. And last, giving up and giving over my life to God by working the steps and being an example for others by my words and deeds.

Only God can change a heart. And only if we let Him.

This story is really about the first three steps.

The genesis of it was a dare by someone who I was in a toxic relationship with. After watching the movie *Adaptation,* the dare came from my partner: "That main character is so you. Why don't you write a story like that."

Well, *Adaptation* was a metaphysical and metafictional meta-mess. It was one of the most deranged movies I'd ever seen. Unforgettable and pythonic. It contained a little of everything.

Mixing fiction and non-fiction with meaning coming in a variety of shallow definitions and irony militant. The tongue was kept firmly in the cheek of truth with this story.

So, I took up the challenge. And started chasing down words. A lot of words.

Since it was Christmastime when the dare had been given, I decided to write about Christmas. But I had no idea of where my own story would take me. Of how much tumultuous change I was in store for.

After that Christmas, I became single. Again. I changed my place of address. Often. I had to rely on my family in order not to be homeless. I changed employers. And professions. Often. I changed lifestyles. I grew. I regressed. I discovered. I lost. I learned. I forgot. I sobered up. I wised up. I loved. I hated. I struggled. I conquered. I forgave. I grudged. I laughed. I saved. I lost. I trusted. I was lied to. I lied. I hid. I cried. I sang. I waited. I grew impatient. I ran. I limped. I walked. I stumbled. I studied. I passed. I won. I failed. A lot.

I tend to get bored very fast.

And still, through all that, this story stayed alive because of the challenge. And I worked on it every Christmas for seven years.

I listened to old Christmas songs. I discovered new Christmas songs. I studied the origins of Christmas. I watched the different generational Christmas movie favorites. I dug out old Christmas pictures. I remembered good and bad Christmas experiences. I shopped and wrapped and returned Christmas. I lived, breathed, and ate Christmas.

But in the writing about it, I failed.

For seven years.

Then I realized what I was missing was structure. I crave structure. I need structure. I was born into a structure (the physical universe) and I exist in a structure (my physical body).

Every story has a structure, like it or not. A beginning, wherever it starts, and where we learn the character and the setting (time and place), a rising action (the character has to have a problem), a climax (will the problem get solved?), a falling action (how does the problem seemed to get solved?), and a resolution (how has the character changed? What have they learned or lost or gained?)

My structure was found in Charles Dickens' *A Christmas Carol.* In some quarters of the world, it is perhaps the *second* best known Christmas story after the original.

CD had created his story in nothing short of a whirlwind. After conceiving it while doing lectures on poor working conditions for children and the needy and after his quick drafting, the short novel appeared as a serial in magazines for the Christmas holiday, and then publication after subscriptions (or pre-sales) were made.

Once I was brave enough to relax and not think about it (thank you, Mr. Bradbury), I let it run away and I chased after the words. Running to keep up with getting them down and getting it down but quick. All of which I did within holiday break periods between 2011 and 2012, when I was a substitute teacher.

Then as I opened, this story was read by my constant reader and put on the shelf. I published my first book in 2021, *Leftwich Blues/Elfwitch Rules* and the marketers were asking for a sequel. This Christmas story was the only thing I had ready enough at the time but I knew it would need a little revising.

I started revising in March 2022, and hoped to be done by summer 2022. Double health tragedies hit my wife and me within the same week. Near the end of summer, I had a minor procedure and she had a major procedure done in back to back weeks. All that put off my revising.

I got my second wind on our holiday breaks and started the New Year sliding into Verse Four. But then tragedy struck again and I was in a one car accident on a foggy morning and fractured my back. I used some of the time God had given to me to recover and heal to finish this revision (in between job duties I could perform from home and multiple doctor's visits).

The first three verses, I did very little changing or pruning (about the first half of the book). But Verses Four and Five were almost entirely re-written and I added about seventy new pages. Because I had to deal with the ugly in various characters' situations. The truth should not be skirted. The truth should be uncovered or discovered or revealed. It needs to be nailed to the cross.

Though, this is a fictionalized memoir involving several characters' stories which may ring true in other people's stories, it all boils down to the ugly truth: We are in charge of very little but we have a choice. To choose life or death. What matters is what do we do when we have problems? Where do we go to get our problems solved? How do we take care of our problems?

We all fall short of the goal: perfection and righteousness. We all need forgiveness and salvation: life and love and light. But no one has any righteousness in and of themselves. No one is perfect, since we all need forgiveness, and no one can make themselves perfect.

This is why Jesus came. For all the other three hundred and sixty-four days of the year that are not Christmas. Jesus came into this world to die for us. Through Grace to extend salvation. To give us hope.

It's the other side of the Christmas story, folks. Resurrection morning.

"For God so loved the world that He gave His only begotten Son, that whosoever believeth in Him should not perish, but have everlasting life"—John 3:16.

Maybe some of you have to been to a meeting that started like this.

(Imagine meeting me at the front door as I greet you): "Hello, my name is Jeff. I am grateful believer who has overcome depression, addiction, suicide ideation, cutting, and toxic relationships. My sobriety date is October 31, 2009."

There is a welcome table with literature and nametags.

Then there is a meal.

Then there are songs, a coining, a recitation of twelve steps, a message over a step or a testimony (which always works far better because rather than someone telling how to do the steps someone is showing you how it worked for them).

There is one final song and often tears shed.

And finally, the Serenity Prayer:

"Lord/God, Grant me the serenity to accept the things I cannot change,

The courage to change the things I can

And the wisdom to know the difference

Living one day at a time, (many people know this part for I've seen it on t-shirts, bookmarks, wall décor, and even tattoos…now, here comes the rest of it…)

Moment by moment

Accepting hardships as the pathway to peace,

Taking, as He/Jesus did, this sinful world as it is and not as I would have it,

Trusting that He will make all things right if I surrender to His will,

That I might be reasonably happy in this life,

And forever happy in the next.

Amen."   --attributed to Reinhold Niebur

So, now this tale is done (put to bed). And in the morning, it's time to start the next tale.

Cont; nue,
Jeffrey Cummins

ABOUT THE AUTHOR

Jeffrey Cummins is very grateful for the blessings and dreams and hardships that have come his way. Over the years, he has worked in retail, the banking industry, as a mental health paraprofessional, and as a public school teacher. Prior to publishing books, he won an Editor's Choice for the short ghost story "Lethe House" in the *Arkansas Anthology*. He published his debut novel *Leftwich Blues/Elfwitch Rules* in 2021 which was well reviewed. *Ex-Mas Song* is his second novel and explores themes of mental illness and forgiveness during Christmastime. He currently lives in the Ozarks with his wife and family and their many dogs.

www.ingramcontent.com/pod-product-compliance
Lightning Source LLC
Chambersburg PA
CBHW060603300726
48975CB00005B/1435